Clueless

I wanted to get rid of Hooker, but I didn't have a plan. Truth is, I didn't have a plan for *anything*. Alexandra Barnaby Girl Detective was stumped. Just pretend it's a transmission, I thought. You take it apart. You see what's broken. You put it back together. Really go through Bill's apartment. My brother was friendly. Surely, he talked to someone.

Hooker pulled the Porsche into a spot in front of Bill's building.

"Thanks for the ride," I said. I was hoping to get into the apartment and close and lock the door before Hooker could elbow his way past me. I got one foot on the sidewalk, and I was yanked back by my purse strap.

"Wait for me," Hooker said.

"Here's the thing," I told him. "You're not invited in."

"Here's the thing about driving NASCAR," Hooker said. "You learn not to wait for an invitation."

Books by Janet Evanovich

Manhunt
Metro Girl
Back to the Bedroom
Love Overboard
The Rocky Road to Romance

One for the Money
Two for the Dough
Three to Get Deadly
Four to Score
High Five
Hot Six
Seven Up
Hard Eight
Visions of Sugar Plums
To the Nines
Ten Big Ones

Coming Soon
Smitten

JANET EVANOVICH

METRO GIRL

HarperTorch
An Imprint of HarperCollinsPublishers

This is a work of fiction. Names, characters, places, and incidents are products of the author's imagination or are used fictitiously and are not to be construed as real. Any resemblance to actual events, locales, organizations, or persons, living or dead, is entirely coincidental.

HARPERTORCH
An Imprint of HarperCollins*Publishers*
10 East 53rd Street
New York, New York 10022-5299

Copyright © 2004 by Evanovich, Inc.
Author photograph copyright © 2004 by Deborah Feingold
ISBN: 0-06-113716-2

First HarperTorch special printing: June 2006
First HarperTorch paperback printing: October 2005
First HarperTorch international printing: May 2005
First HarperCollins hardcover printing: November 2004

HarperCollins®, HarperTorch™, and ◆™ are trademarks of HarperCollins Publishers Inc.

Printed in the United States of America

Visit HarperTorch on the World Wide Web at www.harpercollins.com

10 9 8 7 6 5 4 3 2

ONE

Just because I know how to change a guy's oil doesn't mean I want to spend the rest of my life on my back, staring up his undercarriage. Been there, done that. Okay, so my dad owns a garage. And okay, I have a natural aptitude for rebuilding carburetors. There comes a time in a girl's life when she needs to trade in her mechanic's overalls for a pair of Manolo Blahnik stilettos. Not that I can afford a lot of Manolos, but it's a goal, right?

My name is Alexandra Barnaby, and I worked in my dad's garage in the Canton section of Baltimore all through high school and during summer breaks when I was in college. It's not a big fancy garage, but it holds its own, and my dad has a reputation for being an honest mechanic.

When I was twelve my dad taught me how to use an acetylene torch. After I mastered welding, he gave me some spare parts and our old lawn mower, and I built myself a go-cart. When I was sixteen, I started rebuilding a ten-year-old junker Chevy. I turned it into a fast car. And I raced it in the local stocks for two years.

"And here she comes, folks," the announcer would say. "Barney Barnaby. Number sixteen, the terror of Baltimore County. She's coming up on the eight car. She's going to the inside. Wait a minute, I see flames coming from sixteen. There's a lot of smoke now. Looks like she's blown another engine. Good thing she works in her dad's garage."

So I could build cars, and I could drive cars. I just never got the hang of driving them without destroying them.

"Barney," my dad would say. "I swear you blow those engines just so you can rebuild them."

Maybe on an *un*conscious level. The brain is a pretty weird thing. What I knew was that on a *conscious* level, I hated losing. And I lost more races than I won. So, I raced two seasons and packed it in.

My younger brother, Wild Bill, drove, too. He

never cared if he won or lost. He just liked to drive fast and scratch his balls with the rest of the guys. Bill was voted Most Popular of his senior class and also Least Likely to Succeed.

The class's expectation for Bill's success was a reflection of Bill's philosophy of life. *If work was any fun, it would be called play.* I've always been the serious kid, and Bill's always been the kid who knew how to have a good time. Two years ago, Bill said *good-bye* Baltimore and *hello* Miami. He liked the lazy hot sun, the open water, and the girls in bikinis.

Two days ago, Bill disappeared off the face of the earth. And he did it while I was talking to him. He woke me up with a phone call in the middle of the night.

"Barney," Bill yelled over the phone line. "I have to leave Miami for a while. Tell Mom I'm okay."

I squinted at my bedside clock. Two AM. Not late for Bill who spent a lot of time in South Beach bars. Real late for me who worked nine to five and went to bed at ten.

"What's that noise?" I asked him. "I can hardly hear you."

"Boat engine. Listen, I don't want you to worry if you don't hear from me. And if some guys show up looking for me, don't tell them anything.

Unless it's Sam Hooker. Tell Sam Hooker he can kiss my exhaust pipe."

"Guys? What guys? And what do you mean, don't tell them anything?"

"I have to go. I have to . . . *oh shit*."

I heard a woman scream in the background, and the line went dead.

Baltimore is cold in January. The wind whips in from the harbor and slices up the side streets, citywide. We get a couple snowstorms each year and some freezing rain, but mostly we get bone-chilling gray gloom. In the midst of the gray gloom, pots of chili bubble on stoves, beer flows like water, sausages are stuffed into hard rolls, and doughnuts are a necessity to survival.

Miami, it turns out, is *hot* in January. I'd taken the midday flight out of BWI, arriving in Miami midafternoon. When I left home I was wrapped in a quilted down-filled coat, cashmere Burberry scarf, fleece-lined boots, and heavy-duty shearling mittens. Perfect for Baltimore. Not great for Miami. On arrival, I'd crammed the scarf and mittens into the medium-size duffel bag that hung from my shoulder, wrapped my coat around the duffel bag handle, and went in search of the taxi stand. Sweat was soaking into my Victoria's Secret Miracle Bra, my hair was plastered to my forehead, and I was sucking in air that felt like hot soup.

I'm thirty years old now. Average height and average build. I'm not movie-star gorgeous, but I'm okay. My hair is naturally mousy brown, but I started bleaching it blond when I decided to stop being a grease monkey. It's currently platinum and cut in a medium-length shaggy kind of style that I can punk up with paste if the occasion arises. I have blue eyes, a mouth that's a little too big for my face, and a perfect nose inherited from my Grandma Jean.

My parents took Bill and me to Disney World when I was nine. That's the extent of my in-the-flesh Florida experience. The rest of my Florida knowledge consists mainly of horrific bug stories from my mom's friend Elsie Duchen. Elsie winters in Ocala with her daughter. Elsie swears there are cockroaches as big as cows in Florida. And she says they can fly. I'm here to tell you, if I see a cow-size cockroach fly by, I'm gone.

I gave Bill's address to the cabdriver, and I sat back and watched Miami roll past the window. In the beginning there was a lot of concrete road stretching forward into a confusing jumble of intersections and turnoffs. The turnoffs spiraled away to super highways. And the super highways flattened and went on forever. After a few minutes the Miami skyline appeared in the distance, in front of me, and I had the feeling I was on the road to Oz. Palm trees lined the road. The sky was azure. Cars were clean. Exotic stuff for a girl from Baltimore.

We rolled across the Causeway Bridge, leaving Miami behind, moving into Miami Beach. My stomach felt hollow, and I had a white-knuckle grip on my bag. I was worried about Bill, and my anxiety was increasing as we drew closer to his apartment. Hey, I told myself. Relax. Pry your fingers off the bag. Bill's okay. He's always okay. Like a cat. Lands on his feet. True, he wasn't answering his phone. And he hadn't reported in for work. No reason to panic. This was Wild Bill. He didn't always prioritize in the normal fashion.

This was the guy who missed his high school graduation because en route to the ceremony he found an injured cat on the side of the road. He took the cat to the vet and wouldn't leave until the cat was out of surgery and awake. Of course, he could probably still have made the ceremony if only he hadn't felt the need to seduce the vet's assistant in examining room number three.

The troublesome part about my late-night phone call from Bill was the woman screaming. This was a new twist on Bill's usual call. My mother would freak if she knew about the call, so I'd said nothing and boarded a plane.

My plan was to somehow get into Bill's apartment and make sure he wasn't lying on the floor dead. If he wasn't dead on the floor and he wasn't hanging out watching television, my next stop would be the marina. He was on a boat when he called me. I thought I might have to find the boat. Beyond that, I was clueless.

The Causeway Bridge fed into Fifth Avenue in South Beach. Fifth was three lanes in each direction with a grassy island in the middle. Businesses lined both sides of the road. The driver turned right at Meridian Avenue, went one block, and pulled to the curb.

I was in a neighborhood of single-family bungalows and blocky two-story stucco apartment buildings. The lots were small. The vegetation was jungle. Cars were parked bumper to bumper on both sides of the two-lane street. Bill's apartment building was yellow with turquoise and pink trim and looked a lot like a cheap motel. There were wrought iron security bars on the windows. In fact, most of the buildings on the street had barred windows. In Baltimore, bars on windows would be found in conjunction with gang graffiti, street garbage, burned-out crack houses, and broken-down cars. None of those things were present in this neighborhood. This neighborhood looked modest but neatly maintained.

I paid the driver and trudged up the walkway that led to the apartment entrance. Moss grew between paving stones, overgrown flowering bushes and vines spilled onto the sidewalk and raced up the yellow stucco building, and the air smelled sweet and chemical. Bug spray, I thought. I was probably a step behind the exterminator. Best to keep my eye out for the cow-size cockroach. Lizards skittered across the walk in front of me and clung to the stucco walls. I didn't want to prejudge Miami Beach, but the lizards weren't doing a lot for me.

The building was divided into six apartments. Three up and three down. Six front doors on the ground level. Bill lived in an end apartment on the second floor. I didn't have a key. If he didn't answer his doorbell, I'd try the neighbors.

I rang the bell and looked at the door. There were fresh gouges in the wood around the lock and the dead bolt. I tried the doorknob and the door swung open. *Damn*. I'm not an expert on criminal behavior, but I didn't think this was a good sign.

I pushed the door farther open and looked inside. Small entrance foyer with stairs leading up to the rest of the apartment. No sounds drifting down to me. No television, talking, scuffling around.

"Hello?" I called. "I'm coming up, and I have a gun." This was a big fat lie shouted out for a good cause. I figured in case there were bad guys going through the silverware drawer this would encourage them to jump out the window.

I waited a couple beats and then I cautiously crept up the stairs. I've never thought of myself as being especially brave. Aside from my short career at racing stocks, I don't do a lot of wacky, risky things. I don't like scary movies or roller coasters. I never wanted to be a cop, firefighter, or superhero. Mostly my life has been putting one foot in front of the other, moving forward on autopilot. My family thought it took guts for me to go to college, but the truth is, college was just a way to get out of the garage. I love my dad, but I was up to here with cars and guys who knew nothing else. Call me picky, but I didn't want a romantic relationship where I was second in line to a customized truck.

I got to the top of the stairs and froze. The stairs opened to the living room, and beyond the living room I could see into the small kitchen. Both rooms were a wreck. Couch cushions had been thrown onto the floor. Books were pulled off shelves. Drawers had been wrenched out of cabinets, and the drawer contents scattered. Someone had trashed the apartment, and it wasn't Bill. I'd seen Bill's style of mess. It ran more to dirty clothes on the floor, food stuck to the couch, and a lot of empty beer cans, everywhere. That's not what I was seeing here.

I whirled around and flew down the stairs. I was out the door, on the sidewalk in seconds. I stood facing the building, staring up at Bill's apartment, gulping air. This was something that happened in movies. This didn't happen in real life. At least it didn't happen in *my* real life.

I stood there trying to pull myself together, listening to the steady drone of traffic a block away on Fifth. There was no visible activity in the apartment building in front of me. No doomsday cloud hanging overhead. An occasional car cruised by, but for the most part, the street was quiet. I had my hand to my heart, and I could feel that my heartbeat was improving. Probably it had even dropped below stroke level.

All right, let's get a grip on what happened here. Someone tossed Bill's apartment. Fortunately, they seemed to be gone. *Unfortunately*, Bill seemed to be gone, too. Probably I should go back and take another look.

The voice of reason started yelling at me inside my head. What are you, nuts? Call the police. A crime was committed here. Stay far away.

Then the voice of the responsible older sister

spoke up. Don't be so cowardly. At least do a walk-through. Bill's not always so smart. Remember the time he "borrowed" Andy Wimmer's classic GTO from the garage so he could take his buddies on a joyride and ended up in jail? And what about the time he "borrowed" a keg from Joey Kowalski's bar for his Super Bowl party. Maybe you don't want to get the police involved right away. Maybe you want to try to figure out what's going on first.

Good grief, the voice of reason said.

Shut up, or I'll bitch slap you into tomorrow, the sister voice said to the voice of reason.

Bottom line is, the sister voice grew up in a garage in Baltimore.

I blew out a sigh, hoisted my duffel bag higher on my shoulder, and marched back into the apartment building and up the stairs. I set my bag on the floor, and I studied the room. Someone had been looking for something, I decided. They'd either been in a hurry or they'd been angry. You could conduct a search without making a mess like this.

It wasn't a big apartment. Combination living room and dining room, kitchen, bathroom, and bedroom. The door to the medicine chest was open in the bathroom but not much else was touched. Not much you can do when tossing a bathroom, eh? The top to the toilet tank was on the floor. No stone unturned.

I crept into the bedroom and looked around. Clothes were strewn everywhere. The drawer from the small chest beside the bed was on the floor, and condoms, still in their wrappers, were scattered across the carpet. *Lots* of condoms. Like the entire drawer had been filled with condoms. Yep, this was Bill's apartment, I thought. Although the number of condoms seemed optimistic, even for Bill.

The television and DVD player were untouched. Scratch drug-induced burglary off the list of possibilities.

I went back to the kitchen and poked around, but I didn't find anything of interest. No address book. No notes detailing criminal activity. No maps with an orange trip line. I was feeling more comfortable in the apartment. I'd been there for fifteen minutes and nothing bad had happened. No one had rushed up the stairs wielding a gun or a knife. I hadn't discovered any bloodstains. Probably the apartment was really safe, I told myself. It's already been searched, right? There's no reason for the bad guys to come back.

The marina was next up. Bill worked on a corporate boat owned by Calflex. The boat's name was *Flex II*, and it sailed out of Miami Beach Marina. I'd gotten a map and a guidebook at the airport. According to the map, I could walk to the marina. I'd be a puddle of sweat if I walked in my present clothes, so I changed into a short pink cotton skirt, white tank top, and white canvas tennis shoes. Okay, so I'm a bleached blond and I like pink. Get over it.

I'd looked for a second set of keys while picking through the mess on Bill's kitchen floor. I wanted to leave my duffel bag in the apartment when I went to the marina. I hoped the front door could still be locked. And if I could get it to lock I'd need a key to get back in.

Normally, people keep extra keys on hooks in the kitchen or by the door. Or they were kept in kitchen or bedroom drawers with a collection of odds-and-ends junk. Or, if you were frequently hung over and tended to lock yourself out in your underwear when you stepped off the stoop to retrieve your morning paper, you might hide the keys outside.

I slipped my purse over my shoulder and went downstairs, carefully leaving the door open behind me. At home we kept our emergency keys in fake dog poop. My father thinks fake dog poop is hilarious. Tells everyone. Half of Baltimore knows to look for fake dog poop if they want to burgle our house.

I snooped under an overgrown bush to the right of the front stoop and *bingo*. Fake dog poop. I removed the keys from inside the pile of poop. A house key and a car key. I tried the house key, and it fit Bill's front door. I locked up and followed the path to the sidewalk. I pressed the panic button on the remote gizmo attached to the car key, hoping to find Bill's car among the cars parked there. Nothing happened. None of the parked cars responded. I had no idea what Bill drove. No logo on the key. I aimed the remote toward the other end of the street and didn't get a hit there either.

I set off on foot and found the marina four blocks later. It was hidden behind a strip of condos and commercial real estate, barely visible from the road. I crossed a parking lot, aiming the remote around the lot as I walked. None of the cars beeped or flashed their lights. I crossed a small median of grass and flowers and stepped onto a wide concrete sidewalk that ran the length of the marina. Palm trees lined both sides of the walkway. Very neat. Very pretty. Wood docks with slips poked into the channel. There were maybe ten docks in all, and most of the slips on those docks were filled. Powerboats at one end. Sailboats at the other end.

The huge cranes that serviced container ships off-loading at the Port of Miami were visible directly across the channel. Because I'd studied the map, I knew Fisher Island sat offshore, at the mouth of the harbor. From where I stood I could see the clusters of white stucco high-rise condos on Fisher. The orange Spanish tile roofs sparkled in the sunlight, the ground floors were obscured by palms and assorted Florida greenery.

There were white metal gates at the entrance to each of the marina docks. The signs on the gates read NO ROLLERBLADING, SKATEBOARDING, BICYCLE RIDING, FISHING, OR SWIMMING. OWNERS AND GUESTS ONLY.

A small round two-story structure perched at the end of one of the docks. The building had good visibility from the second floor, with green awnings shading large windows. The sign on the gate for that dock told me this was Pier E, the dockmaster's office. The gate was closed, and yellow crime scene tape cordoned off an area around the dockmaster's building. A couple cops stood flat-footed at the end of the dock. A crime scene police van was parked on the concrete sidewalk in front of the white metal gate.

Ordinarily this sort of thing would generate morbid curiosity in me. Today, the crime scene tape at the dockmaster's office made me uneasy. I was looking for my missing brother, last heard from on board a boat.

I watched a guy leave the dockmaster's office and walk toward the gate. He was midthirties, dressed in khakis and a blue button-down shirt with sleeves rolled. He was carrying something that looked like a toolbox, and I guessed he belonged to the crime scene van. He pushed through the closed gate and our eyes made contact. Then his eyes dropped to my chest and my short pink skirt.

Thanks to my Miracle Bra there was an inch of cleavage peeking out from the scoop neck of my tank top, encouraging the plainclothes cop guy to stop and chat.

"What's going on out there?" I asked him.

"Homicide," he said. "Happened Monday night. Actually around three AM on Tuesday. I'm surprised you didn't see it in the paper. It was splashed all over the front page this morning."

"I never read the paper. It's too depressing. War, famine, homicides."

He looked like he was trying hard not to grimace.

"Who was killed?" I asked.

"A security guard working the night shift."

Thank God, not Bill. "I'm looking for the Calflex boat," I said. "I don't suppose you'd know where it is?"

His gaze shifted to the water and focused one dock down. "Everyone knows the Calflex boat," he said. "It's the one at the end of the pier with the helicopter on deck."

That was the boat Bill was working? It was the largest boat at the marina. It was gleaming white and had two full decks above water. The top deck held a little blue-and-white helicopter.

I thanked the cop guy and headed for *Flex II*. I ignored the gate and the sign that said owners and guests, and I walked out onto the wood-planked pier. A guy was standing two slips down from *Flex II*, hands on hips, looking royally pissed off, staring into an empty slip. He was wearing khaki shorts and a ratty, faded blue T-shirt. He had a nice body. Muscular without being chunky. My age. His hair was sun-bleached blond and a month overdue for a cut. His eyes were hidden behind dark sunglasses. He turned when I approached and lowered his glasses to better see me.

I grew up in a garage in the company of men obsessed with cars. I raced stocks for two years. And I regularly sat through family dinners where the entire conversation consisted of NASCAR statistics. So I recognized Mr. Sun-bleached Blond. He was Sam Hooker. The guy Bill had said could kiss his exhaust pipe. Sam Hooker drove NASCAR. He'd won twice at Daytona. And I guess he'd won a bunch of other races, too, but I didn't pay close attention to NASCAR anymore. Mostly what I knew about Sam Hooker I knew from the dinner table conversation. He was a good ol' boy from Texas. A man's man. A ladies' man. A damn good driver. And a jerk. In other words, according to my family, Sam Hooker was typical NASCAR. And my family loved him. Except for Bill, apparently.

I wasn't surprised to find that Bill knew Hooker. Bill was the kind of guy who eventually knew *everybody*. I was surprised to find that they weren't getting along. Wild Bill and Happy Hour Hooker were cut from the same cloth.

The closer I got to *Flex II*, the more impressive it became. It dominated the pier. There were two other boats that came close to the *Flex* in size, but none could match it for beauty of line. And *Flex II* was the only one with a helicopter. Next time I had a billion dollars to throw away I was going to get a boat like *Flex*. And of course it would have a helicopter. I wouldn't ride in the helicopter. The very thought scared the bejesus out of me. Still, I'd have it because it looked so darned good sitting there on the top deck.

There was a small battery-operated truck at the end of the pier, and people were carting produce and boxes of food off the truck and onto the boat. Most of the navy blue and white–uniformed crew was young. An older man, also in navy blue and white, stood to the side, watching the worker bees.

I approached the older man and introduced myself. I'm not sure why, but I decided right off that I'd fib a little.

"I'm looking for my brother, Bill Barnaby," I said. "I believe he works on this boat."

"He did," the man said. "But he called in a couple days ago and quit."

I did my best at looking shocked. "I didn't know," I said. "I just flew in from Baltimore. I was going to surprise him. I went to his apartment, but he wasn't there, so I thought I'd catch him working."

"I'm the ship's purser, Stuart Moran. I took the call. Bill didn't say much. Just that he had to leave on short notice."

"Was he having problems?"

"Not on board. We're sorry to lose him. I don't know about his personal life."

I turned my attention to the boat. "It looks like you're getting ready to leave."

"We don't have any immediate plans, but we try to stay prepared to go when the call comes in."

I thought it might be helpful to talk to the crew, but I couldn't do it with Moran standing watch. I turned away from the boat and bumped into Sam Hooker.

Hooker was just under six foot. Not a huge guy, but big for NASCAR and built solid. I slammed into him and bounced back a couple inches.

"Jesus Christ," I said, on an intake of breath. "Shit."

"Cute little blonds wearing pink skirts aren't allowed to take the Lord's name in vain," Hooker said, wrapping his hand around my arm, encouraging me to walk with him. "Not that it matters, you're going to hell for lying to Moran."

"How do you know I was lying to Moran?"

"I was listening. You're a really crappy liar." He stopped at the empty slip. "Guess what goes here?"

"A boat?"

"My boat. My sixty-five-foot Hatteras Convertible."

"And?"

"And it's gone. Do you see a boat here? No. Do you know who took it? Do you know where it is?"

The guy was deranged. One too many crashes. NASCAR drivers weren't known for being all that smart to begin with. Rattle their brains around a couple times and probably there's not much left.

I made a show of looking at my watch. "Gee, look at the time. I have to go. I have an appointment."

"Your brother took my goddamn boat," Hooker said. "And I want it back. I have exactly two weeks off before I have to start getting ready for the season, and I want to spend it on my boat. Two weeks. Is that too much to ask? *Two friggin' weeks.*"

"What makes you think my brother took your boat?"

"He told me!" Hooker's face was flushing under his tan. He had his glasses off, and his eyes were narrowed. "And I'm guessing he told you, too. You two are probably in this together, going around ripping off boats, selling them on the black market."

"You're a nutcase."

"Maybe selling them on the black market was pushing it."

"And you have anger management issues."

"People keep saying that to me. I think I'm a pretty reasonable guy. The truth is I was born under a conflicting sign. I'm on the cusp of Capricorn and Sagittarius."

"Which means?"

"I'm a sensitive asshole. Whatcha gonna do?"

It was a great line, and I really wanted to smile, but I didn't want to encourage Hooker, so I squashed the smile.

"Do you follow NASCAR?" he asked.

"No." I hiked my bag higher on my shoulder and headed for the concrete walk.

Hooker ambled after me. "Do you know who I am?"

"Yes."

"Do you want an autograph?"

"No!"

He caught up with me and walked beside me, hands in his pockets. "Now what?"

"I want a newspaper. I want to see what they said about the guy who was murdered."

Hooker cut his eyes to the dockmaster's office. "I can tell you more than the paper. The victim was a forty-five-year-old security guard named Victor Sanchez. He was a nice guy with a wife and two kids. I knew him. They found his body when he didn't check in as scheduled. Someone slashed his throat just outside the dockmaster's building, and then the struggle got dragged inside. The office wasn't totally trashed, but logbooks and computers were wrecked. I guess the guard didn't go down easy."

"Anything stolen?"

"Not at first look, but they're still going through everything." He grinned. "I got that information from the cops. Cops love NASCAR drivers. I'm a celebrity."

Not too full of himself, eh?

Hooker ignored my eye roll. "Do you want to know what I think? I think the guard saw something he wasn't supposed to see. Like maybe someone was smuggling in drugs. All right, I didn't think of that all by myself. That's what the cops told me."

I'd reached the path at the water's edge. The marina stretched on either side of me. There were several high-rises in the distance. They were across from Fisher Island, looking over the harbor entrance. I turned and walked toward the high-rises. Hooker walked with me.

"Are there really boats bringing drugs in here?" I asked him.

Hooker shrugged. "Anything could come in here. Drugs, illegal aliens, art, Cuban cigars."

"I thought the Coast Guard intercepted that stuff."

"It's a big ocean."

"Okay, so tell me about my brother."

"I met him a couple months ago. I was in Miami for the last race of the season. When the race was over I hung around for a while, and I met Bill in Monty's."

"Monty's?"

"It's a bar. We just passed it. It's the place with the thatched roof and the pool. Anyway, we got to talking, and I needed someone to captain the boat for me down to the Grenadines. Bill had the week off and volunteered."

"I didn't know Bill was a boat captain."

"He'd just gotten his certification. It turns out Bill can do lots of things . . . captain a boat, steal a boat."

"Bill wouldn't steal a boat."

"Face it, sugar pie. He *stole* my boat. He called me up. He said he needed to use the boat. I said 'no way.' I told him *I* needed the boat. And now my boat's gone. Who do you think took it?"

"That's borrowing. And don't call me sugar pie."

The wind had picked up. Palm fronds were clattering above us, and the water was choppy.

"A front's moving in," Hooker said. "We're supposed to get rain tonight. Wouldn't have been great fishing anyway." He looked over at me. "What's wrong with sugar pie?"

I gave him a raised eyebrow.

"Hey, I'm from Texas. Cut me some slack," he said. "What am I supposed to call you? I don't know your name. Bill only mentioned his brother Barney."

I did a mental teeth-clench thing. "Bill doesn't have a brother. I'm Barney."

Hooker grinned at me. "You're Barney?" He gave a bark of laughter and ruffled my hair. "I like it. Sort of Mayberry, but on you it's sexy."

"You're kidding."

"No. I'm getting turned on."

I suspected NASCAR drivers woke up turned on. "My name is Alexandra. My family started calling me Barney when I was a kid, and it stuck."

We'd reached one of the high-rises. Thirty-five to forty floors of condos, all with balconies, all with to-die-for views. All significantly beyond my budget. I tipped my head back and stared up at the building.

"Wow," I said. "Can you imagine living here?"

"I *do* live here. Thirty-second floor. Want to come up and see my view?"

"Maybe some other time. Places to go. Things to do." Small fear of heights. Distrust of NASCAR drivers . . . especially ones that are turned on.

The first drops of rain plopped down. Big fat drops that soaked into my pink skirt and splashed off my shoulders. Damn. No umbrella. No car. Four long blocks between me and Bill's apartment.

"Where's your car parked?" Hooker wanted to know.

"I don't have a car. I walked here from my brother's apartment."

"He's on Fourth and Meridian, right?"

"Right."

I looked at Hooker, and I wondered if he was the one who had trashed the apartment.

TWO

"I don't like the way you're looking at me," Hooker said.

"I was wondering what you're capable of doing."

The grin was back. "Most anything."

From what I knew of him, I thought this was probably true. He'd started driving on the dirt tracks of the Texas panhandle, scratching and clawing his way to the top. He had a reputation for being a fearless driver, but I didn't buy into the fearless thing. Everyone knew fear. It was the reaction that made the difference. Some people hated fear and avoided the experience. Some people endured it as a necessity. And some people became addicted to the rush. I was betting Hooker fell into the last category.

The wind picked up, the rain slanted into us, and we ran to the building for cover.

"Are you sure you don't want to visit the casa de Hooker?" Hooker asked. "It's not raining in the casa."

"Pass. I need to get back to the apartment."

"Okay," Hooker said. "We'll go back to the apartment."

"There's no *we*."

"Wrong. Until I get my boat back *we* are definitely *we*. Not that I don't trust you . . . but I don't trust you."

I was speechless. I felt my mouth involuntarily drop open and my nose wrinkle.

"Cute," Hooker said. "I like the nose wrinkle."

"If you're so convinced my brother stole your boat maybe you should report it to the police."

"I did report it to the police. I flew in yesterday and discovered the boat was missing. I tried calling your worthless brother, but of course he isn't answering. I asked for him at *Flex II* and found out he'd quit. I tried the dockmaster, but they have no freaking records left. Blood on everything. How inconvenient is that? I called the police this morning and they took my statement. I expect that's as far as it'll go."

"Maybe someone else took your boat. Maybe the guy who killed the night guard took your boat."

"Maybe your brother killed the night guard."

"Maybe you'd like a broken nose."

"Just what I'd expect from a woman named Barney," Hooker said.

I turned on my heel, crossed the lobby, and exited through the door to the parking lot. I put my head down and slogged through the wind and the rain, walking in the direction of Fourth Street. Just for the hell of it, I pointed Bill's car remote in a couple directions, but nothing beeped or flashed lights.

I heard a car engine rumble behind me, and Hooker rolled alongside in a silver Porsche Carrera.

The driver's-side window slid down. "Want a ride?" Hooker asked.

"I'm wet. I'll ruin your leather upholstery."

"No problem. The leather will wipe dry. Besides, I'm thinking of trading up to a Turbo."

I scurried around to the passenger side and wrenched the door open. "What do you expect to gain by following me around?"

"Sooner or later, your brother's going to get in touch with you. I want to be there."

"I'll call you."

"Yeah, right. That's gonna happen. Anyway, I

haven't got anything better to do. I was supposed to be out on my boat this week."

I wanted to get rid of Hooker, but I didn't have a plan. Truth is, I didn't have a plan for *anything*. Alexandra Barnaby Girl Detective was stumped. Just pretend it's a transmission, I thought. You take it apart. You see what's broken. You put it back together. Really go through the apartment. Bill was friendly. He didn't have a well-developed sense of secret. Surely, he talked to someone. You have to find that someone. You found the key in the dog poop pile, right? You can find more.

Hooker made a U-turn on Meridian and pulled into a spot in front of Bill's building.

"Thanks for the ride," I said, and I hit the ground running. Okay, not exactly running, but I was moving right along. I was hoping to get into the apartment and close and lock the door before Hooker could elbow his way past me.

I got one foot on the sidewalk, and I was yanked back by my purse strap.

"Wait for me," Hooker said.

"Here's the thing," I told him. "You're not invited in."

"Here's the thing about driving NASCAR," Hooker said. "You learn not to wait for an invitation."

When I reached the front door I tried opening it without the key. If the door had opened, I would have sent Hooker in first. The door didn't open, so I unlocked it and stepped inside.

"Someone broke into this apartment," I told Hooker. "You can see where they pried the door open. It was unlocked when I got here this afternoon. I don't suppose it was you?"

Hooker looked at the doorjamb. "I was here around four o'clock yesterday and again this morning. I rang the bell, but I didn't try the door. I was so pissed off I could barely see. No, it wasn't me." He followed me up the stairs and gave a low whistle at the mess. "Bill's not much of a housekeeper."

"Do you think I should call the police?"

"If something's been stolen and you need a report to put in an insurance claim, yes. Otherwise, I can't see where it does much good. I don't see the boat police out searching for my Hatteras."

"I can't tell if anything's been stolen. This is the first time I've visited. The television and DVD player are still here."

Hooker strolled into the bedroom and gave another whistle. "That's a *lot* of condoms," he said. "That's a NASCAR amount of condoms."

"How about giving the NASCAR thing a rest," I said.

He returned to the living room. "Why don't you like NASCAR? NASCAR's fun."

"NASCAR's boring. A bunch of idiots, nothing personal, driving around in circles."

"What's *your* idea of fun?"

"Shopping for shoes. Having dinner in a nice restaurant. Any movie with Johnny Depp in it."

"Honey, that's all girl stuff. And Depp's done some pretty weird shit."

I was going piece by piece, picking through the clutter on the floor. I was torn between wanting to put things away and restore order, and feeling like I needed to keep the integrity of a crime scene. I decided to go with restoring order because I didn't want to believe something terrible had happened.

"Maybe you shouldn't be touching this stuff," Hooker said. "Maybe there's something bad going on."

"I'm doing denial," I told him. "Try to be supportive. Help me look."

"What are we looking for?"

"I don't know. A place to start. An address book. A name scribbled on a piece of paper. Matchbooks he picked up in bars."

"I don't need matchbooks. I know the bars Bill liked. We went out drinking together."

"Do you know any of his friends?"

"It looked to me like Bill was friends with everyone."

An hour later, I had everything put away. Couch cushions were back in place. Books were neatly shelved. Knives, forks, assorted junk, and condoms were returned to drawers.

"What have we got here?" I said to Hooker. "Did you find anything?"

"A black lace G-string under his bed. Your brother is an animal. What have you got?"

"Nothing. But he made that phone call to me and he cleaned out his refrigerator. The only thing left is a can of Budweiser."

"Barney, that doesn't mean he cleaned his refrigerator. It means he had to go shopping for more Bud."

"These days most men call me Alex."

"I'm not most men," Hooker said. "I like Barney. Tell me about the phone call."

"Bill said he had to leave Miami for a while. I could hardly hear him over a boat engine. He said if some guys showed up looking for him, I shouldn't talk to them. And, he said I should tell you to kiss his exhaust pipe. I heard a woman scream and the line went dead."

"Wow," Hooker said.

It was six-thirty, and it was getting dark. It was still raining, I didn't have a car, and all that was standing between me and starvation was a single can of Bud. What's worse, I suspected if I opened it I'd have to share it with Hooker.

"Do you have any ideas?" I asked Hooker.

"Lots of them."

"About how to find Bill?"

"No. I don't have any of *those* ideas. My ideas run more to food and sex."

"You're on your own with the sex. I wouldn't mind hearing your ideas about food."

Hooker took his car keys out of his pants pocket. "For starters, I think we should get some."

I did a raised eyebrow.

"Some *food*," Hooker said.

We went to a diner on Collins Avenue. We had beer and burgers, French fries and onion rings and chocolate cake for dessert. There was healthier food on the menu but we weren't having any of it.

"The all-American meal," Hooker said.

"Did you ever eat here with Bill? Do you think anyone knows him here?"

"Pick out the prettiest waitress and I bet she knows Bill."

I had a photo with me. A picture of Bill smiling, standing beside a big fish on a big hook.

The waitress dropped our check on the table and I showed her the photo.

"Do you know him?" I asked.

"Sure. Everyone knows him. That's Wild Bill."

"He was supposed to meet us here," I said. "Did we get the time wrong and miss him?"

"No. I haven't seen him in days. I haven't seen him hanging out at the clubs, either."

We left the diner under clear skies. The rain had stopped and the city was steaming itself dry.

"You're getting better at lying," Hooker said, when we were belted into the Porsche. "In fact, you were frighteningly convincing."

He turned the key in the ignition and the car growled to life. When you grow up in a garage you learn to appreciate machinery, and I got a rush every time Hooker revved the Porsche. As vocal as I was about hating NASCAR, I've been to a couple races. Last year I was at Richmond. And the year before that I was at Martinsville. I wouldn't want to admit to anyone what happened to me when all those guys started their engines at the beginning of the race, but it was as good as any man had ever made me feel in bed. Of course, maybe I was just sleeping with the wrong men.

"Now what?" Hooker wanted to know. "Do you want to flash that photo some more tonight?"

It had been a long, exhausting day with a whole bunch of terrifying moments, starting with the takeoff from BWI. Nothing had turned out as I'd hoped. My sneakers were wet, my skirt was wrinkled, and I needed a breath mint. I wanted to think that the day couldn't get any worse, but I knew worse was possible.

"Sure," I said. "Let's keep going."

We were on Collins, heading south. The art deco buildings were lit for the night and neon was blazing everywhere. There were surprisingly few people on the street.

"Where's the nightlife?" I asked. "I expected to see more people out."

"The nightlife doesn't start until midnight."

Midnight! I'd be comatose by midnight. I couldn't remember the last time I stayed up that late. It might have been New Year's Eve three years ago. I was dating Eddie Falucci. I was a lot younger then. I pulled the visor down to take a look at my hair in the mirror and shrieked when I saw myself.

Hooker swerved to the right, jumped the curb, and skidded to a stop.

"Ulk," I said, flung against the shoulder harness.

"What the hell was that?" Hooker asked.

"What?"

"That shriek!"

"It was my hair. It scared me."

"You're a nut! You almost made me crash the car! I thought there was a body in the road."

"I've seen you drive. You crash cars all the time. You're not going to pin this on me. Why didn't you tell me my hair was a wreck?"

Hooker eased off the curb and cut his eyes to me. "I was worried it was *supposed* to look like that."

"I need a shower. I need to change my clothes. I need a nap."

"Where are you staying?"

"At Bill's apartment," I told him.

"You're kidding."

"I've thought it through, and it's perfectly safe. It's already been searched. What are the chances of the bad guys returning? Low, right? It's probably the safest apartment in South Beach." I almost had myself convinced.

"Do you have club clothes with you?"

"No."

"I can probably come up with something."

Hooker eased the Porsche to a stop in front of Bill's building. "I'll be back at eleven," he said.

The last thought in my head was of Hooker scrounging a dress for me. He probably had a bunch of them under his bed, rolling around like dust bunnies. It was still in the front of my mind when I woke up. It didn't stay there for long.

I opened my eyes and stared up at a very scary guy. He was at the side of the bed, snarling down at me. Hard to tell his age. Late twenties to midthirties. He was maybe six foot four, and his muscles were grotesquely overdeveloped, making him look more science fiction creature than human being. He had a thick neck and a Marine buzz cut. A ragged white scar ran from his hairline, through his right eyebrow, down his cheek, and through his mouth, ending in the middle of his chin. Whatever had slashed through his face had taken out his eye, because his right eye was fake. It was a big shiny glass orb, larger than his seeing eye, inexplicably terrifying. His mouth was stitched together in such a way that the upper lip was always held in a snarl.

I stared at him in stupefied horror for a heart-stopping second, and then I started screaming.

He grabbed me by my shirtfront, picked me up off the bed like I was a rag doll, and gave me a shake.

"Stop," he said. "Shut up or I'll hit you." He looked at me dangling at arm's length. "Maybe I'll hit you anyway. Just for fun."

I was so freaked out my mouth felt frozen. "Wha do wha whan?" I asked.

He gave me another shake. "What?"

"What do you want?"

"I know who you are. I know lots of stuff and I want your brother. He has something that belongs to my boss. And my boss wants it back. Since we can't find your brother, we're going to take you instead. See if we can't swap you out. And if your brother won't deal, that's okay too, because then *I* get you."

"What does Bill have that belongs to your boss? What's this about?"

"Bill has a woman. And it's about fear and what it can do for you. And about being smart. My boss is real smart. And someday he's going to be real powerful. More powerful than he is now."

"Who's your boss?"

"You'll find out soon enough. And you should cooperate or you'll end up like that night watchman. He didn't want to tell us nothing, and then he tried to stop us from going into the dockmaster's office to get the occupancy list. What a dope."

"So you killed him?"

"You ask too many questions. I'm gonna put you down now, and you're gonna walk out with

– 39

me, and you're not gonna give me any trouble, right?"

"Right," I said. And then I kicked him as hard as I could in the nuts.

He just stood there without breathing for a couple beats, so I kicked him again.

The second kick was the home run because the big guy's glass eye almost fell out of his head. He released his grip on my shirt and went to his knees. He grabbed his crotch, threw up, and then went facedown into the mess he'd just made.

I fell back on my ass and scrambled away crab style. I got to my feet and bolted, out of the bedroom, through the living room, down the stairs. I was on the sidewalk, ready to start running and not stop until I reached Baltimore, when Hooker pulled to the curb in the Porsche.

"B-b-big guy," I said. "B-b-big guy in Bill's apartment."

Hooker felt under his seat, brought out a gun, and got out of the car.

This did nothing to make me feel safe. If anything, it added to the panic.

"Don't worry about the gun," Hooker said. "I'm from Texas. We give guns as baptism presents. I knew how to shoot before I could read."

"I don't like g-g-guns."

"Yeah, but sometimes you need them. Lots of people need to shoot varmints in Texas."

"Like coyotes?"

"That would be in the country. In my neighborhood it was mostly pissed-off husbands shooting guys in their naked ass as they jumped out bedroom windows." Hooker looked to the open door and then up to the windows. "Tell me about this big guy."

"He was big. Real big. Like he didn't even fit in his skin. Like the Hulk, except he wasn't green. And he didn't have a neck. And he had a scar running down the side of his face into his mouth where he was all drooly and snarly. And his eye . . . his eye. Actually he didn't have an eye. Only one. The other one was fake, but it was a cheap fake. Like it was sort of too big for the *real* eye. And it didn't move. No matter what the real eye did, the one big cheap fake eye just stared out at me. Didn't blink, or anything. It was . . . frightening."

"Did he have a name?"

"I'm calling him Puke Face."

"Did Puke Face say anything interesting? Like why he was in Bill's bedroom?"

"He said Bill had a woman who belonged to his boss, so he was going to trade me. And that his boss was smart, and that this was all about fear and what it can do for you."

A blind was slightly pulled aside at one of Bill's windows. Hooker aimed his gun at the window. The blind dropped back into place, and a moment later we heard a crash from the other side of the apartment building. "Unh," someone said. And then there was the sound of receding footsteps. *Ka thud, ka thud, ka thud.*

"Sounds to me like he just jumped out Bill's window," Hooker said. "And he's limping."

"I kicked him in the nuts."

"Yeah, that might make him limp. Do you still want to do the club scene?"

I nodded. "I have to find Bill."

Hooker beeped the Porsche locked, and he tossed a shimmery scrap of material at me. "I hope this fits. It was the best I could do on short notice."

"It's still warm."

"Yeah, you probably don't want to know all the details."

I held the dress up by its little string straps. "There's not much here."

"Trust me, you don't want a lot of dress. This is Miami. They really mean it when they say *less is more.*"

I followed Hooker back into the apartment, and we cautiously looked around.

"I'm a little flustered," I said.

"Perfectly understandable. If you need help getting into the dress . . ."

Yeah, right. Not that flustered.

"This is disgusting," Hooker said, upper lip curled at the mess on the rug.

"He threw up after I kicked him the second time."

Hooker instinctively put his hands to his package. "I could throw up just thinking about it."

I dragged myself and the dress into the bathroom. I did some deep breathing and got myself calmed down enough to keep going. Hooker was out there with his gun, and I was safe in here, I told myself. Just get changed and get out.

I stripped my clothes off and exchanged my bikini undies for a thong. I dropped the dress over my head and tugged it down. It was silver metallic with some spandex. It had a V-neck that plunged halfway to my doodah, and the skirt fell two inches below my ass. I swiped some mascara on my lashes, sprayed my hair into a style that looked like maybe my brain had exploded, and I tarted up my mouth. I'd brought two pairs of shoes with me . . . the sneakers and a pair of silver strappy sandals with four-inch stiletto heels. Shoes for every occasion. I slid my feet into the sandals and swung out of the bathroom.

"Holy cow," Hooker said.

"Too short?"

"Now *I'm* flustered."

Hooker had his hair gelled back. He was wearing black linen slacks, a short-sleeve black silk shirt patterned with fluorescent purple palm trees, and loafers without socks. He had a Cartier watch on his wrist, and he smelled nice.

"Easy to see how Puke Face got in. The door is completely broken," Hooker said. "If there's anything of value here, you should hide it or take it with you."

I gave Hooker the photo of Bill to put in his pocket. "The only thing of value is the television, and it's not that great."

I followed Hooker down the stairs and out to the Porsche. Hooker drove a block and a half over to Washington and valet parked the car in front of a club.

"We could have walked," I said.

"Boy, you don't know much. You probably think owning a Porsche is about power and bling. Okay, power and bling is part of it, but it's mostly about valet parking. It's about the sucking up and the ogling and the envy. It's about the *arrival*, baby."

He was being funny, but there was some truth to what he said. There were about a hundred people milling around outside the club. These were the people who weren't thin enough, young enough, rich enough, or famous enough to get on the A list. None of them had arrived in a Porsche. And none of them had given the doorman enough money to compensate for their short-comings.

The doorman smiled when he saw Hooker and motioned him forward. I guess being a famous NASCAR guy has its compensations. The smile widened when he saw me attached to Hooker. I guess having legs that went from my ass all the way down to the ground had its compensations, too.

We took a moment to adjust to the dark and the lights and the pulse from the DJ. The women dancing onstage were all wearing feathers. Big feather headpieces, feathered G-strings, feathered bikini tops on their big fake boobs. The feathers were peach and aqua and lavender. Very South Beach avian.

"You do the men," Hooker yelled at me over the music, pressing the photo of Bill into my hand. "Hit up the bartenders and security guys. I'll do the women. I'll meet you at the exit in a half hour. If you see Pukey, get up on a table where people can see you and start dancing."

If you want to chat with someone in a club you have to yell in their ear or hope they read lips. I found a bunch of guys who knew Bill but none who knew where he was. A bartender gave me a cosmo. I felt a lot more relaxed after I slurked it down. I even started to feel a little brave. I met Hooker in a half hour and we left together.

"Did you get anything?" he asked.

"A cosmopolitan."

"Anything else?"

"Nope. That was it."

"I didn't get a lot either. I'll fill you in later."

The valet brought the car around. We got in and drove three blocks to another club. The experience was almost identical, except this time the women performing were dressed like Carmen Miranda. Lots of fruit on their heads, colorful rumba ruffles on their G-strings, and rumba ruffles on the bikini tops that held up their big fake boobs. I drank another cosmo. And I found out nothing.

"Do you suppose it's possible that we're being followed?" I asked Hooker. "I keep seeing this same guy. Someone different from Puke Face. He's all in black. Slicked-back hair. He was in the diner. And now he's here in the club. And I think he's watching me."

"Sugar, everyone's watching you."

We hit a third club, and I belted back my third cosmopolitan. I screamed at a couple guys, asking about Bill. And then I danced with a couple guys. I had part of a fourth cosmo, and I danced some more. I was liking the music a lot. And I was feeling very unconcerned over Puke Face. In fact, I was feeling pretty darned happy.

In this club, the women onstage were men. They were all dressed in a jungle theme, and they were excellent, except I'd gotten used to seeing a lot of big fake boobs and it felt like something was missing here.

I'd stopped worrying about the time, worrying about meeting Hooker at the designated exit. Probably a half hour had passed, but for some unexplainable reason the numbers on my watch had gotten blurry. Actually, it occurred to me that I might be just a teensy drunk.

Hooker plastered his hand against the small of my back and he guided me off the floor.

"Hey," I said. "I was dancing."

"I noticed."

He maneuvered me out the door and into the warm night air. He gave the parking attendant his ticket and ten dollars.

"So," I said to him. "What's up?"

"I've been watching you dance in this little dress for the last half hour, and you probably want to rephrase that question."

"Are we going to another club?"

"No. We're going home." He looked down at my shoes while we waited for the car to be brought around. "Don't your feet hurt in those shoes?"

"Fortunately, I lost the feeling in my feet an hour ago."

I woke up in Hooker's guest bedroom with the sun pouring in on me. I was still wearing the little dress. I was alone. And I was pretty sure I hadn't done anything romantic before I fell asleep. Hooker had refused to drive me back to Bill's. He said it wasn't safe. I guess he could be right, but it didn't feel safe here either.

I rolled out of bed and padded barefoot across the room to the window. I looked down and had a moment of vertigo. The ground was *w-a-a-ay* down there. Now here's the thing . . . I don't love *high*. Hurtling around a race track at 120 mph, in a metal enclosure resting on four wheels, feels natural to me. Being shot up thirty-two floors in an elevator does not. And the thought of dropping thirty-two floors turns everything in my intestines to liquid.

I carefully backed up and made my way out of the room, down a short hall, and into a large living-dining area. An entire wall of the living room and dining room was glass. I could see a balcony beyond the glass. And beyond the balcony was air. And a seagull flying backward.

The kitchen opened off the dining area. Hooker was lounging against a kitchen counter with a mug of coffee in his hand.

The kitchen was very white with splashes of cobalt blue. The living room and dining room mirrored the white-and-blue color scheme. Very contemporary. Very expensive looking.

"Why is that seagull flying backward?" I asked Hooker.

"Wind. We've got a front blowing through."

And then I noticed it. The sway of the building.

There was a loud *crash*, and I turned to the window in time to see a seagull bounce off the glass and drop like a rock onto the patio.

"Omigod!" I said.

Hooker didn't blink. "Happens all the time. Poor dumb buggers."

"We should do something. Will he be okay? Maybe we should take him to a vet."

Hooker walked over and looked out. "He might be okay. Oops. Nope, he's not okay." Hooker drew the curtains. "Vulture food."

"You're kidding! How awful."

"It's the chain of life. Perfectly natural."

"I'm not used to being this far off the ground," I said. "I don't really love being up this high."

Alexandra Barnaby, master of the understatement.

Hooker sipped some coffee. "It didn't bother you last night. Last night you loved *everything.* You tried to get me to take my clothes off."

"I did not!"

"Okay, I'm busted. You didn't. Actually, I volunteered but you'd already passed out."

I cautiously crept to the kitchen and poured myself a mug of coffee.

"Why are you walking like that?" Hooker wanted to know.

"It's spooky being up here. People weren't meant to live way up here. I feel . . . insecure."

"If God didn't intend for people to live up here he wouldn't have invented reinforced concrete."

"I'm not much of a drinker. My tongue feels like it's stuck to the top of my mouth."

"You keep talking dirty like that and I'm going to get excited."

"You get excited, and I'm leaving."

"It would help if you weren't wearing that dress." His eyes moved north to my hair. "Although, the hair is enough to make most men go limp. Not me, of course. But *most* men."

I could hear flapping and scuffling sounds coming from the patio. "Is that the seagull?" I asked.

Hooker pulled the drape aside and peeked out. "Not exactly." There were some loud angry bird sounds, and Hooker jumped back and pulled the drape shut. "Food fight," he said.

There was a breakfast bar separating the kitchen from the dining room. Four stools lined up in front of the bar. A photo in a silver frame sat on the far end of the breakfast bar. It was a picture of a boat.

"Is this your boat?" I asked, picking the picture up to see it better.

"It *was* my boat. Prettiest boat ever made. And fast . . . for a fishing boat."

"Last night I talked to a bunch of guys who knew Bill, and the consensus is that Bill made a last-minute decision to take off. Apparently, *Flex II* had just returned from a trip to the Bahamas. Bill went clubbing the night he got back, but he was supposed to sail the following morning, so he cut out early. Around one AM. And that's the last anyone's seen him."

"When did he call you?"

"Around two AM."

"So he comes back from a trip to the Bahamas," Hooker said. "He goes clubbing until one AM. He calls me at two AM. And he calls you right after he hangs up with me. He's on a boat. *My* boat!"

"*Maybe* he's on your boat."

"It's the only boat missing in the goddamn marina. I checked. He tells you some guys are going to be looking for him. A woman screams. That's the last we hear from him. An hour later, someone kills the night watchman."

I told him about the night watchman conversation I had with Puke Face. "So what does all this mean?" I asked Hooker.

"Don't know, darlin'."

"I need to go back to Bill's apartment. I left my duffel bag there. I wasn't thinking clearly."

Hooker palmed a set of keys off the bar. "I can help with that. NASCAR Guy to the rescue. After we get you out of the dress and into some shorts we can get on with the Bill search."

I followed him out the door, into a foyer with two elevators. Hooker pushed the button and looked at me.

"Are you okay? You just went white."

That's because my heart stopped pumping when I saw the elevators. "I'm fine," I said. "A little hung over."

We stepped into the elevator, Hooker hit the lobby button, and the doors closed. I sucked in some air and squinched my eyes shut. I didn't whimper or yell out "we're gonna drop like a rock and die." So I was sort of proud of myself.

"What's with the closed eyes?" Hooker wanted to know.

"I don't like to see the numbers changing."

Hooker slid his arm around me and hugged me close to him. "Cute."

Hooker parked the Porsche in front of Bill's apartment building, and we both got out. Bill's front door swung open when I pushed it. No key necessary. Definitely broken.

We went upstairs and froze at the entrance to the living room. The apartment had been tossed. Again. Not trashed, like the first time, but clearly searched. Couch cushions were slightly askew. Drawers weren't entirely closed. My duffel bag wasn't exactly as I'd left it.

"Why would someone go through twice?"

"Maybe we've got two different people."

We walked through the bedroom and bathroom. Nothing appeared to be missing. The Puke Face mess was sort of caked into the rug and not smelling too good.

"Give me ten minutes to shower and change my clothes. And then I'm out of here," I said.

I took a fast shower, blasted my hair with the hair dryer, and got dressed in shorts, T-shirt, and the white sneakers.

Hooker wasn't in the apartment when I came out of the bathroom, so I slid the duffel bag strap over my shoulder and went downstairs to look for him. I found him talking to one of Bill's neighbors. Smart. NASCAR Guy had a brain. Not to give him too much, I thought motivation helped. He really wanted his boat back.

It was late morning, and the sky was a glorious blue, no clouds in sight. The wind had cut back to a gentle stirring of air. The pale stucco buildings with the peach and aqua trim sparkled in the sunlight. Flowers were blooming everywhere, on trees, on vines, on bushes. Lizards rustled in the undergrowth. I was keeping guard for the cockroach.

Hooker left Bill's neighbor when he saw me emerge from the building. He walked over to me and took the duffel bag off my shoulder. Fine by me. No reason to get carried away with women's rights.

"I didn't want to interrupt," I said. "I assume you were asking about Bill?"

"Yeah. I've been going door to door. Most were no answers. I found the super's unit and told him about the broken lock. I said Bill was cruising, and you were here on vacation. He's going to take care of it. I also suggested he get someone in to shampoo the rug. The guy I was just talking to is retired and stays home all the time. His name's

Melvin. His wife doesn't let him smoke in the house, so he's out on the front porch a lot. Said he has trouble sleeping and lots of times he just sits out and smokes."

I smiled at Hooker. "And he saw the guys who broke into Bill's apartment?"

"Both times."

THREE

Hooker dropped the duffel bag into the back of the Porsche. "According to Melvin, the first break-in occurred around eleven, Tuesday night. He said there were two guys. He didn't see them go in. He just saw them leave. He said he thought they were Bill's friends. It turns out Bill has lots of parties. Big surprise, hunh? He said they got into a black Town Car when they left. He didn't know any more than that."

"He give you a description of them?"

"It was dark. He couldn't see much. Medium build. Average height. He thought they were Cuban."

"And the second time?"

"He said they were Caucasian. Two guys again. This time, one went in and one stayed out. Dark slacks. Dark short-sleeve shirts. He was pretty sure they weren't wearing uniforms, but the *Flex* crew wears navy, so I'm not ruling that out. He said the one guy had slicked-back hair like a gangster."

"That sounds like the guy in the diner and the club. Remember I told you he was watching me?"

"It also sounds like half the guys in Miami. Melvin said the one guy walked right in, like he was expected."

"The lock was broken."

"Melvin didn't know about that. Melvin said he saw us leave. And then about five minutes later, the guys in black showed up. Melvin figured Bill was home. I think he felt bad that he didn't report it."

"Did Melvin see Puke Face just now?"

"No. Melvin was inside watching TV."

"Melvin isn't too smart."

"Melvin is at least three hundred years old."

"There seem to be a lot of people involved in this."

"We have the guys who tossed the apartment the first time. We have Puke Face. And we have the guys who tossed the apartment the second time."

"Unsettling."

"Yeah, but don't worry. I could clean their clocks if I had to."

"Because you're the clock cleaner?"

"Because I'm NASCAR Guy!"

"Frightening."

"Get in the car," Hooker said. "I'm taking you to breakfast at the News Café. *Everyone* eats breakfast at the News Café."

Five minutes later, we were on the sidewalk in front of the outdoor eating area of the News Café. We were waiting for a table, and we weren't alone. There were lots of people waiting for tables. We were all milling around on the sidewalk, gawking at the lucky people who had food, gawking at the people across the street who were rollerblading in thongs.

"This is Ocean Drive," Hooker said. "And as you can see, across the street there's a small green belt with a bike path, and beyond the green belt is the beach and the ocean."

"Would you rollerblade in a thong?"

"I wouldn't rollerblade in body armor."

"What happens when someone falls?"

"I move in closer to get a better look," Hooker said. "There's usually a lot of blood."

Hooker waded into the diners, stopping here and there to say hello and ask about Bill. He made the rounds, and he came back to the sidewalk. "Nothing," he said.

After ten minutes of waiting, we got a table. Hooker ordered eggs, a stack of pancakes, sausage, juice, and coffee. I got a bran muffin and coffee.

Hooker poured syrup on his pancakes and looked over at my bran muffin. "Yum," he said.

"If there's one thing I can't stand it's a skinny wiseass."

"I'm not skinny," he said. "I'm buff. I'm ripped. Geeky guys are skinny."

There was a steady stream of guys coming up to Hooker, clapping him on the back, doing weird handshakes with him. "Hey, man," they'd say, "how's it going? What's happening?" And Hooker would say, "It's going good, man." Sometimes Hooker would say, "I'm looking for Wild Bill. Have you seen him?" And the answer was always the same. "Haven't seen him. What's up with that?"

A Miami Beach cop car parked at the curb across the street, followed by two trucks and an RV. A bunch of people got out of the trucks and began off-loading equipment.

Hooker forked pancakes into his mouth. "Two possibilities," he said. "A movie with a volleyball scene, or else it's a fashion shoot. You can tell which it is when the girls come out of the RV. If they have big boobs, it's a volleyball scene."

"I seem to be the only one interested."

"At this time of year Ocean Drive is filled with this stuff. It gets old. Just like the club scene gets old."

"I can't believe you said that. NASCAR Guy thinks the club scene is boring. You keep that up and you'll ruin your image."

"I'll try to be extra shallow today to make up for it."

I finished my muffin, and I was working on a second cup of coffee when my cell phone rang. Hooker and I locked eyes at the first ring, both of us hoping it was Bill. I pulled the phone out of my bag and did a mental groan at the number on the screen. It was my mother.

"Where are you?" she wanted to know. "I've been calling your apartment, and there's never any answer. Then I called your work number, and they said you took a couple days off."

"I felt like I needed warm weather, so I flew down to Miami to visit Bill."

"You hate to fly."

"Yes, but I did it. And here I am. And it's warm."

"How is your brother? He never calls me."

"Bill isn't here. He's at sea, but he should be back any day now."

"When you see him, tell him his friend called yesterday looking for him."

"What friend is that?"

"He didn't leave a name, but he had a Hispanic accent. He said Bill was expecting his call. Something about a property dispute. Apparently Bill inadvertently took something that belongs to this man."

I talked to my mom for another minute, promised I'd be on guard for the roaches, and then I disconnected.

"You're going straight to hell," Hooker said. "You just lied to your mother, didn't you?"

"I don't want her to worry."

"Lying for a good cause. That's the worst kind of lying." He threw some money on the table and stood. "Let's go to the marina and see if my boat's drifted in."

I followed Hooker through the crowd to his Porsche. "Are you telling me you don't lie once in a while for a good cause?"

"I lie all the time. It's just that I'm going to hell for so many other reasons, lying doesn't hardly count."

"You didn't call my mother, did you?"

"No. Was I supposed to?"

"Someone with a Hispanic accent called and asked for Bill. They said it was regarding a property dispute."

*   *   *

Hooker parked at his condo building, and we walked up to the marina. The crime scene tape was still restricting entrance to the dockmaster's office, but it had been removed from the entrance to Pier E. We walked past Pier E to Hooker's pier. *Flex II* was tied up at the end of the dock. No one was on deck. The helicopter was still in place.

"How often does a boat like that cruise?" I asked Hooker.

"The corporate boats are out a lot when the weather's good. The executives use them to sweet talk clients and politicians. It's always nice to have a politician in your pocket."

We stopped at Hooker's slip. No boat.

"Shit," Hooker said. It was more a thought than an exclamation.

There was movement on board *Flex*, and we both turned to check it out. A couple crew members were setting out lunch at the back of the boat.

"Someone's on board," Hooker said.

Two pretty young women in bikini tops and wrap skirts came on deck. They were followed by two men who were in their late sixties, maybe early seventies. Moments later, they were joined by a man in a *Flex* uniform and a poster boy for the young, up-and-coming corporate executive.

"Do you recognize anyone?" I asked Hooker.

"The tall gray-haired guy in the uniform is the captain. I don't remember his name, but he's been around forever. He captained *Flex I* and then moved over to *Flex II* last year when the boat was launched."

"Is there still a *Flex I*?"

"No. It's been scrapped."

"Do you know anyone else?"

"The bald guy with a face like a bulldog. He's a state senator. The guy modeling for Tommy Bahama looks like corporate chum. I don't know who the women are. Entertainment probably."

"And what about the remaining man?"

"Don't know him."

The remaining man was average height and chunky. His thick, wavy hair was silver. His face was doughy. He was wearing tan slacks and a floral-print short-sleeve shirt. We were some distance from him, but something about his body language and the set to his mouth was repelling and sent my thoughts back to the giant flying cockroach.

"Want to share your thoughts?" Hooker asked.

"I was thinking about a cockroach."

"That would have been my second guess."

"He's probably a perfectly nice guy," I said.

Hooker was blatantly staring, hands in his pants pockets, back on his heels. "He looks like he kills people and eats them for breakfast."

The man looked our way and Hooker smiled and waved. "Hi," Hooker said.

The man watched us for a moment without expression and then turned his back on us and continued his conversation with the senator.

"Nice," I said to Hooker. "Now you've annoyed the professional killer."

"I was being friendly. For a minute there I thought we were bonding."

We turned away from *Flex* and walked back to the concrete path. There was a lot of activity around us. The weather was perfect, if you like hot and hotter. It was noon Friday, and by Miami standards this seemed to constitute weekend. Hooker was wearing sandals, totally washed-out jeans with a lot of rips and holes in them, a bleach-stained black sleeveless T-shirt, sports sunglasses, and a ball cap that advertised tires. I had sunglasses but no hat and no sunblock. I felt like I could cook an egg on my scalp, and if I looked cross-eyed I swear, I could see my nose blistering.

A guy was walking toward us on the path. He had a schnauzer on a Burberry leash, and the dog was prancing along, head high, eyes vigilant under bushy schnauzer eyebrows. The guy caught my attention because he was everything Hooker wasn't. His brown hair was perfectly cut and styled. His face was clean shaved. His white three-button knit shirt was stain free and unwrinkled. His khaki shorts were crisply ironed and a perfect fit. He was maybe an inch shorter than Hooker, and he had only slightly less muscle. My best friend, Marjorie, says you can always tell if a guy is gay by the size of his pores. And, even from a distance I could see that this guy exfoliated.

The dog and his walker got even with Hooker and me, and the dog stopped and growled at Hooker.

"I am *so sorry*," the guy said. "He's just been in a mood today. I think he must need a bran muffin."

"No problem," Hooker said. "You've got a good grip on the leash, right?"

"Absolutely. *Down, Cujo*," the guy said to the dog.

"His name is Cujo?"

"No. Not really. His name is Brian."

I smiled at the dog walker. "Jude?"

"Yes?" He looked over at me, recognition slammed into him, and his eyes opened wide. "Barney? Omigod. I don't believe this!"

"This is Jude Corker. We went to grade school and high school together," I said to Hooker. "Jude Corker, Sam Hooker. Sam Hooker, Jude Corker."

"Everyone calls me Judey now," he said, extending his hand to Hooker. "Barney and I were such good friends, and then we went off to college and completely lost touch."

"How long have you been down here?" I asked him.

"I went to school here and decided to stay. I met a lovely man my junior year and that was it. He had a thriving business here, so of course we couldn't move."

"And you're still a couple?"

"We broke up a year ago. Just one of those things. But I'm a Miamian now. What brings you here?"

"Bill lives here."

"No! I didn't know that. I haven't run across him." He looked back at Hooker. "And who is this person? Is this a love interest?"

"Associate."

"Nice body," Judey said. "But the hat has to go. Tires. Ick."

Hooker smiled at him. Friendly.

"I don't suppose you're gay?" Judey asked Hooker.

"Nope," Hooker said. "Not even a little."

"Too bad. The sleeveless tee is a good look for you."

Hooker kept smiling. NASCAR Guy wasn't threatened by Gay Guy.

"And so what does 'associate' mean?" Judey asked. "Because girlfriend, I don't see associate in his eyes. He's looking at you like you're lunch. And shame on you," Judey said, turning to Hooker. "You have her standing out here in the sun without a hat. Look at her little pink nose and her poor pink scalp. You're never going to get to first base if you let this pretty little blond sunburn."

Hooker took his hat off and put it on my head.

"Not *that* hat," Judey said. "That hat belongs in a garage. She's already been there done that. Go get her a nice hat."

Hooker blew out a sigh. "You're going to be here when I get back, right?" he said to me.

"Where would I go?"

"God only knows," Hooker said. And he ambled off.

"He's gorgeous," Judey said. "In a brutish kind of way. Totally ripped."

"He drives NASCAR. And he's from Texas."

"Omigod. Say no more. He's an asshole, isn't he?"

I looked after Hooker. "Truth is, I've known worse. As far as assholes go, he isn't all that bad."

I told Judey about the phone call and the missing boat and the searched apartment. I told him about Puke Face, and I was on a description of the second search when Hooker returned. He took his hat off my head and replaced it with a pink hat that said SEXY in pasted-on rhinestones.

"Much better," Judey said. "Totally tasteless. Very trashy. It's perfect Miami."

"I don't suppose you know any of the *Flex* crew members?" Hooker asked him.

"Well, of course I do. I know a very nice young man named Todd. And since the boat is tied up at the dock and doesn't seem to be going anywhere, Todd is most likely on the beach."

Ten minutes later we were all crammed into Hooker's Porsche. Hooker had the top down, and Judey and Brian were scrunched into the tiny backseat.

"Park at Eleventh," Judey said. "Todd is always at Eleventh Street."

The beach was broad at Eleventh and stretched far in both directions. The sand was white and hard packed. Vendors parked on the beach, selling iced coffee and assorted stuff. And bodies seeking skin cancer were everywhere. The bodies were fat and thin and everything in between. Some of the women were topless. Thongs were the order of the day. And a lot of the thongs were sucked into more cheek than I ever wanted to see.

Traffic buzzed in the background, competing with cell phones and MP3 players and with the *shushhhh* of waves breaking far out and calmly rolling in, swirling around the people who ventured into the water to wade and splash.

Freighters and tankers hung on the horizon. A prop plane flew overhead trailing a banner that advertised a club.

We walked into the crowd of greased-up abs and flabs with Judey leading the way and Brian straining at the leash, snapping and snarling at passing dogs.

"He's *so* alpha," Judey explained. "It's the German in him."

"There's so much on display here," I said to Hooker. "Doesn't it ruin the romance? Would you want to date one of these topless, thonged women?"

Hooker looked around. "I want to date *all* of them. No wait a minute. Not that fat one with the hair on her chin."

"That's a man."

"I don't want to date him."

"Jeepers," Judey said. "I don't want to date him either."

"It's like being in a bakery," Hooker said. "You look at the doughnuts and you want to eat them. Admit it, you walk into a bakery and you get hungry, right?"

"It's not the same."

"It is to a man. This beach is just one big bakery."

"You are so eloquent!" Judey said to Hooker.

"That's because I'm NASCAR Guy," Hooker

said. He slung an arm around my shoulders and dragged me close to him. "This conversation isn't doing much to improve my chances of scoring with you, is it?"

"There he is," Judey said. "That's Todd. He's the luscious thing on the blue beach towel. And he's wearing his red thong. Don't you love it? He's such a Mr. Pickle Pants!"

Todd was stretched on a beach towel, broiling himself on the sand, halfway to the water's edge. He looked like he was probably in his early twenties. And Judey was right . . . Todd was luscious. He stood when he saw us, so we could better appreciate his lusciousness. His body was toned and golden, and the red thong showed off a terrific ass and a bunch of lumpy things in the front. I was trying to think positive about the bakery concept, but the bagels in his bathing suit weren't doing a lot for me.

Todd bent over to pet Brian, and I made an instant mental note to *never* bend over in a thong. Brian didn't share my perspective and thought it was all just fine. In fact, Brian was beside himself, wagging his tail, vibrating with happiness.

Judey introduced us to Todd and told him Bill was missing.

"Missing," Todd said. "What do you mean?"

"Gone. Poof. Disappeared," Judey said.

"We were told he quit."

"Yes. But then he disappeared. And his apartment has been searched. Twice!" Judey said.

"I don't know what to say. He didn't seem to be into anything weird. One minute he was there, and then he was gone. I was sorry to see him take off. He was a good guy."

Brian was dancing around, wanting to be petted some more. He was kicking sand up with his schnauzer toenails, and the sand was sticking to Todd's oiled, perfectly waxed legs.

"Did you work with him on the last trip?" I asked Todd, trying hard not to stare at the lumpy banana sling.

"Yeah. We were out for five days."

"Anything unusual happen?"

"No. It was a routine run, except it was cut short. We were supposed to be out for a full week. A Calflex vice president and a Calflex security guy were on board. A couple South Beach ladies. And four executives from some software company."

"Do you know why it was cut short?"

"No, but it happens. Usually it's because Calflex needs the boat to entertain someone more important. The drill is that the resident Calflex company man says he's sick, and we head back to port. We off-load the cargo, pick up the new VIP, and head back out again. This was a little strange because we were told we were sailing the following day, but then it was cancelled. And the boat's been sitting at the dock ever since. Not that I mind. I'm getting paid for beach time."

Brian wasn't getting any attention with the dancing around so he added some barking. *Arf, arf, arf.*

Judey gave a tug on the Burberry leash. "Stop it!" Judey said to Brian. "Behave yourself."

Arf, arf, arf, arf, arf.

"I got him in the property settlement when we split," Judey said. "I should have taken the Boxster."

Todd looked down at his legs. "I'm going to have to wash this sand off. It's going to ruin my tan."

We walked to the water's edge and waited while Todd plunged into the surf. A roller came in and caught him midthigh.

"Eeeeee. *Cold!*" he shrieked, jumping around, flapping his arms, splashing back to us, doodles bouncing in the silky red pouch.

Brian was at the end of his leash, panting, choking himself, trying to get to Todd. Judey was busy trying to control Brian. And Hooker and I were mesmerized. The bouncing doodles were hypnotic.

"Holy crap," Hooker said.

"You see my problem with the bakery theory."

"Yeah, but just so you know, my 'boys' would look better."

"Let me guess. You've got NASCAR 'boys.'"

"You betcha."

Todd stopped jumping around, and we all pulled ourselves together.

"There were some people on board *Flex* for lunch today," I said to Todd. "One of them was a state senator."

"Bulger. He's around a lot. Doesn't usually sail with us. Just comes to socialize. He pals around with Luis Salzar. Salzar was probably there, too."

We were back at the beach towel, and Todd stood air-drying his legs before reapplying oil.

"Is Salzar a chunky guy with a lot of silver gray hair? Looks like a professional killer?" I asked him.

"Yeah. That's Salzar. I hate when he's on board. The ship always gets locked down."

"Locked down?"

"The main deck is off limits to everyone but Salzar's personal crew. He's got his own steward, two bodyguards, and two-man helicopter crew. Plus the captain and the purser are company men, so they have access. And sometimes Salzar brings one or two members of his family. And I don't necessarily mean relatives when I say family. It's like cruising with Al Capone. Always lots of guns. Conversations that stop when a nonfamily member enters a room. It's pretty darn creepy."

"Salzar's a Cuban businessman," Judey said to Hooker and me. "Got his finger in a lot of pies. He lives in Miami, but the rumors go that he's mucho friendly with Fidel."

"Yeah," Todd said. "We fly Salzar to Cuba on poker night."

We all looked at Todd.

"Not really for poker night," Todd said. "That's just the joke on the boat. When Salzar sails with us we tie up at Shell Island Resort in the Bahamas. And in the dark of night, the helicopter mysteriously takes off and returns with the first light of dawn the following morning."

"You think it takes Salzar to Cuba? Isn't that illegal?" I asked.

Todd shrugged. "Lots of people go to Cuba these days. Not Americans, but everyone else."

"I thought we monitored flights."

"We monitor for drug flights and boat people. Anyway, I imagine a helicopter could go in low, under radar. This is all just conjecture, anyway. Like I said, the second deck is off limits when Salzar's in residence. Junior crew members, like me, don't have access to flight plans. In fact, sometimes we're not even sure where we are. If you want to keep your job on this boat, you do a lot of smiling, you don't ask questions, and you don't stick your nose in where it doesn't belong."

"That doesn't sound like Bill," I said.

Todd grinned. "No. Bill wasn't a total fit. Bill was like Brian. Into everything, tail wagging, kicking up sand."

"Was Salzar on the last trip?"

"Salzar hasn't sailed with us for a while. Maybe two or three weeks. I'd say on an average he goes out once a month. Sometimes his crew goes out without him. Sometimes the second deck gets locked down for just the Salzar people." Todd turned to Hooker. "You're a couple slips down from *Flex*, right? The name of your boat is *Happy Hooker*?"

"Yeah, the boat disappeared with Wild Bill."

"That's a good-size boat. Bill would have a hard time taking it in and out by himself."

"We think he had a girl with him," Hooker said. "You have any idea who it might be?"

"I could probably narrow it down to two or three hundred women."

"No one special?" I asked.

"They were all special," Todd said. "Last I talked to Bill, he was going clubbing. He probably brought someone home with him."

"Someone who could handle a boat," Hooker said.

"Someone who didn't mind a quickie," Judey said. "If they left the club at one, and they were stealing the boat an hour later, they didn't have a lot of foreplay time."

"Maybe Bill ran off with someone's wife and now the enraged husband is after him," Todd said.

A perfectly logical assumption, but the boat part of it bothered me. "I don't get the boat-stealing part," I said. "Bill's running from someone. Let's say it's the husband. Why does Bill take a boat? If you wanted a fast getaway you'd use a car. If you were going any distance you'd take a plane. A boat seems so limiting. And snatching the boat seems extreme. And what about the apartment trashing?" Not to mention Puke Face and the fear speech.

No one had an answer.

"Maybe it was that the boat was the fastest way out," Hooker finally said. "Or maybe it was the only way out. Maybe Bill didn't go home to his apartment. He was supposed to sail in the morning. So maybe he went back to *Flex*, and something happened, and he had to take off."

"We were supposed to sail early. Almost everyone stayed on the boat," Todd said. "I went to dinner with some friends, and I was back on the boat by ten."

"I have twin diesels. Combined they give me fifteen hundred fifty horses," Hooker said. "Didn't you hear *Happy Hooker* leave?"

"You can't hear a whole lot in crew quarters. Mostly you hear the generator. I can ask around, though. Maybe one of the other guys knows something." Todd's eyes opened wide. "Hey, wait a minute. *Happy Hooker* wasn't in its usual slip. There was something wrong with the electrical hookup, so they had her at the end of Pier F. Bill moved her. He had your key. He was listed as captain with the dockmaster."

"I walked every square inch of this marina, and I didn't see my boat," Hooker said. "Why didn't the dockmaster tell me the boat was moved?"

"It was a real mess when they discovered the guard. Nobody was thinking about anything but the murder. And then the office was a mess and the records were trashed. I guess it was a real bloody struggle. Probably no one even remembered about your boat."

"One last thing," I said to Todd. "Have you ever run into a big guy with a scar on the right side of his face? Glass eye?"

"That sounds like Hugo. Don't know his last name. He's one of Salzar's henchmen. Sails with us sometimes."

*   *   *

Hooker swung the Porsche into the lot that serviced Monty's. It had only been a ten-minute drive, but it felt like a lifetime. It looked like Bill had snatched a woman who belonged to Salzar. I didn't know what to think. Was this woman a daughter? A girlfriend? Personal chef?

Hooker and I got out. I took Brian. And Hooker hauled Judey out of the Porsche's pretend backseat.

"What sort of business are you involved in?" I asked Judey.

"Interior design. And I'm much sought after. Calvin and I were making a nice living . . . until he dumped me. The jerk." Judey took Brian's leash from me. "How about you? What have you been up to?"

"I work for Salyer Insurance Group. Property damage. I'm the supervisor over six claims adjusters." Not the world's most glamorous job, but it paid the rent. And paying the rent was important, since I wasn't doing so good in the finding-a-husband department. Unfortunately, it also wasn't a very forgiving job. Salyer Insurance Group wasn't going to be happy if I didn't show up for work on Monday.

"You were always the brain," Judey said. He turned to Hooker. "When we were kids, Barney always won the spelling contests in school. I was a complete loser, but Barney always got a perfect report card."

"You were smart," I said to Judey. "You just had a concentration problem."

"I was conflicted. I was having an identity crisis," Judey said.

"Right now I'm having a hunger crisis," I said. "I need lunch."

"There's a wonderful deli next to Monty's," Judey said. "They have spice cookies that Brian adores."

Brian's ears perked up at the mention of spice cookies.

"Isn't he the clever one," Judey said. "He knows 'spice cookies.'"

Hooker looked doubtful, and I was guessing Hooker wasn't a schnauzer person. Hooker looked more like an English bulldog sort of person. Hooker looked like the sort of guy who'd feed his dog beer. I could see Hooker sitting in front of his television, in his underwear, getting wasted with his bulldog.

"You're smiling," Hooker said to me. "What's that about?"

I didn't think it was a good idea to tell Hooker I was smiling about him in his underwear, so I popped out a lie. "It's Brian," I said. "Don't you think he's cute?"

80 –

"That's not a cute-dog smile," Hooker said. "I know a cute-dog smile when I see it, and that's not it."

"Are you calling me a liar?"

"Yeah."

"Uh-oh," Judey said. "Are we having a lovers' quarrel?"

"We're not lovers," I said to Judey.

Hooker steered me in the direction of the deli. "Not yet," he said.

FOUR

The deli was on the second level on the street side, and leaned more toward Williams-Sonoma than 7-Eleven. An overhead blackboard advertised large chilled shrimp and fresh grilled vegetables. A couple small round tables with chairs had been stuck between polished chrome racks holding gourmet staples.

I cruised past the glass and stainless display cases filled with salads and pasta, hand-rolled cigars, fresh baked bread, soups, chips, the shrimp, fruits, and fancy tapenades. I considered the Häagen-Dazs, cheesecake, and snack packs of Oreos. And then I settled on a turkey roll-up and a bottle of water. Judey got the same, plus an oatmeal raisin cookie for himself and a spice cookie for Brian. Hooker got a roast beef with cheese and coleslaw on a sub roll, a bag of chips, a Pepsi, and three giant chocolate chip cookies.

We sat outside at one of the scrolled concrete and blue tile picnic tables and ate our lunch. When we were done we followed Hooker up and down the piers, looking for his boat.

There were a lot of piers and a lot of boats but none of the boats was Hooker's. Hooker looked like he was thinking dark thoughts. Judey didn't look like he was thinking any thoughts. And all I could think about was Brian's spice cookie, and how I wished I had one. Finally, I gave up the fight, and I left the guys sitting in the sun while I ran back to the deli. I got a cookie and, on impulse, a newspaper, hoping there might be more information about the marina murder.

I joined Hooker and Judey and paged through the paper while I ate my cookie. Nothing new about the murder. I checked out the movie section and read the comics.

I was about to set the paper aside when a photo and headline caught my attention. The photo was of a pretty young woman with lots of wavy dark hair and dark eyes with long dark lashes. She was smiling at the camera, looking a little mysterious. The headline said she was missing. Maria Raffles, age twenty-seven, disappeared Monday evening. She'd been clubbing with her roommate but decided to leave early and went home alone. Foul play was feared. Her apartment had been broken into and violently searched. Maria had been born in Cuba but had managed to reach Florida four years ago. She was an accomplished diver and sailor. And she worked in a Miami cigar factory.

The article went on to explain the immigration service policy of allowing Cuban nationals to remain in this country if they touch U.S. soil, as opposed to being intercepted at sea.

I was holding the paper and my eyes were wide and my mouth was open.

"Let me guess," Hooker said. "Ben and Jerry came out with a new flavor."

I read the piece to Hooker and Judey.

"By God, Watson," Hooker said. "I think you've found something."

"Maybe not," Judey said. "This is Miami. Probably a lot of women disappear after clubbing."

"Don't rain on my parade," I told Judey. "I haven't got anything else. I'm at a dead end in the how-to-find-Bill idea department."

"Yes, but how would this woman relate to Salzar?"

"I don't know. They're both Cuban. There could be a connection."

"Maybe you should go to the police," Judey said. He followed up with a grimace. "I take that back. What was I thinking? This is Wild Bill we're talking about."

"In the past the police haven't totally shared Bill's relaxed attitude to the law," I explained to Hooker.

"Bill's a great guy," Judey said, "but he has a history of getting his brains caught in his zipper."

This had us both looking at Hooker, who we suspected suffered from the same dilemma.

"NASCAR Guy knows enough to wear button fly," Hooker said.

Judey and I smiled. NASCAR Guy was being a good sport.

"I think we move on this," Judey said. "The newspaper doesn't give Maria's address, so let's start with the cigar factory. There aren't that many of them. They're all in Little Havana, around Seventeenth and Calle Ocho."

Hooker took the Causeway Bridge out of Miami Beach into the city of Miami. He wound around some, crossed the Miami River, and found SW Eighth Street. We were now in a neighborhood where businesses advertised in both Spanish and English. *Sopa de pescado, camerones, congelados*. The street was wide and the buildings were low, with

strip mall–style fronts. Stunted palm trees occasionally grew out of concrete sidewalks. The
Porsche was common in South Beach. We were
odd man out in Little Havana. This was the land
of the family sedan. It was midafternoon and the
air was hot and thick. It stuck on my face and
caught in my hair. It was the McDonald's milk
shake of air. You had to work to suck it in.

Hooker swung the Porsche onto Seventeenth
and pulled to the curb. "Here we are," Hooker
said. "Cigar factory number one."

I'm from Baltimore. Factories are big and noisy.
They're in industrial parks. They're filled with
guys in hard hats. They make machine parts, ce-
ramic pipes, conduit wire, molded sheet metal.
This left me completely unprepared for the cigar
factory.

The cigar factory was half a block long, the inner
workings visible behind large plate glass windows. One end of the factory was devoted to a
small retail store. And at the other end, six women
sat at individual tables. Barrels filled with tobacco
leaves had been positioned beside the tables. A
woman selected a leaf and then rolled it into a
cigar. A man stood supervising. The man and all
the women were smoking cigars. They looked up
and smiled when they realized we were watching.
It was a silent invitation. Come in and buy a cigar.

"I'll wait here," Judey said. "Brian is very sensitive to smoke."

Hooker sauntered in and admired some tobacco leaves. He bought a cigar, and he asked one of the women about Maria Raffles.

No, she said solemnly. Maria didn't work there. It was a small community. They'd heard she was missing. The woman thought Maria worked at the National Cigar Factory on Fifteenth.

We climbed into the Porsche and Hooker drove to the National Cigar Factory. Again, there was a small retail store. And beside the store there were women rolling cigars in the window. There were six tables. But there were only five women.

I followed Hooker into the store and took a step back when one of the women jumped up and shrieked at Hooker.

"Omigod!" she yelled. "I know you. You're what's his name!"

"Sam Hooker?" he said.

"Yeah. That's it. You're Sam Hooker. I'm a huge fan. *Huge*. I saw you on television when you crashed at Loudin. I started crying. I was so worried."

"I got pushed into the wall," Hooker said.

"I saw that, too," I told him. "You were hotdogging and you deserved to crash."

"I thought you didn't watch NASCAR," Hooker said to me.

"My *family* watches NASCAR. I was at the house mooching dinner, and I was forced to watch." All right, so maybe sometimes I still enjoyed NASCAR.

"Who's she?" the woman wanted to know.

"I don't know," Hooker said. "She's been following me around all day."

I gave him a shot to the shoulder that knocked him back a couple inches.

Hooker said "*ow*," but he grinned when he said it.

"Alexandra Barnaby," I said extending my hand. "I'm looking for Maria Raffles."

"Rosa Florez," she said.

Rosa was my height, but more round. Fat round breasts. Round brown eyes. Flushed round cheeks. A round Jennifer Lopez bootie. A small, soft roll of fat circling her waist. She had pale Cuban skin, and she had a lot of wavy brown hair cut short. Hard to tell her age. In her forties, probably.

She was wearing a white V-neck knit shirt that showed a lot of cleavage, and jeans that were rolled at the ankle. If you stuck a quarter in Rosa's cleavage and turned her upside down the quarter wouldn't move. She was wearing clear plastic, open-toed four-inch heels that clacked when she walked. She was wearing minimum makeup and lots of flowery perfume.

"Maria isn't here," Rosa said. "She hasn't been here all week. I have to tell you, I'm real worried. It's not like her to miss work. Or not to call anyone. We were real good friends. She would have told me if she was going away."

"Were you at the club with her?"

"No. I don't go to those clubs. I mostly stay in Miami. Maria didn't used to go to those clubs either. She's a Cuban girl, you know. She always stayed in the neighborhood. Then one day a couple months ago she decided she wanted to be by the marina in South Beach. When she was in Cuba she lived in a little town right on the water. She said she missed the diving and the boating since she's been here." Rosa lowered her voice. "I think she was looking to get out of the cigar factory, too. She thought maybe she could meet someone and maybe get a job on a boat. I think that's why she started clubbing. She was pretty. She could get in for free and look at the rich men with the boats. And she was crazy about the diving. Always looking at charts. Always talking about the diving."

"Did she ever mention Luis Salzar?"

"Not that I remember. Maybe just in conversation. Everyone in Little Havana knows of Salzar."

Rosa looked beyond us to the parked Porsche. "Is that your car?" she asked Hooker.

"Yep."

"It's a Porsche, right?"

"Yep."

"So what's the deal here?" Rosa asked. "Why are you looking for Maria?"

"My brother is missing, and we think Maria and Bill might be together."

"On my boat," Hooker said.

"What would they be doing on your boat?" Rosa wanted to know.

"They stole it," he said.

I pressed my lips together. "Borrowed it."

Rosa liked that. "No kidding?"

"The newspaper article didn't give her address," I said.

"I know her address!" Rosa said. "I could show you. I could go with you in the Porsche. I always wanted to ride in a Porsche."

I looked over at the other women. They were older than Rosa and their roundness had turned blocky. They'd all stopped working and were openly staring, waiting to see what would happen next.

"What about your job?" I asked.

"It's almost the end of the day," Rosa said. "I could take off a half hour early."

"You take off a half hour early and you're fired," the lone male foreman said.

"Kiss my ass," Rosa said. "Kiss his ass. Kiss all their asses."

The women burst out laughing and made kissing sounds at the foreman.

"Rosa Louisa Francesca Florez, you're a bad influence," the man said.

"It's true," Rosa said to Hooker and me. "I'm a big *bitch*." She grabbed her purse off the table and shoved her cigar in her mouth. "Okay, let's go."

We all pushed through the door and stood on the sidewalk by the Porsche. Judey was already in the backseat, hugging Brian to his chest.

"News flash," Hooker said. "We're not going to fit."

"Who's the gay guy with the hairy rat?" Rosa asked.

"That's Judey," I told her. "How do you know he's gay?"

"Look at his complexion," Rosa said. "He exfoliates. I'd kill for skin like that. And he's got two eyebrows."

Hooker raised a hand to feel his eyebrows. "I have two eyebrows, don't I?"

"I'm not getting out," Judey said. "I was here first."

Rosa shoved past Hooker and me and climbed

over the car, into the backseat. "Just move your skinny little gay ass over and we can both fit," she said to Judey.

"It's too small," Judey said. "You're going to squish my Brian."

"Your Brian?" Rosa asked.

"My dog!"

"Oh jeez," she said. "I thought you were talking about your thingy. You know how guys are always naming their thingy."

"I've never named my thingy," Hooker said. "I feel left out."

"It's important to get the right name," Rosa said, trying to maneuver her ass onto the seat. "They all have their own personality."

Judey was trying to make himself very small in the backseat. "It should have something to do with NASCAR."

I slid a look at Hooker. "Speedy?"

"Sometimes," Hooker said.

Rosa was wedged into the back with one leg hanging outside the car and one foot on the console. "I'm ready," she said. "Take me to South Beach."

Maria lived a couple blocks from Bill on Jefferson. The building was similar but larger. Tan stucco. Six floors. Small balconies opening off each apartment. A small front foyer with two elevators. Not totally decrepit, but it looked like it had the potential to be home to the cow-size cockroach. The ever-present lizards skittered away from us as we approached the foyer door.

"Maria has a roommate," Rosa said, punching the button for the second floor. "She's a waitress working the dinner shift, so she should be home now getting ready to go to work."

There were six apartments to the floor. Maria lived in 2B. Rosa rang the doorbell and the chain slid back on the inside and the door was opened.

Maria's roommate was young. Twenty, maybe. She had long straight blond hair and lips so pumped up with collagen I took a step back in case they exploded. She had a tiny waist, and a tiny nose, and big boobs with big nipples jutting out of a tiny white T-shirt. She was pretty in a painful, manufactured generic sort of way.

"Rosa!" she said. "Omigod, this isn't bad news, is it? Tell me they didn't find her dead. She's okay, right?"

"Nobody's heard from her," Rosa said.

"That's good. I mean, at least she's not dead or maimed. I mean, not that we know of."

"These are friends of mine," Rosa said. "We're all looking for her. And this is Barbie," Rosa said by way of introduction.

Barbie. Judey, Hooker, and I went momentarily speechless.

Barbie's eyes opened wide at the sight of Brian. "Look at the cute doggie. And *hello* handsome," she said to Hooker.

"I'm handsome," Judey said.

"Yes, but your complexion is flawless, you're perfectly shaved, and you have two eyebrows. Gay, gay, gay."

Hooker did another eyebrow feel. "I'm starting to really worry about this eyebrow thing."

"We were hoping you'd have some ideas about Maria," Rosa said to Barbie. "Were you clubbing with her the night she disappeared?"

"Yeah, sort of. We went together, but then we got separated. You know how that is. I'm breaking into modeling so I try to work a room."

"Do you think she hooked up with anyone?"

"Don't know. I lost sight of her. She called me on my cell and told me she was leaving. That was around twelve. We had only just gotten there."

"What about before that?" I asked. "Did she talk about going away? Was she upset? Was she scared? Was she excited?"

"No, no, no. And yeah, sort of. She was working on some project. Some dive thing. I don't know anything about diving. *Hello*. Don't care either. *Boring*. But Maria was into that stuff. She had a bunch of maps in her room. Water maps."

"Charts?" Hooker said.

"Yeah. Charts. But they got stolen. Or maybe she took them. Or maybe someone took Maria *and* the charts. The apartment was trashed the night she disappeared, and so far as I can see the only things missing are the charts from her room. And I know this is really weird but the apartment got broken into and trashed a second time two days later. How's that for shitty luck?"

"Do you mind if we look at her room?" I asked.

"Knock yourself out. I have to get ready for work. I'm waiting tables until I get my big break into modeling. Don't mind her room. I tried to put it back together the first time, but I haven't gotten to cleaning up the second time."

Barbie disappeared into her bedroom and we all trooped into Maria's room.

"This is a mess," Rosa said. "Maria would die if she saw this. She was real organized. That's why she was so good with the cigars. She was neat. And she had good fingers."

"You won't really get fired, will you?" I asked.

"Nah. They're already down Maria. And there's not many people can roll a cigar. Most young people don't want to learn. Rather work at Burger King. When my generation retires they'll probably close down the factories."

I was combing through the clutter, looking for anything interesting, anything that might tie Maria to Bill. Rosa was doing the same. Judey, Hooker, and Brian took the rest of the apartment.

Judey danced into the bedroom and waved a little leather book at me. "I found her address book," he said. "I am the master detective. I am the Magnum of South Beach." And he handed the book over to me with a flourish. "I also found bags of chips and boxes of crackers in the microwave. And you know what *that* means."

I had no idea. "What?" I asked.

"Cockroaches," Rosa said. "They got roaches as big as a barn cat in here. They keep the chips in the microwave so the roaches don't get them."

Damn. "Do they fly?"

"I've never seen them fly," Rosa said. "But I wouldn't be surprised. We're talking major mutant roaches."

Hooker ambled in. "What's up?"

"Judey found an address book. Rosa and I didn't find anything."

Hooker looked around, his attention focusing on the small desk. "She has a laptop. Let's see where she goes on the net." He turned the laptop on and studied the icons at the bottom of the screen. "No AOL. Looks like she uses Explorer as her browser of choice." He went to the top of the screen and clicked on the phone connection. When he had a connection he hit the Explorer icon and the home page came on. He had several choices at the side of the page. He hit *history* and a chronology of Maria's Internet use appeared.

"Wow," I said. "I'm impressed."

"Not that impressive," Hooker said. "I have a lot of downtime, and I kill time by surfing. I lucked out here. Maria uses the same browser I use, so I sort of know where to go." Hooker started working his way through the dates. "Okay, I'm getting a little freaked," he said. "She's pulling some nasty stuff up. She started out with Cuban history. To be more specific, the Kennedy Missile Crisis. From there she went to sites detailing Soviet munitions brought onto the island. She looks at nuclear warheads. And then she goes to sites detailing chemical agents."

"Maybe someone else used her computer," Rosa said. "Like her roommate."

We all stared at Rosa.

"You're right," she said. "What was I thinking?"

"She's also been reading up on gold," Hooker said. "Weights and measures stuff."

"Anything else?"

"Nothing interesting. As you can see, the rest is more typical. Mostly eBay and weather."

Hooker shut the computer off, and we all trooped out of Maria's bedroom. We called good-bye to Barbie and let ourselves out. We silently entered the elevator and dropped to the ground floor. No one said anything until we were out of the building, at curbside, standing next to the Porsche.

Judey had been holding Brian the whole time. He put Brian down and Brian lifted his leg and peed on the Porsche's right rear tire.

"What a good boy," Judey cooed to Brian. "He had to go pee, and he held it all that time."

"You know there are places where they *eat* dogs," Rosa said.

I thumbed through the address book. "Bill's name isn't in here," I said.

We were on a corner, and just for the hell of it, I took Bill's keys out of my purse and pointed the automatic lock gizmo down the street. Nothing. I turned and tried the cross street. A red-and-white Mini Cooper, two cars away, beeped at me.

"Do it again," Hooker said.

I pointed the gizmo at the Mini and got the same response. The Mini flashed its lights and beeped.

"I don't get it," Rosa said. "What's with the car?"

"It's Bill's," I said. Leave it to Bill to drive a Mini Cooper.

We walked over to the car and looked inside.

"No bloodstains," Hooker said.

"That is *so gross*," Judey said.

Rosa made the sign of the cross.

"It looks like Bill and Maria were together the night they disappeared," I said.

"Maria was excited about a dive project and her charts are missing. Plus Hooker's boat is missing. So I'm guessing Wild Bill and Maria are off on a sunken treasure hunt," Judey said. "Mystery solved."

"It must be the mother of all treasure hunts," Hooker said. "They both walked out on their jobs. Two different groups of people are after them. And one of those groups includes Salzar. A night watchman was killed at the marina. They 'borrowed' my boat. And Maria's been researching gold and warheads."

"I don't know anything about a night watchman getting killed," Rosa said. "And why is Salzar involved?"

"I'm surprised you didn't read about the murder in the paper," Judey said. "It was splashed all over."

"I live in a neighborhood where murder isn't big news. Guess I overlooked the fancy pants marina murder that was in the paper. I was probably in a hurry to see what Snoopy was doing."

"Monday night my brother and Maria went clubbing and it looks like they left together, took Hooker's boat, and disappeared. That night the watchman at the marina was stabbed and killed outside the dockmaster's office. And one of Salzar's employees broke into Bill's apartment last night and tried to kidnap me."

Rosa gave a single shake to her head. "I don't like this. Maria is mixed up in something bad. Such a nice girl, too."

"I'd like to know about the dive project," I said. "Maria must have talked to someone about it."

"Maybe family," Rosa said. "She hasn't got a lot. Just a cousin. She's never seen her father. She doesn't talk about it, but I think maybe he was killed or maybe put in prison. She has a hatred of Castro. Her mother died four years ago. That was when Maria left Cuba."

"No sisters or brothers?"

"No. Her mama never remarried."

"Do you know the cousin?"

"Felicia Ibarra. She lives a couple blocks from me. I know her from Maria, and sometimes I see her at showers and things. She's probably at work now. The Ibarras own the fruit stand on Fourth."

"Oh my goodness," Judey said. "Look at the time. I have to go. I have a dinner date tonight. I hate to punk out on the investigation, but this guy I'm dating knows someone at Joe's Stone Crab. And you know how hard it is to get into Joe's."

"Do you need a ride home?" I asked him.

"No. I live one block from here." He took a card out of his wallet and scribbled a number on it. "This is my cell phone. And my home phone is on the card, too. Call me if you need help. I'll get Todd to sniff around on *Flex*."

I gave Judey my cell number. "It's been great seeing you again," I said.

Judey gave me a hug, and he and Brian left.

I opened the driver's side door on the Mini, and Hooker grabbed me by the back of my T-shirt.

"What do you think you're doing?" he asked.

"I'm going to the fruit stand on Fourth."

"By yourself?"

"Sure."

"I don't think so."

"Well, I was going to take Rosa."

"Remember me? I'm the guy who's been driving you around?"

"Yes, but I have a car now."

"And you were going to leave me standing here?"

"Yeah."

Hooker smiled. "You're teasing me. That's a sign of affection, you know."

Actually, I hadn't been teasing.

"Don't forget about me," Rosa said to Hooker. "I could *really* give you a sign of affection. I'm a divorced woman. I'm desperate."

"Everybody in," I said. "Let's see what this little guy can do."

I positioned myself behind the wheel and felt like I was in a sports car whose growth had been stunted in childhood. The Mini had black leather trim and black leather bucket seats. It was deceptively comfortable and had great visibility. I turned the key and stepped on the gas, and the car leaped forward. When I'm at home I drive a Ford Escape. Compared to the Escape, the Mini had the feel of a turbocharged roller skate.

I rocketed to the corner and hung a left without braking.

Rosa had both hands braced on the dash. "Holy mother," she said.

Hooker slid off the backseat, righted himself, and reached for the shoulder harness.

"Corners like a dream," I told them.

"Yeah," Hooker said, "but you drive like a nightmare. I don't suppose you'd want to relinquish the reins on these horses to me?"

"No chance."

I took the Causeway Bridge into Miami, sailing through traffic, enjoying the feel of the car. The car handled like a hummingbird—hovering at a light, zipping ahead, cutting in and out of gridlock.

The reality of my life is that I love to drive, and I probably would have been happier driving a truck for a living than I am working for an insurance company. But you don't spend all that time and money on a college education so you can drive a truck, do you?

Little Havana was busy at this time of day. It was Friday afternoon, and people were on their way home from work, running errands, gearing up for the weekend. I followed Rosa's directions to the fruit stand and pulled into the lot. I parked the Mini and heard Hooker mumble from the backseat.

"What was that?" I asked.

"You're a maniac."

"You're not used to being a passenger."

"True," Hooker said, climbing out of the car. "But you're still a maniac."

And that was probably also true. By reputation, I was the sensible, smart sibling. But that was only by comparison.

The stand was packed with people buying produce, fried polenta, and pulled pork to go. Rosa found Maria's cousin and brought her over to Hooker and me.

Felicia Ibarra was from the same mold as Rosa. A little shorter. Just as round. Different shoes. Ibarra was wearing wood clogs. Probably in deference to the smushed fruit that littered the pavement around the fruit stand. Ibarra was older. Maybe in her early sixties. And Ibarra had a heavy Cuban accent. Clearly, not U.S. born.

"Rosa tells me you're looking for Maria Raffles," Felicia said. "I have to tell you, I'm worried. She has so much trouble behind her. And now she's missing. I worry that this is more trouble. Heaven help her." And Felicia Ibarra crossed herself.

"What kind of trouble?" I asked.

"Just trouble. Some families carry the trouble. It happens. They have a curse. Or an obsession. Or just bad luck."

"And Maria's family?"

Felicia shook her head. "They have Cubano trouble. Sometimes it can be bad on the island. And what I know are only things whispered. Not from Maria. She never says anything. But I hear from my cousin who hears from her sister, Maria's mother, rest in peace. I was told there was trouble with Maria's grandfather. Enrique Raffles. He was a fisherman. He fish from a little town to the west of Havana. Nuevo Cabo. He owned a boat and sometimes he would use the boat for other things. Sometimes a boat would come from Russia and the cargo would be best kept secret. Maria's grandfather was good at not seeing things, so he would go out to the big boat and let them put things in the hold of the little boat to be taken ashore. He would do this at night, when there was no moon. And he would also bring things from Cuba to the Russian sailors."

"Maria's grandfather was a smuggler?" Rosa asked.

"Yes. And he work with another man because the boat was too big for one man. But I don't know this other man.

"Then one night the men went out to get special cargo, and somehow the little fishing boat ran into a reef and went down. The one man got to shore, but Maria's grandfather did not.

"Maria's father, Juan, was fourteen years old when this happened. He took a vow to bury his father and he started diving, looking for the boat. Many people looked for the boat, but no one found it.

"Juan married, and still he kept diving, even when his wife was pregnant. It was the vow to bury his father. And then one night, a month before Maria was born, the police came and took Juan away. He was never seen again. When the relatives came to help with the birth of Maria they found a fresh grave in the little backyard and a cross with *E. R.* hand carved into it. And everyone knew Juan had found his father.

"Some say there was gold on the boat that night it went down. Gold that belonged to Castro. And that's why Juan was taken away. Because Castro wanted his gold. And there are other rumors too. Rumors about a very bad weapon. Something new the Russians were sending into Cuba.

"Maria's mother never remarried. She stayed in the little village, always hoping Juan would return. She died four years ago. That is when Maria escaped the island and illegally sailed her little boat here to Miami."

"Such a tragic history," Rosa said. "I had no idea."

"She was marked by her family history. Like a thumbprint on her forehead. How you say it in this country . . . destiny? She was called to dive. Like her father. Always looking for the ship-wreck."

FIVE

I took Rosa home and then I took Hooker back to his car. I parked behind the Porsche, and we sat in silence for a couple minutes. Both of us thinking about Maria.

"Fuck," Hooker finally said on a sigh.

I nodded my head in agreement.

"Your brother is involved in some serious shit," Hooker said.

"We don't know for sure."

"You're worried."

"Yeah."

"Never fear," Hooker said. "NASCAR Guy is here to help you."

Hooker was a nice guy, I decided, but he wasn't James Bond. I needed James Bond.

Hooker looked at me, his eyes hidden behind his dark sunglasses. "Don't underestimate NASCAR Guy."

"Does NASCAR Guy have any ideas about where to go from here?"

"Yep. NASCAR Guy thinks we should go to Monty's. Get a sandwich. Have a beer. Hang out. NASCAR Guy has some other ideas, too, but he's going to wait until he gets a beer in you before he shares those ideas."

"Do you want to follow me over?"

"You follow me. We'll use the garage at my condo. It'll be impossible to get a parking place at Monty's at this time of night."

"Okay," I said. "I'll follow you."

Now here's the thing, this wasn't the first time I'd gotten a middle-of-the-night call from Bill. Usually he was stranded somewhere and needed a ride home. Usually there was a woman involved. Twice he needed me to bail him out of jail. Neither of those incidents was serious. When I couldn't reach Bill after this latest call I was concerned enough to get on a plane, but truth is, I wasn't a wreck over it. I'd suspected it was business as usual. I thought I'd find Bill, help him out of a messy situation, and go home. When I discovered his apartment had been ransacked, I was thinking irate husband or boyfriend. When there was a murder at the marina I was trying to convince myself it was a meaningless coincidence. Pukey showing up to kidnap me raised my level of alarm by about two hundred percent.

Now I was thinking Bill had finally done it. Bill had finally managed to get himself involved in something serious. He'd put his nose someplace it absolutely didn't belong. He'd stolen a boat and gone off with a woman who was diving for God-knows-what.

I had a gnawing ache in my stomach that wasn't going to be fixed with pizza. I was afraid I might not be able to clean up the mess this time. I was afraid it might be too big and I might be too late.

I looked at the Porsche, turning into the parking garage in front of me and admitted to myself that I was happy to have Hooker involved. It didn't have anything to do with Hooker being NASCAR Guy. In fact, gender wasn't the comforting factor. It was just nice not to be afraid and alone.

Hooker and I parked and walked over to Monty's. The sun was starting to drop in the sky, and another day was passing without word from Bill.

Hooker slung an arm around my shoulders. "You're not going to cry, are you?" he asked me.

"No," I said. "Are you?"

"NASCAR Guy doesn't cry."

"What are we looking to accomplish at Monty's?"

"We're going to eat. And while we're eating we can check out the boats. Who knows, maybe Bill will come cruising in."

We sat at the bar, and we looked at the boats. We watched the people. We looked down the pier at *Flex*. Not much happening. No Florida politician or Cuban businessman in sight. I ordered a Diet Pepsi and a turkey club. Hooker got a beer, a cheeseburger, fries, a side of potato salad, and cheesecake for dessert. Plus he ate the chips that came with my club.

"Where does it go?" I asked him. "You eat enough food for three people. If I ate all that food I'd weigh seven hundred pounds."

"It's about metabolism," Hooker said. "I work out, so I have muscle. Muscle burns calories."

"I have muscle."

"Do you work out?"

"I take the escalator to get to the nosebleed seats at the Orioles games and then I jump up and down and scream my lungs out once in a while when they score."

"Strenuous."

"Damn straight."

Maria's address book was lying on the table. I'd thumbed through the little book twice now and nothing significant had jumped out at me. Of course there'd have to be a notation that hit me over the head before a name seemed significant. It would have to read *Riccardo Mattes, Cuban mafia hit man* for me to figure it out. Because I didn't have anything better to do, I ran through the book again. *Delores Daily, Francine DeVincent, Divetown . . .*

The lightbulb went on in my head. "Here's something," I said. "Maria was obsessed with diving. Now Maria has disappeared. Her charts have disappeared. Your boat has disappeared. What else does she need?"

"Dive equipment," Hooker said.

"Did you have dive equipment on your boat?"

"No. I tried diving a couple years ago, but it wasn't my thing."

"The roommate didn't say anything about dive equipment. And it's sort of bulky, right? The roommate would have seen it."

"I'm not an expert, but when I was diving I had a buoyancy compensator vest, some tanks, a regulator, flippers, a light, a compass, a bunch of gauges."

"So where's her dive equipment?"

Hooker pulled a folded sticky note out of his pocket and punched a number into his cell phone.

"What's that?" I asked.

"It's the roommate's phone number."

"You got her phone number?"

"Hey, she gave it to me. She *forced* it on me."

I did an eye roll.

"I can't help it. I'm a hunk of burning love," Hooker said. "Women like me. Most women, anyway. Except for you. I get a *lot* of phone numbers. Sometimes they write them on their underwear."

"Eeeuw."

"It's not that bad. It's a variation of the bakery thing," Hooker said.

He connected with the roommate, did some preliminary flirting, and asked about the dive equipment.

"Maria has dive equipment," Hooker said, putting his phone back in his pocket. "It's in a storage locker in the apartment building. And it's still there. The roommate keeps her bike in the locker. She used the bike this morning, and she remembers seeing the dive equipment."

"So maybe this isn't about diving."

"Or maybe Maria and Bill knew someone was

after them, and they only had time to get the charts. You can always buy more dive equipment."

I saw Hooker's eyes focus beyond my shoulder, and I turned to find a man smiling at us. He was nicely dressed in a black shirt and black slacks. His hair was slicked back. His face was perfectly tanned. His teeth were shockingly white and precisely even. Full veneers I was guessing. I was pretty sure it was the guy from the diner and the club. And maybe he was the guy Melvin saw coming out of Bill's apartment.

"Sam Hooker," he said. "I'm a fan. This is a real pleasure."

"Nice to see you," Hooker said.

"And this is Miss Barnaby, if I'm not mistaken?"

Hotshot NASCAR drivers are recognized all the time. Claims adjusters are rarely recognized. Actually, we're *never* recognized. And I was okay-looking, but I wasn't Julia Roberts. So being approached by a total stranger who knew my name (and maybe had been following me) was disconcerting.

"Do I know you?" I asked.

"No," he said. "And my name isn't important. What's important is that you pay attention, because I like watching Hooker drive, and I'd hate to see that end."

"And?" Hooker asked.

"And I'm going to have to take steps if you continue to look for Maria Raffles. My employer is also looking for her, and you're muddying the water."

"My brother—"

"Your brother made a bad decision, and there's nothing you can do now to help him. Go home. Go back to your job. Forget your brother."

"Who's your employer?" Hooker asked.

The guy in black dismissed the question with a small humorless smile. "I'm the one you need to worry about. I'm the one who will pull the trigger."

"Or hold the knife?" Hooker said.

He gave his head a slight shake. "That wasn't my work. That was clumsy. Ordinarily I wouldn't give a warning like this, but like I said, I enjoy watching you drive. Take my advice. Both of you. Go home."

And he turned and left.

Hooker and I watched him walk away, past the pool, disappearing into the dark shadows of the taproom and beyond.

"He was a little creepy," Hooker said.

"I *told* you I was being followed by some guy with slicked-back hair who dressed in black! Maybe we should turn this over to the police."

"I thought you were worried about your brother's involvement."

"That was before someone threatened to shoot us."

Bob Balfour met us at Bill's apartment. Balfour was plainclothes Miami PD. He was in his early thirties, and he reminded me of a golden retriever. He had brown retriever eyes, and sandy blond retriever hair and a pleasant retriever personality. He was easy to talk to, and easy to look at, but if I'd had a choice I would have preferred a cop who reminded me of a Doberman. When I called the police I'd hoped to get a cop who could corner a rat and snatch it out of its hiding place.

Balfour looked around Bill's apartment and wrote in his little cop notebook. He listened carefully when I told him about the guy in black. He looked slightly disbelieving when I told him about Puke Face. He took down Bill's neighbor's name for possible future interrogation.

I told him about Maria surfing bomb sites. He included this in his notes. He asked if I thought she was a terrorist. I said no.

He said Bill would be added to Missing Persons. He said I should call him if I was threatened again. He suggested I follow the hit man's advice and go home. He asked Hooker what he thought

about the restrictor plates NASCAR was impos-
ing on the cars. And he left.

"Sort of unsatisfying," I said.

"Cops are like that. They have their own way of
working."

"Mysterious."

"Yeah. Are you going home?"

"No. I'm going to keep bumbling along, looking for Bill. Let's check out some dive shops."

We drove back to Hooker's building and stood
in front of the bank of elevators. Hooker pushed
the up button, and I refused to crack my knuckles
or faint or burst into tears. It's just a stupid elevator, for crying out loud, I told myself.

Hooker looked at me and grinned. "You really
do hate elevators. You didn't blink when that guy
threatened to kill us, but you're breaking into a
sweat over this elevator."

The doors opened, Hooker stepped in and held
the door, waiting for me.

I was thinking, get in the elevator, but my feet
weren't moving.

Hooker reached out and grabbed me and
pulled me into the elevator. He hit the button for
the thirty-second floor, and I inadvertently whimpered. The doors closed, and he pulled me to him
and kissed me. His tongue touched mine, and I

think I whimpered again. And then the elevator doors opened.

"Do you want to go up and down a couple more times?" Hooker asked.

"No!" I jumped out of the elevator.

He slung an arm around my shoulders and steered me toward his condo. "Do you have any more irrational fears? Snakes? Spiders? Monkeys? Fear of eating pizza? Fear of making love to NASCAR drivers?"

"The NASCAR fear and the monkey fear might be redundant," I said.

Hooker unlocked his door, stepped in, and looked around. "Everything looks okay," he said. "I was worried I was going to find it had been destroyed. Every place we go into lately has been searched at least twice." He got a phone book and turned to the dive shop advertisements. "You're going to call," he said. "People are more willing to give information out to women. And besides, you're getting good at lying."

"What am I supposed to say?"

"Tell them your roommate called and asked you to pick up a regulator, but you don't know anything about diving, and she didn't say what kind of regulator. Ask if they know her, and they remember what she bought."

There were two dive shops in South Beach, a couple in Miami and one in Coral Gables. I called all of them. The store that was listed in Maria's book, Divetown, remembered her but hadn't seen her in weeks. The others had no knowledge of her.

"Maybe we're looking too close," Hooker said. "If they were running from someone, they might have stopped under way. Like in the Keys."

I got a hit on the second try. Scuba Dooba in Key West. Maria and Bill had been in on Wednesday.

"Hold a regulator for me," I said. "I'll pick it up tomorrow."

Fifteen minutes later, we were in the garage, arguing over cars and driving.

"We should take the Mini," I said. "The shooter with the slicked-back hair probably knows your car."

"Fine," Hooker said, "but I'm driving."

"No way. It's my brother's car. *I'm* driving."

"Yeah, but I'm the man."

"What the heck does that have to do with anything?"

"I don't know. It was all I could come up with. Come on, give me a break and let me drive. I've never driven one of these little things. Besides, I know the roads."

Knowing the roads got him a couple points. "Okay," I said, "but don't expect to *always* drive."

Hooker took the bridge out of South Beach, and I kept my eyes on the road behind us, watching to see that we weren't followed. Hard to do while we were in the multilane tangle of roads going through the city. Easy to do once we got out of the greater Miami area and traffic thinned.

Florida is flat, flat, flat. As far as I can see, the highest point in Florida could very well be a sanitary landfill. You don't notice the flatness so much when you're in a city like Miami. The planted palms, the flashy buildings, the waterways, the beautiful people, the expensive cars, and international influences add interest to the cityscape. As you leave the city and Route 1 dips south to Florida City and Key Largo, the tedium of the landscape becomes painfully apparent. The natural vegetation is scrubby, and the towns of south Dade County are small and unmemorable, hardly noticed in the relentless stream of strip malls lining the road.

The Mini engine hummed in my head and the concrete moving toward me was hypnotic. Thank God Hooker was driving because I was barely able to keep my eyes open. It turns out Hooker is unflappable in traffic and tireless on the open road. Not much of a surprise since he is, after all, NASCAR Guy.

I became more alert when we got to the bridge to Key Largo. Florida has never held much interest for me . . . with the exception of the Keys. The Keys conjured images of Ernest Hemingway. And the ecosystem was unique and as foreign to downtown Baltimore as I could possibly get. I know all this because I watch the Travel Channel.

We passed through Largo and began skimming along on bridges that felt inches above the water, hopping key to key. Plantation Key, Islamorada, Fiesta Key. The sun was setting and the sky was washed in Day-Glo flamingo pink broken by magenta slashes of cloud. The roadsides were cluttered with fried-food shacks, real-estate offices, Froggy's Gym, some chain restaurants, gift shops specializing in trinkets made from shells imported from Taiwan, gas stations, and convenience stores tucked into small strip malls.

We motored through Marathon, over the Seven Mile Bridge, through Little Torch Key. It was dark when we got to Key West. It was a weekend, and Key West was packed with tourists. The tourists clogged the sidewalks and streets. Lots of overweight men in brown socks and sandals and baggy khaki shorts. Lots of overweight women wearing T-shirts that advertised bars, bait shops, their status as grandmothers, ice cream, motorcycles, Key West, and beer. Restaurants were lit, their tables spilling onto sidewalks. Shops were open selling local art and Jimmy Buffet everything. Vendors hawked T-shirts. Ernest Hemingway look-alikes offered themselves up on street corners. Ten dollars and you can have your picture taken with Ernest Hemingway.

"I thought it would be a little more . . . island," I said.

"Honey, this *is* island. If Ernest was alive today, he'd be living in South Beach doing the clubs."

"I don't see a lot of hotels. Are we going to be able to get a room?"

"I know a guy, Richard Vana, who has a house here. We can crash there overnight."

Hooker turned down a side street, away from the crush of tourists. He drove two blocks and pulled into a driveway. We were in a pocket of small elaborate Victorian houses and plantation-shuttered island bungalows that were lost in shadow, tucked back from the narrow street behind tiny yards filled with exotic flowering bushes and trees.

I took my bag and followed Hooker to the house. It was a single-story bungalow. Hard to see the color in the dark, but it looked like it might be yellow with white trim. The air was heavy with the scent of night-blooming jasmine and roses. No lights on inside the house.

"It looks like your friend isn't home," I said to Hooker.

"He's never here. A couple weeks out of the year. I called before we left Miami and asked if we could use his house." Hooker ran his hand above the doorjamb and came up with a key. "One of the advantages to driving NASCAR. You meet a lot of interesting people. This guy has a boat I can borrow, too . . . if we need a boat." Hooker opened the door and switched on the foyer light.

The house wasn't big, but it was comfy. Furniture was rattan and overstuffed. Colors were crimson, yellow, and white. Floors were cherry.

"There are two guest bedrooms down the hall to the right," Hooker said. "Take whichever one you want. They're both pretty much the same." He dropped his bag, wandered into the kitchen, and stuck his head in the refrigerator. "We've got Corona and Cristal champagne and diet cola. I'm going for the Corona. What would you like?"

"Corona. Looks like you know your way around the house."

"Yeah. I probably spend more time here than Rich. I like the Keys."

"Do you like it better here than South Beach?"

He took a long pull on his Corona. "Not better. I guess it depends on my mood. If I had a house here it wouldn't be Key West. It would be on one of the quieter Keys to the north. I like the fishing. I'm not crazy about the hordes of tourists. There are a lot of NASCAR fans here, and once I get recognized on the street I have to worry about a mob scene. I don't get much attention in South Beach. I'm low on the celebrity watch list there."

"Richard Vana sounds familiar."

Hooker slouched onto the couch in front of the television and remoted it on. "He's a baseball player. Houston."

My cell phone chirped, and I had a moment of terror, debating answering, worried it was my mother. But then I thought it could also be Bill, and I wouldn't want to miss that call.

It turned out it wasn't my mother, and it wasn't Bill. It was Rosa.

"Where are you?" Rosa asked. "I have to see you. I went back to talk to Felicia. And we asked around the neighborhood. Does anybody know anything? And they tell us to go to crazy Armond. Armond came to this country when they opened the prisons in Cuba and sent those people here to Miami. Armond says he was in the prison with Maria's father, and Armond says Juan would sometimes talk about the diving. And then he showed me on a map where Juan would like to dive."

"Can you tell me?"

"I have no names. The names aren't the same. But I have this little map Armond drew for us. I need to give you the map."

"Hooker and I are in Key West."

"What are you doing in Key West? Never mind. We'll bring you the map. We'll leave here early in the morning. Make sure you have your phone on. I'll call you when we get there." And Rosa hung up.

I rolled out of bed and followed my nose to the kitchen where Hooker had coffee brewing. He was dressed in wrinkled board shorts and a T-shirt that advertised motor oil. His hair was uncombed and his feet were bare. He looked very island, and I hated to admit it, but he also looked sexy . . . in an unkempt, fashion-disaster slob kind of way.

"We have coffee and creamer," Hooker said. "The only other food in the house is some microwave popcorn. Usually I have wasabi peas and beer nuts for breakfast when I stay here, but we ate them last night."

I poured myself a mug of coffee and added two packets of creamer. "Do you think that guy with the slicked-back hair was for real yesterday?"

"Yeah. I think he was for real. I think the night watchman was really dead. I think Maria Raffles is really screwed up. And I think your brother is an even bigger moron than I am when it comes to women."

"Anything else?"

"I think Maria and your brother are trying to bring something up from Cuban waters."

"Don't say that out loud. I don't want to hear that! Americans aren't supposed to go to Cuba. Cuba is closed to American citizens."

"There are a lot of people who think we'll resume relations with Cuba in the near future, and it'll create economic havoc for south Florida. The island is only one hundred and sixty-five miles from Miami. Ninety miles from Key West. It could steal away a lot of tourism and manufacturing dollars. I know a guy who's brokering a land deal for future development."

"Isn't that risky?"

"Sure, but I guess you weigh the risk against the potential payoff."

"I'd think it was impossible for an American to make that sort of deal."

"Apparently there are ways if you know the right people."

I took my coffee into the shower with me, and a half hour later Hooker and I were ready to roll.

The streets were much less crowded. It wasn't quite 8 AM and the shops were closed. A few bars were open, serving breakfast. We got breakfast burritos to go and ate them as we made our way to the docks. A giant cruise ship sat offshore. In a couple hours it would dump thousands of people into Key West, and Key West would be like the old lady in the shoe who had so many children she didn't know what to do. Personally, I didn't think it would be such a bad thing to divert some of the cruise ships to Cuba.

"I guess this isn't much of a vacation for you," I said to Hooker.

"It's not that bad," Hooker said. "I'm in Key West with a pretty girl. So far you haven't put out, but I still have hopes. Someone's threatening to kill me. I'm on sort of a treasure hunt. And the breakfast burrito was first-class."

"My fantasy is that we'll walk along these docks and stumble across your boat, complete with Bill and Maria."

"That's a decent fantasy. Want to hear mine?"

"No."

"It involves wild gorilla sex."

"Gee, that's a surprise."

Hooker grinned. "I didn't want to disappoint you."

We walked the entire marina, but we didn't see

Hooker's boat. We showed Bill's picture to a couple people, but no one recognized him. We stopped in at the dockmaster's office and got a hit. The boat came in on Tuesday and stayed one night. Bill paid for the space with a credit card Hooker had left on board.

Hooker called his credit card company to see if there'd been any further charges or cash withdrawals. There hadn't.

"Now what?" I asked.

"Now we hope Rosa's map is worth something."

We were at the edge of the marina parking lot, debating a latte and a bag of doughnuts when my phone rang.

"We're here," Rosa said. "We just crossed the bridge onto the island."

"Tell her we'll meet her in the marina parking lot," Hooker said. "Uh-oh."

"What uh-oh?"

"You see that family, by the trolley stop? I don't like the way they're looking at me."

"They're probably thinking you need a fashion makeover. Or maybe they're looking at me. Maybe they think I'm adorable in my pink hat."

"You don't know what it's like. It can get damn scary. Before you know it there are people running at you from all over the place. I don't have any security here."

"Don't worry. I'll protect you."

Hooker was still in the motor oil T-shirt and wrinkled shorts. He was wearing sunglasses, ratty sneakers without socks, and the hat advertising tires. He turned his back to the family and kept his head down. "Tell me when they're gone. I like my fans. I swear, I really do, but sometimes they scare the crap out of me."

"They aren't going away," I told him. "They're slowly creeping toward us. They look like a nice family. A couple little boys. And the mother and father are nicely dressed."

"They're all nice. It's just when you put them together and they turn into a mob."

"Well maybe if you weren't wearing a hat advertising tires and a T-shirt advertising motor oil . . ."

"My sponsors give this shit to me. I'm supposed to wear it. And anyway, I've got a billion of these T-shirts and hats. What am I supposed to do with them if I don't wear them?"

"It's *him*," the mother screamed. "It's Sam Hooker!"

The two kids ran up to Hooker. Hooker turned and smiled at them. Mr. Nice NASCAR Guy.

"Hey, how's it going?" Hooker said to the kids. "Do you guys like cars?"

The mother had a pen and the father had his

hat in his hand. "Would you sign my hat?" he asked Hooker.

A couple more people trotted over. Hooker was smiling at them all, signing whatever was handed to him.

"See," I said to Hooker, "isn't this fun? Look how happy you're making these people."

"You're not doing your bodyguard thing," he said. "You have to keep them back a little so they don't crush into me. I can't sign if I've got my arms pinned against my chest."

I looked around. He was right. They were crushing into him, pushed by the people at the back. He was right about the numbers, too. There were suddenly *a lot* of people trying to get close to Hooker. They were waving hats and napkins and T-shirts and they were yelling at him. "Hooker. Hey Hooker, sign this. Sign this!"

I'd been standing next to him, but somehow I got elbowed aside and shoved to the rear. In a moment's time I was pushed so far back I couldn't see Hooker at all. I was looking for an opening to get back in when Rosa and Felicia showed up.

"What's all the excitement about?" Rosa wanted to know.

"Hooker's up there, autographing stuff," I said. "I was supposed to be doing crowd control, but I got pitched out. I'm worried about Hooker. I just saw a woman run by with a piece of his shirt in her hand."

"We gotta get Hooker away from this mob or there'll be nothing left of him but a grease spot on the sidewalk," Rosa said. "There's people coming from all over."

"I don't know what to do," I said. "I tried yelling at them and they laughed at me."

Rosa hiked her purse up on her shoulder. "Get out of my way. I'll take care of this." She leaned forward and shouted at the crowd. "Omigod! It's Britney Spears! *Britney Spears.*"

The people at the outermost edge turned to look. A murmur rippled through the mob.

"Now they're vulnerable," Rosa said. "Now we gotta ram our way through."

Rosa went first with her head down. She knocked people out of her way, and she kept going. "Britney Spears is back there," she kept saying. "Did you see Britney?"

Felicia followed Rosa. And I followed Felicia.

By the time we reached Hooker he'd climbed onto the roof of a Subaru. He only had one sneaker, and his hat and his shirt were gone.

The Subaru was surrounded by fans trying to grab Hooker. They were still shoving things at him to get signed. The fans were all yelling things

like: *"This is for my son. He's dying. Brain cancer . . .
It's his birthday . . . It's for my mother. She tried to kill
herself when you lost at Taledega . . . It's for my daughter. She sold her trailer so she could come to Daytona
to see you race, and now she's homeless. It would mean
a lot to her if you'd sign my sock . . . I haven't got any
paper. Could you sign my forehead? . . . Could you
sign my right breast? Look I've got it out for you.
Here's a pen."*

Rosa and Felicia and I climbed onto the Subaru
with Hooker.

"Lady, you suck as a bodyguard," Hooker said
to me. "Where were you when they ripped my
shirt off?"

"These people are crazy!"

"They're just a little excited. I don't understand
it, but this happens to me a lot."

Two cop cars pulled into the lot, lights flashing.
A couple cops got out and waded through the
crowd.

"Hey look," one of the cops said. "It really is
Sam Hooker. Man, I love to watch you drive," the
cop said to Hooker. "You're the best. I almost lost
it when you took out the Bud car last year at
Miami."

"Yeah," Hooker said. "That was a good one.
I'm in sort of a bind here, guys. I'm turning into
fan food."

One of the cops got knocked to the ground. "Call for backup," he yelled to his partner. "We need riot control."

A half hour later, the crowd was dispersed. The cops all had autographs. A property damage report had been filed for the Subaru. One of the cops had gotten Hooker's shoe back. The hat and the shirt were never to be seen again.

"Thanks guys," Hooker said to the cops. "Appreciate the help."

We all piled into Rosa's gray Nissan Sentra, and the cops escorted us out of the lot and waved us away.

SIX

Rosa, Felicia, and I sat on the crimson-and-yellow couch in Rich Vana's living room and waited while Hooker went off to get another motor oil T-shirt.

"So," Felicia said to me. "Are you sleeping with him?"

"No!"

"That's a good thing. He's hot-looking, but he's probably diseased. I read the magazines, and I watch the celebrity shows on television. These race car drivers have sex on the brain. They're like barnyard animals."

"It's not just race car drivers," Rosa said. "It's men. All men have sex on the brain. That's why they can't multitask. Their whole brain is taken up with sex."

"Not all men are diseased, though," Felicia said.

"Puleeze," Rosa said, eyes rolling, hands in the air. "*All* men are diseased. What about herpes and genital warts? Do you honestly think there's a man in Miami without one of those?"

"Well, no. But I wasn't counting those. Do you think they count for disease?"

Hooker strolled into the living room. He was wearing a new hat and a new T-shirt that were exact replicas of the ones he'd lost. "What counts for disease?"

"Herpes," I said.

"Not if it's on your lip," Hooker said. "If it's on your lip you can call it a cold sore. And everyone knows a cold isn't a disease."

"I rest my case," Rosa said. "All men are sex-crazy and diseased."

"Yeah," Hooker said. "But we're fun, right?" He turned to me. "Just for the record, I'm not diseased."

Felicia put two maps on the coffee table. One was a fold-up road map of Cuba, and the other was crazy Armond's map, drawn on a piece of lined paper. The road map was dog-eared and worn at the folds. It had a coffee cup stain over

Havana and an arrow drawn in red Magic Marker pointing to Club Med Varadero.

"Here, you see, is Maria's little town, Nuevo Cabo," Felicia said. "It is a very good place to be a fisherman because the fish are not far offshore, and because there is a safe harbor. It is also a good place to smuggle things you would like kept secret because it is a little remote, but it is still close to Mariel. There were many Russian ships going into Mariel when Maria's grandfather was looking to make money. The first of the missiles came into the port of Mariel to be taken to the site at Guanajay.

"Remember, there was the blockade by the U.S. Navy, and still Maria's grandfather went out that night. It was craziness. And it started the curse."

"There's no curse," Rosa said. "Just greed."

Felicia made the sign of the cross. "Greed is a curse," she said. "If you look on crazy Armond's map, you will see where he puts Nuevo Cabo and Mariel. It was always thought the fishing boat went down in the harbor of Mariel. Or maybe that it started to sail to Havana. Armond says Juan found his father far west of there. Juan told Armond he found his father's bones still with the wedding band on his finger and with a bullet hole in his skull. There are islands and underwater caves to the far side of the Bahia de Cabana, and this is where Armond says Juan found his father. Armond has drawn three islands. One he calls the boot. And another he calls the bird in flight. And he says it is here that Juan did his final diving."

Hooker took the piece of paper and studied it. "How reliable is crazy Armond?"

"He's crazy," Felicia said. "How reliable is crazy?"

"Great."

"Tell me again why you are doing all this looking," Felicia said.

"I want to find my boat," Hooker said.

"And I want to find my brother," I said.

"But won't they come home by themselves when they are ready?"

"We're not the only ones looking for them," I said. "I want to find them before the bad guys find them."

"Is that possible?"

"Anything's possible," Hooker said. He had his cell phone in his hand, and he was scrolling through his phone book. He found what he was looking for and pushed *send*.

"Hey," Hooker said when the connection was made. "It's Sam Hooker. What's up? Un hunh. Un hunh. Un hunh." There was some NASCAR talk. Then there was some talk about cigars. And then

Hooker asked the guy on the other end if he wanted to buzz some islands off the coast of Cuba. There was some laughing after that. Hooker disconnected and stood. "I'm going to the airport," Hooker said. "Anyone going with me?"

Key West International Airport is on the easternmost part of the island. The terminal is single story white stucco with an orange tile roof, and it seems too pretty, too relaxed, and too small to belong to something calling itself an international airport. We parked in the lot, under a couple palms, and we all followed Hooker into the building.

"You seem to know what you're doing," I said to Hooker.

"I've flown out of here before on fishing and sightseeing trips. Other than that, it's an illusion. I have no idea what I'm doing."

We stood to one side of the entrance and looked around. A slim guy with a great tan trotted over to us. He was wearing sandals and shorts and a short-sleeve, open-necked shirt with a lot of red and green parrots printed on it. His hair was long, pulled back into a ponytail, his sport sunglasses were on a cord around his neck, his eyes were blue and crinkled at the corners, his smile was wide.

"Where the hell have you been?" he said to Hooker. "I haven't seen you in months."

"End of the season always gets nutty. And then I had to go back to Texas for the holidays."

"So what are you doing, shopping for Cuban real estate?"

"My boat's wandered off. I thought I'd go out looking for it. This is Barney, Rosa, and Felicia. Barney's going with us."

The ponytail guy nodded to us. "Chuck De-Wolfe. A pleasure, ladies."

"Isn't it illegal to fly over Cuba?" I asked Chuck.

"Not for me," he said. "I'm a Canadian citizen."

"So, what have you got?" Rosa wanted to know. "Seaplane?"

"Helicopter," Chuck said.

Helicopter! I'd never been in a helicopter. Never wanted to try one out. I'd take an elevator to Mars before I'd go a hundred feet in a helicopter.

"Barney gets a little nervous over heights," Hooker said.

"No problemo," Chuck said to me. "We'll fly nice and low."

Felicia was crossing herself and saying the rosary in Spanish. "You'll crash and die," she said. "No one will ever find you. The sharks will eat you, and there'll be nothing left. I can see it all."

"Yeah, you have to be nuts to go in a helicopter," Rosa said. "Only men go in helicopters. Women know better." She shook her finger at me. "Don't you let him talk you into going up in that helicopter. Just because he's a hottie doesn't mean he has any brains."

"Cripes," Hooker said. "Cut me some slack here."

"Yeah, that's harsh," Chuck said. "On the other hand, dog, they think you're a hottie."

Hooker and Chuck did a complicated variation on the high five.

"Probably there's no need for all of us to go," I said. "Why don't I wait here?"

Hooker locked eyes with me for a couple beats. "You're going to be here when I get back, right?"

"Right."

"Promise."

"Don't push it," I said.

Rosa and Felicia and I watched the two men walk away, out to the helicopter.

"He might be worth a disease," Felicia said. "Nothing major. A little one."

"I'm gonna tell your husband," Rosa said. "You're thinking dirty thoughts about another man."

"Thinking doesn't count," Felicia said. "A woman's allowed to think. Even a good Catholic woman can think."

"Here's the plan," Rosa said. "First we eat, and then we shop."

We went back to Old Town, parked by the harbor, and walked up Duval Street. We sat outside at a tourist-trap café, and we ate fried fish sandwiches and key lime pie.

"I make better pie," Felicia said. "The trick is you use condensed milk."

A flash of black caught my attention. Not a lot of people wearing black in Key West. I looked up from my pie and locked eyes with the shooter with the slicked-back hair. He seemed as surprised to see me as I was to see him.

We stared at each other for maybe ten seconds, and then he turned and crossed the street and walked toward the corner. He stopped outside a store, and I realized the store was Scuba Dooba. A guy who looked like he was in the Rent-A-Thug training program came out of Scuba Dooba and stood talking to the shooter. The two men swiveled their heads to look at me. We all stared at one another for what seemed like two years. The shooter made a gun with his hand, index finger extended, aimed it at me, and pulled the trigger.

Rosa and Felicia had been watching.

"Hey!" Rosa said. "Shoot this." And she gave him an entirely different hand gesture, *middle* finger extended.

Felicia did the same. And I didn't want to be left out, so I gave him the finger, too.

The shooter smiled at us. He was half a block away, but I could see the smile went to his eyes. The shooter thought we were funny.

"What's with him?" Rosa asked.

"I think he wants to kill me," I said.

"He's smiling."

"Yeah," I said. "Men. Go figure."

Rosa leaned forward, across the table at me. "Any special reason why he wants to kill you? Because aside from that, he's not too bad to look at."

I told them about the conversation at Monty's.

"You got a lot of nerve to stay here like this," Rosa said to me. "I'd be on a plane going home."

"I can't do that. It's my brother."

"What about the police?"

"I went to the police, but I couldn't tell them everything. I'm afraid Bill might be doing something illegal."

"You're a good sister," Felicia said.

The shooter and his partner turned away from us and disappeared down a side street.

"This is like a movie," Rosa said. "One of those scary ones where everyone gets murdered. And John Travolta is the hit man."

Felicia was crossing herself again.

"I wish you'd go light on that crossing," Rosa said to Felicia. "It's freaking me out."

"What crossing?" Felicia asked. "Was I crossing? I didn't notice."

We paid our bill, and we wandered down the street, past Scuba Dooba, to the next block. We looked at T-shirts, jewelry, sandals, and cotton shirts with island prints. Not high fashion here. This was tourist town. Fine by me, because I couldn't afford high fashion. Felicia bought T-shirts for her grandchildren, and Rosa bought a Jimmy Buffet shot glass. I didn't buy anything. It was Saturday, and I was very possibly two days away from being unemployed.

"It's almost four," Rosa said. "We should be heading back. I don't want to be driving too late at night."

We did an about-face and walked back on Whitehead Street. Felicia turned around twice and looked behind us.

"I got one of those feelings," Felicia said. "Anybody else got a feeling?"

Rosa and I looked at each other. We didn't have any feelings.

"What kind of a feeling are you talking about?" Rosa asked.

"Creepy. Like we're being followed by a big black bird."

"That's friggin' weird," Rosa said.

Felicia turned around for the third time.

"There's something back there. I *know* there's something . . . what do you call it? Stalking! There's something stalking."

Rosa and I looked all around, but we didn't see anything stalking.

"Okay, now you've *really* got me freaked out," Rosa said. "I'm not crazy about being stalked by a big black bird. I don't even like birds all that much. What kind of bird is it? Is it, like, a crow?"

We were on a cross street, heading for the Sentra. The street was for the most part residential. Single-family homes and small bed-and-breakfasts. Cars lined both sides of the street. We walked past a yellow Hummer and the Rent-A-Thug stepped from between two parked cars and stood in front of us. He was followed by the shooter with the slicked-back hair.

"Excuse me, ladies," the shooter said. "I'd like to speak to Miss Barnaby, alone."

"No way," Rosa said, moving between me and the shooter. "She don't want to talk to you."

"I think she does want to talk to me," the shooter said to Rosa. "Please step aside."

"Take a hike," Rosa said. "I'm not stepping anywhere."

The shooter flicked a glance at the Rent-A-Thug. The Rent-A-Thug reached for Rosa, and Rosa bitch slapped him away.

"Watch it," Rosa said. "No touching."

The Rent-A-Thug pulled a gun out of his jacket pocket. Rosa screamed. I ducked behind a car. And Felicia whipped a gun out of her handbag and shot the Rent-A-Thug in the foot, and winged the shooter. The Rent-A-Thug went down to the ground like a sack of wet sand.

"Fuck," the Rent-A-Thug said. "The old lady shot me!"

The shooter stood in speechless astonishment, watching blood seep into the sleeve of his black shirt.

"Run!" Rosa yelled to us. "Run!"

We took off down the street, partially dragging Felicia. Felicia could shoot, it turned out, but she wasn't much good at running. We reached the Sentra, jumped in, and Rosa pulled away from the curb and floored it.

"I told you we were being stalked!" Felicia said.

"You said it was a bird," Rosa said. "I was looking for a bird."

I was in the backseat, and my heart was racing, and my lips felt numb. I'd never seen anyone shot before. In the movies and on television, but never in person. And I'd never had anyone pull a gun on me. Hard to believe, since I was born and raised in Baltimore. One time Andy Kulharchek chased me around the garage with a tire iron, but he was drunk off his ass and he kept falling down.

"I can't believe you shot them," I said to Felicia.

"It was one of those reactions."

"You don't look like someone who'd carry a gun."

"I always carry a gun. Do you know how many times the fruit stand has been robbed? I can't count that high. Now when someone tries to rob me I shoot them."

"You go, girl," Rosa said.

My heart was still skipping around. I could still hear the gunshots echoing in my ears. In my mind's eye I could see the two men getting shot.

Felicia pulled the visor down and looked at herself in the mirror. "He called me an old lady. Did you hear that? I don't think I look so old."

"He deserved to get shot," Rosa said. "He had no tact."

"I've been using this new cream from Olay," Felicia said. "It's supposed to make your skin luminous."

"I should get some of that," Rosa said. "You can never be too luminous."

I couldn't believe they were having this conversation. Felicia just shot two men! And they were talking about skin cream.

"We have to go home," Rosa said. "Do you have someplace safe where you can wait for Hooker?"

"You can take me back to Vana's house. I'll be okay there," I said.

"Just in case, you should take the gun," Felicia said, handing the gun to me. "It's a revolver. Easy to use. Still got four shots left."

"No! I couldn't take your gun." Don't want to. Won't use it! Terrified to touch it!

"It's okay. I always get rid of them after I shoot somebody," Felicia said. "It's simpler that way. When you're done with it, just throw it in the ocean. Make sure it's someplace deep. When I'm in Miami I throw them in the Miami River. Probably if the police dive down they find the Miami River filled with guns. Probably so many guns in the Miami River it raises the high-water line."

"I don't know anything about guns," I said.

"I thought you were from Baltimore," Rosa said. "Doesn't everyone in Baltimore have a gun?"

"Not me."

"Well, now you have a gun," Felicia said. "Now you just like everyone else from Baltimore and Miami."

"It won't go off all by itself, will it?"

"No," Felicia said. "You got to pull the hammer

back and then squeeze the trigger. If you don't pull the hammer back the gun won't go *bang*."

Five minutes later we were idling in front of Vana's house.

"You be careful," Rosa said. "You call us if you need help."

"And don't go out of the house until Hooker gets back," Felicia said. "Maybe I should have killed those two guys, but I would have to say a lot of Hail Mary for that."

They waited until I got in the house and waved at them through the window that I was okay, and then they cruised off.

I had Felicia's gun in my handbag, and there was no way the shooter could know my location. None of this stopped me from mentally cracking my knuckles every ten seconds. I made sure the curtains were all drawn, and then I sat myself down in front of the television. I put the sound on low, so I could hear suspicious noises on the porch or in the bushes under the windows. And I waited for Hooker.

A little after eight a car pulled into the driveway and idled behind the Mini. I peeked from behind a curtain and saw that it was Hooker getting dropped off by his pilot friend.

I opened the front door, Hooker swaggered

in, grabbed me by the front of my shirt, and kissed me.

"I'm home," he said. "And I'm hungry."

"For dinner?"

"Yeah, that too. I don't suppose food has magically appeared in the kitchen?"

"Must be the food fairy's day off."

"That's okay. I know a place where we can get sauce up to our elbows eating ribs."

"Probably that's not a good idea. We might want to order in." And I told him about the shooter and his partner.

Hooker had a full-on smile. Lots of perfect white teeth showing. Crinkles around his eyes. "Let me make sure I got this right. Felicia shot the guy in black? And she also shot his Rent-A-Thug."

I had to smile with him. Now that I had some distance it was sort of funny, in a surreal kind of way. "Yep. She shot them. One in the foot. One in the arm."

"And then you all ran away, they dropped you off here, and they left."

"Yeah. And Felicia gave me her gun."

"I'm jealous. You had a better day than I did."

"Did you find your boat?"

"Maybe. We found the islands. They're about ten miles offshore and a good distance from Nuevo Cabo. We couldn't see any sign of habitation. The vegetation is thick. And there are places where a boat could go up an arm of the sea and not easily be seen. Apparently some of these waterways are deep. We saw light reflecting from something on one of those cross-island arms. No way to know if it was off the *Happy Hooker*. We were afraid to spend too much time there or to go too low. I didn't want to chase Bill into a different hiding place."

"Now what?"

"Now we get some pizza delivered, and tomorrow we take Rich's boat and go look for Bill."

I'd left my cell phone on the coffee table, and it started to buzz and dance around.

"Hey girlfriend," Judey said when I answered. "I've got news. I just got a phoner from Todd. He was called back to *Flex*. They're leaving first thing in the morning. And Salzar is on board with a diver."

I dragged myself out of bed at 4 AM, took a shower to try to wake up, brushed my teeth, and gave my hair a blast with the dryer. I stumbled into the kitchen and found Hooker drinking coffee and eating cold leftover pizza.

"Good morning," Hooker said.

"This isn't morning. Morning has sun. Do you see sun?"

"We don't want sun. We want to board the boat and get under way without being seen. I know where there's an all-night convenience store. We'll clean them out of water and granola bars, and then I'll stash you and the food on the boat. I'll park the Mini somewhere and walk back. I don't want to leave Bill's car in the marina lot."

"You know all about boats, right?"

"I know enough to get us to the island and back . . . if there are no problems. We're supposed to have good weather. Calm water. No storms predicted. Rich has a sixty-foot Sunseeker Predator Powerboat. It can cruise at thirty-two knots. And it can carry enough fuel to take us where we want to go. You'll have to help me get away from the dock. Once we're under way the computer takes over."

"How long do you think we'll be gone?"

"I don't know. A couple days, I'm hoping. I haven't got a lot of time. I'm supposed to start doing promotions at the end of the month."

I grew up in Baltimore, on the harbor, but I know nothing about boats. I can tell the difference between a powerboat and a sailboat, and that's where my expertise ends. So it looked to me that Rich Vana had a boat with a big nose. The boat was sparkling white with a wide navy stripe running along the side. The place where you drive was at the back of the boat and was enclosed and cozy. When you went down a set of stairs, the inside of the boat was all high-gloss wood and luxuriously upholstered couches and chairs. It had a state-of-the-art kitchen, two bedrooms, two bathrooms with showers, and a small living room with a dining area.

Hooker dropped me off with the groceries and immediately left to park the Mini. I stashed the bread and peanut butter, cereal, milk, beer, bags of cookies, sealed packets of bologna, sliced ham, cheese, pretzels, granola bars, and cans of SpaghettiOs. And then before Hooker returned, I took a quick peek at the engines. I don't know boats, but I *do* know engines. And these were big boys. Two twin Manning diesels.

Okay, so I was more excited about the engines than the kitchen. Not that the kitchen wasn't great. A side-by-side Sub-Zero refrigerator and freezer, a microwave plus convection oven, a built-in coffeemaker, dishwasher, and a Sub-Zero wine cooler. Nice appliances but hardly in the same league as the diesels. Plus there was a 20kw generator, ten 24 V batteries, two 12 V batteries and chargers.

I scrambled back to the kitchen when I heard Hooker on deck. In an instant, he was down the ladder, moving around me, checking the mechanicals. He looked around and I guess everything was okay. He went up to the pilothouse and started the generator. He unplugged and stored the shore power electrical cord. He flipped breaker switches for the main engine start. He turned on the VHF radio, autopilot, radar, GPS receiver, depth sounder, and boat computer. He entered the GPS course from Key West to Cuba into the boat's computer. He did a test of the bow thruster.

All the while he was telling me what he was doing, and I was trying to remember in case I had to do this myself. You never know, right? He could get washed overboard. He could have a heart attack. He could get drunk and pass out!

"Vocabulary," Hooker said. "The ropes are called lines. The bumper things are called fenders. Right is starboard. Left is port. Front is the bow. Back is the stern. The steering wheel area is the helm. The kitchen is the galley. The crapper is the head. I don't know why any of these things have their own names. It makes no sense to me. Except maybe for the head."

Hooker handed me a walkie-talkie. "As soon as the engines are warmed up we're pulling out, and you're going to have to help me. I'm going to give you directions on the walkie-talkie. Ordinarily I'd have someone on the dock to help untie the lines, but we're trying to sneak off this morning, so we're going to have to manage without help. I'm going to hold the boat against the dock and you're going to untie the lines and throw them onto the boat. You're going to start at the bow and work your way back."

I was ready. First Mate Barney, at your command. I climbed over the rail that ran around the bow, and I scrambled onto the dock. I was wearing shorts and sneakers and my pink ball cap. I didn't need sunglasses because the sun was still struggling to rise out of the water. I had the walkie-talkie in my hand. And I was pretty darned excited.

Hooker was standing at the wheel, and I saw him put the walkie-talkie to his mouth. "I've got her steady," he said. "Start throwing the lines. Do the bow line first."

"Okay," I said. "Doing the bow line."

I reached for the bow line, the walkie-talkie slid from my hand, bounced off the dock, splashed into the water, and disappeared from sight. I looked up at Hooker, and his expression was a lot like the expression on the shooter's face when he watched his blood seep into his shirt.

"Sorry," I said to Hooker, knowing full well he couldn't hear me.

Hooker gave his head a small shake. He was saddled with a moron for a first mate.

"Give me a break here," I yelled at him. "I'm new at this."

Hooker smiled at me. Either he was a very forgiving kind of guy, or else I looked really sexy in my pink hat.

I threw the rest of the lines onto the boat and climbed on board. Hooker crept the boat back, inching away from the dock. He got clear of the dock and he reversed his direction and swung the boat around to leave the marina.

"We need to stay at idle speed, five knots, until we leave the marina," he said. "Once we get into open water I can increase the throttle to bring us to cruising speed."

I had no relationship to knots. I was strictly a miles-per-hour kind of person. And on my salary, which was going to be zero as of tomorrow, I didn't think I had to worry about cruising at thirty-two knots much beyond this trip. Still . . .

"I don't know what the hell a knot is," I said to Hooker.

"One knot equals 1.15 miles per hour."

The sun was finally above the horizon and the water in front of us looked like glass. We plowed through some small swells at the mouth of the harbor and then we were in the open water. I stored the lines and the fenders away as best I could. When I had everything tidy Hooker took the boat up to speed, and engaged the autopilot.

"The autopilot interfaces with the GPS chart plotter," Hooker said. "And it's a lot smarter than I am."

"Can you just walk away from it now?"

"In theory, but I wouldn't walk far. Especially not on this cruise. I need to keep my eyes open."

"Worried about pirates?"

"I don't know who I'm worried about."

SEVEN

After two hours of ocean cruising, the whole boat thing started to get old. There's not a lot to look at when you're in the middle of the ocean. The boat was noisy, making conversation a pain, and I got nauseated when I went below while we were under way.

After three and a half hours, I was looking for land.

"Cuba is off the port bow," Hooker said. "We're about fifteen miles offshore, and I don't want to get closer. The islands we're looking for are about ten miles out."

"You're pretty good at this boat stuff," I said.

"If the computer punks out, I'm a dead man."

I couldn't eyeball the island, but I could see the island approaching on the GPS screen. It was possible that Bill was just miles away. An unnerving thought. Chances were good that he wouldn't be happy to see Hooker and me. And chances were *very* good that *I* wouldn't be happy after hearing his story.

"You look tense," Hooker said.

"How confident are you that the boat you saw in the river was yours?"

"Not confident at all. In fact, I'm not even sure it was a boat."

Suddenly there were three dots on the horizon.

"The island we're after is in the middle," Hooker said.

My heart skipped a beat.

"Are you carrying Felicia's gun?" Hooker asked.

"Yes."

"Do you know how to use it?"

"Sure." In theory.

I had my eyes fixed on the island. It looked relatively flat and heavily vegetated with the exception of a narrow strip of sugar sand beach. "Pretty beach," I said.

"This island alternates between beach and mangrove. The back of the island is all mangrove."

Hooker disconnected the autopilot and eased back on the throttle. "We're going to have to watch the depth finder and make sure we've got enough water under us. My boat displaces a lot more than Rich's, so we should be okay . . . if it's my boat in there."

Hooker brought us into the cove at idle speed and we looked around. No sign of activity. No traces of civilization. No cute little beach shacks, no docks, no Burger King signs. There were seagulls and long-legged shorebirds among the mangroves, and the occasional fish jumped in front of the boat. The water was calm. Very little breeze. Nothing moved on the palms.

We'd seen other boats when we got within fifteen miles of Havana, but they were always far away. Planes occasionally passed overhead. Not a threat since no one knew to look for Vana's boat. Hooker and I were out of sight, at the helm, under a hardtop.

A helicopter came out of nowhere and buzzed the boat. Hooker and I held our breath. The helicopter disappeared over the treetops, and we both expelled a *whoosh* of air.

"It wasn't military," Hooker said. "Probably just some rich tourist seeing the sights."

"Are we going up the waterway?"

"I'm going to try. I'd feel more comfortable if

we had a smaller boat. I'm probably going to have to back out. I'd like to back in, in case we have to leave fast, but I'm afraid to go in propellers first."

So here's the thing about a NASCAR guy. He might be an asshole, but at least he knows how to drive. And he's got *cojones*. Not even ordinary *cojones*. We're talking big brass ones.

Hooker approached the estuary and began creeping forward.

"Go to the bow," he said, "and watch for problems. Floating debris, narrowing of the water, signs that the water is getting too shallow. I've got a depth finder, but by the time it tells me I'm in trouble it could already be too late."

I carefully walked across the white fiberglass bow to the pointed prow. I dropped to hands and knees for better stability and leaned forward, studying the water ahead.

Hooker leaned around the windscreen and looked out at me. "I know you're trying to be helpful," he said, "but I can't drag my eyes off you when you're in that position. Maybe you could try lying flat to the boat, or at least swinging your ass more to the side."

I turned slightly to look at him. "Deal with it," I said. And then I went back to watching the water. I was from Baltimore. I grew up in a garage. I had my own set of *cojones*. And there wasn't much a man could say that would surprise me.

The width narrowed, but the depth stayed constant. Trees from both banks formed a canopy over our heads, and the sun dappled the water through holes in the canopy. Hooker eased the boat around a bend, and a boat lay at anchor directly in front of us. The bow of the boat faced us, so no name was visible. I turned to look at Hooker, and he nodded yes. He brought the boat to a standstill, and I scrambled back to the pilothouse.

"Are you sure it's your boat?" I asked him.

"Yep."

It was slightly bigger than Vana's boat, and the proportions were different. I didn't know a lot about boats, but I knew Vana's boat was more speed boat. And Hooker's boat was for deep-sea fishing.

"Do you think they see us?"

"They could be below decks. Or they could be off exploring the island. I'd think they could hear the engine, no matter, even at idle. We aren't visible behind this tinted sunscreen, so most likely they're watching us from someplace, messing their pants, wondering who the hell we are."

"There's some satisfaction to that," I said.

Hooker smiled at me. "Sugar pie, you've got an evil streak in you. I think I'm getting turned on."

"Everything turns you on."

"Not everything."

"What doesn't turn you on?"

"Dennis Rodman in a wedding gown."

Hooker shifted to the side and leaned out the open window. "Hey Bill, you jerk-off," he yelled. "Get your ass out on deck where I can see you."

Bill popped into view. "Hooker?"

Hooker turned to me and kissed me. He was smiling when he broke away.

"I don't know," he said. "I just felt happy, and I wanted to kiss you."

Seemed to me that there was a lot of tongue in it for just a happy kiss, but hell, he was NASCAR Guy. What do I know? He probably kissed his mother like that. Not that I was complaining. Hooker was a terrific kisser.

Bill was on deck, squinting at us, hand shielding his eyes from the splotches of sun. "Hooker?" he asked again.

Hooker shoved his head back out the side window. "Yeah. I need to talk to you."

"Hey, I can explain about the boat."

"Just get your sorry ass over here. I have to talk to you."

"How's he going to get over here?" I asked.

"I carry a small rigid inflatable boat with an outboard motor. RIB for short. He's probably got it in the water, tied up behind the *Happy Hooker*."

Bill disappeared, and minutes later I heard an engine kick in and Bill reappeared in the RIB. He maneuvered the inflatable to the dive platform at the back of the Sunseeker and tied up to us.

Bill has red hair that's cut short and is sort of Hollywood messy. He's got a little nose and blue eyes that smile 24/7. He's tanned and freckled. And he's five feet ten inches of solid Scottish-Irish muscle and bullshit. He was wearing Teva sandals and baggy flowery shorts that hit just above his knees. He climbed onto the dive platform and his cheeks went red under his tan when he saw me. "What the hell?" he said.

And I lost it. "You jerk!" I yelled at him. "You self-absorbed, inconsiderate miserable excuse for a brother. You irresponsible bag of monkey shit! How dare you make a phone call like that and then drop off the face of the earth. You scared the crap out of me. I'm going to lose my job because of you. My nose is peeling. My hair is a wreck. I've got seven messages from Mom on my cell phone that I'm afraid to access."

Bill smiled at me. "I'd almost forgotten how much fun you could be."

"Fun?"

I was right up there, in his face. I was so angry the roots of my hair felt like they were on fire. I gave Bill a shot to the shoulder that knocked him off balance and pitched him into the water.

Hooker gave a bark of laughter behind me. I whirled around and caught him with a kick to the back of the knee that doubled him over and rolled him off the edge of the dive platform, into the water with Bill.

Both men surfaced still smiling.

"Feel better?" Hooker asked.

"Yes. Sorry about the kick. I got carried away."

He pulled himself onto the platform and peeled his shirt off. "You're lying again. You're not sorry about the kick."

"I might be a *little* sorry."

Bill followed Hooker onto the platform. "You don't want to mess with her. She's always been a dirty fighter. And she used to be engaged to a kickboxer." Bill grabbed me and gave me a bear hug, leaving me almost as wet as he was. "I've missed you," he said. "God, it's good to see you."

Hooker raised his eyebrows at me. "Engaged?"

"She's been engaged three times," Bill said. "First there was the kickboxer. Then there was the photographer. And then the bartender. Barney's hell on men. I hope you haven't got any ideas."

I gave Bill the squinty eye. "You keep talking and I'm going to knock you into the water again."

"What should I do about anchoring this boat?" Hooker asked Bill.

"Who owns it?"

"Rich Vana."

"Anyone know you and Barney are on it?"

"No," Hooker said.

"We can probably chance dropping anchor in the cove. There's not enough room for both of us back here." Bill went to the helm. "Make sure the RIB is secure, and I'll start pushing her back."

A half hour later we were anchored in the cove.

"I can't believe you found me," Bill said. "I didn't think I left a trail."

"We're not the only ones looking for you," I said to Bill.

"Yeah, it was scary in the beginning, but I thought we were safe tucked away upstream. So what's going on with you two?"

"We're looking for *you*," I said.

"Well, here I am. And as you can see, I'm fine. And I've got a girl back there. So, probably I should be getting back."

"Excuse me," Hooker said. "That's *my* boat you're getting back to."

"I know," Bill said. "And I wouldn't have borrowed it if I wasn't really in a bind. If you could just give me a couple more days I'll have it back, tied up in South Beach, good as new. Swear to God."

"I want it back now," Hooker said.

"I can't give it back now. I'm involved in something here. It's important."

"I'm listening," Hooker said.

"I can't tell you about it."

"I know he's your brother," Hooker said to me, "but I think you should shoot him."

"My mother would hate that," I told Hooker. "And the gun's downstairs in my purse."

"Okay," Hooker said. "I'll get the gun. And I'll shoot him. *My* mother won't mind at all."

"Hey dog," Bill said. "It's just a boat."

"It's a three-million-dollar boat. I had to crash into a lot of walls to pay for that boat. And I was supposed to be out fishing this week. It's perfect weather."

"Maria's going to be pissed off if I tell you."

"We already know some of it," I said. "It's about her father and her grandfather, right?"

Bill grinned. "Actually it's about seventeen million, three hundred thousand dollars in gold bars."

"That's a lot of gold," Hooker said.

"A hundred bars, each weighing twenty-seven pounds."

"Is it on my boat?" Hooker asked.

"We're taking up the last load tonight."

"And then?"

"I'm taking it to Naples. I rented a house in Port Royal when we stopped in the Keys. It's on a canal. I just tie the boat up to the dock and off-load the gold."

Hooker grinned. "You're going in through Gordon Pass?" He turned to me. "Naples is a pretty little town on the Gulf. It's built around canals and filled with multi-million-dollar houses. It's the most respectable place in Florida. Not as much flash as Miami Beach or Palm Beach. Just tons of money. Very safe. And the Port Royal neighborhood is the richest. A three-million-dollar house in Port Royal is considered a tear-down."

"What are you going to do with these gold bars?" I asked Bill.

"I'm not doing anything with them. They belong to Maria."

Hooker and I exchanged glances.

"We need to have a conversation with Maria," Hooker said.

The rigid inflatable was about twelve feet long with an outboard. We all piled in. Bill took the wheel and motored us upstream to Hooker's boat. At this lower level, the tropical forest was beautiful but claustrophobic. Ground vegetation was dense and dark. The second tier was wrapped in flowering vines and occasionally dotted with roosting waterbirds. The air was liquid, soaking into my hair and shirt, sitting like dew on my forearms, trickling down the sides of my face. It was South Beach air magnified, and the cloying scent of flowers and damp earth and plant rot mixed with the brine from the sea.

We tied up to the small dive platform at the back of *Happy Hooker* and climbed on board. Everything was shiny white fiberglass, which I assumed was for easy cleanup when fishing. A fighting chair was bolted to the cockpit deck. A door and large windows looked into the salon from the cockpit, but the glass was darkly tinted and it was impossible to see inside.

Bill opened the salon door and we all trooped in. Maria stood in the middle of the salon with a gun in her hand. She was maybe five three with a lot of wavy dark brown hair that swirled around her tanned face and brushed the tops of her shoulders. Her features were delicate, her mouth naturally pouty, her eyes were the color of melted chocolate. She was slim with large breasts that swayed under her white cotton T-shirt when she moved.

"I'm understanding everything now," Hooker said to me.

170 –

I gave him raised eyebrows.

"Probably you don't want to shoot this guy," Bill said to Maria, "since he owns this boat."

"All the more reason," Maria said.

"Yeah, you're right," Bill said. "But don't shoot Barney. She's my sister."

Maria went off in Spanish, waving her hands, yelling at Bill.

I looked to Hooker.

"She's unhappy," Hooker said.

I didn't need a translator to figure that out.

"And she's calling him some names I've only heard in Texas stockyards. She's going so fast I can't get it all, but there's something about the size of his privates with the size of his brain and neither of them are looking good." He cut his eyes to me. "Just so you know, I've never had any problems with size in the privates department. The size of my brain has sometimes been questionable."

"Gee, I'm glad you shared that with me," I said.

"I thought you might want to know."

Now Bill was shouting back at Maria. He was shouting in English, but it was hard to tell what he was saying, since the two of them were nose to nose, both yelling at the same time.

"*Hey!*" Hooker said. "*Chill.*"

Maria and Bill turned and looked at Hooker.

"You've got bigger problems than us," Hooker

said. "You should be worrying about the guys who trashed your apartments, twice. And the guy who threatened to kill us. And probably you should be worrying about whoever it is that actually owns the gold. Not to mention the Cuban government."

"I own the gold," Maria said. "It was on my grandfather's boat."

"I'm guessing not everyone shares that point of view," Hooker said.

Bill locked eyes with Maria. "The truth is," he said to her, "we could use some help."

Maria looked at Hooker and me, and then she looked back at Bill. "And you trust them?"

"Hooker, yes. Barney, I'm not so sure of."

"You'd better watch your step," I said to Bill. "You'll be in big trouble if I tell Mom you stole a boat."

Bill gave me another bear hug.

Maria put the gun on the black granite galley counter. "I guess it's okay. You start to tell them the story."

"I met Maria at a club a couple weeks ago. We talked but we never got together. Then I saw her Monday night. Again, it was just hello. She left real early."

"I met a guy the night before," Maria said. "I didn't like him, and when I saw he was at the club again I decided to leave. I wasn't in a club mood anyway. I walked home, and I was about to go into my apartment building when a man stepped out of the shadows and put a gun to my head. There were two more men waiting in a car at the curb, and they drove me to the marina. When we got to the boat I asked them what this was about and they said I was going back to Cuba. They said I was going to take a helicopter trip to Cuba. That was when I started to struggle."

"I decided to leave the club early too," Bill said. "We were supposed to go back out first thing Tuesday morning, and I didn't want to get wasted. I was in the marina lot, heading for *Flex*, when the car pulled in with Maria. I saw them help her out of the car and walk her down the pier. I recognized the car and the men as Salzar's. He's brought women on board before, so I didn't think much about it. It wasn't until she started struggling at the end of the pier that I realized she was being forced onto the boat. Probably I should have called the police, but all I could think of was to get her off *Flex*.

"I waited for about ten minutes and then I boarded. Everything was quiet. The rest of the crew was asleep. There was a light on in the pilothouse, but that was it. I crept around, trying doors, and found her bound and gagged in one of the VIP staterooms on the second deck."

"Wasn't the door locked?"

"Yeah, but I accidentally came into possession of a master key the first week I worked on *Flex*. You never know when you might need a master key, right?"

Yessir, this was my brother.

"Anyway," Bill said, "I cut Maria loose, and we hauled ass out of there. Maria didn't want to call the police. She just wanted to get some stuff out of her apartment."

"I knew when they discovered I was gone they would go to my apartment and search for my charts," Maria said. "Before this night, I didn't realize anyone knew about me. I didn't bother to hide my charts. I thought the shipwreck had been forgotten. Gone with my father."

"So you think Salzar wants either you or the charts so he can salvage the wreck?"

"My father discovered gold when he went diving for my grandfather. He came back with my grandfather's remains, and he told my mother. My mother told me on her deathbed. She always said to everyone that she didn't know where my father went to dive, but she always knew. And she knew about the gold."

A small prop plane buzzed the treetops, and we all went still until it passed.

"I can tell you what I think," Maria said. "I

think the gold was for Castro. My grandfather was lost at sea two days after President Kennedy put the blockade up. I think one of the big Russian ships had gold for Castro. The ship couldn't get to port, so perhaps they sent my grandfather out to get the gold. It was always a rumor in my village. I never believed it until my mother told me."

"And?"

"And something happened. My grandfather's boat hit a reef and never arrived at Mariel. There were two men on the boat. The one man was rescued at sea in a lifeboat. He said my grandfather's boat was damaged and taking on water, but my grandfather wouldn't leave the boat. For years the man who survived looked for the boat, but he always looked in the shoals around Mariel. Everyone thought he was looking for my grandfather, but now I think he was looking for the gold."

"Oh boy," Hooker said. "I have Castro's gold on my boat."

Maria cut her eyes to him. "It's *my* gold on your boat."

"How did your father know where to look for the shipwreck?"

"He heard that a fisherman from Playa el Morrillo was catching fish off a wreck in this harbor. When my father heard of a wreck he would go to investigate. It didn't matter how far."

Hooker went to the refrigerator and got a beer. "Anyone?" he asked.

Bill took a beer. Maria and I declined.

"If I brought the gold up while I lived in Cuba it would do me no good," Maria said. "The government would come and take it. And they might throw me in prison like my father. So I came to Miami and I looked for someone to help me."

"That would be me," Bill said.

Maria smiled at Bill. "An unlikely hero."

Bill slid a protective arm around Maria, and she leaned into him. It was a simple gesture, but it was surprisingly tender.

"I'm in love," Bill announced to Hooker and me.

I smiled at Bill and Maria, and I mentally wished them well, but I'd heard this *a lot*. Bill fell in love easily. And often. Bill was four years old the first time he made this announcement. Carol Lazar had allowed him to take a peek at her panties and Bill was in love. And Bill has been peeking at girls' panties and falling in love ever since. I think it would be nice if Bill could find the right woman and commit, but in the meantime, at least his sex life wasn't without love.

Hooker smiled at Bill, too. Hard to tell if Hooker's smile was cynical or wistful.

"To love," Hooker said. And he took a pull on his beer.

"What was the scream about at the end of your phone call to me?" I asked Bill.

"We were casting off and the night watchman showed up with a gun. I guess he thought we were stealing the boat."

"Imagine that," Hooker said.

"The night watchman is dead," I said to Bill. "Knifed an hour after you took off. Both of your apartments have been searched, twice. Once by two Cuban guys. And once by two Caucasians. One of the Caucasians always wears black and has slicked-back hair. The slicked-back-hair guy threatened to kill me and Hooker if we kept looking for you. I was attacked by a mutant named Hugo, who I prefer to call Puke Face. Puke Face tried to kidnap me with hopes of trading up to you. Puke Face works for Salzar. And Puke Face's message was that you were in possession of Salzar's property. I imagine he was talking about Maria. Oh yeah, and they called Mom and left a message for you. Those are pretty much the high points."

"And then there's your computer," Hooker said to Maria. "With the gold and the warhead research. The gold I get. Maybe you should tell us about the warhead."

"It was part of the rumor. That besides the gold, there was some new weapon on board my grandfather's ship. My mother said my father was afraid it was true. My father told her there was a canister not far from the gold. He said it looked like it might be a bomb. He didn't want Castro gaining control of this weapon, so he wouldn't talk. When they came to take him away, he told my mother he would never reveal the wreck. My mother told me some of the markings on the canister, and I tried to identify it on the Internet, but I couldn't find anything."

"You've been diving," Hooker said. "Is the canister down there?"

Maria nodded. Solemn. "Yes."

"Do we know the connection between Salzar and Calflex?" I asked Bill.

"There was a rumor a while back that Salzar was brokering a Cuban land deal for Calflex. Not sure if it's true."

"A better question," I said. "How does Salzar know about the wreck?"

"He's originally from Cuba, no?" Maria said. "He's of an age where he might have heard the rumors."

"Seems like he's investing a lot of energy in a rumor," Hooker said. "I can be a pretty aggressive guy, but I don't think I'd kidnap someone on the basis of a rumor."

"There could be others who would know the

ship's cargo," Maria said. "My grandfather's partner would know. My mother spoke of him sometimes. His name was Roberto Ruiz. And he could have told people. The men on the Russian ship might know. Someone had to put the gold and the canister on board the fishing boat. And Castro would know. Maybe some of his aides."

"Salzar could be working for Castro," Bill said. "They're supposed to be buddies."

"Why is Salzar going after you now?" I asked. "Why did he wait so long? You've been in Miami for four years."

"I don't know. Maybe he just found out. Not long ago, there was an article in the newspaper about the cigar factory with my picture and my name in it. The newspaper man spoke to me because I am the youngest of all the women who roll the cigars."

Another plane flew overhead.

"You're reflecting light through the trees," Hooker said to Bill.

"I know. I was hoping it wasn't too bad. If this had been planned out I would have gotten a tarp. We only need one more night, and we'll be out of here. We've been diving at night, so we wouldn't be seen. The harbor is deep in the middle. Sixty feet. And that's where the boat went down. Maria brings the gold up using lift bags, and we ferry it back to the boat in the RIB. Tonight we'll bring the boat out and take off when we get the last of the gold . . . if it's okay with you."

"Sure," Hooker said. "I wouldn't want to see Castro's gold go to waste."

The birds had stopped chattering and had settled in for the night. The water was still. No trace of a breeze. The sun was a fireball, sinking into the island palms. Hooker and I were on deck, waiting for Bill and Maria.

"That was nice of you to let him use your boat," I said to Hooker.

"I didn't see where I had much choice."

"You could have asked for some of the gold."

Hooker was slouched in a deck chair, bare legs outstretched, eyes closed, arms crossed over his moth-eaten T-shirt. "I don't need the gold." He opened his eyes and looked over at me. "We've got a few minutes, in case you want to jump my bones."

"I've got your number."

"Oh yeah? What's my number?"

"Every time you do something nice you have to follow it up with some asshole remark. Just to keep the balance. To keep things at a safe distance."

"Think you're pretty smart, hunh? Maybe I meant what I said. Maybe I'd really like you to jump my bones. Maybe bones jumping is what Texas NASCAR drivers do best."

"There's no doubt in my mind that Texas NASCAR drivers are excellent bones jumpers. It was the unromantic announcement that guaranteed failure."

"Damn, I thought that was a good line. I thought I was being real classy. I didn't even say anything about what a great rack you have."

"You're doing it again!"

Hooker smiled and closed his eyes. "Just funnin' with you. We haven't got enough time. When I finally let you jump my bones it's going to go on for hours. And sugar pie, you won't even see it coming."

And the horrible part was . . . I believed him.

EIGHT

I heard the boat engine turn over upstream. Bill was moving out before he was in total darkness.

"He's good at this, isn't he?" I asked Hooker.

Hooker sat up. "At working the boat? Or at looting gold?"

"Working the boat."

"He's very good at working the boat. He's one of the few people I'd trust to captain her. The *Happy Hooker* is a big boat with a deep draft. I'd need a whole crew to get me out of that estuary if I was at the helm. Even then I'd probably run into a bank."

"But you think Bill and Maria can do it?"

"Yep. He couldn't do it alone, but it sounds like

Maria's been around boats all her life. She's probably a good mate. Bill would have asked if he needed my help. He doesn't take chances with boats."

The engine noise drew closer, and the boat appeared and stopped before moving into the more open water of the cove. Bill went to the prow, attached the remote to the windlass, and dropped anchor.

A half hour later, in total darkness, I heard the hoist swing out and set the RIB on the water. The sky was black and moonless. We knew the course of the RIB more by sound than by sight. A low-level hum. It was moving toward the middle of the small harbor. Then the outboard cut off. Snatches of muted conversation carried over to us. There was a soft splash and all was quiet.

"She's diving to sixty feet," Hooker said. "It'll take her two minutes to get down and a minute to get up. And she's probably got a little over an hour work time. She's using lift bags to bring the gold up, so you'll know she's coming up when you see the white bags."

Forty minutes later, the lift bags bubbled to the surface like giant marshmallows, and a light appeared at the side of the RIB.

Hooker had taken a walkie-talkie from the *Happy Hooker*, and the talkie came to life.

"She has to go down again," Bill said. "If you bring Vana's boat around to the far side of the lift bags we can load onto your dive platform. I'll talk you through it. Keep your running lights off."

Hooker cranked the boat over and we raised anchor.

Bill was back on the talkie. "Follow my light beam," he said. "I'm going to bring you around to the far side of the RIB."

When we were in position I resumed breathing.

Hooker looked over at me and grinned. "You look like you're about ready to pass out."

"I was worried we were going to run them over. Our boat is so big, and the RIB is so small."

"Barney girl, you need to learn to trust people. Your brother's a good guy. He's kind of a horn dog, but he knows what he's doing when he's on a boat. It's like when I'm racing, and I've got spotters telling me I can make it through a wall of smoke and fire. You figure out who you can trust and then you go with it."

"So you weren't scared just now?"

"Almost messed my pants twice. Don't tell your brother."

Maria was sitting on the side of the RIB. She adjusted her mask and mouthpiece. She touched hands with Bill. And she went over, into the black water, and disappeared. I followed Hooker to the dive platform, and we started working with Bill, hauling the gold out of the water, onto the platform, being careful not to damage the bricks.

"This is a lot easier than trying to get the gold into the RIB," Bill said. "I didn't want to bring the *Happy Hooker* out until I was ready to make a run for it. I know the *Flex* chopper is doing airtime looking for us."

"You've never cared that much for money," I said to Bill. "I'm surprised you're risking your life for this."

"I'm risking my life for Maria," Bill said. "This is her gold, not mine. She thinks her father might still be alive in prison. She's hoping she can buy him out with the gold."

"Oh shit," Hooker said. "We're doing this for a good cause. How crappy is that?"

The lift bags bobbed to the surface for the second time. Maria followed them up, and we tugged the bags over to the dive platform. Bill helped Maria come on board and get out of her equipment.

"This is it," she said. "This is everything that was down there. At least everything I could find." She slipped back into the water to guide the last bag while Hooker and Bill hauled it onto the boat.

We opened the bag, and we all stood back, looking at the contents. A single metal canister, approximately a foot and a half wide by three feet long. Very heavy. Maybe eighty pounds. Russian writing barely visible running along one side. The end cap had been painted red. And there were two thin green-and-black bands painted onto the rear of the canister.

Hooker toed the canister. "Anyone read Russian?"

Nope. No one read Russian.

"It *does* sort of look like a bomb," Bill said.

"Probably we shouldn't open it," I said.

Hooker squatted beside it for a better look. "Probably we *can't* open it. At least not without an acetylene torch and a crowbar. This baby is *sealed*."

If this came off a Russian ship that was stopped by the blockade, I didn't even want to speculate on its purpose. "I keep going back to what Puke Face said about fear," I told Hooker. "He said this was about fear and what it can do for you."

"And maybe this is something to fear? Not a good thought. I don't want to go there."

"I brought it up because I was worried it was no longer safe to leave it in the cove. It should be turned over to the authorities," Maria said. "My father suffered to keep this out of Castro's hands. I don't want that suffering to have been in vain."

We heard the beat of a helicopter coming at us

from the north. We scrambled to get the lift bags out of sight and ducked into the cabin. The copter did a flyby, sweeping the water with its light. The beam missed the boat, and the helicopter continued south.

The instant we could no longer hear the chopper, Bill and Maria were off the dive platform, into the inflatable.

"I'll bring *Happy Hooker* around, and we can use the hoist to load," Bill said.

A half hour later the boats were in position to transfer cargo, and Bill was on the talkie to Hooker.

"I've got a problem here. I can't get the boat out of idle."

"What do you mean, you can't get it out of idle?"

"If I try to increase speed it cuts out."

"So?"

"So that's not good."

"Can you fix it?"

"Not my thing, pardner. Send Barney over."

"Barney? Did I copy you . . . Barney?" Hooker asked.

"She's good with engines."

"You're kidding."

I was standing behind Hooker, listening to the conversation broadcast over the walkie-talkie, and I had a real strong urge to kick him in the knee again.

"Do you know anything about marine engines?" I asked Hooker.

"Not a damn thing," Hooker said. "I don't even know anything about car engines."

"How could you make a living driving cars and not know anything about engines?"

"I drive them. I don't repair them."

Truth is, I was itching to see his engines. I scrambled across to the Hatteras and followed Bill into the mechanical room.

"He's got twin CATs," Bill said. "Twice as big as the Sunseeker's Mannings. I took a quick look but nothing jumped out at me. I guess that doesn't mean much. I was never that interested in garage stuff."

"Holy Toledo," I said, eyeballing the CATs. "This is *way* over my head. I can take a car apart and put it back together again, but I don't know *anything* about *any* of this."

"Take a deep breath," Bill said. "They're just engines . . . only bigger."

Maria was at the helm on the walkie-talkie. "The helicopter's coming back," she said. "Kill the lights."

Hooker, Bill, and I stood in the darkness, waiting for Maria's all clear. My mind was racing and my heart was skipping around. I was in a broken boat that was filled with Castro's gold and something that looked like a bomb. And the bad guys were looking for us.

"All clear," Maria said.

Hooker flipped the lights back on. "How bad is this loss-of-power problem?"

"I don't know how bad it is," Bill said.

"Executive decision," Hooker said. "Let's use the hoist to transfer the gold over to the Sunseeker while Barney pokes around down here. It's probably better to have it in Rich's boat anyway. No one's looking for his boat. You guys can take off as soon as you're loaded up, and we'll follow when we can."

I found the service record and some manuals and I began walking my way through basic troubleshooting. At the very least I thought we could limp out of the harbor and get far enough out of Cuban waters to radio for help and not get arrested.

I was checking hoses and seals when I heard the Sunseeker's engines turn over. I looked at my watch. I'd been working for two hours. I stepped out of the mechanical room and went on deck. Bill was pulling away, moving toward open ocean. Maria was flat on the prow with a handheld halogen, periodically searching the water in front of them.

Major lump in the throat time.

"He'll be okay," Hooker said.

I nodded, sucking back tears, not wanting to go hormonal in front of Hooker.

"I think I found the problem," I told him. "You had water in the fuel, probably from condensation over a period of time. And it affects both engines. I was able to drain the water that collected in the fuel filters, and we should be good, unless they fill with water again. I don't know why they didn't catch this when the boat was last serviced. I have a few more things to check and then I'll be done."

"Take your time. Bill's a lot more skilled than I am when it comes to running this boat. I'd rather wait and get under way at dawn when I can see where I'm going."

"Do you think it's dangerous to wait?"

"Yes. Unfortunately, chances of us getting stranded on a sandbar are good if I try to go out in the dark. I got this boat with the idea in mind that I'd always have a captain. I've learned how to do the minimal, but I'm not a pro."

I went below deck to finish and Hooker followed me down with two glasses and a bottle of wine.

"Do you mind if I watch?" he asked.

"Nope."

"Do you mind if I talk?"

"Nope. I'm a multi-tasker."

"I thought you worked for an insurance company."

"Your use of the past tense is probably appropriate."

"So what's with the mechanic thing?"

"My dad owns a garage. I helped out."

"You must have more than helped out. Bill thinks you're a mechanical genius."

"Bill's my brother. He has to think things like that."

He handed me a glass of wine. "Not true. I have two sisters and I think they're both airheads. What did you study in college?"

"None of your business."

"Art? American history? Mechanical engineering?"

I sipped some wine. "Engineering, but I never did anything with it. By the time I graduated I was disenchanted with job prospects."

I finished my wine and my checklist at precisely the same time. "I think we're good to go," I told Hooker. "Start her up and check out the gauge."

Hooker came back two minutes later. "We have a problem," he said.

"The gauge?"

"The gauge isn't in the same league as this

problem. There's a boat sitting at the mouth of the harbor. Not the Sunseeker. It's got its lights off, but I can see the white hull reflecting in the water."

"Could it be *Flex*?"

"No. It's not nearly that big."

Hooker and I went topside and looked at the boat.

"Maybe it's here for the fishing or snorkeling," I said. "Maybe it's just an innocent pleasure boat."

"Innocent pleasure boats don't arrive at two in the morning and turn off all their running lights. I'm worried that someone did a flyover and picked us up and motored out here. Calflex has a bunch of smaller boats. It could be one of those."

"Looks to me like they're blocking our way out. If they think Maria is on board, maybe they'll just send a couple henchmen out in the morning. Or maybe at this very moment, the henchmen are getting into scuba gear."

"I really hate that idea," Hooker said. "Especially since I gave Bill the gun. The RIB is tied up to the dive platform. Throw a couple bottles of water and some granola bars into it and get in. I'll be right behind you."

I grabbed the water and granola bars and ran to the RIB. And in the dark, I crashed into the canister.

"What the heck is this?" I said. "They didn't take the canister!"

Hooker came up behind me. "Shit, we were rushing to get the gold on board and forgot about this thing back here on the dive platform."

"What should we do with it?"

"We're going to have to take it with us. I don't know what it is, and I don't want to chance leaving it here."

We struggled to get the canister into the RIB, Hooker climbed in with a backpack, and we set off for the island interior. We were about fifty feet upstream when we saw the flash of a penlight on the double H deck.

"Fuck," Hooker said.

That pretty much summed up my feelings, too.

Hooker pulled the outboard up and went the rest of the way using oars. Not especially easy but quieter and safer, and we were able to get farther upstream, poling most of the way. It was so dark under the canopy I couldn't see the hand in front of my face. When we ran aground we got out and dragged the boat above the waterline. Then we got back into the boat and searched for a comfortable position to spend the night.

I was stumbling around, and I felt Hooker's hand grab hold of my leg.

"You're like a hound dog looking for the perfect spot," Hooker said. "Just sit down."

"I can't see anything. I don't know what I'm sitting on."

"You have no spirit of adventure," Hooker said. "Take a chance." He yanked me down and pulled me back against him. "Now you're sitting on me. Relax."

"You've got your hand on my breast."

"Oh. Sorry. It's dark. I didn't know."

"You didn't know you had your hand on my breast?"

"Okay, so I knew. Did you like it?"

"Good grief."

"I was hoping you liked it."

I was sitting between his legs with his arms around me and his chin against my temple.

"*I* liked it," he said. And he kissed me just in front of my ear.

I liked it too. And I liked the kiss. And I couldn't believe I was sitting between Hooker's legs, feeling randy when there were scuba guys combing the *Happy Hooker*, looking for the gold, probably hoping they'd get to kill someone.

"This isn't a good time," I told him.

"I know. No condoms. I don't suppose you picked up any of Bill's?"

"I was talking about the frogmen and the fact that they might want to kill us."

"I'd forgotten about the frogmen. Hell, if we're going to die, we don't have to worry about condoms."

"What time is it?"

"Three-thirty."

I closed my eyes, and I was instantly asleep. When I woke up the sun was shining through tiny pinpoints in the tree cover, and Hooker's hand was back on my breast.

"I can't believe this," I said. "You've got your hand back on my breast."

"It's not my fault. It goes there all by itself. I'm not responsible for what my hand does when I'm sleeping."

"You're not sleeping. You're wide awake."

"Good point." And he fondled me. "Are you sure you don't like it?"

"Maybe a little, but it doesn't matter. I need a shower. I need a toothbrush. I need to shave my legs. *Omigod!*"

"What?" Hooker was on his feet, looking around. *"What?"*

"There's no bathroom."

He had his hand to his heart. "You scared the bejeezus out of me."

"I need a bathroom."

Hooker's eyes strayed to the jungle.

"No way!"

"Don't wander too far," Hooker said. "It wouldn't be good to get lost. And watch where you step."

"This is all my brother's fault," I said. "Every mess I've ever been in has been his fault."

"The three engagements?"

"Men!" I said. And I huffed off, viciously kicking and slashing my way through the tangle of vines and bushes. I did what I had to do, and I followed the trail of smashed vegetation back to the stream.

Hooker was sitting on the side of the boat, eating a granola bar. He looked at me and his eyes got wide and his mouth dropped open.

"What?" I said. "All right, so I know I tinkled on my sneaker. It's not easy doing this when you're a girl."

He dropped the granola bar on the ground and reached for an oar. "Honey, I don't want you to panic, but you've got something in your hair."

I rolled my eyes up, trying to see through my skull, and reached for the top of my head.

"No! Don't touch it!" Hooker said. "Don't move. Stand perfectly still."

"What is it?"

"You don't want to know."

"What are you going to do with the oar?"

"I'm going to flick it off."

"Why don't you just use your hand?"

"What are you, nuts? That's the biggest fucking spider I've ever seen. That motherfucker is the size of a dinner plate. I don't know how it's even staying on your head."

"*Spider!*" And I started screaming and doing the yucky dance. "*GET IT OFF! GET IT OFF! GET IT OFF!*" Everything went cobwebby and I fainted.

When I came around, Hooker was bending over me looking worried.

"What happened?" I asked him.

"You fainted. You were screaming and then your eyes rolled back and went over like *CRASH.*"

"I never faint. You probably hit me with the oar and knocked me out."

"Honey bunch, if I hit you with the oar you'd still have your eyes closed."

"Help me up. At least I got rid of the spider." I looked up at Hooker. "I *did* get rid of him, didn't I?"

He got me to my feet. "Yeah, you got rid of him."

I picked a long slim black thing off the front of my shirt. "What is this?"

"Spider leg," Hooker said. "You fell on him

when you went down, and he's sort of smushed all over the back of you."

"Not even."

"The good news is . . . he's dead."

I started to cry. I know it was stupid to cry, but there it was. I'd held it back lots of times, and I couldn't hold it back anymore. I had spider guts on me, and I was crying.

"Listen, we can fix this," Hooker said. "We'll just wash you off in the stream. Most of it fell out of your hair already, anyway. Well, *some* of it. But, we can get the rest out. Damn, I wish you'd stop crying. I really hate when you cry."

Okay, get a grip, I told myself. Get out of the spider guts clothes, wade into the water, and wash your hair. Simple.

"Here's the plan," I said to Hooker. "I'm going to get undressed, and you're not going to look. Then I'm going to wash off, and you're not going to look. And if you look, I'm going to cry."

"Anything! Just no more crying."

I walked to the edge of the stream, got undressed, and dropped the clothes with the spider guts attached into the water to soak. Then I waded out and dunked myself. I swished my hair around a lot, hoping that would do it in the absence of shampoo. I waded back to the bank and caught Hooker looking at me.

"You're really pretty," Hooker said.

"You're looking!"

"Of course, I'm looking. I'm a man. I have to look. I'd lose my union card if I didn't look. I'd have my testicles repossessed."

"You promised."

"Promises never count when naked women are involved. Everybody knows that. If it would make you feel better, I could get naked, too."

"Tempting, but no. Is my hair clean? I got all the spider guts out, right?"

Hooker looked at my hair. "Oh shit."

"Now what?"

"Leeches."

I started crying again.

"It's not that bad," Hooker said. "There are only a couple of them. Maybe three. Or four. And mostly they're not attached. Well okay, probably they're not *real* attached. Stay right there, and I'll get a stick."

"A *stick*?"

"To pry them off."

Now I was up to openmouthed sobbing.

"Oh man, I'm sorry you've got leeches. I'll pick them off. Look, I'm picking them off. Do you think you could stop crying?"

"I don't know why I'm crying," I said, tears streaming down my sunburned face, sliding past my peeling nose and blistered lips. "I never cry. I'm really brave. And I'm a good sport."

"Sure you are," Hooker said, flipping a leech into the bushes. "Anybody could see how brave you are." He tossed another leech. "Yuk," he said. "Ick."

"I don't usually lose it like this. I'm always the sensible, dependable person. Okay, so I don't like heights and I don't like spiders, but I'm pretty good with snakes."

"I hate snakes. And I'm not too crazy about leeches. *Oh man,* this is a big one. Hold still."

I wiped my nose with the back of my hand. "Life sucks," I said.

"Life isn't so bad. You'll feel better about life now that the spider guts and the leeches are all gone." He took half a step backward and his gaze wandered south. "Maybe before you get dressed I should check out the rest of you for leeches. They seem to like ah, hairy places."

I started shrieking and Hooker clapped a hand over my mouth.

"Not so loud!" Hooker said. "The bad guys could still be out there."

I felt around and was relieved not to find any more leeches.

"Sorry," I said. "I got a little hysterical."

"Perfectly natural," Hooker said. "Even NASCAR Guy would get hysterical if he thought he had leeches on his stick shift. You just need to relax. You know what you need? Sex."

"Sex? You just finished picking leeches off my head and you want to have sex?"

"Yeah."

Men never cease to amaze me. I remembered reading somewhere a description of men and women in terms of boxes. The female box had a bunch of knobs and buttons and complicated instructions. And the male box had an *off/on* switch. That was it. Just a single switch. Hooker's switch was always turned to *on*.

"I'm not feeling really sexy right now," I said.

"I just thought since you were already naked it would be a good idea. This way we wouldn't have to go through that awkward getting undressed part."

"Speaking of clothes . . ."

"Seems like a shame to cover you up, but if that's what you want, NASCAR Guy is here to help." And he scooped my panties out of the boat and dangled them by one finger.

I took the panties and the bra that followed and put them on. Hooker waded into the stream, swished my shorts and shirt around, looked them over, and threw them into the jungle. "Not gonna happen, sweetie. Trust me, you don't want to *ever* wear those clothes."

"They're the only clothes I have!"

He took his shirt off and gave it to me. "Wear my shirt until we get back to the boat."

"Do you think we can go back to the boat?"

"I don't know. I'm going to walk back and take a look. Stay with the RIB. If you hear any noise at all, hide in the jungle."

An hour later, Hooker crashed through the brush behind me.

"The boat is still there," he said. "It looks like a Sea Ray. No sign of life on it. I watched the *Happy Hooker* for a while, and I didn't see any activity there either, but I think chances are good that someone's on board. It's what I would do. I'd sit and wait. I have a hoist, so it's obvious I have the ability to carry an inflatable. Since no one's come upstream, I can only assume they decided to wait for Bill and Maria to return."

"They're going to be disappointed when we show up."

"Yeah, they're going to torture us and make us tell them where to find Bill and Maria."

"I'd faint but I've already done that."

"We can stay here until we starve to death, or we can go back and rat on Bill and Maria. What do you think?"

"I think I'm tired of sitting here in my underpants."

We moved to get into the RIB, and we both stopped and stared at the canister.

"We don't want to take this with us," Hooker said. "If there's someone on the boat, we don't want to chance dropping this into their hands . . . whatever the hell it is."

"Don't expect me to help you carry it into the jungle. I've already done the spider-leech thing."

"We can drop it in the water. It's about fifteen feet deep at the first bend. No one will find it there."

We got into the RIB and Hooker motored us downstream. We dropped the canister and continued on to the harbor entrance, where we sat for a half hour, watching Hooker's boat. It was midday and the jungle was steaming. No breeze and a hundred percent humidity. The air was condensing on my forehead and running down the sides of my face, dripping off my chin.

"Do you have air-conditioning on that boat?" I asked Hooker.

"Yep."

"Take me to it."

We cruised over to the *Happy Hooker* and circled it. No sign of life.

"Do you think the bad guys are on board, waiting for us?" I asked Hooker.

"Yep."

"Do you think we could make Miami in the RIB?"

"What's your relationship with God?"

"It's shaky."

"Then I wouldn't count on making Miami in the RIB."

"I'm feeling a little vulnerable in my underwear."

Hooker gave his head a shake. "I'm sorry I didn't do a better job of protecting you. I should have been smarter."

"Not your fault. You were great. You picked leeches off my head with your bare hands."

"I almost threw up. Good thing I can drive, because I sure as hell couldn't wrangle leeches for a living."

We sat off the starboard side for another ten minutes. Neither of us said anything. We were listening. Finally I got restless.

"Let's get on with it," I said to Hooker. "I'm tired of waiting. Let's tie up to the dive platform."

"I'm not going to tie up," Hooker said. "Stay in the RIB and I'll look around. You know how to work this thing if you have to, right?"

"Yes."

Hooker looped the line once around to stabilize the RIB and climbed out. "If you have to take off, try to get to the mainland. It's all I can come up with."

I watched him cross the deck behind the fighting chair and open the cabin door. The door partially closed behind him. I heard him yell *"Barney, go!"* There was a gunshot. And Hooker reeled out of the cabin and collapsed onto the deck.

The guy with the slicked-back hair and his partner appeared in the doorway. The partner had his foot completely wrapped in a bandage. The guy with the slicked-back hair had his arm in a sling. Slick and Gimpy, I thought. They both had guns, and they didn't look happy to see me. No surprise there.

"Lucky me," Slick said. "My favorite person. I can't get rid of you. You're like a bad rash. Where's your brother?"

NINE

I couldn't believe they shot Hooker. He was face-down on the deck, and he wasn't moving. My heart was in my throat, and I was so enraged my vision was blurred.

"Get in the cabin," Slick said, motioning at me with his gun.

"Listen to me, you sack of slime," I yelled, coming out of the RIB wielding an oar. "I've had a really bad day. First the spider and then the leeches. My underwear's riding up my ass, and I hate this freaking humidity. I'm not going into the cabin. The only way you're going to get me into the cabin is to shoot me, like you shot Hooker."

"Lady, that's really tempting, but I need to get some answers from you."

"You're not getting *any* answers from me. And get off our boat."

Both guys blew out a sigh.

"Get her," Slick said to Gimpy.

Gimpy stepped over Hooker and reached for me. I spun around and caught him square in the stomach with the oar. *Thwack.* And Gimpy went down to the deck with the wind knocked out of him.

The move had been instinctual, the result of a bad engagement to a great kickboxer. Bruce Leskowitz didn't have a lot upstairs, and his Mr. Stupid had a tendency to roam. On the plus side, Leskowitz had a fabulous body, and he brought me up to a brown belt. Who would have thought I'd ever use the moves? God works in mysterious ways.

Slick leveled his gun at me. "Put the oar down."

"No."

"Don't make me shoot you."

"Go ahead, shoot me," I said to Slick. "If you don't shoot me, I'm going to kick your ass."

Okay, I admit it. I was a little nuts. I was rolling on adrenaline and desperation. The bad guy had a gun, and I had an oar. And the truth is, even though I knew some karate, I didn't have a lot of history behind me in the ass-kicking department. It just seemed like the thing to say. It's what The Rock would say, right?

Since I don't have entirely the same presence as The Rock, Slick started laughing. It was a perfectly appropriate response, but it's not something you want to do to a woman on the edge.

I lunged at him with the oar, and he stepped to the side. He didn't have a lot of room to maneuver away from me. I whirled and tagged him in the bad arm with the blade. He got off a wild shot. I shoved the oar at him, knocked him off balance, and he went sailing into space, off the side of the boat.

Gimpy was on hands and knees, sucking air. I grabbed the revolver that had fallen out of his hand when he went down, and I jumped back to a safe distance. I dropped the oar, and I two-handed the gun. Even with two hands, the gun was shaking.

Gimpy's eyes were on me, wide with terror. And I thought my eyes probably looked like that, too.

"Don't shoot me," he said. "Take it easy. Jesus, I never believed in gun control until I met you."

"Into the water," I said.

"What?"

"Jump!"

"I got a bad foot. I'll sink like a stone."

I sighted down the gun barrel, pulled the hammer back, and he jumped off the boat.

He bobbed to the surface beside Slick, and the two of them hung there, about fifteen feet off the starboard side.

"Swim!" I yelled at them.

Gimpy was floundering, taking in some water, and Slick wasn't doing much better.

"For Pete's sake," I said. "Take the RIB."

There was a lot of splashing and sputtering, but they weren't making much progress moving, so I grabbed the line to the RIB and dragged the RIB around to them. They hung on for a while, catching their breath, coughing up seawater. Then they dragged themselves into the RIB and lay there like a couple dead fish.

I gave the RIB a shove with the oar, and the RIB drifted off. When I turned back to Hooker he was sitting on the deck, knees bent, head down.

I knelt beside him. "Are you okay?"

"Give me a minute. I've got a real bad case of the whirlies."

I went back to looking at the guys in the RIB. They were just sitting there, letting the RIB drift. Not far enough away for me to feel safe. I fired off a shot that I knew would go far right of them. They looked at me like I was Demon Woman. Gimpy cranked the outboard over and headed for shore.

Hooker was beside me, holding on to the fighting chair. "They've got the RIB?"

"Yeah, they were going to drown."

"Isn't that a good thing? Dead bad guys?"

"I've never killed anyone."

"This would have been a great place to start."

Hooker leaned over the rail and threw up. When he was done throwing up he flopped back onto the deck and lay spread-eagle, eyes closed. "What happened?"

"They tranked you."

"Tranked me?"

"I know all about it because I watch *Wild Kingdom* reruns on television. I thought you were shot, but you aren't bleeding, and there's a dart stuck in your chest. Don't move."

I pulled the dart out and looked at it. I was having a hard time seeing it because my hands were still shaking, and the dart was surprisingly small.

"Lucky for you they weren't using the big-game dart gun," I said. "This must be the dart they use to tranquilize rabbits."

"How'd you get them off the boat?"

"I asked them nicely."

Hooker smiled and rubbed his chest where the dart had gone in. "It stings," he said. "Want to kiss it and make it better?"

I bent and kissed him just to the side of the puncture.

"I'd kiss you back, but I just threw up," he said.

NASCAR Guy's sensitive side.

I stood and checked on the bad guys. They were pulling the RIB onto the shore. They looked okay.

"We should get out of here," I said to Hooker. "Can you help me get the anchor up?"

"No problemo." He crawled to the dive platform, leaned over, and stuck his head in the water. He dragged his head out of the water, crawled to the fighting chair, and pulled himself to his feet. "You really should have killed them," he said.

We hauled the anchor up, and we got under way with Slick and Gimpy watching us. They didn't wave good-bye.

Hooker inched his way over to the Sea Ray. "Throw out a couple fenders on the port side. Let's see if we can tie up to their boat and get you on board so you can *fix* their engines."

Ten minutes later I was climbing off the Sea Ray, back onto the *Happy Hooker*, bringing in the fenders. I'd sliced through fuel lines and sabotaged the electrical system. If Slick and Gimpy got back to the States, it wasn't going to be in the Sea Ray.

"Next stop, Florida," Hooker said. And he took the *Happy Hooker* up to cruising speed.

I played the binoculars across the water for a while, but there wasn't anything else to see. Just azure sky and gently undulating ocean.

Hooker stayed in the chair, at the helm, and I stretched out on the banquette behind him. It was Monday, and I supposed I was unemployed. It didn't seem especially important anymore. I fell asleep, and when I woke up we were plowing through heavy seas.

"We're going into Key West," Hooker said. "The weather's changed, and I'm not feeling comfortable with waves this size. I need to refuel anyway. If I can use Vana's slip I'll stay in Key West. If I can't, I'll try to get a captain to take her to Miami with me."

Ten minutes later, Key West was in sight and Hooker was on the radio, calling the Key West dockmaster, arranging to use Vana's slip.

"I got the slip," Hooker said to me, "but this is going to be messy. This is way too much boat for me to dock by myself in these conditions."

We rode into the marina on whitecapped rollers, and Hooker cut to an idle. We found our spot, and Hooker sent me to the back of the boat with a walkie-talkie. There were two dockhands from the dockmaster's office already in place, waiting to help us tie up.

"Watch your footing back there," Hooker said to me. "I've got wind and tide pushing me, and I'm probably going to ram the pier. I don't want to dump you into the water."

When we were finally secure, Hooker thanked the dock hands, and then he turned and rapped his head on the control panel. *Thunk, thunk, thunk.*

"I need a drink," he said. "A big one."

"It wasn't so bad. You only rammed the pier twice. And you didn't do any damage when you drifted into that other boat. Well, not a *lot* of damage."

"On the bright side," Hooker said. "You did great. You didn't even drop the talkie."

We collected some food, grabbed our duffel bags, and walked three blocks to the Mini. Hooker drove around a little, making sure we weren't being followed, before parking at Vana's. We went inside and collapsed on the couch.

"I'm exhausted," Hooker said.

"You've had a full day. You wrangled leeches. You got tranked. You trashed a pier."

"I'd chase you around the house," Hooker said, "but I don't think I can get off the couch."

I took the food into the kitchen and made us sandwiches. I brought the sandwiches out to the living room with a bottle of vodka and a single glass.

"Not drinking?" Hooker asked, taking a plate from me.

"Maybe later. I have seventeen messages I have to answer, and I don't want to be drunk when I talk to my mother."

"Yeah, mothers hate that."

Ten minutes later, Hooker was asleep on the couch. I draped a blanket over him and tucked myself into a guest room. I slipped under the covers of Vana's comfy guest bed, but it was a while before I fell asleep. Too many things to worry about. Too many loose ends

Hooker was showered and dressed in fresh clothes, drinking coffee in the kitchen when I shuffled past him in a guest robe and poured out a mug of coffee.

"Morning," I said.

"Morning." He wrapped an arm around me and dropped a friendly kiss on the top of my head, like we were an old married couple.

"Nice," I told him.

"It's going to get nicer. Unfortunately, not immediately. I just got off the phone with Judey. Todd called him first thing this morning. Todd said *Flex* moved from Miami to Key West. We didn't see her because they're anchored on the other side of the island. Todd said the helicopter's been flying non-stop, and that everyone was told to take shore leave today. Todd went to the marina to have breakfast with a friend and saw the *Happy Hooker*. He thought maybe Bill was living on the boat."

"Good thing we're safe in this house."

"We're not that safe. If someone halfway tried, they'd come up with Vana's name and address, since the boat's in his slip."

"Are we scrambling to get out of town?"

"Darlin', we're scrambling big time."

I took a three-minute shower and threw some clothes on. We grabbed our bags, made sure the lights were out, locked up the house, and followed the stepping-stones to the Mini. The instant we were in the car, a black Town Car pulled in behind us, blocking our exit. Two men came out of nowhere, one on either side of the Mini. They had guns drawn.

"Stay cool," Hooker said to me.

The doors were wrenched open and we were walked back to the Town Car. One of the men got in the back with us and one got in next to the driver.

"Mr. Salzar would like to talk to you," the guy in the back said. "He's invited you onto *Flex*."

Flex was still anchored offshore. No place big enough for it in the marina, I guess. Or maybe they wanted to be far enough away so the tourists couldn't hear me screaming while I was being tortured. Whatever the reason, we were put in a large RIB and motored out to the boat. The RIB tied up at the stern and we were escorted to the second deck.

Even under these circumstances it was hard not to be impressed. There was a lot of high-gloss wood and polished brass. Fresh flowers in vases. The furniture was perfectly restored Biedermeier. Couches and comfy chairs were upholstered in the ship's colors of navy and gold.

Salzar was waiting for us in the salon. He was at a writing desk. A laptop and a mug of coffee sat to one side on the desk. Puke Face stood behind Salzar. There were two chairs in front of the desk.

"Be seated," Salzar said. As if this was some friendly little meeting. Like maybe he was a mortgage broker. Or a marriage counselor.

Hooker slouched into his chair and smiled at Salzar. "Nice boat."

"Thank you," Salzar said. "It's quite unique. Calflex is very proud of it."

"Nice of you to invite us on board," Hooker said.

This got a weird little cat-playing-with-the-mouse smile from Salzar. "You have something that I very much desire. I've been on your boat. The object that I desire isn't there. And I've just received a call from my associate. The object isn't in Richard Vana's house. And it isn't in the Mini Cooper. So I have to assume you've hidden this object."

"What object are we talking about?" Hooker asked him.

"A canister. Red cone. Black-and-green stripe. Sound familiar?"

"We turned that over to the navy when we arrived," Hooker said.

Salzar shifted his eyes to an aide by the door, and the aide left the room. "That would be unfortunate," Salzar said. "That would make me unhappy. And it would mean I'd have to torture you for no good purpose. Other than pleasure, of course."

"What's so special about this canister?" Hooker asked him.

"It's filled with fear," Salzar said, smiling again. "And fear is power, isn't it?"

The aide returned and shook his head, no.

"My source tells me the canister was never delivered to the navy," Salzar said. "You might want to rethink your answer."

"Your source is wrong," Hooker said.

Salzar hit a button on his laptop and a photo appeared on the screen. He turned the laptop so Hooker and I could see the photo. It was a picture of Maria. Her hair was lank and stuck to her face. She had a swollen lip and a bruise just under her left eye. She was looking into the camera, and she was spewing hatred.

"This picture was taken earlier this morning," Salzar said. "The chopper picked up the Sunseeker leaving the island. Infrared technology is so helpful. It allows you to see all sorts of things, like people and very dense cargo such as gold bricks. Bottom line is, we followed Bill and Maria to Port Royal and paid them a visit. My men found the gold, but unfortunately, not the canister. As you can see, we gave Maria an opportunity to share with us, but it turned out she didn't have much to share. Now you have a similar opportunity." He leaned forward on the desk. The line of his mouth compressed, and his pupils shrank to pinpoints. "I want that canister. I'll stop at nothing to get it. *Nothing*. Do you understand?"

Hooker and I didn't say anything.

"I have another picture you might enjoy," Salzar said. "The resolution isn't as good as I'd like . . . picture phone quality. Still, I think it's a compelling photo." He clicked on an icon and a second photo filled the screen. It was Bill, sprawled on a carpeted floor, bleeding. He'd been shot in the upper arm and chest. Hard to tell if he was dead or alive.

I heard someone sob. I guess it was me. And then Hooker reached over and grabbed my wrist and squeezed. And that was all I felt. Hooker at my wrist. No thoughts in my head. No emotion. Just Hooker squeezing my wrist. How's that for a defense mechanism? Can I do denial, or what?

There was absolute silence in the room. Time stood still for several moments. And then the silence was pierced by a siren. Everyone stood, me included. My first thought was *police siren*, but the siren was internal to the ship.

Salzar closed the laptop and handed it over to Puke Face. The door to the salon was opened, and aides were running outside the salon. The siren stopped and the captain came on over the intercom.

"We have a fire below decks. All guests are advised to leave the ship."

Salzar moved from behind the desk. "Hugo, you come with me. Roger and Leo, take Ms. Barnaby and Mr. Hooker to shore and see that they're safely transported to the garage."

Smoke was beginning to seep into the salon, so we all migrated to the sundeck at the stern. Before we could get to the stairs, there was an explosion below decks and the lower deck was engulfed in flames. Salzar and Puke Face moved forward along the outside rail and were swallowed up in black billowing smoke. The smoke roiled around us, and the next thing I knew I was flying through the air. Hooker had picked me up and sailed me out over the rail like a Frisbee.

I splashed down and immediately kicked myself up to the surface. Hooker was a couple feet away.

"Swim for shore," he yelled at me.

I did a couple strokes and an RIB pulled up to me. It was Todd. He dragged Hooker and me into the RIB and took off. I was choking on smoke and seawater, holding on for dear life as the RIB bounced through the chop. There were a lot of boats in the area now. Emergency vehicles screaming in the distance. The shoreline was filling up with gawkers. Todd aimed for a small sand beach away from most of the traffic. He rammed the RIB aground, and we splashed to shore.

"I have the Mini parked close by," he yelled. And we ran after Todd.

Hooker took the wheel. I took the seat next to

Hooker. And Todd crammed himself into the backseat. No one spoke. We just hunkered down, teeth chattering, and rocketed out of there. We got onto Route 1 and crossed the bridge to Cow Key.

Todd was the first to talk. "I guess I'm out of a job," he said.

"Holy fuck," Hooker said. "Saved by a fire. What are the chances?"

"Pretty good, since I set it," Todd said. "Judey called me back and filled me in. I was staying with a friend not far from Vana's house, so I walked over to see if I could help with anything. I saw them load you into the car and take off. Another car immediately showed up and did a fast search of the house and the Mini. When they left I borrowed the Mini. Lucky the keys were still in the ignition. I parked at Wickers Beach and saw them ferrying you out to *Flex*. So, I ran and got a RIB. No one noticed me tie up to *Flex*. The only people left on the boat were Salzar's people, and they were all in the main deck salon and in the pilothouse. I knew you were in trouble, so I thought I'd set the fire alarm off. I was down in the engine room, holding my lighter up to a sensor, and I don't know what happened, but I heard something go *pop* and then there was fire everywhere. I ran out and got back into the RIB. I didn't know what else to do. And then all of a sudden Barney came flying through the air!"

"Do you know anything about Bill?" Hooker asked Todd.

"No. What about Bill?"

Hooker took his cell phone out of his pocket. He shook the phone and water sloshed out. "Do you have a cell phone on you?" he asked Todd.

"Yep."

"Salzar had a picture of Bill bleeding," Hooker said. "It looked like he'd been shot. I know Bill was in Naples, so let's start there. Call the hospital in Naples and see if Bill's been brought in."

Todd got connected to the hospital and asked about Bill. There was a lot of un hunh, un hunh, un hunh. And Todd disconnected.

"Okay," Todd said when he got off the phone. "There's good news and there's bad news. The bad news is Bill has been shot. The good news is he's in stable condition. They said he was in the recovery room. That he was out of surgery. And he was stable."

I leaned back and closed my eyes and took a deep breath. "I don't like when Bill's hurt. I know he's all grown up, well, sort of grown up . . . but he's still my little brother."

"Bill's going to be okay," Hooker said, his hand

back at my wrist with a reassuring squeeze.
"We'll try calling in an hour. Maybe you can talk
to him."

We passed through the lower Keys and then we
were on the Seven Mile Bridge. The water was
choppy below us and the Mini was buffeted by
wind, but she held the road. We came up to
Marathon Plaza and Hooker slowed for two guys
fixing a flat on the shoulder. The car was a white
Ford Taurus. We got closer and Hooker shook his
head. Disbelieving. It was Slick and Gimpy.

"I'd really like to run them over," Hooker said,
"but I don't think I could get away with it this
close to the Plaza."

"Too bad we threw Gimpy's gun away. We
could shoot them."

"God knows how many people that gun has
killed," Hooker said. "It wouldn't have been
smart to get caught in possession of that gun."

Slick looked up just as we blew by them, and I
saw the shock of recognition register.

"I think we got busted," I said to Hooker.

He looked in the rearview mirror. "They still
have to get the tire on. Maybe we can get off the
Keys before they catch us. Once we pass Largo I
have more road choices."

A half hour later, just when I was beginning to feel comfortable, Todd saw the car behind us.

"Your friends have caught up to us," Todd said. "This is turning into *one of those days*, isn't it?"

It was midmorning, midweek and there weren't a lot of cars on the road. Three rolled by going south. The road behind them was empty. No cars behind Slick and Gimpy.

"Here's where they'll make their move," Hooker said. "This is going to be fun. Slick's going to force us to pull over."

The white Taurus swung out to pass, and Hooker smiled and watched his side-view mirror.

"Gimpy's got a gun sighted on us," I said. "I don't think it's a dart gun."

"I see it," Hooker said.

Todd ducked down below window level. *"Criminy!"*

They were directly abreast of us, and Gimpy was motioning with the gun to pull over. Hooker nodded acknowledgment and dropped the Mini back a couple inches.

"It's all in the timing and placement," Hooker said. "Hang on." Then he jerked the car to the left and slammed into the Taurus.

"Omigod," Todd said, head still down. "What are you doing? This isn't a demolition derby!"

The Taurus careened across the road, caught air going off a small embankment, rolled once, and came to a smoking stop, tires up, in a strip of mangrove.

"Amateurs," Hooker said, back in his lane, his foot still steady on the accelerator.

Todd popped up in time to see the roll. "Ouch."

"It was a good hit, but it seems pretty lame compared to blowing up a billion-dollar ship," Hooker said.

"I didn't do that," Todd said. "I was never there."

"Do you think we should go back to see if they're okay?" I asked.

"Darlin', they just pointed a gun at you," Hooker said. "If we go back for anything it'll be to set fire to their car."

"I've still got my lighter," Todd said.

We passed Largo and stayed on Route 1. Hooker pulled into a strip mall when we got to Florida City, so we could stretch and check the damage to the car.

I was out, but Hooker couldn't get his door open and his window wouldn't slide down.

"Sit tight," I said. "I'm good at this."

I poked through the junk in the cargo area and came up with a big ass screwdriver. I shoved the screwdriver between the door and the frame and pried the door open.

"Lesson number one from my father," I told Hooker. "Never go anywhere without a Maglight and a screwdriver. The bigger the better."

"Lesson number one from my father had to do with opening a beer bottle," Hooker said. He got out and looked at the Mini. "This is a tough little car. Considering how small it is, it really stood up. The side needs some body work. Well, okay, Bill probably needs a whole left side."

"Nothing structural," I said, on my back, under the car. "At first look, I don't see any damage to the frame or wheel wells."

We all went into a convenience store, got some cold sodas, and came back to the car.

"I'm cutting north here to the Tamiami Trail," Hooker said to Todd. "I'm taking Barney to Naples, so we can check on Bill. I have some of my crew in Homestead. Some sort of schmooze thing going on at the track. I can get one of them to pick you up here and take you back to Miami Beach, or wherever. Since you just destroyed *Flex* you might not want to go home for a while. Not until we get this straightened out."

"Thanks. That would be great. I have someone I can stay with in North Miami."

Hooker used Todd's phone again, and ten minutes later he swung the Mini out of the lot and back to Route 1.

"I'm taking the Trail instead of going all the way up to Alligator Alley. It's a slower road, but the distance is shorter. We should make Naples in two hours," Hooker said.

The Tamiami Trail cuts across the bottom tip of Florida, running through mile after mile of flat swampland, the tedium occasionally broken by signs advertising Indian-guided airboat rides. For the most part, it's a two-lane road used by people who aren't in a hurry. Hooker didn't fall into the *not in a hurry* category. Hooker was doing ninety, weaving in and out of traffic like this was just another day at the job. If anyone other than Hooker had been driving, I would have had my feet braced on the dash, ready to escape the car at the first opportunity.

"What's this schmooze thing going on in Homestead?" I asked him.

"Some kind of a preseason sponsor event. They wanted me to participate, but I refused. The season is long and hard, and I never shirk my corporate responsibilities, but this is my time, and I'm not giving it up. I told them to send a car instead. We have a couple cars that roll around in a transporter and are used for this stuff. They look like my car, but they can be used to give rides to the fans. They're cars we've raced and retired so they're pretty authentic."

Hooker dropped to the speed limit as we approached Naples, the scenery suddenly changing from swamp to civilization. Movie theaters, shopping malls, golf course communities, high-end furniture stores, and car dealerships lined the Trail. I'd called ahead and gotten an address for the hospital. I'd been told Bill was in his room but sedated and not able to talk.

By the time we got to the hospital Bill was more or less awake. He was hooked up to an I.V. and a respiration monitor. I'd learned from a nurse that no vital organs had been damaged, but he'd lost some blood.

"I know my eyes are open," Bill said, his words soft and slurred. "But I'm feeling a little slow."

"We aren't going anywhere," I told him. "Take a nap. We'll be here when you wake up."

It was early evening when Bill opened his eyes again. "Hi," he said. His voice was stronger, and his pupils were no longer dilated to the size of quarters. "How did you know I was here?"

"That's a long story," I said. "We might want to save it for another time."

"Yeah, and parts of it are too good to waste on you in your drugged-up condition," Hooker said.

I was standing at bedside, and I could feel
Hooker pressed into my back with his hand lightly
resting at the base of my neck. Probably worried
I'd faint. I was pretty sure his fear was un-
grounded, but it was still nice to have the support.

"They found us," Bill said. "I don't know how.
The helicopter probably. It did a couple flyovers
when we were in the Gulf. I didn't think they saw
me go into Gordon Pass, but hell . . ."

He was white again and his breaths were shallow.

"Are you okay?" I asked. "Are you in pain?"

"Pain that you can't fix, Barney. They've got
Maria, don't they? We were in the house I rented,
in bed, sleeping, when they came in," Bill said.
"Two Cuban guys. They grabbed Maria. She was
screaming and crying, and I tried to get to her,
and they shot me. That's the last I remember."

"There's a cop outside, waiting to talk to you.
He said you were shot in your driveway."

"I guess I dragged myself out there."

Good thing, too. The cop in the hall told us Bill
was found by a passing motorist who saw him
lying on the driveway. If Bill had stayed in the
house, no one would have found him. He most
likely would have bled to death.

"I'm going to tell the cop about the Cubans and
Maria, but not about the gold," Bill said. "You
need to go to the house and see if the gold is still

there. I left it on the boat. The boat is tied to the dock directly behind the house." His eyes filled. "I love her, Barney. I really love her. It's going to work out okay, isn't it?"

"Yeah, it's going to work out okay."

"We'll get her back, right?" Bill asked.

I nodded, barely able to speak. "We'll get her back."

TEN

I talked to Bill's doctor while the cop talked to Bill. If Bill's signs stayed stable he'd be allowed to go home tomorrow. He had a flesh wound in his upper arm, and the bullet in his chest had cracked a rib but missed everything else. Bill had been lucky . . . if you can call getting shot twice lucky.

The cop was expressionless when he left Bill. I don't imagine he was all that happy. He had a kidnapping and shooting without motive. It didn't take a genius to figure out there were holes in the story.

I could have told the cop I'd been kidnapped and threatened by Salzar. I could have told him Salzar had photos of Bill and Maria. Problem was

I didn't have the photos in my possession. And the kidnapping was Salzar's word against mine and Hooker's. And our only witness was a guy who blew up a billion-dollar boat.

So, I didn't especially want to talk to the cop. Not to mention, my cop experience to date wasn't impressive. What I really wanted to do was scoop Bill up and take him someplace where he'd be safe. And then figure out a plan to defuse everything.

We stayed until nine. Bill was sedated and drifted off to sleep. Hooker and I dragged ourselves out of the hospital, into the parking lot.

"I'm adding this to my list of really shitty days," Hooker said. "I've had a bunch of them. Not a lot of people get shot in NASCAR, but people get hurt and people die. It's always awful."

"Why do you drive?"

"I don't know. I guess it's just what I do. It's what I'm good at. I used to think it was for the fame, but it turns out the fame is a pain in the ass. I suppose it could be for the money, but the truth is I've got enough. And I still keep racing. Crazy, hunh?"

"You like it."

Hooker grinned. Boyish. Caught by the simple truth. "Yeah, I like it."

"You're a good driver."

"I thought you didn't follow NASCAR."

"I was at Richmond last year. You were brilliant."

"Damn. I'm all flummoxed. I'm not used to you being nice to me."

"You have a short memory. I kissed your dart wound."

"I figured that was a pity kiss. I was pathetic."

"Well yeah, but I was still being nice to you."

We got into the battered Mini, and Hooker drove south toward town.

"I haven't spent a lot of time in Naples, but I think I can find my way to the house," Hooker said. "Bill gave me directions."

Hooker turned right at Fifth Avenue and drove past blocks of restaurants and shops. People were eating at outdoor tables and strolling into art galleries. The pace was slower than South Beach. The dress was more conservative. Palm trees were wound in twinkle lights. Cars were expensive.

We took a left onto Gordon Drive and watched the houses get larger as we drove south. No more restaurants or shops. No high-rise condos. Just block after block of expensive houses and professionally landscaped yards. And beyond the houses to our right was the Gulf of Mexico.

When we reached the Port Royal Beach Club, Hooker turned left into a neighborhood of curving streets that we knew followed a series of man-made canals. Half the houses were 1970s ranches and half the houses were new mega McMansions. The McMansions filled their lots and were hidden behind wrought iron gates that opened to brick drive courts and lush gardens. I suspected there were some older residents of Naples who might roll their eyes at the McMansions. I thought the McMansions were glorious. For that matter, I thought the ranches weren't bad either.

In my mind I imagined movie stars living behind the wrought iron gates, or possibly *Fortune* 500 CEOs. The reality was probably much less fun. Probably these houses were all owned by realtors who'd made a killing in the grossly inflated housing market.

Bill had rented one of the ranches. It was easily recognized by the yellow crime scene tape stretched across the front of the property, preventing people from using the circular drive.

Hooker parked at the side of the road, and we ducked under the tape and walked to the front door. Even in the dark it was possible to see the bloodstains on the yellow brick drive and concrete front porch.

"Maybe you should go back to the car," Hooker said. "It's not necessary for both of us to do this.

I'm just going to collect Bill's things and check out the boat."

"Thanks," I said, "but I'm okay."

In the absence of fake dog poop, Bill had hidden the key under a flowerpot on the front porch. Hooker found the key and opened the door. We stepped inside, and Hooker hit the light switch. The foyer was white marble and beyond that beige wall-to-wall carpet. There was a grisly trail of blood through the foyer to the carpet. The blood was smeared where Bill had fallen and dragged himself up. In the middle of the foyer was a perfect bloody handprint. Bill's handprint. Drops splattered out in an arc.

I felt my stomach sicken, and I went down hard on my knees. I was on all fours, fighting back nausea, shaking with the effort.

Hooker scooped me up and carried me into the powder room off the foyer. He sat me on the toilet seat, shoved my head between my legs, and draped a soaking wet hand towel over my head and neck.

"Breathe," he said. His hand was on the towel at the back of my neck. "Push against my hand. *Push.*"

"I guess I wasn't okay," I said.

"No one should ever be okay when they see something like that." He replaced the towel with a fresh one, and water ran down my neck and soaked into my shirt and my shorts. "I'm going to leave you here while I get Bill's things. You have to promise me you won't move an inch."

"I promise."

Ten minutes later, he came back for me. "I have Bill's and Maria's things in the back of the Mini. Can you stand?"

"Yes. I'm horrified and disgusted and angry, but I'm not sick. And I'm not going to turn to mush when I see the blood on the way out. It caught me by surprise."

Hooker took my hand and led me past the blood in the foyer and out the door. He turned the lights off, locked the door, and pocketed the key.

"I want to show you something out back," he said. "Take a walk with me."

We followed a footpath around the side of the house, past trees filled with oranges and grapefruits and flowers that were still fragrant in the warm night air. A pool stretched the width of the yard, and beyond the pool was a swath of manicured lawn and beyond the lawn was a dock and beyond the dock was the canal. A full moon hung in the lower sky, reflecting light that shimmered across the black water.

"It's pretty, isn't it?" Hooker said.

It was more than pretty. It was calming. Standing there, looking out at the canal, it was hard to imagine anything bad had happened in the house behind us.

"No Sunseeker," I said.

"No. But then we already knew they had the gold."

We returned to the car and left Port Royal. Hooker retraced his route and got back onto the Trail, heading north. This part of the road was clogged with traffic. Professional buildings, strip malls, furniture stores, and chain hotels lined both sides of the highway. Hooker pulled into the first hotel he came across and parked in the unloading zone.

"I'll run in and see if I can get a room," he said. "I don't suppose you'd want to sleep with me?"

It was said with such little boy hopeful hopelessness that I laughed out loud. "I'm not ready for that," I told him.

He curled his fingers into my T-shirt, pulled me close to him, and kissed me. His fingers were pressed into my breasts, his tongue slid over mine, and I felt my engine turn over and hum.

"Let me know when you're ready," he said. "Because I've been ready since the first day I met you."

Okay, so maybe I wanted to rethink the little boy part. I wasn't seeing any evidence of a little boy here. In fact, I was thinking Hooker showed the same single-mindedness of purpose when he focused on a woman that he showed on the track. Hooker kept his eye on the prize.

Hooker gave the battered door a good hard shot with his fist to get it to open. He angled himself out of the Mini and jogged to the hotel's revolving front door. He came back ten minutes later and got our bags out of the trunk.

"Darlin', we're in business," he said. "We've got rooms without bad guys."

The next morning, Bill's doctor assured me that Bill's signs were all good and he was strong enough to leave the hospital. You wouldn't know by looking. Bill was still pale. His arm was bandaged and in a sling. His chest was wrapped and double wrapped. He had blood caked under his fingernails and a bump on his forehead the size of a walnut. I had him dressed in khaki shorts and an orange-and-blue flowered shirt, hoping it would cheer him. It turned out Bill didn't need anything to cheer him because Bill was shot up with painkillers and happy juice for the ride home.

The hospital and police had assumed Bill was returning to the rental house. Hooker and I hadn't said anything to change their minds, but we had other plans. We loaded Bill into the front seat of the Mini, and we took off for Miami Beach.

It was noon when we rolled across the Causeway Bridge and into South Beach. It was a brilliant blue-sky day with temperatures in the low eighties and not a breath of air stirring. Hooker turned onto Alton Avenue and drove straight to Judey's condo building.

"We're leaving you with Jude," I said to Bill. "Do you remember Jude?"

"Ju-u-u-de," Bill said.

Bill was wasted.

"I don't know what they gave him," Hooker said. "But I wouldn't mind having some."

Hooker parked in the condo garage, we maneuvered Bill out of the car, and we locked arms around his back and steered him to the elevator.

Hooker hit the button for the twenty-seventh floor and looked over at me. "Are you going to be okay?"

"Sure. Twenty-seven. Piece of cake." I was just grateful it wasn't thirty-two.

We shuffled Bill out of the elevator, down the short hall, and rang Judey's bell.

"Oh my goodness," Judey said, throwing the door wide open to us. "Just look at this poor little sad sack."

"He's a lot higher than the twenty-seventh

floor," I told Judey. "They gave him some painkillers for the ride home."

"Lucky duck," Judey said. "I have my guest room all ready. We'll just tuck Wild Bill in, and I'll take good care of him. I'm very nurturing. And I won't leave him alone for a minute. Nothing bad is going to happen to him while I'm on the job."

Judey's condo was decorated in bold warm colors. Tangerine walls and hot red couches. A zebra skin coffee table ottoman. Black granite counters in the kitchen. It was striking, but it was a little like looking through your eyelids when you have a hangover.

We walked Bill into the guest room and put him to bed.

"Everything's red," he said. "Am I in hell?"

"No," I told him. "You're in Judey's guest room."

"J-u-u-deeee."

I handed the bag containing Bill's antibiotic and pain medication over to Judey. "Instructions are on the labels," I said. "There's also a sheet with instructions for changing the dressings and for doctor's visits."

"Never fear. Judey's here." Judey cut his eyes to Hooker. "And you take good care of Barney."

"I'm trying," Hooker said.

We left Judey and Bill, and we walked the

short distance to the elevator. The doors opened, we stepped in, and Hooker hit the lobby button.

"If you're afraid of the elevator, big brave NASCAR Guy would be willing to hold you close and make you feel safe," Hooker said.

"Thanks, but I'm too numb to be afraid."

"Could you pretend?"

When we were kids Bill was always bringing stray animals into the house. Dogs, cats, birds with broken wings, baby bunnies. My parents didn't have the heart to turn the strays away, but the rule was that the animals were only allowed in the yard and in Bill's room. Of course, eventually the blind dog and the cat with half an ear chewed off found their way into the living room. The birds were healed and set free but refused to leave. The bunnies grew up and migrated throughout the house, eating the wires and gnawing on the baseboards. And we loved them all. The point to this is that Bill loves easily and immediately. And the rest of my family, me included, loves more slowly.

Against my better judgment, Hooker was growing on me like one of Bill's adopted animals. The smart part of me was saying *are you kidding?* The soft squishy part of me that let the one-eared cat sleep on my chest all night long, almost smothering me for five years, was finding Hooker endearing. And the sex part of me was thinking the bakery theory was one of those male things I'd never fully understand. My way was to develop a craving for a particular pastry, to obsess about it, to dream about it, to desire it. And finally to lose control and buy it and eat it.

And now Hooker was looking tasty. Scary, hunh?

We took the elevator to the parking garage and found our way back to the Mini. Hooker and I had new cell phones. Mine rang just as I was about to buckle up.

"Barney," my mother said. "Where are you? Is everything all right?"

"Everything is fine. I'm still in Miami."

"Are you with Bill?"

"I just left him."

"He never answers his phone. His message machine is filled. I can't leave any more messages."

"I'll tell him to call you. Maybe tomorrow."

"When are you coming home? Should I go over to your apartment and water your plants?"

"I don't have any plants."

"What do you mean you don't have plants? Everybody has plants."

"Mine are plastic."

"I never noticed."

I hung up and Hooker smiled at me. "Do you really have plastic plants?"

"So sue me, I'm not a gardener."

My phone rang again. It was my boss.

"Family emergency," I told her. "I left you a message on your voice mail. Yes, I know this is inconvenient. Actually, I'm not sure when I'll be back, but I think it'll be soon."

"Did that work out okay?" Hooker asked when I hung up.

"Yep. Everything's great." I was fired, but what the hell, I didn't like the job anyway.

I had two more phone calls. One from my friend Lola. And the other from a woman who worked with me at the insurance company. I told both of them I was fine and I'd call them back.

Finally a call came in from Rosa. It was the call I'd been waiting for. I'd asked Rosa to do some research for me.

"I got it," Rosa said. "I got a list of all the properties Salzar owns in Miami. Felicia helped me. She has a cousin who works in the tax office. We even got his girlfriend's address."

I disconnected and turned to Hooker. "Rosa's got the list."

*　　*　　*

Hooker found a parking space half a block from the cigar factory. We had sodas and burgers from a drive-thru, and we took a couple minutes to finish eating. Hooker's cell phone rang. He looked at the readout and shut his phone off. He drank some soda and saw that I was watching him.

"My publicist," he said. "That's the fourth call today. This guy never gives up."

"This is about the schmooze thing in Homestead?"

"Yeah. I talked to him earlier. The transporter's there with the PR car. He's still trying to talk me into making an appearance."

"Maybe you should go."

"Don't want to go. And who'll protect you if I go?"

"In the beginning you were following me around because you didn't trust me."

"Yes, but all that's changed. That was only partly true, anyway. I was mostly following you around because of the little pink skirt and your long pink legs."

A blue Crown Vic parked on the opposite side of the street at the far end of the block, and Slick and Gimpy got out.

"I don't believe this," Hooker said. "What are the chances?"

Slick still had his arm in the sling, plus he had

a huge Band-Aid across his nose, and both his eyes were black and blue. Gimpy was wearing a neck brace and a knee brace. His foot was still bandaged and wrapped in a thing that looked like a Velcro sandal, and he had a single crutch to help him walk.

Neither of the men saw us. They crossed the street and walked into the cigar factory.

"Maybe we should call the police," Hooker said.

"The police won't get here in time. We should go in to see if we can help Rosa."

We were half out of the Mini when the door to the cigar factory crashed open and the crutch flew out, followed by Slick and Gimpy. They went to the ground, stumbled up, and scrambled for the Crown Vic.

The entire factory emptied onto the sidewalk, yelling in Spanish. Rosa and two other women had guns. *Pow!* Rosa squeezed off a shot that ripped into the rear quarter panel of the Crown Vic. *Pow, pow.* The other women fired.

Slick cranked the Crown Vic over and laid a quarter of an inch of rubber on takeoff.

"Silly butthole," one of the old women yelled at the fleeing car.

We walked over to the group.

"What happened?" I asked.

"Some losers came in and tried to take Rosa away, can you imagine?"

"It was those two guys from Key West," Rosa said. "They say they want to talk to me outside. I say to them I don't think so. I tell them they can talk to me *inside*. Then they start to get smart mouth, threatening me if I don't go outside."

A chunky old woman with short gray hair and a cigar in her mouth elbowed Rosa. "We show them, hunh? You don't get smart mouth in this shop. We kick their asses good. We get all over them."

"You wait here," Rosa said to Hooker and me. "I'll get the list."

The crutch was still in the middle of the road.

A dusty pickup truck with gardening equipment in the back rattled up to the crutch and stopped. A man got out, walked to the crutch, and examined it. Then he threw the crutch into the back of the truck and took off.

"You never know when you're going to need a crutch," Hooker said.

Rosa swung out of the cigar factory with her big straw bag over her arm and a piece of paper in her hand. She was wearing clear plastic open-toed shoes with four-inch spike heels, blue cotton pants that came to midcalf, and a red T-shirt that advertised a crab house.

"All right," Rosa said. "I'm ready to go. All we have to do is pick up Felicia."

Hooker grinned at me. "And to think I was going to waste my time on a fishing trip."

We stopped at the fruit stand and Felicia crammed herself in next to Rosa.

"You know those two guys you shot?" Rosa said to Felicia. "They stopped by the cigar factory just now and tried to get me to go with them."

"They did not."

"They did!"

"What'd you say to them?"

"I said they should eat some lead."

"Maybe they going to stop here next, and I'll miss them. That would be disappointing," Felicia said.

"If they want to talk to you bad enough, they'll be back," Rosa said. "In the meantime, maybe your husband will shoot them." Rosa leaned forward. "Turn right at the next corner," she told Hooker. "And then go two blocks. The first property will be on the right. It's an apartment building."

The apartment building was four stories tall, and the ground-level wall was covered with gang graffiti. The front door was missing. Just some hinges left on the jamb. Inside there was a small dark foyer with four mailboxes built into the one wall and a scary-looking stairwell to the right. We all squeezed into the foyer and read the names on the mailboxes.

"I don't know none of these people," Felicia said. "They must be foreign. Some of those South Americans."

The foyer didn't smell great. And the stairwell smelled even worse.

"No point to all of us trooping up the stairs," Hooker said. "I'll go, and you three wait here."

"Be careful," Felicia said. "Watch for the big cockroaches."

Hooker went upstairs, and Rosa, Felicia, and I stepped out of the foyer, onto the sidewalk.

"This building could use some bleach," Rosa said. "That's the best thing to clean up a building like this."

"Be better if it had a fire," Felicia said. "Urban renewal. Start over."

Ten minutes later I was looking up at the windows, worrying about Hooker.

"He should be down by now," I said.

"No gunshots," Rosa said.

"Yeah, and no screaming," Felicia said. "We give him some more time."

A couple minutes and Hooker appeared at the bottom of the stairs, followed by a bunch of smiling people.

One man had *Hooker* written on his forehead.

"Good-bye, Sam Hooker," they were saying.

"Thank you for autographing my hat."

"Thank you for calling my sister."

A woman came running with a camera, and the group posed for a picture with Hooker smiling in the middle of it all.

We got into the Mini and pulled away.

"Race fans," Hooker said. "Maria wasn't in there."

We searched two more apartment buildings with similar results. The fourth property on the list was a warehouse. We all thought this had some potential, since a truck filled with gold could be hidden in the warehouse.

The warehouse was three stories tall and took up half of a city block. There were three garage bays and a standard door. All were closed and locked. Windows were dark above the doors. Second-floor windows were broken. We drove down a refuse-strewn alley that intersected the block and backed up to the rear of the warehouse. There were a couple Dumpsters back there, and there was a rear door, also locked. Ground-floor windows were painted black and secured with iron bars.

"Get on the Dumpster," Felicia said to Hooker. "Then you can go in through the window above it."

Hooker looked at the Dumpster and the window. "Wouldn't that be breaking and entering?"

"Yeah, so?"

"What if someone's in there?"

"Then we run like hell. Unless they're race fans, and then you can stay to sign autographs."

"I guess I'd look like a hero if I found Maria. And since I'm doing this for your brother, you'd be real grateful," Hooker said to me.

Felicia shook her finger at him. "Shame on you. I know what you're thinking."

"I'd be grateful," Rosa said.

"Something to remember," Hooker said.

Hooker dragged a crate over to the Dumpster and used it as a step. He stood on the Dumpster and tried the window.

"It's locked," he said. "And it's too high. I can't see in."

"And?" Felicia said.

"And I can't get in."

"Break it."

"I'm not going to break it! You can't just go around breaking windows."

Rosa climbed onto the crate and then onto the Dumpster.

"Hand me the crate," she said to Felicia.

Felicia passed the crate up to Rosa, Rosa swung

the crate in an arc and smashed the window. There weren't any alarms. No one came running.

"I'm gonna look in," Rosa said to Hooker. "Give me a boost."

And Rosa started climbing up Hooker. She had her heel on his thigh and her big boobs in his face. Hooker had a grip on her leg. Rosa got her foot on Hooker's shoulder and Hooker got his hand under her ass and pushed her up to the window.

"What do you see?" Felicia asked.

"Nothing. It's just a big empty warehouse. There's nothing in it. It's three stories high, but it's all space. There's no other doors in it, so it doesn't even have a bathroom." She looked at Hooker. "You can put me down now."

Hooker was braced against the building. "Be careful where you put the heels."

Rosa had one heel snagged into Hooker's waistband and her other leg crooked around his neck. She grabbed his shirt and swung her leg free, and Hooker lost his balance.

"Oh shit!" Hooker said. He was flailing his arms, looking for a handhold, and Rosa was hanging on for all she was worth, wrapped on him monkey style.

Hooker hit the Dumpster flat on his back with Rosa on top of him.

"This isn't so bad," Rosa said.

"Call 911," Hooker said.

I was on tiptoes, peeking over the Dumpster at Hooker. "Are you hurt?"

"No. I'm going to kill Rosa."

ELEVEN

We got Hooker and Rosa off the Dumpster and back into the Mini.

"There's two more warehouses," Felicia said. "One down the street and one on the next block."

We drove to both warehouses and found the garage doors open on both of them. Rosa volunteered to go in and look around while she asked directions. "We're lost," she'd say. "We're looking for Flagler Terrace. And what do you guys do here, anyway? And do you have a ladies' room?"

Both warehouses came up zero.

We checked out a parking lot, a Laundromat, several deli marts, and two more slum apartment buildings. We skipped Salzar's house and his girlfriend's condo.

"The only thing left is an office building on Calle Ocho," Felicia said. "That is where Salzar has his offices."

We all did a silent groan. None of us wanted to run into Salzar.

"He don't know me," Felicia said. "I'll go in and ask around."

"I'll go with you," Rosa said. "He don't know me either."

There was a small, unattended parking lot adjacent to the office building. The lot was full so Hooker pulled the Mini into the lot and idled in an exit lane while Rosa and Felicia went into the building. Hooker and I sat in the car, facing Calle Ocho. We watched the rush hour traffic and we kept an eye on the building's front door.

A black Lincoln Town Car dropped out of the traffic and parked at the curb. Puke Face exited the building and held the front door open. Salzar strode through the door, crossed the wide sidewalk, and paused at the Town Car. He turned and glanced at the lot where we were parked. His face showed no expression but his eyes locked onto the Mini.

Hooker did a little finger wave. "Hi," Hooker said, smiling. "Nice to see you survived the fire."

Salzar turned from us, disappeared into the backseat of the Town Car, and the car eased from the curb and rolled down the street.

I looked over at Hooker.

"What?" he said.

"I can't believe you did that."

"He was looking at us. I was being friendly."

"Give me a break. That was announcing your dick was bigger than his."

"You're right," Hooker said. "He brings out the NASCAR in me."

Hooker put the Mini into gear and drove out of the lot and circled the block. Rosa and Felicia were waiting for us when we returned.

"We didn't find anything," Rosa said. "But Salzar has a fancy ass office. We didn't go in. We just looked through the big glass door."

"I could smell brimstone," Felicia said. "Good thing I'm wearing my cross."

We took Felicia back to the fruit stand, and we dropped Rosa off at her apartment.

"Now what?" I asked Hooker.

"I don't know. I'm a race car driver. I'm not a detective. I'm just stumbling along here."

"What about Columbo, James Bond, Charlie's Angels? What would they do?"

"I know what James Bond would do."

"Forget James Bond. James Bond probably isn't a great role model for you."

"Okay, how about this. Let's find a convenience store and get a load of junk and park and eat."

We got the bag of junk, which consisted of soda, nachos, Twizzlers, a box of cookies, a couple shrink-wrapped sandwiches, and a big bag of chips, but we couldn't find a place to eat.

"It has to be someplace romantic so I can make a move on you," Hooker said. "Hey, look here, we can park in this alley. There's some space just past those garbage cans."

"Garbage cans aren't romantic."

"See, that's the difference between a man and a woman," Hooker said, jockeying into a parking space. "A man has imagination when it comes to romance. A man is willing to overlook a few things in the interest of romance." He pushed his seat back and handed me a sandwich. "This isn't so bad. It's nice and private. Here we are in this little car. Just the two of us."

Okay, I have to admit, it was cozy. And I *had* been thinking Hooker had nice legs. Tan and muscular, the hair on them sun bleached. And I *had* been wondering what it would feel like to lay my hand flat against his washboard stomach. That didn't mean I wanted to have car sex in an alley next to some garbage cans. Been there, done that.

"We're in a public alley," I said. "You're not really thinking of doing anything dumb, are you?"

"You mean like having my way with you? Yeah, I was thinking about it. It's what James Bond would do."

"I should never have mentioned James Bond. James Bond had a sex addiction."

"Hey, if you're going to have an addiction, pick a good one. Why waste time on smoking and cocaine when you can have a sex addiction."

"Would you like some cookies? How about more chips? There are some chips left."

"No good, darlin', I'm in James Bond mode now."

"James Bond didn't call women *darlin'*."

He leaned close and slid his arm around my shoulders. "I'm a Texas James Bond."

"Get away from me."

"You don't mean that. Women always put out for James Bond."

"*Put out?* You expect me to *put out?*"

"I guess that was an unfortunate choice of phrase. Probably you don't think that's romantic, eh? What I meant was . . . oh hell."

And he kissed me. A lot. And after a couple minutes of this I was thinking the alley was pretty private, and I could hardly smell the garbage cans, and maybe car sex would work after all. His hands were under my shirt, and his tongue was sliding over mine, and somehow I'd gotten onto my back in the Mini. I had my ass half on the gearshift between the two front seats and a leg draped around the steering column. I had my head pressed into the side door and suddenly I couldn't move. My hair was tangled in the door handle.

"Help," I whispered to Hooker.

"Don't worry, darlin'. I know what I'm doing."

"I don't think so."

"Just give me some direction. I'm good at taking direction."

"It's my hair."

"I love your hair. You have great hair."

"Thank you. The problem is . . ."

"The problem is we're talking about your *other* hair, right? I've already seen it, darlin'. I know you're not a natural blond. It's okay by me. Shit, I wouldn't care if you were bald."

"Hooker, my hair's *caught!*"

"Caught? Caught in what? Caught in your zipper?"

"Caught in the door handle."

"How could that be . . . you don't even have your pants off. *Oh! CRAP!*"

He got his knee on the floor and examined my hair.

"Is it bad?" I asked him.

"No. It's just a little tangled. I've seen worse. I'll have you back in action in a minute. I'll just unwrap a few of these little hairs. . . . Actually, we've got more than a few hairs involved in this. Well, okay, we're talking about major hair involvement. Jesus, how did you do this? All right, don't panic."

"I'm *not panicked*."

"That's good. No reason for *both* of us to be panicked. Maybe if I just . . ."

"*Yow!* You're pulling my hair out."

"I wish it was that simple."

I rolled my eyes up and saw a cop looking down, in the window at me.

"Excuse me," he said. "You're going to have to leave."

"Back off," Hooker said. "I'm having a problem here."

The cop smiled at me. "Jeez, lady, you must have needed it real bad to end up on your back in a little car like this."

"It was my boyish charm," Hooker said.

"Gets them every time," the cop said.

"I just . . . slipped," I said.

A second cop arrived and looked down at me. "What's the delay?"

"He was diddlin' her, and she slipped, and she got her hair caught in the door handle."

"He was *not* diddling me!" Unfortunately.

Hooker looked up at them. "I don't suppose either of you guys would have scissors on you?"

"Scissors?" I said, my voice up an octave. "No! *No cutting.*"

"I got a knife," the first cop said. "You want a knife?"

"No!" I said.

"Yeah," Hooker said.

I narrowed my eyes at Hooker. "You touch a single hair with that knife, and I'll make sure you sing soprano for the rest of your life."

"Wow, she's scary," the first cop said to Hooker. "You might want to think about this relationship."

"Are you kidding?" Hooker said. "Look how cute she is with her hair all wrapped around the door handle. Well, maybe not with the hair wrapped around the door handle . . . but usually."

"All I know is, you gotta get out of here. This is a public alley. Hey, are you Sam Hooker?"

Oh great.

"Yep, that's me," Hooker said. "In the flesh."

"I saw you win at Daytona. That was the best day of my life."

"*Hello,*" I said. "Remember me? How about someone untangling my goddamn hair!"

Hooker blew out a sigh. "Darlin', unless you want to be a Mini Cooper accessory for the rest of your life, you're going to have to get cut free."

"Can't you just drive me to a hair salon?"

Hooker looked out at the two cops. "Do you guys know of any all-night hair salons around here?"

They mumbled something about me being a nut and shook their heads.

"Fine. *Great.* Cut me free," I said. "What am I worried about? I haven't had a good hair day since I've been in this state. It's a swamp for crying out loud."

"That's real negative," the first cop said. "It's hard to live with a woman who's negative. Maybe she's not the one, you know what I mean? You're a NASCAR guy. You can probably have anyone you want."

Hooker sawed at my hair with the knife. "Just a little bit more . . . *oops.*"

"What *oops?*" I asked. "I don't like *oops.*"

"Did I say *oops?* I didn't mean *oops.* I meant thank goodness you're untangled." He handed the knife back to the cop "Now all we have to do is get you to sit up."

"My leg is caught on the steering wheel and my foot is asleep."

The first cop ran around to the other side of the car to help get my leg free. And the second cop opened the passenger-side door, grabbed me under my armpits, and pulled me out.

"This is a little embarrassing," I said to the two cops, "but thanks for the help."

I got back into the car, buckled my shoulder harness, and gave Hooker a death look. "This is all your fault."

Hooker gave the Mini some gas and motored out of the alley, down the street. "My fault?"

"You started it all with that kiss."

Hooker smiled. "It was a pretty decent kiss."

"Sure, easy for you to think that. You didn't get *your* hair caught."

"Seems like it's a good idea to be on top when you're having car sex."

"Do you have a lot of car sex?"

"Yeah, but I'm usually alone."

"I'm afraid to look in the mirror. How bad is my hair? It looks like there's an awful lot of it stuck in the handle."

Hooker cut his eyes to me and ran off the road onto a lawn. He made a fast correction and was back on the road. "It's not bad."

"You just ran off the road."

"I was . . . distracted."

I reached for the mirror on the sun visor and Hooker knocked my hand away.

"Don't do that. You don't want to look," he said. He grabbed the visor and gave it a twist and snapped it off at the pivot point. He powered his window down and threw the visor out the window.

My eyes were wide. "You just broke my brother's car!"

"Darlin', your brother's car is a wreck. He'll never notice the missing visor."

I put my hands up to feel my hair.

"I'm telling you it's not so bad," Hooker said. "Well, okay, it's pretty bad, but I'm really sorry. I'll make it up to you. I'll buy you another hat. A nicer one. Hell, I'll buy you a car. Would you like a car? And you're still cute. I swear, you're still cute. If you put your little pink skirt on, no one's gonna notice your hair."

I just stared at him. I could feel that my mouth was open, but there weren't any words coming out of it. I was all out of words.

"Oh boy," Hooker said. "You're upset, aren't you? I really hate when you're upset. You're not going to cry again, are you? I'll do anything. Honest to God, I'll do anything. What would you like?

A vacation? A good seat for Daytona? Marriage? Do you want to get married?"

"You'd marry me?"

"No, not me. But I could find someone."

I sucked in some air.

"Only foolin' with you," Hooker said. "Of course I'd marry you. I mean, it isn't like your hair won't grow back, right? Any man would be lucky to get married to you."

"And you'd marry me, why?"

"Because I just feel so sorry for you. No, wait a minute that's not it. That's a bad answer, isn't it? Because . . . I don't know why. I was trying to make you happy. You know, take your mind off your hair. Women always want to get married."

"I appreciate the effort, but I don't want to get married."

"Really?"

"Not now, anyway. And not to you."

"What's wrong with me?"

"For starters, I hardly know you."

"I could fix that."

"No! I can't afford to lose any more hair."

I put my pink hat on, settled back in my seat, and called Judey to check on Bill.

"He's sleeping like a little lamb," Judey said. "I'm keeping him comfy. Don't worry about a thing."

Hooker had a country western station on the radio. Some woman was singing about her man dying and her heart breaking. And if that wasn't bad enough it sounded like she didn't have a home and then her dog ran off.

"See," Hooker said. "You don't have it so bad. You could be like that poor woman singing. Her boyfriend died and left her all alone. And you just lost a patch of hair."

"Do you like country western music?"

"I hate it. Depresses the shit out of me. I just get sucked into it every now and then. One of those Texas things."

I searched for a rock station, didn't have a lot of luck, and finally settled on Latin dance music.

"Unless you have a better idea, I'm taking us back to my condo," Hooker said. "I don't know where else to go, I could use some new clothes, and I wouldn't mind trading this car for my Porsche."

"Don't you think that might be dangerous? We're the only ones who know where the canister is located. Suppose the bad guys are waiting for you to go home?"

"I'll deal with it. I need a place to think."

Hooker drove down Alton Road and turned left onto First Street and then onto Washington. "I'm still hungry," he said. "I'm going to run into Joe's and get some take-out stone crabs."

He double-parked and ran into the restaurant. A parking place opened up in front of me, so I scooted over behind the wheel and parked the Mini. Ten minutes later, Hooker came out with a bag of food and slid in next to me.

I returned to Alton Road and entered the parking garage. Hooker had two numbered spaces. His Porsche was in one. I pulled the Mini into the other, beside the Porsche. I caught a flash of movement in my rearview mirror. I looked up and saw Slick move toward us, his white sling standing out in the dim light.

I threw the Mini into reverse and gave it gas. The car jumped back, there was a shriek and a thud, and Gimpy tumbled off to the side. Slick jumped in front of the Mini, arms wide in a *stop* gesture. I shifted into drive, stomped on the accelerator, and bounced Slick off the hood. I swung the car around and headed for the exit. Gunshots echoed in the cavernous space. I gritted my teeth, put my head down, and sped out of the garage.

I cut across a couple streets, hit Collins, and drove north. Hooker was slumped in his seat, looking dazed, clutching the food bag.

"Are you okay?" I asked him.

"Hunh?"

There was a fine line of blood trickling down the side of his face. I slid to a stop under a streetlight. The blood was oozing from a gash in Hooker's forehead. It wasn't a gunshot wound, and it didn't seem to be deep. The area around it was red and swollen. I shifted my attention to the windshield and saw the point of impact. Hooker'd released his shoulder harness and hadn't rebuckled in time. At some point in the garage fiasco I'd pitched him into the windshield.

"Good thing you're such a tough guy," I said to Hooker.

"Yeah," he said. "And I'm going to protect you, too. Both of you. You're going to have to hold still, though. I can't protect you when you keep spinning like that."

"Hang on. I'm going to take you to the emergency room."

"That's nice," Hooker said. "I like going places with you."

I called Judey and got directions to South Shore Hospital. It was a weeknight, and Hooker and I arrived after the hospital'd had a flurry of rush-hour road-rage victims and before the hospital got into the late-night parade of drug- and alcohol-induced disasters. Since we were between peak hours Hooker was seen almost immediately. His head was examined and a Band-Aid applied. Some tests were taken. He was diagnosed as having a moderate concussion. I was given a sheet with instructions regarding his care for the next twenty-four hours. And we were dismissed.

I had Hooker by the elbow, guiding him down the hall to the exit. A gurney rolled toward us, pushed by a male nurse. A man was on the gurney, most of him covered by a sheet. His chart had been placed on his stomach. I passed close by the gurney and made eye contact with the man. It was Gimpy.

Gimpy gave a startled gasp. *"You!"* he yelled, suddenly sitting up, clawing out at me, sending the chart clattering to the floor.

I jumped away, and the nurse gave the gurney a quick shove ahead.

"You didn't hit him hard enough," Hooker whispered to me. "It's like he's the living dead. You can't kill him."

Good to know Hooker was feeling better.

I helped him get into the Mini, which now had one side entirely crumpled, a missing visor, and a scattering of bullet holes in the lower part of the hatchback.

I crossed South Beach and drove north on Collins. I didn't want to chance going back to Hooker's, or Bill's, or Judey's. For that matter, I didn't want to chance staying in South Beach.

Hooker had his eyes closed and his hand to his

head. "I have a massive headache," he said. "I have the mother of all headaches."

"Don't fall asleep. You're not supposed to sleep."

"Barney, I'd have to be dead to fall asleep with this headache."

"I thought I'd drive north of town and look for a hotel."

"There are lots of hotels on Collins. Once you get north of the Fontainebleau we should be safe."

I tried four hotels, including the Fontainebleau, and none had a vacancy. This was high season in Florida. The fifth hotel had a single room. Fine by me. I was afraid to leave Hooker alone anyway.

I moved us in, and I called Judey to tell him everything was okay. The room was clean and comfortable. The hotel was on the beach, but our room faced Collins.

Hooker stretched out on the king-size bed, and I crept into the bathroom to check my hair. I stood in front of the mirror, held my breath, and whipped the hat off.

Shit.

I blew out a sigh and put the hat back on. It'll grow back, I told myself. And it's just one chunk. And it's not like I'm bald. I must have at least an inch or two of hair left where he chopped it.

I returned to the bedroom, and I sat in an armchair and watched Hooker. He opened one eye and looked at me.

"You're not going to sit there and watch me all night, are you? It's creepy."

"I'm following the instruction sheet they gave me at the hospital."

"Those instructions were for a *bad* concussion. I've only got a moderate concussion. They gave you the wrong instructions. Your instructions should read that you go to bed with the concussed."

"I don't think so."

"You can't sit in that chair all night. You'll be tired in the morning. You won't be able to outsmart the bad guys."

He had a point.

I lay down next to him. "We'll leave the lights on so I can check on you. And you have to behave yourself."

"I'll be fine as long as you don't fondle me when I'm sleeping."

"I'm not going to fondle you! And you're not supposed to be sleeping."

I closed my eyes and instantly fell asleep. When I woke up the lights were off and the room was dark. I reached over to check on Hooker.

"I knew you couldn't help yourself," Hooker said.

"That wasn't a fondle. That was a bed check. You were supposed to leave the lights on."

"I couldn't sleep with the lights on."

"You aren't supposed to sleep."

"I can nap. Anyway, it's impossible to sleep with the sound effects."

And that's when I heard it. *Thump, thump, thump, thump.* It was the bed in the next room hitting the wall. "Omigod."

"Wait. It'll get better. She's a moaner and a screamer."

"Not even."

"Swear to God. Wait until you hear her. If it wasn't for the headache I'd have a woody."

"I don't hear anything but thumping."

"You have to be quiet."

We lay there together in the dark, listening. There was some muffled moaning and then some mumbled talking.

"I can't hear what they're saying," I said to Hooker.

"Shhh!"

The thumping resumed and some more moaning. The moaning got louder.

"Here it comes," Hooker whispered.

"Yes," came through the wall. "Oh yes. Oh God. Oh God. Oh God."

Thump, thump, thump, thump. BANG, BANG, BANG.

I was afraid the picture hanging over our headboard was going to get knocked off the wall and crash down on us.

"OH GOD!"

And then it was quiet.

"Well," Hooker said. "That was fun."

"She faked it."

"It didn't sound fake to me."

"Give me a break. No woman sounds like that unless she's faking it."

"That's a disturbing piece of information."

Hooker was feeling better in the morning. He had dark circles under his eyes, and he had a lump on his head, but his headache was gone, and he wasn't seeing double.

We ordered room service breakfast, and halfway through breakfast my phone rang.

"He's gone!" Judey wailed.

"Who?"

"Bill! Wild Bill is gone. I took a shower and when I came out he was gone. I don't understand it. We were having such a good time. He was feeling so much better this morning. He came out and sat at the table for breakfast. I made him pancakes. How could he leave after I made him pancakes?"

"Did he say anything about leaving? Did you hear anything? Did it look like someone broke in and took him?"

"No, no, and no. The little shit just left. He got dressed in *my* clothes. And he left."

"Did he leave a note?"

"A note," Judey said. "I was so upset, I didn't look for a note."

I sat with my lips pressed tight together, listening while Judey searched.

"I found it!" Judey said. "It was on the kitchen counter. It says he went to get Maria back. That's all. I'm so sorry. This is terrible. I was supposed to be watching him."

"It's not your fault. This is why we call him Wild Bill. Call me if you hear from him."

Hooker pushed back from his breakfast. "That didn't sound good."

"Bill went to get Maria."

"Unless he knows something we don't know, he'll be sniffing around Salzar. How do you think he'll do that? From what I've seen, Salzar's never alone. He's always got a couple big guys with him."

"Bill's not known for his cunning. Bill just goes after whatever it is he wants. I wouldn't be surprised if he walked up to Salzar and put a gun to his head."

TWELVE

It was a little after ten when I drove past Salzar's office building on Calle Ocho. It was a perfectly nice-looking building, in a nice neighborhood. And this would have been a perfectly nice day, if only things were different. I must have been doing a lot of unconscious sighing because Hooker reached over and put his hand at the nape of my neck.

It seemed to me we were always taking one step forward and two steps backward. And with each step, no matter that it was forward or backward, Hooker and I got dragged deeper into the mess, Bill's future got increasingly precarious, and I didn't know what to think about Maria. I hoped she still *had* a future.

Until a week ago, my life had been so easy. No major illnesses, no big disasters. Nothing to make me uncomfortable. Okay, I had a couple aborted romances that caused me some pain. And sometimes I felt like I was aimlessly drifting, marking time. But I'd never had to fear for my life or for the premature death of someone I loved. Until a week ago, I'd never looked down the barrel of a gun.

Now I know what it's like to live with real fear . . . and I'm not crazy about it. I'd get on a plane and go home, but that wouldn't make it all go away. I suspect the bad guys would track me down, no matter where I ran. And I couldn't live with myself if I bailed on Bill. Sometimes his brain isn't fully engaged, but his heart's always in the right spot.

And then there's this other thing that I'm struggling over. The canister. The truth is, I'm a person who pretty much lives day to day. I haven't got a lot of large heroic ambitions. I'd like a better job, but up to this point I was always working too hard to pay the rent to take a chance on a move. And even with a better job, I guess my aspirations are small. It's not like I want to be a movie star or an astronaut or the queen of England. I'd just like to find something that's a little more fun. Not that it has to be fun all the time . . . but some of the time would be a good thing. And God knows, I never wanted to save the world. So I'm a little unprepared for the current responsibility of knowing where a canister (that could possibly be a warhead) is hidden. And I'm a *lot* unprepared for the almost violent resolve I have that it won't fall into the wrong hands.

"We need help," I said to Hooker. "This isn't like the time Bill stole the keg. This is serious, and it's not going away. We need to get some sort of law enforcement involved here."

"I agree," Hooker said. "What kind of help should we get?"

"I don't know. Who would be in charge of possible bomb disposal?"

"I'm a little stumped on that one. I can drive, and I can dance, and I can even scramble an egg, but I don't know a whole lot about possible bombs. I guess we could start with the FBI."

I drove around the block three times. Finally a space opened up a half block from Salzar's building, and I maneuvered the Mini into it.

"Do you want to get in touch with authorities now?" Hooker asked. "Or do you want to try to head Bill off first?"

"Bill first. If possible."

There was a decent amount of traffic on Calle Ocho at this time of day. Cars would slow when they came up to the Mini, the occupants' eyes would widen, and then the cars would speed up.

Hooker slouched in his seat. "You'd think this was the first time anybody ever saw a car riddled with bullet holes."

We let a half hour go by. No Bill in sight. I couldn't call him. He didn't have his cell phone. I called Judey. Judey hadn't heard from him.

"We should go in and ask around," Hooker said. "See if he went past the front desk."

I did an inadvertent grimace.

"Hey, it could be fun," Hooker said.

"You're not worried?"

"You want the truth? My boys got the creepy crawlies. When this is done you're gonna owe me large."

We got out of the car and walked the half block to the building entrance. We pushed through the glass doors, crossed the lobby, and went to the front desk.

"I was supposed to meet my brother here," I told the guy behind the counter.

"Bill Barnaby?"

My stomach went into free fall. "Yes."

"He's with Mr. Salzar. They're expecting you."

Great. I turned to Hooker. "They're expecting us."

Hooker had his hand back at my neck. "No need for both of us to go up. Why don't you wait here? I know you need to use the ladies' room."

I bobbed my head at the desk guy. "Ladies' room?"

"Take the corridor to the side of the elevators. It's on the right."

Hooker and I walked to the elevators together.

"Get out of here," Hooker said. "Make it look like you're going to the ladies' room and find a way out. I'll call your cell when Bill and I are out of the building. If you don't hear from me in the next ten minutes, go to the police."

I walked down the corridor to the ladies' room and looked around. Security camera at the end of the hall. I went into the ladies' room and took a couple deep breaths. I was the only one in the ladies' room. It was on the ground floor. There was a window next to the sink. Frosted glass. I unlocked the window and opened it. The window backed up to a service driveway. I climbed out the window and dropped to the ground. I looked for security cameras. One at the far end of the building over the rear entrance. I walked in the opposite direction.

I cut through another service driveway and circled the block. I didn't want to go to the Mini. Hooker had been in the building for ten minutes now and he hadn't called. Time to call the police. I was back on Calle Ocho. I was standing in a doorway one building down from Salzar's building. From where I stood I could see Salzar's small parking lot and the front entrance.

A man left the building and went to one of two Lincoln Town Cars parked in the lot. He got into the car and drove out of the lot. I ran to the corner and saw the car make its way down the cross street and turn into the service road. I ran to the service road and stood on the corner and watched. The car stopped at Salzar's rear entrance. After a moment the door opened and Bill and Hooker were marched out and loaded into the Town Car. There were three other men with them. Two of the men got into the car, and the car drove off.

There was a slim chance that I could follow the Town Car if I could get a ride fast enough. No time to run back to the Mini. I was afraid to go back to it anyway. I jogged down the cross street, looking in car windows for keys left in the ignition. I found one almost immediately. Honda Civic with the door open and the keys dangling. It was parked in front of a hole-in-the-wall restaurant advertising fast food and takeout. Someone had been in a hurry and was way too trusting.

I slid behind the wheel, turned the key in the

ignition, and took off. I got to the corner, and the Town Car cruised by, going west on Seventh Street. I was several cars back by the time I was able to make the turn, but I had the Town Car in sight. Traffic was slow on Seventh. We inched along. The Town Car turned north on Seventeenth.

After three blocks, I caught a flash of lights in my rearview mirror. Cop car. Damn. Take another deep breath, I told myself. Don't panic. Pretend they're an escort. This could be a good thing, right? Just have them follow and help to get Bill and Hooker out of the Town Car.

Three more blocks. The cop car was still behind me, lights flashing. I could be wrong, but it looked like a second cop car was behind the first one. I saw the Lincoln sail across First Street. I approached the intersection and a third cop car came from First, angled in front of me, and stopped me from going any farther.

I got out of the car. Someone yelled for me to put my hands on my head. I did as I was told, and I walked back to the first cop car.

"I need help," I said. "I was following the black Lincoln Town Car. It belongs to Luis Salzar, and he's kidnapped my brother."

"That's pretty original," the cop said. "Usually we just get PMS stories."

"It's true!"

"Radio for a female," he said to his partner. "We're going to need to search her for drugs." He snapped a cuff on my wrist. He brought it to my back and snapped the second cuff on my other wrist.

"You're making a big mistake," I said. A tear trickled down my cheek. I'd totally screwed up.

"Oh man," the cop said. "I hate this part." He swiped the tear away with his finger. "Lady, you shouldn't be doing drugs. You're real cute in your little pink skirt and hat. You don't need drugs."

"Thanks," I said. I was obviously a loser, but at least I looked cute. I tried to tell myself that was worth something, but I wasn't convinced.

One of the cop cars left. Two stayed. The two that remained had their lights flashing, and I suspected there would be a big rush at the hospital for strobe-induced seizures. Traffic slowly moved around the police circus, gawking at me in cuffs, gawking at the cops who were standing, hands on gun belts, in case I made a run for it.

After a couple minutes I realized there was one more cop car involved. It was an unmarked car parked behind the two cop cars to my rear. It had blue grille lights flashing. I couldn't see inside the car. Too far away and too much glare on the windshield. One of the uniforms had walked back and was talking to the driver. The uniform turned his head and looked over at me. He turned back to the driver and shook his head. More discussion. The uniform went to his car and got on the radio. After a five-minute radio conversation the uniform returned to the unmarked cop car. The uniform didn't look happy.

"What's going on?" I asked one of the cops.

"Looks like a fed pulling rank," the cop said.

After a short conversation between the uniform and the government car, the driver's door to the unmarked car opened and a guy got out and walked over to me. It was Slick.

I instinctively edged closer to the cops.

"You're being released into my custody," Slick said.

"No way!" I pressed myself against a uniform. "I don't want to be released. I demand that I stay arrested."

"Not my call," the uniform said, uncuffing me.

Slick wrapped his hand around my arm and tugged me toward his car. "Just shut up and come with me," he said. "The last thing we need is for you to get arrested. Although it wouldn't bother me much to see you behind bars. You've been a real pain in the ass."

"Who are you?"

"Federal agent. One of those three-letter organizations. I'd tell you, but then I'd have to kill you."

The only thing more frightening than thinking this buffoon was working for Salzar was knowing he was on my side. "You're not exactly competent."

"You're not exactly a model citizen."

"Are you kidding? I'm a good citizen. And I'm thinking I might report you to somebody. You shot Hooker."

"I tranked him. And just for the record, your friend Felicia shot me when I didn't have a weapon drawn. That's a little illegal."

"I thought you were trying to kill me."

"I asked you to step aside so I could talk to you. How does that translate to kill?"

"When you came up to me at Monty's you said you'd kill me."

"I'm supposed to be undercover. Don't you ever go to the movies? Don't you watch television?"

"You shot real bullets at my car last night."

"Okay, I admit it. I got carried away. Hell, you ran over me. What did you expect me to do, yell *thank you*?"

"You're lucky I didn't back up and finish the job."

"Tell me about it."

Slick was driving a sedan. He opened the back door for me, and Gimpy looked over his shoulder from the shotgun seat.

"Look who's joining us," Slick said to Gimpy. "Devil Woman."

"This is a bad idea," Gimpy said to Slick. "She's deranged."

"She's all we've got."

Slick got behind the wheel, shut his grille flashers off, and hit the door locks.

"I had them take the cuffs off," he said to me. "I'd appreciate it if you don't try to climb out a window or strangle me while I'm driving."

"Where are we going?"

"Early lunch. My pain pills are wearing off, and I don't want to take more on an empty stomach."

"My brother and Hooker . . ."

"Would have been fine if you hadn't stolen a car. We were staking out Salzar when you bumbled in . . . like always. All we ever wanted you to do was butt out."

"Why didn't you say that? Wait, I know, because then you'd have to kill me."

Slick slid a look at me in the rearview mirror. "Yeah. Doesn't seem like such a bad idea anymore."

"You'd better be nice to me, or I'll kick your ass again."

"Lady, this has been humiliating enough for two lifetimes. And painful. It'd be a real treat if you kicked someone else's ass for a while."

"We need to do something about Bill and Hooker and Maria."

"There's not a lot we can do right now. We lost the Town Car. I got stuck in the police roadblock, so I went to Plan B and rescued you."

Slick pulled into a fast-food drive-thru, and we all put in an order. I got a burger, fries, and a chocolate milk shake. Slick got a burger and a diet soda. Gimpy sulked in the front seat. Slick parked in the fast-food lot, and we ate our food with the motor running and the air-conditioning on.

"Here's the deal," Slick said. "You and your brother have screwed up this whole operation and now you're going to have to help us salvage it."

I sucked some milk shake up the straw and slanted a look at him in the mirror.

"There are things about Calflex that you don't need to know. . . ."

"That's not a good way to start," I said.

Slick washed two pills down with some soda.

"Where's the pain?" I asked him.

"Cracked rib."

"Sorry."

"Yeah, right," he said. "Change places with my

partner so I can see you without twisting. The looking-in-the-mirror thing is getting old."

Gimpy got out and held the door for me. His foot was still bandaged. His knee was still in the brace. His face was a mess of cuts and bruises. And he was bent.

"Do you have a cracked rib, too?"

The line of Gimpy's mouth was thin and tight. "Just get in the car, okay?"

Slick grinned. "It's his back. He tore a muscle when he tried to get off the gurney to choke you."

I did more milk shake sucking. "Tell me about Calflex."

"Salzar has been negotiating a Cuban land deal for Calflex. Prime real estate that will be used for a variety of purposes. The deal is being made with a member of the Cuban politburo who has large aspirations."

"Large aspirations?"

"He wants to be king."

"Would he be king through the normal chain of events?"

"He would not."

"A coup?"

"Possible. He needs money for the coup."

"This would be supplied by Calflex in exchange for the land?"

"Yeah. Unfortunately, this is not an individual who would be a good neighbor. In addition to Calflex money, he's demanded an item that would give him military leverage. Salzar has been shopping for such an item without much success. These things are available, but the purchase requires time and connections. When the agency learned Salzar was making inquiries, we got involved. We've spent the past year penetrating Salzar's organization."

"A year's worth of work shot to hell," Gimpy said from the backseat. "Shot to hell by a blond in a pink skirt."

Slick helped himself to some of my French fries. "Just for the record, you look great in the skirt."

"What's the Salzar connection to Calflex?" I asked Slick.

"Salzar *is* Calflex. It's not widely known. The ownership goes through holding companies and filters back under his wife's maiden name. If the deal goes through, Salzar will not only get land, he'll also get significant behind-the-scenes political power. Maybe even a seat on the politburo."

"Scary."

"You bet. He's a ruthless sociopath. And he's not aging gracefully."

"The Maria connection?"

"Maria arrived in Miami four years ago. Just another boat person washed ashore. Only it turns out she's more than that, and she blipped onto Salzar's radar screen a couple months ago. We had a man on the inside, and he said Salzar saw Raffles mentioned in a newspaper article. Salzar asked around Little Havana and found out Raffles came to Miami when her mother died. And then he found out she was a diver and that she had charts of Cuban waters.

"I don't think Salzar knew anything for sure until Maria took off in Hooker's boat with her charts. Once she took off, his gut instincts told him she was going to the wreck. He had the helicopter working overtime looking for her. And somehow, he knew there was more than gold down there. Our man inside overheard Salzar talking about the canister. Salzar knew the canister went down with the gold. The gold is worth millions, but it's the canister he really wants. With Russian help we were able to identify it. And it's not good. It's exactly what Salzar's politburo friend needs."

"Why didn't you go to Maria and get the canister first?"

"We want to catch Salzar with his hands dirty. So far, Salzar's been careful not to directly involve himself in anything illegal. And the few times when he has become involved, people who might have been helpful have disappeared. Forever. Probably encased in concrete two miles off Fisher Island. Persuading Maria to help us get the canister is only part of the problem. Unfortunately, there's a lot of bad shit out there, and if we don't nail Salzar, he'll keep looking and eventually he'll find something."

"Yeah, and anyway, we tried and she wouldn't cooperate," Gimpy said.

Gee, let me help you out with some charges against Salzar, I thought. Kidnapping, murder, assault with a deadly weapon.

"We had a man in place on the boat when Maria was brought on board. We could have gotten Salzar on a number of charges and recovered the canister if only Maria had *stayed* on board. They wouldn't have killed her until after the wreck location was confirmed and the canister brought up. We had a team ready to move in before anything bad happened to her. Once your brother got involved things went downhill fast."

I was thinking Slick was pretty cavalier about risking a civilian life for his operation.

"Unfortunately, we no longer have a man on the inside, and there's something I don't understand," Slick said. "Maria and Bill brought the gold up. And they brought the canister up, too. I dove down to the wreck site after you left. It was picked clean. Salzar tracked Bill and Maria, shot Bill and took Maria. I got a police report. So here's what I don't understand. Why did they take Maria? Why not just take the gold and the canister? Why not kill Bill and Maria on the spot? The obvious answer is . . . because they didn't get what they wanted. So they've got Maria. They encourage her to talk to them. Why don't they go get what they're after? Why do they grab Bill and Hooker?"

"I don't know," I said. "Why?"

"Because as much as they encouraged Maria to talk she couldn't tell them something she didn't know."

I sent Slick my very best dumb blond look. I didn't trust him. And I wasn't going to tell him something *he* didn't already know.

"I don't suppose you'd know anything about this?" Slick asked.

"Sorry. I wasn't on deck at the end when Bill and Maria took off. There was water in the fuel line, and I was in the engine room trying to get the *Happy Hooker* up and running. That's why they transferred everything over to the Sunseeker. Or at least I thought they transferred everything."

Slick locked eyes with me for a couple beats.

"You should work with us," he said. "We can help you."

"What happened to the inside guy?"

"Disappeared."

"Tell me about the canister," I said.

"You don't want to know about the canister."

"I can find out for myself. I was there when they brought it up, and I know what it looks like. I can go on the Net and research the markings."

There was a silent exchange between Slick and Gimpy.

"I'll give you a history lesson first," Slick said. "Because if I just tell you the contents of the canister you're going to think I've been seeing too many doomsday movies.

"Khrushchev launched Operation Anadry in June of '62 and began sending troops and weapons to Cuba. The Soviet military deployment to Cuba by fall of '62 included medium- and intermediate-range ballistic missiles, surface-to-air missile systems, coastal defense missiles, MiG fighter aircraft, medium-range bombers, and battlefield artillery. Plus there were forty-two thousand Soviet troops on the island, operating the equipment and training Cubans.

"The warheads in place included nuclear, conventional HE, chemical, and cluster munitions that were capable of penetrating the United States and of defending Cuba.

"Khrushchev decided more was needed. So the Soviet freighter *Indigirka* left the Soviet Union on September fifteenth, 1962, and arrived in the Cuban port of Mariel on October fourth. The *Indigirka* was carrying forty-five SS4 and SS5 warheads, thirty-six FKR warheads, which were approximately twelve kilotons each, and twenty-eight warheads containing a new-generation chemical agent, SovarK2.

"Kennedy went nose to nose with Khrushchev on October twenty-second, and in November the Soviets started pulling their strategic weapons out of Cuba. To date, twenty-seven of the SovarK2 warheads have been accounted for and removed. The twenty-eighth SovarK2 warhead was smuggled out of the country, along with one hundred bars of gold from the bank of Cuba, hours after Kennedy enforced the blockade of Soviet ships en route to Cuban ports.

"Intelligence indicates that this was a back door for Castro, should he need to leave the country. He'd have money, and he'd have a bargaining chip. The gold and the canister of SovarK2 were secretly given over to Maria's grandfather for transport to possibly Grand Cayman, and from there it would go by plane to South America.

"We're not sure what happened, but the fishing boat never reached its scheduled destination."

"The story I heard was that Maria's grandfather was bringing gold *into* Cuba," I said to Slick.

"When the gold and the canister of SovarK2 went missing Castro launched a search, and that was the cover story. It wouldn't have done much for his image if it became known he was planning to flee in case of invasion. The part about Maria's grandfather being a smuggler is probably true. There was money to be made off the Russians. In fact, the advance information Enrique Raffles had that night might have been the story circulated. It's possible Raffles didn't know until the very last moment, when the truck arrived on the dock with the gold and the SovarK2, what the true mission would be."

"And this canister of SovarK2?"

"Is essentially a bomb. It contains somewhere between forty-six to fifty-three pounds of liquid SovarK2. SovarK2 is similar to the nerve agent Sarin used during the Gulf War, but SovarK2 is far more potent. It has an indefinite shelf life and is highly volatile. It's colorless and odorless in both gas and liquid forms. Skin absorption can cause death in one to two minutes. Respiratory lethal doses kill in one to ten minutes. Liquid in the eye kills almost instantly. And you want to hope for a lethal dose of this stuff because the pain and suffering and permanent neurological damage will make you *wish* you were dead.

"The agent in the canister in question is in relatively stable form unless the canister is accidentally pierced or intentionally combined with a device to disperse. On a modest estimate, the canister has the ability to deliver six million lethal doses. If disseminated over Miami there would be tens of thousands to hundreds of thousands of people killed. And under the right conditions, millions could be incapacitated beyond help."

"So, if Salzar got his hands on this and turned it over to his friend in Cuba, they could use it to persuade us to accept their government?"

"Or possibly to persuade Castro to step down and allow them to take over."

"Would they actually use it? Are they that crazy?"

Slick shrugged. "Hard to say. The original intent was that the canister would be the payload on a warhead, and it would be exploded over a target area. But it might be possible to put a dispersion mechanism on the cylinder that would allow dissemination of a small amount and hold the rest in reserve. It would cause a lot of damage, and Salzar and friend would still have cards to play."

The thought that this stuff even existed made my skin crawl. And the realization that we'd had it on board the *Happy Hooker* took my breath away.

"Here's the thing," Slick said. "We need to get to the canister before Salzar. And don't for a minute think that Hooker won't talk. Salzar will make him talk.

"And by the way, I don't suppose you'd know anything about an explosion that sunk *Flex*?"

And here's *my* thing, I thought. I'm with two guys who impressed the police enough to get me released into their custody but won't show me any identification. They could tell me anything. How would I know fact from fiction? Call me a cynic but I have no reason to trust them. And no reason to like them.

"Wish I could help you," I said. "But I don't know anything."

We were back in Little Havana, and I wanted to put physical distance between me and Slick and Gimpy. I was going to move the canister. I'd made up my mind. I wasn't entirely sure how I'd do it, but I'd find a way. And I'd find it fast before Salzar beat me to it. I'd do what I could to check up on Slick and Gimpy. In the meantime, I'd work independently.

"I'm feeling stressed," I said to Slick. "I have a headache. Maybe you could drop me at a hotel."

"Do you have a preference?"

"I remember one on Brickell. The Fandango. It looked nice."

"The Fandango's expensive," Slick said. "You sure you don't have a gold bar hidden away?"

"I have Hooker's credit card."

I turned my back on Slick and Gimpy and entered the Fandango lobby. The floor was polished black marble. The vaulted ceiling was two stories above me, painted a soft blue and white to simulate sky and clouds. The support columns were cream-colored marble that had been carved into floor-to-ceiling palm trees. Fred Astaire and Ginger Rogers could have tap tap tapped their way through the lobby and looked perfectly at home. Registration counter at the far end. Concierge desk to one side. Couches and chairs and potted plants were scattered around, arranged in conversation areas.

I thought I'd performed well in the car. I held it together, and I didn't show a lot of emotion, but deep inside I was ruined. I'd left the car with

Slick's cell phone number and a promise that I'd call him if Salzar contacted me. I kept my head down and walked to an unused conversation area on the perimeter of the room.

Hundreds of thousands of deaths from the disbursement of a vile liquid into the air over a city filled with kids and puppies. It was horrific and disgusting. I wasn't on a career track to save the world, but I was going to move this one canister out of harm's way.

I gave a startled yelp when my cell phone rang.

"Miss Barnaby?"

"Yes."

"You're missing the party. Everyone else is here . . . your brother and your boyfriend. Wouldn't you like to join them?"

"Who is this?"

"You know who I am. And you know I'm looking for something, don't you?"

"Mr. Salzar."

"I will make life very unpleasant for you and the people you care about if I don't get what I want. Never in your worst nightmare could you imagine how unpleasant life will become. Do you understand?"

I disconnected and searched through my purse for Chuck DeWolfe's card. My hands were shaking and I couldn't find the card. It was in there, somewhere. I dumped everything into my lap and fingered through it. I finally found the helicopter pilot's card and punched his number into my cell.

DeWolfe answered on the third ring. "Hey!" he said. "Chuck here."

"Hey," I answered back. "It's Barney. I need help."

THIRTEEN

I chose to get dropped at the Fandango because
I'd driven past a bunch of times since I'd been in
Miami, and on a couple of those passes I'd no-
ticed a helicopter coming and going off the roof.
It was a huge, expensive, high-rise hotel, and it
made sense that it would have a helipad. Chuck
DeWolfe had confirmed my suspicions.

My plan was basic. Get the canister before anyone else. Figure out what to do next when the
canister was safely hidden. It wasn't hard to come
up with the plan. It was obvious. Everyone's welfare hung on the canister . . . Bill's, Maria's,
Hooker's, the world's.

I got off the phone and crossed the lobby to the

hotel gift shop. My heart was beating with a sickening thud, and I was doing my best to ignore it. I bought a pair of shorts and changed out of the pink skirt. I went back to the chair, and I called Rosa.

"I've been thinking about Salzar's property," I said to Rosa. "Some of his financial transactions go through holding companies and then filter back to his wife under her maiden name."

"Gotcha," Rosa said. "I'm on it. I'll dig around for the maiden name and I'll check for more properties."

"I'm especially interested in property north of the Orange Bowl Stadium." That was where I lost the Town Car.

After an hour I went out to the pool and sat in the shade, waiting. Forty-five minutes later, I heard the *wup, wup, wup* of the approaching chopper. I quickly walked to the elevator and I took it to the rooftop. I stepped out just as the chopper was touching down.

Chuck was at the controls. He smiled at me and gave me a sign that I shouldn't approach. He had a guy in the seat next to him. The guy got out and ran over to me as the blades slowed.

The guy was my age and reminded me a lot of Bill. Sandy hair and freckles. Ratty sneakers, baggy rumpled red-and-white shorts, washed out T-shirt. Lean and muscular.

"I have a harness," he yelled. "I'm going to strap you in."

I was holding my hat on my head with both hands. "Sure," I said. "Whatever."

Minutes later I was buckled into something that looked like a full-body chastity belt. The guy tugged on the straps, and when he was satisfied everything was secure he threw an arm around me and moved me forward. "Show time," he yelled. "Come with me."

We hunkered down and ran to the helicopter and climbed in. I was directed to the seat next to Chuck and given a headset with a microphone. The second guy took a seat behind me. Chuck revved the engine, and before I had a chance to throw up, the chopper lifted off. It's amazing what you can force yourself to do when you're saving the free world.

I could hear Chuck talking in the headset.

"This is Ryan behind you," Chuck said. "He's going to help us. We need a third person for this kind of a maneuver."

I nodded. I was disoriented, fighting panic, not wanting to look like an idiot in front of the two men. My lips were numb and there was a lot of clanging in my head. I leaned forward and put my head between my legs. I felt Chuck's hand on my back.

"Breathe," he said. "You'll be okay as soon as we get away from the city. I'll be flying over water and you'll lose the vertigo."

I kept my head down and concentrated. I thought about Bill as a kid. No help there. I thought about Hooker. Hooker thoughts were better. I got him naked. Okay, I was on to something. Here was an image that could compete with the panic of flight. I had the naked Hooker walking around in my head, and I realized we were over open water, and Chuck was right about the vertigo. It disappeared when we left Miami.

I could see the reef below us as we skimmed along the Keys, passing over pleasure boats and schools of fish. And then we were over ocean, flying toward Cuba, heading west of Havana.

My stomach rolled when the three islands appeared in front of us. The boot, and the bird in flight, and a third island that looked like a cupcake iced in bright green frosting.

"There it is," Chuck said over the headset. "The island is coming up. It's the one shaped like a boot. I'm going to do a couple flyovers to make sure nothing is going on down there."

We took a straight route to the island and flew over high enough to get an overview.

"No boats in sight," Chuck said. "That's good."

He circled the island at a lower altitude and

then he followed the stream, buzzing the tree-tops.

"Okay," he said to me. "This is it, Barney. Tell me where you want me to drop you."

"What?"

"That's the plan, right? You want to go down to pick up the canister."

"Yeah, but not me!"

"You're all we got, honey," Chuck said. "That's why we've got you in the harness. I have to fly. And Ryan's the drop-and-pull man. You can't do either of those."

"Omigod."

"You said this was important. And that we had to get the canister up fast," Chuck said to me. "Life or death?"

I swallowed and nodded.

"Then do it. Ryan's going to hook you up to the cable. Don't make a move until he tells you. He'll drop you to the water. He's a pro at this. He does search-and-rescue and adventure diving. I'm not flying my usual sightseeing mosquito. This heli-copter is designed for this sort of thing. We're going to give you a collar and an extra line for the canister. When you get into the water I'll give you some slack. You said the canister was only about fifteen feet down?"

"Yes. At the mouth of the estuary, dead center."

"You're not going to have great visibility. The blades are going to move the water and churn up sediment. Don't waste time. Get down there and try to find the canister. Ryan's going to take your headset and put you into some foolproof scuba gear. You're going to have a flashlight on your wrist. Shine the light at us if you want to get pulled up, or just follow the cable to the surface. Once you get the canister secured we'll bring you in. We'll bring the canister up after we get you on board. There's not a breath of wind today. This should be pretty easy."

Here's the truth. I was beyond scared. I couldn't believe I'd actually come up with this stupid idea. And I couldn't believe I'd talked two other men into being accomplices. The phrase *not thoroughly thought through* came to mind.

Chuck looked over at me. "Are you breathing?"

"No."

"You're going to have to remember to breathe. It's hard to pull someone in when they're dead weight."

We were directly over the stream, slightly above treetops. I looked down and caught a glimpse of the canister in the swirling water.

Chuck was smiling. "I see it," he said. "Piece of cake. Go back with Ryan, and he'll suit you up."

I crawled back and Ryan sat me on the floor and started walking me through the equipment.

"This is a no-brainer," he said. "Try to enjoy yourself. It's not every day you get a chance to swing from a helicopter."

I did an inadvertent whimper.

Ryan was grinning. "You're going to be great," he said. "I'm going to take your headset off now, and replace it with a full face mask. All you have to do is remember to breathe. When I get the mask on, you're going to scoot over to the door. You'll feel me holding you. Don't worry about anything. I'm going to take good care of you. Stay as still as possible while you're dropping. Look down so you know when you get to the water. Keep concentrating on the water and stay focused on your goal." And then he took the headset and fixed the mask over my face. I felt his hand at my back, and I knew I was supposed to scoot to the door, but I was paralyzed. My heart was pounding so hard it was shaking my whole body. I turned and grabbed hold of Ryan's shirt with both hands. We're talking genuine death grip, my fingers curled into the fabric, possibly drawing blood. I was shaking my head *no, no, no,* and I was babbling gibberish into the mask.

Ryan tapped a finger on the visor to get my attention. He pried my fingers loose from his shirt, and he eased me over in a crab-walk to the open doorway. And then somehow, I was dangling from the cable, slowly dropping to the water.

I have a dim memory of screaming. My screams getting lost in the whoosh of air in my mask and the beat of the chopper blades. I was swinging under the chopper, and I was choking on a fresh wave of panic. I tried to conjure up Hooker naked, but I was way beyond that as a mental health aid. Water was whipping up from the chopper's downdraft and spraying onto my mask. My mind was scrambling. I didn't realize at first that my feet were splashing in water. Ryan was holding me at stream level, waiting for me to get calm and give him the signal to drop me farther.

I started an internal dialogue. Okay, Barney, it's up to you now. Get it together so you don't screw up when you're underwater. Remember to breathe. Focus. Do the job.

I waved at Ryan, and he started letting out more cable. I was in water up to my knees, my waist, my chest, and then the water was over my head. More panic. Push it away, I thought. Trust Ryan. Get the job done. I realized I was breathing underwater and the panic became manageable.

The water was murky. I flashed my wrist light

around, but I didn't see the canister. I was disoriented, and I was reluctant to move from my drop point. And then I saw a slim, fluorescent green laser beam cut through the water in front of me. Ryan could see the canister from the air and was trying to guide me. I followed the beam, and I found the canister. It had only been about ten feet away. I attached the collar and made sure it was secure. Then I flashed my light at Ryan, and he pulled me up.

This time the trip was exhilarating. The fear was gone. Or maybe I'd learned to enjoy the fear. At any rate, I was smiling when Ryan pulled me through the door and removed my mask.

"I did it," I said. "I did it!"

Ryan was grinning, too, "You were amazing!" he yelled.

I took my seat and watched as Ryan raised the canister from the water. Six million lethal doses of SovarK2 swinging below me. I closed my eyes for a moment, and my hand reflexively went to my heart. I didn't know all the mechanical details, but I suspected it wouldn't be good if the canister dropped from this height. Ryan got the canister to the door and hauled it in. His expression turned sober when he saw the markings. It didn't take a lot of imagination to figure this was some sort of bomb. He secured the canister in the back of the cargo area without comment. Before Ryan was even back in his seat, Chuck lifted the chopper, our eyes held for a moment, and then he angled off, and we were over open ocean, on our way to Key West.

I rented a car and drove it across the runway to the helicopter where Chuck and Ryan were waiting. They were sitting in the open door, feet dangling, guarding the canister. I could see the bulk of a gun on Chuck's hip, under his orange-and-purple flowered shirt.

"Do you always carry a gun?" I asked, getting out of the car.

"Need it for gators," Chuck said.

They transferred the canister to the trunk of the rental and took a step back.

"Be careful," Chuck said.

I gave them both a hug, got into the car, and left the airport behind. I took South Roosevelt Boulevard to Route 1 and began my trek through the Keys. I checked my rearview mirror from time to time to make sure I wasn't being followed. I kept the radio silent so I could listen for a helicopter. I was pretty sure I was a couple steps ahead of Salzar and Slick and Gimpy, but I was being careful.

I hadn't heard from Hooker. No messages on

my cell. No missed calls. That wasn't good. It meant Bill and Hooker were still being held captive . . . or worse. The sadness took over my heart and radiated out into every part of me. Not an emotion I wanted to embrace. Better to channel my emotional energy in more positive directions, I thought. Stay alert. Get the job done. That was my mantra. *Get the job done.*

The job was simple to articulate. Not so simple to complete. Rescue Bill and Hooker and Maria without letting the canister fall into the hands of the bad guys. And that meant I had to make sure the good guys weren't bad guys.

The sun was low in the sky when I reached Key Largo. I'd felt especially vulnerable in the Keys. One road in and one road out didn't leave a lot of escape routes. Scary when traveling with a much-sought-after warhead in the trunk. I drove onto the last bridge and was relieved to be back on the mainland.

I was still wearing the same clothes I'd worn diving, and I was anxious to get out of them. When I approached Homestead I made a fast stop at a Wal-Mart and got a complete new outfit, including sneakers. I got a bag of food at the snack bar. And I got a charger for my cell phone.

I didn't have much direction, other than north to Miami. I needed a place to spend the night (or at least to take a shower), and I thought I would be safer in Homestead than I was in Miami. I took the first motel that popped up. It was an affordable chain. I paid cash, and I gave a fake name. If you're going to be paranoid, go all the way. The canister was in the trunk of the rental car, in the parking lot. I couldn't do much about that.

I took a shower and dressed in the clean clothes. I flipped the television on and dug into the food.

My cell phone rang. It was Rosa.

"I just got off the phone," Rosa said. "I got another list of Salzar's properties, but there's only one property on it that's north of the Orange Bowl. It's not a good neighborhood."

I got the address from Rosa and told her I'd get back to her. I scrounged in my purse and came up with Slick's cell phone number.

"Yeah?" he answered.

"It's Devil Woman."

There was a moment's pause. I'd caught him by surprise.

"Where are you?" he asked.

"The Fandango."

"No you're not. You never checked in."

"Where are you?"

"Coral Gables."

They were probably back to following Salzar. Salzar lived in Coral Gables.

"Do you know anything about Bill and Hooker?" I asked.

"Haven't seen them."

"I know where they are."

Okay, so this was sort of an exaggeration. I knew where they *might* be located. The thing is, I needed to get Slick's attention.

"And?" Slick asked.

"And I want you to go get them."

"Have you planned out any of the details of this rescue?"

"I figured that was your arena."

"I'm not much of a break-down-doors, shoot-'em-up agent. I'm more of a sneaky, *listen*-at-doors agent."

Easy to believe from what I'd seen. "Look, I don't care how you do it," I said. "Bring in the Marines, for crying out loud. Just do it."

"All right, here's the truth. It would screw up everything. I'm after Salzar, and I'm not going to tip my hand by staging a Waco to rescue your brother."

"Here's *my* truth. I've got the bomb, and I'm going to FedEx it to Cuba if you don't help me."

Silence. "I don't believe you've got the bomb," Slick finally said.

"I'll phone you a picture tomorrow morning. You have a picture phone, right? In the meantime you should be thinking about a rescue operation." And I disconnected.

Then just for the hell of it, I dialed Hooker's cell phone and let it ring until his message service came on. I finished the food and watched more television. I slept in my clothes, waking every couple hours with a start. At five o'clock I gave up on the sleep thing and checked out. It was still dark, and the lot was eerie, lit by overhead halogens spooked up by fog. I checked the trunk for the bomb and took off. I thought I was probably less than an hour from Miami. My timing was good. I'd be able to check out the address Rosa gave me just as it was getting light.

The closer I got to the address, the more depressed I became. Houses were squalid cinder block cells. Windows were barred. Exterior walls were covered with gang graffiti. Trash collected against buildings and on roadsides. There were no lush gardens. No rows of palms. The yards surrounding the stucco bungalows were barren, the dirt hard packed and cracked from sun exposure.

The address Rosa had given me was actually an entire block of condemned houses. They were little stucco bungalows in varying degrees of decay. Windows and doors were secured with hammered-on boards to keep squatters and users out.

One of the houses had been gutted by fire. The roof was collapsed into the house and the stucco was stained with soot. A few pieces of charred furniture—a couch and two chairs—were left in the small front yard.

And one of the houses had a car in the driveway. The windows were boarded shut on the house, but the boards on the door had been removed and tossed on the ground.

I drove by the house twice, and I swear I could feel Hooker's heart beating inside. There were no other cars on the street. No one rattling off to work. No one parked at the curb. The structures on the opposite side of the street had already been razed. Nothing left but concrete slab foundations and an occasional piece of pipe that had escaped the demo.

Because there were no houses obstructing my view I was able to park a block away and watch the occupied bungalow. I had my doors locked, and I was hunkered down in my seat, trying to be invisible. I was wearing a new plain black ball cap with my hair tucked up, a black T-shirt, jeans, and black-and-white Converse sneakers. Not especially cool in the Miami heat, but it was unisex and practical.

There were a few other cars parked at the curb and in driveways. Mostly junker pickups and rusted-out muscle cars. The rental didn't totally fit, but it wasn't glaringly conspicuous either.

At precisely seven o'clock, a silver Camry rolled down the street and parked in front of the occupied house. Two guys got out and walked to the front door. The door opened, and the guys went in. Five minutes later, two different guys came out. One of the guys was carrying a black plastic garbage bag. He put the bag into the trunk of the Nissan Maxima in the driveway, both guys got into the Nissan, and took off.

Shift change.

Okay, I was excited. I was pretty sure I'd found Hooker and Bill. And I was pretty sure they were being guarded by two guys. I followed the Maxima out of the neighborhood and dropped back when they pulled into a restaurant parking lot. They drove to the back of the lot, the one guy got out, took the bag from the trunk, and left it sitting by the Dumpster. I continued following them when they left the lot, and I lost them when they turned south on Seventeenth Street. They were heading for Little Havana, and I didn't want to go there.

I returned to the abandoned house and cruised by very slowly, taking it all in. Then I went back to the restaurant parking lot and parked by the Dumpster. Call me crazy. I wanted to see what they were throwing away. Who knows, right?

I pawed through the bag and found a bunch of large plastic soda bottles and cardboard pizza boxes. I looked at the top of the box. Pizza Time. It was one of those chains that advertise on-time delivery or no charge. The orders were taped to all the box tops. These guys were living on pizza and soda. And it was being delivered. I went through all the boxes. The day shift ordered a large pizza with green pepper, sausage, onions, extra cheese. They got a big bottle of Dr Pepper with the pizza. Yesterday the order went in at noon and again at five. The night shift ordered pizza at ten. Large pie. Plain. Large bottle of Sprite.

I took one of the day shift boxes and headed out of the lot.

I went east, looking for a safe place to call Slick. I found a spot I liked on North River Drive. It was a church with an empty parking lot. The lot was large and only partially visible from the road. I pulled in, parked in a far corner and placed the call.

Slick's cell rang five times before he answered. "Unh," he said.

"Are you awake?"

"Barely."

"I have something to show you."

"I'm hoping it's you with your clothes off."

"Not nearly."

He blew out a sigh. "Okay, let's see it."

I got out of the car, went around to the rear, and opened the trunk. I'd angled the car to get as much early-morning light as possible into the open trunk. I aimed the phone at the bomb.

"Fuck," Slick said.

I closed the trunk and got back into the car. "I know where they've got Bill and Hooker," I said to Slick. "I want you to go get them."

"Okay, but you have to transfer the item over to me first."

"Can't do that."

"Why not?"

"I don't trust you."

"You think I'd go back on my word?"

"Yeah."

"Boy, that hurts."

"Here's the thing," I said. "I'm not all that patriotic. What I really want is to get the two guys I care about someplace safe. So if you won't help me, I'll deal directly with Salzar."

This was a flat-out lie. I trusted Salzar less than I trusted Slick. And I had no intention of handing a deadly chemical bomb over to possible terrorists.

"Gonna call your bluff on that, Barney," Slick said.

"You're not going to help me?"

"I am helping you. I just can't do it your way. You need a little patience here. And you really need to turn that item over to me. And I'm also assuming you have the gold?"

I disconnected, immediately left the lot, crossed over the Miami River, and drove west. I didn't think there was much showing in the photo other than the trunk and the bomb, but I wasn't risking getting caught because Slick identified a corner of the church.

I found a small bakery parking lot off Seventh and hid between two other cars. I ran into the bakery and got a bag of doughnuts and a large coffee. I ate a doughnut, drank some coffee, and called Judey.

"I think I found Bill and Hooker," I told Judey. "I'm pretty sure they're being held in one of those condemned houses in Northwest. I checked it out this morning, and it looks like they're being guarded by two guys. I can't see in the house at all because it's all boarded up, but two guys went in at seven and two guys came out and drove away."

"Let me guess . . . you want to rescue Bill and Hooker?"

"Yeah."

"I'm in. Do you have a plan? Are we gonna do

- 321

a SWAT thing and kick some ass? What do you need?"

Good thing I watch a lot of television. If it wasn't for television I wouldn't have any ideas at all. Sometimes I worried that I didn't have a single thought in my head that wasn't already a cliché.

It was almost noon, and I was sitting in a Pizza Time parking lot. Judey and Brian were with me. Judey was holding a small vial. Brian was in attack-dog mode, alert at the back window.

"It would have been much easier if you'd wanted an erection extender," Judey said. "*Everyone's* got that. Fortunately, I happen to know a pharmacist who works out of the trunk of his car. Of course he works at night, so I had to wake him up, but I got just what we need. And he gave me instructions on use. Five drops per piece of pizza will render the diner unconscious in less than five minutes and have him sleeping for over an hour. It's the date rape drug of choice when you're in a hurry."

I dialed the Pizza Time number off the box top I'd gotten out of the Dumpster. "I want to check on a pizza order," I said. "It's going to 9118 NW Seaboard."

"Is that a large pie, peppers, onions, sausage, extra cheese?"

"That's the one. I want to pick it up instead of having it delivered."

"You got it. Five minutes."

A woman walked by the car. She had a mixed breed on a leash, and the dog was walking placidly beside her. Brian was nuts in the backseat, bouncing around, clawing at the window.

"Arf, arf, arf, arf."

Judey took a spice cookie out of his pocket. "If you're a good doggie I'll give you some cookie," Judey said. "Does 'ou wanna spice cookie? Does 'ou? Does 'ou?"

Brian stopped arfing and sat at attention, ears up, body vibrating, totally focused on the cookie. His eyes were so wide they were surrounded by white and looked like they might roll out of his head.

Judey held the cookie out and Brian lunged for it. *Snap!* The cookie broke into about twenty pieces, and Brian was nuts again, tracking the cookie pieces.

"He really likes spice cookies," Judey said.

There were two Pizza Time delivery cars parked in reserved slots by the back door. They were old Ford Escorts that had been painted pink with powder blue palm trees, and PIZZA TIME was written in fluorescent green all over the cars.

"I could use one of those cars," I said to Judey.

"That shouldn't be a problem for you," Judey

said. "You and Bill have been stealing cars since you were ten years old."

"Not stealing. Borrowing. And I only borrowed cars from the garage."

I turned the key in the rental and pulled it up into the slot next to the Pizza Time car. I left the rental, walked into Pizza Time, and picked up my pizza and soda. I rushed back to Judey, and we very carefully lifted the cheese and added five knockout drops to each piece of pizza.

The driver's side door to the Escort was unlocked. I got in with my nail file and had the car running in less than two minutes.

"You are *so* clever," Judey said. "There's not a car made that you can't steal."

"Thanks, but the newer ones are impossible. Lucky this was an old Escort."

I took off in the Pizza Time car with Judey following in the rental.

FOURTEEN

I drove by the condemned bungalow once to check things out. Nothing had changed. Same car at the curb. Judey was following me. When I did my second lap around the block, Judey dropped back and parked the rental in the spot I'd vacated earlier.

Now or never, I thought. I took a deep breath and yanked the Pizza Time car into the driveway. I got out, walked around the car to the passenger side, and got the pizza box and the soda. I marched up to the front door and rang the bell. Nothing. No bell sound. The bell wasn't working. Great. I knocked as hard as I could. Still no action.

"Hey!" I yelled. "Anybody home?" And I gave the door a good kick.

I could hear someone mumbling behind the door. The door opened and a big sweaty guy looked out at me.

"What?" the guy said.

"Pizza."

"You're late."

"I would have been on time if you'd opened the door when I got here. You need to get your bell fixed. What are you doing here, anyway? It looks like all these houses are condemned."

"I work for the guy who's gonna build here. We're doing . . . research."

"That's twelve-fifty."

"I'm gonna give you fifteen 'cause you're cute."

He gave me fifteen. I told him to have a nice day. And I got into my stolen car and left. I got to NW Twentieth Street and saw flashing lights behind me. *Shit.* I pulled over, got out, and walked back to the cop car. As luck would have it, it was the same cop who pulled me over yesterday.

"Oh man," he said. "Not you again. Give me a break."

"I'm on a secret mission."

"Of course you are."

"And that's my partner behind you."

Judey was idling behind the cop car, a forced smile on his face. Brian was in the seat next to

Judey, front paws on the dash, schnauzer eyebrows drawn together in concentration, staring the cop down.

The cop looked back at Judey. "The gay guy with the dog? Are you kidding me?"

"How do you know he's gay?"

"I'm a cop. I know these things. And his dog's wearing one of them rainbow collars."

"Maybe it's just his dog that's gay."

"Lady, I don't want to go there. My nuts are shrinking up in my scrotum just thinking about it."

"Listen, I sort of have things to do . . ."

"Like go to jail?"

"You're not going to make me call the guys with the blue flashy grille lights, are you?"

"Scala and Martin? No! Don't do that. I *hate* those guys."

"Tell you what. I'm done with the car. How about if I just leave it here, and you can call it in."

"Fine. Great. But you gotta stop stealing cars on my watch. Steal them on the night shift. Steal them from Coral Gables or Miami Beach."

I ran back to Judey, shooed Brian into the backseat, and buckled myself in.

"You are *so good*," Judey said.

Fifteen minutes later, we were back in front of the abandoned bungalow. I was hunkered down, out of sight in the backseat. Judey was driving. The plan was that he'd park behind the silver Camry, run up to the house, tell them he was lost, and ask directions. If no one answered after he yelled and pounded and kicked, we were golden.

"If I don't come back you have to promise to take Brian," Judey said.

I looked up at Brian sitting on the backseat. If there was a God in heaven, Judey would come back.

"He's very smart," Judey said. "If you mix up the letters in his name it spells *brain*."

I kept my head down and listened to Judey walk up to the house. He knocked. He yelled. And then quiet. I popped my head up. No Judey. I looked at Brian.

"Where is he?" I said to Brian.

Brian just sat there. He looked worried. Most likely not crazy about the prospect of maybe living with me.

Judey appeared at the back of the house, and I let out a *whoosh* of air. He'd circled the house, probably looking for an open window. He returned to the front and waved me over.

I got behind the wheel and pulled the rental into the driveway.

"I was able to look in through the back windows," Judey said. "There's some good news and some bad news. The good news is that both goons are out for the count. The bad news is, it looks like they shared the pizza with Bill and Hooker."

I got a tire iron out of the trunk.

Judey was looking over my shoulder. "What's that thing in the trunk?"

"Bomb. Probably a warhead, to be more precise."

"I wouldn't expect any less," Judey said. "You never disappoint."

I hustled across the yard with the tire iron and wedged it between the jamb and the door, just below the doorknob. I put my weight behind it, the jamb splintered away, and the door popped open.

The inside of the bungalow was even more depressing than the outside. The air was stale, smelling of poor sanitation, mold, and cold pizza. The furniture was Dumpster pickings. The light was dim.

Salzar's men were facedown on the floor, having fallen off their chairs at the rusted chrome and Formica kitchen table. The empty pizza box was open on the tabletop. Nothing left in the box but smudges of tomato sauce and a few scraps of cheese.

A short hallway opened off the living room,

dining room, kitchen area. There were two bedrooms and a small bathroom at the end of the
hallway. The bedroom doors were open. Bill and
Hooker were handcuffed together in one of the
bedrooms. They were sprawled on the bed, out
like a light. A half-eaten piece of pizza was stuck
to the threadbare yellow chenille bedspread,
inches from Hooker's open hand.

"Hey, wait a minute," I said. "Where's Maria?"

We looked in the second bedroom and bathroom. No Maria.

"She's probably at a different location," Judey
said.

Neither of us entirely believed it, but it was a
good thought for now. Worry about one thing at
a time.

"How are we going to get these big boys out of
here?" Judey asked. "They're hooked together,
and together they must weigh about three hundred and sixty pounds. And then we have to get
them through the door."

I ran to the kitchen and checked the goons'
pockets for a key. I did a fast scan of the house.
No key. I looked back at the bedroom door. Not
wide enough to drag them through side by side.
"We're going to have to make them into a sandwich and pull them through."

We wrestled Bill and Hooker off the bed and

onto the floor, trying to be careful with Bill's gunshot wounds. We took the ratty chenille spread off the bed and worked it under Hooker. Then we put Bill facedown on top of Hooker.

Judey and I grabbed the chenille spread and pulled Hooker and Bill through the bedroom door, across the living room, and out the front door. We got them as far as the rental car, and we were stumped again.

"I guess we have to try to sit them up in the backseat," I said.

We pushed and pulled and managed to get them more or less sitting in the backseat. Hooker was hanging in the shoulder harness, head down and drooling. Bill was leaning on Hooker, looking like Zombie Bahama.

Brian had retreated to the front and was peeking between the seats, not sure he was liking what he saw.

"You know what we should do?" Judey said. "We should take one of the goons. And then we can interrogate him and maybe find out where they've got Maria."

We went back to the house and took the smallest of the two men. We dragged him out the door to the car and around to the trunk. I opened the trunk and threw the spare tire away. Now I had room for the goon *and* the warhead. I took a good look at the warhead to make sure it'd be safe back there with the goon. It didn't look like anything could break off. We heaved the goon into the trunk, folded him up, and closed the lid.

"Now we need a good porn store," I said. "One that sells *devices*. Handcuffs have a universal key. I know that from watching *Cops* on television."

"I *love* that show," Judey said.

I drove across the Miami River, went south on Seventeenth Street and into Little Havana. After a few blocks I saw what I was looking for. Adult Entertainment. I swung into a strip mall parking area and came to a stop in front of the store.

"I don't want to buy an expensive pair of hand-cuffs just to get a key," I said to Judey. "See if you can borrow one."

Judey ran into the store and a couple minutes later came out with a guy who looked like Ozzie Osbourne on a bad day.

"Whoa," the guy said when he saw Hooker and Bill. "Kinky."

We got the cuffs off, and the porn guy shuffled back into the store. Judey and I made a half-hearted attempt to revive Hooker and Bill. Hooker opened one eye halfway, smiled at me, and went back to slumberland.

"We should put those cuffs to good use," Judey said.

We got out of the car, went around to the trunk, and made sure no one was looking. We opened the trunk, twisted the goon until his arms were behind his back, and cuffed him.

"Much better," Judey said. "It's a little creepy to have him back here with the warhead."

I know this is weird, but I was getting used to carrying the warhead around. I wouldn't go so far as to say I was going to miss it when I got rid of it, but I wasn't nearly as freaked out that it was back there. It was sort of like . . . luggage.

Judey and I got back into the car and watched Hooker and Bill. They seemed to be comfortable, breathing normally, good color. Still, I was worried. It would be a relief when they came around.

"I appreciate your help," I said to Judey. "Probably I should take you and Brian home."

"You'll do no such thing. I'm staying with you until these bad boys wake up."

So we sat there in front of the smut shop, waiting for Hooker and Bill to wake up.

"This is just like when we were in school," Judey said, smiling. "We were always getting Bill out of scrapes. And usually they involved young ladies."

Sometimes the more things changed, the more they stayed the same.

After an hour, Hooker opened an eye again. "Did I miss something?" he asked.

"We rescued you," I said.

"The last thing I remember I was eating pizza."

"Yep," I said. "I did the old date-rape-pizza-delivery routine."

"What's this big wet spot on my shorts?"

"Drool."

"That's a relief." He glanced out the window. "And we're parked in front of adult entertainment, why?"

"We needed a key for the handcuffs."

Bill opened his eyes. "Adult entertainment?" He put his hands to his head. "Wow, killer headache."

"Your sister delivered poison pizza to the bad guys, and we ate it," Hooker said.

"Did I tell you? Barney always comes through," Bill said. "She's been rescuing me for years."

"Not a minute too soon for me," Hooker said. "Things were about to get really ugly."

"Hooker sang like an *American Idol* wannabe," Bill said. "They tied him to a chair, gave him one punch in the face, and he told them everything they wanted to know."

"Yeah," Hooker said. "I told them we buried the canister about ten feet into the jungle about an eighth of a mile upstream. I thought that would keep them busy. Bill was sure you'd ride in with the Marines and save our asses."

"The Marines were booked," I said. "Fortunately, Judey was available."

"I figured this was the day Salzar would find out I sent him on a wild goose chase, and he'd order his goons to come back to beat the living crap out of me," Hooker said. "He wants that canister real bad."

"It's filled with a chemical nerve agent," I said. "SovarK2. It's estimated that it contains about six million lethal doses. If dispersed as a gas over Miami it would kill tens to hundreds of thousands of people. It turns out Slick and Gimpy are with one of those three-letter government agencies, and they've been trying to retrieve the canister and nail Salzar."

"Had me fooled," Hooker said.

"Me too. And I don't entirely trust them. I could use their help, but they worry me."

"I don't know anything about this," Judey said. "Nobody tells me anything."

"When Maria dove down for the gold, she also found a canister. We didn't know it at the time but it turns out it's a chemical bomb."

"The bomb we've been carrying around in the trunk?" Judey said.

Hooker looked over at me. "In the trunk?"

"I was worried about Salzar finding it. So I went back and got it and it's . . . in the trunk."

Everyone turned and looked at the backseat, as if they could see through it into the trunk.

"This trunk?" Hooker asked.

"Yep."

"You've been riding around with a chemical bomb in the trunk?"

"Yep."

"I hate to change the subject," Bill said. "But they still have Maria."

"I don't know where she is," I told him. "We ran through all Salzar's properties, and we didn't turn anything up. No Maria and no gold bars."

A car parked next to us and a middle-aged, balding guy got out and walked into the smut shop.

"I know him!" Judey said. "That's my dentist."

"Wait a minute," Hooker said. "I want to go back to the bomb in the trunk. How did you get it out of Cuba?"

"Chuck helped me. And his friend Ryan."

"They flew to the island, got the bomb, brought it back, and put it in your trunk?" Hooker said.

"That's the big picture."

I put the car in gear and pulled out of the lot, into traffic. I had no idea where to go next, but it seemed like it was time to move on.

"I might know where they've got Maria," Bill said. "When they first brought us out of Salzar's office there was some confusion about where we were going to go. They were talking about a garage on the Tamiami Trail."

Bill wasn't looking great. His face was ashen and there were dark blue smudges under his eyes. Blood had seeped through the bandage around his ribs and stained his shirt.

"How are you feeling?" I asked him.

"Fine," he said.

"You look awful."

"Bad pizza."

"Here's the deal," I said to him. "I'm sending you back home with Judey. If you promise to stay in bed, Hooker and I will look for Maria."

"Not good enough," Bill said. "You have to promise to *find* her. And you have to help her get her father out of Cuba."

"I'll do my best," I said.

There was some thumping and muffled yelling from the trunk.

"The goon is awake," Judey said.

I turned to Bill and Hooker. "I almost forgot. I have a goon in the trunk, too."

"We thought it might be helpful to be able to interrogate one of Salzar's men," Judey said. "So we put him in the trunk . . . with the bomb."

"It was Judey's idea," I said. "He's a crime fighter mastermind."

"Some people think I look like Magnum," Judey said. "Do you think I look like Magnum? Maybe around the mouth a little?"

"I'm awake, right?" Hooker said. "This is real?"

FIFTEEN

By the time we got to Judey's condo building, the guy in the trunk had quieted down.

"What's Salzar like?" Judey wanted to know. "I only know what I read in the paper."

"He's scary," Hooker said. "Obsessed with the canister. Obsessed with one last grab at power in Cuba. I think at this point he might not be playing with a full deck. I think what probably started out as a smart political move has turned into a last-ditch nightmare. Castro's time is coming to an end, and the politburo is in a power scramble. If Salzar doesn't come through with that canister, I'm guessing he's lost his place in history."

"I got a creepy phone call from him," I said.

"He got your number out of my cell phone. He went nuts when he found out you'd escaped," Hooker said.

It was late afternoon. There were big puffy clouds in the sky and the wind was picking up. It would have been a nice day to be on the beach or drifting around in a boat. A couple blocks over, the almost naked sun worshippers were packing up, and the Ocean Drive waiters were arriving for work. And here I was wearing day-old underwear, sitting in a parking lot with a bomb and a goon in my trunk.

"All righty then," Judey said. "Let's get Bill upstairs and comfy. And you're welcome to come up, too. I could put a pot of coffee on. And I have a cake."

"Anybody have any ideas about the goon?" I asked.

"He can come, too," Judey said. "I have plenty of room. We can lock him in my powder room. And before we put him in the powder room we can put on a salsa CD and beat the crap out of him."

"That sounds like fun," Bill said.

We opened the trunk and hauled the goon out. He was wild-eyed and soaked through with sweat.

"It's Dave," Hooker said. And then he punched Dave in the face.

"Stop that!" Judey said, clutching Brian to his chest. "I was kidding about the beating." He put his hand over Brian's eyes. "Don't look."

"I owed it to him," Hooker said.

NASCAR Guy was back in the saddle.

We dragged Dave up to Judey's condo, locked the door behind us and propped Dave up against a wall.

"We need to know where Maria's hidden," I said to Dave.

"Eat shit," Dave said.

"Can I hit him again?" Hooker asked.

"No!" Judey said. "He'll bleed on the carpet."

"This is your last chance," I said to Dave. "Or else."

"Or else what?" he asked.

"Or else we'll turn Brian loose on you," Judey said.

Brian was running in circles, happy to be home. "Arf, arf, arf, arf."

"Yeah, that's gonna worry me," Dave said.

Judey took a spice cookie out of his pocket and held it out, waist level. Brian rushed over, jumped into the air, and *SNAP!* The spice cookie was dust.

Hooker was smiling. "Allow me," he said, unzipping Dave's slacks. The slacks slid down and pooled at Dave's feet, leaving Dave standing there in his tighty whities.

Judey scooped Brian up and tiptoed over with Brian under his arm. With his free hand, Judey dropped three spice cookies into the front of Dave's briefs, crushing them up a little, releasing a lot of spice cookie fragrance, making sure the crumbs settled in the pouch.

"Rawffff!" Brian said, watching the spice cookies disappear from view.

Judey held Brian out so he could better smell the cookies. And Brian started to salivate. Brian's ears were up and his legs were treading air. He was squirming and running in place, eyes bugged out of his head, and schnauzer spittle was flying everywhere. "Arf, arf, arf, arf!" Brian was in a spice-cookie frenzy.

"Okay, now I'm going to put Brian down," Judey said.

"Jesus, no!" Dave said. "You people are freaky."

"So, what about Maria?" I asked him. "Do you know where she is?"

"Yeah," Dave said. "I know where she is. Get the dog away from me."

"Where's Maria?" I asked again.

"Salzar's got a garage on the Trail. She's in the garage," Dave said.

"She's alive?"

"Yeah. She's alive."

When we were done questioning Dave we

pulled his pants up and shoved him into the powder room.

"Hey," he said, "you can't leave me in here like this with my hands cuffed behind my back and cookies in my drawers. And what if I have to use the facilities?"

Judey smiled at him. "Just give me a holler, big boy, and I'll be glad to help you."

We closed the door on Dave, and Judey rolled his eyes.

"Wouldn't touch him with a long stick," Judey said, "but I couldn't resist scaring him one more time. Now if you'll all get comfy, I'll make some coffee, and we can sit down and plan out the rescue operation."

"We need help," I said when we were at the table. "We need someone in government that we can trust."

"I know a guy," Hooker said.

Hooker called his assistant and minutes later had a phone number. Hooker dialed the phone number, made some required small talk when the connection was made, and then got to the point.

"I found something that might be dangerous," Hooker said to the person on the phone. "I want to turn it over to the authorities, but I'm not sure how to go about it. I think giving it to the local police isn't the route we want to go." There was some talking on the other end. "I don't want to go into details on a cell phone," Hooker said. "Let's just assume the government would like to gain possession of this item that's chemical in nature. I've been approached by two losers who claim to be feds."

"Scala and Martin," I said. "Working out of Miami."

Hooker repeated the names to his connection. "And something else," Hooker said. "I want to get someone out of prison in Cuba. Maybe buy him out." There was some more small talk, and Hooker hung up.

"He's going to get back to me," Hooker said.

"He have a name?"

"Richard Gil."

"Senator Richard Gil?"

"Yeah. He's a real good guy."

"And a NASCAR fan?"

"That too."

"Let's make a list of everything we have to accomplish," Judey said. "We have to rescue Maria. We have to get the gold and use it to buy Maria's father out of Cuba. We have to give the bomb over to the authorities."

"It would be good if we could neutralize Salzar," Hooker said.

"Neutralize?" Judey said. "You mean like whack him?"

"NASCAR Guy doesn't whack people," Hooker said. "NASCAR disapproves of whacking. Neutralizing is broader in scope."

Brian was whining at the powder room and sniffing under the door. He wanted the cookies.

"Now let's review what we know," Judey said. "We know the location of the garage on the Tamiami Trail. We know what it looks like inside and that there are always four guys there. We know they have the gold crated for shipment to Cuba."

"We know the helicopter can land in the parking lot out back of the garage," Bill said.

"I think my man can help facilitate things like swapping out an old Cuban guy for a shitload of gold," Hooker said. "And I think he can coordinate this with canister pickup. What he's probably not going to be able to do is round up the goods. We're going to have to round up the goods. And then we're going to have to deliver them."

"I don't want to be left out," Bill said.

"You look awful," I told him.

"I can deal," he said.

It was midafternoon, and by six we had a plan pretty much in place. It sounded ridiculous on paper. Straight out of a bad movie. But it was the best we could do. We couldn't move on the plan until we heard from the senator.

The phone rang at seven-thirty and Hooker answered. It was Senator Gil. Hooker took notes while he talked. His face was flushed when he got off the phone.

"It's a go," he said. "Everything will be in place tomorrow at ten AM." He turned to me. "NASCAR Guy's a little flummoxed."

We were all flummoxed.

"Gil says Slick and Gimpy are part of a combined agency task force that keeps tabs on international arms sales. He didn't know much about them. They've been with the task force for three years. Before that they were ATF, pushing paper. Gil's sending them over to help us. He thought we could use some extra firepower."

This set off a mental alarm. "They're coming here?"

"Yeah. Is there a problem?"

"I don't know. There's something about those guys that doesn't feel right. Maybe we should do something with the bomb."

"Damn," Hooker said. "We left the bomb in the trunk. I forgot all about the bomb."

We all trooped out and got in the elevator and rode to the garage. Judey had a blanket so we could wrap the bomb and bring it upstairs unnoticed.

Hooker opened the trunk. "It's gone!" he said.

We all gasped.

He winked at me. "Only funnin'."

NASCAR Guy humor.

Hooker wrestled the bomb out of the trunk, we wrapped the blanket around it, and Hooker headed for the elevator.

"This is like carrying a giant eighty-pound watermelon," he said. "Somebody hit the button. Barney'll be all disappointed if I get a hernia from this. She's got plans for me."

Bill grinned at Hooker. "A hernia's the least of your problems if Barney has plans for you, you poor dumb sonovabitch."

We got to the condo and Judey ran ahead clearing the way. "Put it in my closet. It'll be safe there. No wait, not on the Gucci loafers. Right there, next to the Armani dress shoes."

We closed the closet door on the bomb and the doorbell sounded. Slick and Gimpy.

Judey looked out at them through the peephole.

"They don't look happy," Judey whispered to me. "And they look like they've been run over by a truck . . . several times."

"Guess it's tough being a federal agent," I said.

Judey opened the door and I introduced Slick and Gimpy to Judey and Bill.

"So, you gentlemen are *agents*," Judey said,

making quotation signs with his fingers when he said *agents*. "That must be pretty exciting."

"Whatever," Gimpy said. "I'm hanging on for my pension. I don't know why . . . it's a freakin' pittance."

"Yes, but the job must be rewarding."

"Real rewarding. We sit on our ass for a year watching Salzar, trying to set him up, and then some politician calls our boss and we're told to take orders from a NASCAR driver."

"Gotta go with the flow," Slick said, sliding a cautionary look to Gimpy.

"I haven't got a lot of orders," Hooker said. "I figure we'll all meet downstairs in the garage tomorrow at nine AM and we'll take it from there."

"Cake anyone?" Judey said. "I have a coffee cake."

"Things to do," Slick said. And Slick and Gimpy left.

"I'm going out for stone crabs," Hooker said. "I didn't get to eat them last time." He draped an arm around me. "C'mon, Barney. I'll take you for a ride."

I followed him into the hallway and into the elevator. "Since we had decided to move out at five AM and you told Slick and Gimpy to show up at nine, I'm assuming you don't trust them either, do you?"

"They're not on my list of favorite people." He tossed me the keys when we got to the car. "You drive, and I'll run."

As usual, there weren't any parking places by Joe's. I double-parked and watched Hooker jog off. Eye candy, I thought. Hooker always looked relaxed . . . as if motion was effortless, and all the body parts were working perfectly in sync. He had a nice gait when he ran and when he walked. I was betting his stroke was good, too. Holy cow! Did I just think that? Okay, truth is I've been having a lot of erotic thoughts lately. I'm sexually deprived. My love life is a barren wasteland. And I'm locked in an adventure with a sexy guy. Yes, he's sort of a womanizer, but he's a *nice* womanizer. I think his heart might be in the right place. And the rest of him seems to line up pretty good too. Damn. There I go again.

I wasn't paying a lot of attention to what was going on around me. I was watching Hooker through the big windows in the take-out section. He was standing in line with his hands in his pockets and his shorts were pulled tight across his butt.

So by the time I saw Puke Face, it was already too late. He had the door to the rental open. He reached across, released my seat belt, and yanked me out of the car like I was a ground squirrel and he was a grizzly.

I was tumbled into the back of a Town Car, Puke Face got in next to me, and before I could scream or kick or even haul myself off the floor, the Town Car was in motion.

No one said anything. No music from the radio. A driver. And a man on either side of me. Everyone stared straight ahead. Although, the truth is I could see only one of Pukey's eyes, the fake one. I wasn't sure where his other eye was going. We crossed the bridge into Miami and took Route 1 south. When we got to Coral Gables the driver turned off Route 1 and took a road that ran along Biscayne Bay. It was a service road, leading to a small marina. There were no other cars on the road. We stopped before we got to the marina entrance, and I realized there were lights shining in the rearview mirror. A car had come up behind us.

Pukey opened his door and yanked me out. Headlights blinked off on both cars, and I could see that the second car was a black stretch limo. Six seater.

I thought I was going to die. My chest felt constricted, and I had a sick feeling in my stomach. Beyond that there wasn't much. No tears, no diarrhea, no fainting. Maybe girls who grow up in a garage in Baltimore aren't real fragile. You learn early on that parts are recycled. Even scrap metal has some worth. Maybe that was my religion. Junkyard reincarnation. The soul as a rebuilt carburetor.

I was walked back to the stretch, Pukey opened the back door, and I was shoved in. There were two bench seats facing each other. Luis Salzar sat on one. A man Salzar's age sat next to him. There was enough ambient light that I could see the men clearly. Both were dressed in expensive summer-weight suits, white shirts, and conservative ties. Their trousers were pressed. Their shoes were polished.

"We meet again," Salzar said. "Please sit down." And he gestured to the seat across from him, where Maria was sitting. But then maybe sitting is the wrong word. Maria was so rigid she seemed to be levitating, hovering a fraction of an inch above the cushy black leather.

"You've caused me some inconvenience," Salzar said to me. "Perhaps I can rectify that now."

Some inconvenience. I supposed he was talking about his boat going down in a blaze of nonglory. Plus there was the canister.

"I believe you've already met Miss Raffles."

I looked over at Maria. Her hair was unwashed, pulled back from her face, and held at the nape of her neck with a rubber band. Her face was pale. Her eyes were rimmed in dark circles, slightly sunken. Her expression was pure unadulterated rage. Her hands were cuffed behind her back, probably to keep her from ripping Salzar's eyes out of his head. She barely acknowledged me. She was concentrating every scrap of hatred she could muster on Salzar.

"Pig," she said to Salzar.

"She's unhappy with me," Salzar said. "She's just received some unpleasant news about her grandfather and her father."

"You killed my grandfather," she said. "And you had my father imprisoned."

Salzar showed a brief, slightly loopy smile. "True. But it wasn't much of a loss. Your grandfather's passing was a nonevent. Unfortunately, my gold and my SovarK2 were lost with your worthless grandfather. And your dim-witted father preferred beatings to divulging the location of the wreck."

Maria spit at Salzar, but it fell short.

"Allow me to finish my introductions," Salzar said, returning his attention to me. "This is Marcos Torres, my very good friend and the next President of the Council of State and Ministers of Cuba. You have something that belongs to me . . . and to Marcos. Would you like to tell me where our property is located?"

I didn't say anything.

"I was hoping Miss Raffles would encourage you to cooperate."

Neither Miss Raffles nor I responded.

"Very well," Salzar said. "It's only a matter of time. And it's always much more rewarding when you have to beat information out of a woman. Plus, I have some men who would enjoy you." He turned his attention to Maria. "What do you think of my men?"

Maria continued to give him the death look.

"You killed Maria's grandfather?" I asked Salzar.

"I was his partner many years ago in Cuba. I changed my name when I came to this country. I erased my past. Now I am going to reclaim it. In Cuba, I was a government officer, attached to the Council of Ministers. It was a good position, but not especially well paying, so sometimes when the occasion presented itself, I would supplement my income with an entrepreneurial enterprise. Maria's grandfather and I had a very profitable, but short-lived entrepreneurial enterprise."

"Smuggling?"

Another of the crazy half smiles. "Yes, but it was women we were smuggling. The Russian sailors wanted women, and we would supply them. We would run them out in the fishing boat.

Maria's grandfather and I were common pimps."
He gave a bark of laughter at that.

Maria continued to glare at him. No laughter
from Maria.

"When the blockade went up, and Castro
wanted to hide some things away for a rainy day,
our fishing boat was the perfect choice," Salzar
said. "I was a trusted aide, and the boat wouldn't
raise suspicions. Unfortunately, Maria's grandfather and I had a difference of opinion. He thought
we should follow orders. And I thought we
should take the gold and the SovarK2 and never
look back. Marcos was the silent partner, the partner Enrique knew nothing about, really the mastermind of the plan. Even then, Marcos had a
taste for power, eh Marcos?"

There wasn't a lot of light in Marcos's eyes.
They were focused on me and they weren't smiling. And it occurred to me that Marcos was probably crazier than Salzar.

"Enrique and I were arguing on the little fishing boat and not paying close attention to navi-
gating and somehow we hit a reef," Salzar said.
"The boat began taking on water, so I shot
Maria's grandfather in the head and left him for
dead. Then I set out in the dinghy we carried and
watched for the boat to go down. I knew exactly
where we were. Salvage would be easy. But the

boat didn't go down. Maria's grandfather didn't die fast enough. He managed to get the boat moving away from the reef, leaving me behind. I don't know how he did that with a head wound. A hard head, I guess.

"Can you imagine? There I was in the dinghy and I had to watch the boat cruise off away from me."

"You must have felt pretty stupid," I said.

Salzar's eyes narrowed, and I thought he might hit me, but he reined himself in and continued. "We searched for that boat for years without finding it. Who would have thought it could have gotten so far away? When he left me he was moving toward Havana. Those were the waters where I concentrated my search."

"You disgust me," Maria said. And she spit at him again. This time scoring a direct hit on his perfectly polished shoe.

Salzar flicked his arm out and caught Maria on the chin with his fist. Her head snapped to the side, and a small trickle of blood appeared at the corner of her mouth.

Maria was concentrating so hard on hating Salzar, I wasn't sure she felt him hit her.

"Where were we?" he said, settling back in his seat, forcing his cold, thin-lipped smile on me. "Oh yes, the gold and the SovarK2. Isn't it interesting that it's been returned to me after all this

time? True, I don't have the SovarK2 in my possession, but that's just a technicality." He leaned
close to me. "Where is it?"

"Uh . . . I don't know," I said.

Salzar rapped on the tinted glass window and
Pukey opened the door.

"Miss Barnaby and Miss Raffles are going to
the garage now," Salzar said to Pukey.

I cut my eyes to Maria, and she gave an almost
imperceptible shake to her head. Going to the
garage wasn't a desirable thing to do.

My hands were cuffed behind my back, and
Maria and I were transferred to the Town Car.
There was a guy driving. And there was Pukey.
Pukey looked like he had a different opinion of
the garage. Pukey was looking forward to it.

Once we got on the Trail there wasn't a lot to
see at night. A lot of dark. Occasionally rectangles
of light from a house. A few headlights from cars
en route to Miami or points south. Maria didn't
say anything. She'd lost the angry energy and
was slumped in her seat, smaller than I'd remembered her.

Hard to keep track of time when you can't see
a watch, but I was guessing we drove for somewhere between thirty to forty minutes before
slowing and turning onto a dirt road. After
maybe a quarter of a mile we reached our desti-

nation. I was pulled out of the limo, and I stood for a moment looking around. I was in a large hard-packed dirt field, and beyond the dirt was tall grass and swamp. A large cinder block building with a corrugated metal roof hunkered in the middle of the dirt field. The *Flex* helicopter was parked behind the building. A large military-type helicopter was parked beside the *Flex* chopper. A couple cars were parked in the front of the building, not far from where I stood. A single light burned over a door at one end. A bunch of bugs were beating themselves senseless against the light. Not a good omen, I thought. Four portable latrines sat off to one side. Another bad omen.

The building was large enough to hold maybe eight eighteen-wheelers. Only one was parked at the rear of the building. The floor was poured concrete, stained with oil drips, transmission fluid spills, and the rest of the crud that accumulates when cars and trucks are involved. Plus, I thought there were some stains I'd rather not identify.

There were no windows. A large fan droned on the far wall, providing ventilation. Lighting was overhead fluorescent. The air was damp and tasted metallic. The door was solid metal. Heavy-duty fire door. Two garage doors were built into the far end. Again, heavy duty. This wasn't a mechanic's garage. This was a storage garage, reinforced to serve as a bunker.

A wood crate sat on a forklift. The gold was ready to go. A motley assortment of chairs had been gathered around a rectangular scarred wood table. A single can of Coke had been left on the table. A small television tethered to a wall outlet had been placed on a folding chair. A makeshift kitchen with a rusted refrigerator, coffeemaker, and hot plate occupied an area behind the table.

We'd been told by Dave that there were four men in the garage keeping watch over Maria. This evening there were twenty. The men were working, cleaning out the garage, moving crates of guns, massive amounts of consumer goods that probably had been hijacked, and several metal file cabinets into the eighteen-wheeler. Dave told us that Salzar had a small army of dedicated men, and that almost all were illegal immigrants, handpicked by Marcos Torres, brought over one at a time on *Flex*. This was obviously some of that army.

I didn't see any rooms partitioned off. No bathroom. No office. A wood bench had been placed more or less in the middle of the floor. It was long and narrow and it had heavy metal rings screwed into the seat.

Maria and I were handcuffed to the bench.

"What are we supposed to do with them?" one of the men asked.

"Nothing," Puke Face said. "Salzar wants them left alone until he gets here."

After several hours my ass was asleep and my back ached. Thank God I didn't have to use the latrine because I'd already been told that wasn't one of my options. I had both wrists shackled, which meant I couldn't lie down. I now understood the sunken eyes and dark circles on Maria. She was exhausted. Probably the sunken eyes had other sources as well, but I didn't want to dwell on that. I was making a large effort not to freak.

No one came near Maria or me. Not complaining about that. Only occasionally Puke Face. He'd look down at us, drool a little, and move on. Hours passed. Once in a while the door would open for someone to use the latrine, and I'd look out to see if the sky was showing signs of light. I dozed off very briefly, head between my legs. When I awoke the men were still working, but the garage was close to empty of goods.

Another horn sounded outside the garage bay. The bay was opened and the stretch rolled in, followed by an SUV. Beyond the open garage door, the sky was still dark, but I thought it had to be almost daybreak. I looked over at Maria.

"I'm sorry," she said. "This is all my fault."

I knew that Hooker'd had a plan. It was pretty straightforward. Go into the garage like gangbusters and overwhelm whoever was in there. He couldn't get help from law enforcement or military. Too much process involved. Too much chain of command to wade through. Hooker's plan was to use a few friends. That was before I was captured. That was before Slick and Gimpy sold me out. I figured it had to be them. Senator Gil gave them the address. And they gave it to Salzar. There was no other way Salzar would know to follow Hooker and me from Judey's condo. No one knew about Judey.

Salzar and Torres left the limo and crossed the garage. They stopped to talk to Pukey and then they moved to me.

"Are you ready to talk to me?" Salzar asked.

I didn't say anything.

"You're not going to get rescued," he said. "We know all about the plan, and we'll be long gone before anyone reaches this garage on your behalf. All they'll find is an empty garage."

"Let me guess. Scala and Martin?"

"Very good. I'm impressed. They were unhappy with the way their lives were shaping up and decided they could use one of my gold bars.

Of course, down the line they'll get one of my bullets."

"No honor among thieves, hunh?"

Salzar motioned Pukey over with a crook of his finger. "We need to persuade Miss Barnaby to talk to us," Salzar said.

Pukey looked down at me. "My pleasure."

I was thinking now would be a good time for Hooker to show up. Although, I wasn't sure how that would play out, considering the number of armed men in the garage.

I heard a roll of thunder in the distance, and I knew it was starting.

Salzar heard the thunder, too. "A storm," he said to Pukey. "Make sure the helicopters are secure."

That's not a storm, I thought. That's NASCAR.

Two men ran to the door to secure the helicopters. They opened the door and stood momentarily dumbfounded. They slammed the door shut and yelled something to Salzar in Spanish.

I looked to Maria.

"They say we're under attack," Maria whispered.

And then there was chaos. Footsteps and shouting overhead on the corrugated roof. Salzar's men firing off rounds at the ceiling only to have them ricochet off the metal and embed themselves in the concrete floor. There were a couple heavy thuds on the roof and then the unmistakable sound of acetylene torches at work. Dave had told us the doors were impenetrable. Hooker knew the roof was vulnerable. Especially since he had access to a mobile metal shop. NASCAR did on-site body work. I couldn't tell how many people were on the roof, but it sounded like a lot. When Hooker put the call in for help, after we'd come up with the plan, he didn't know exactly what he could muster. We knew we could bring in the people at Homestead on short notice, but it sounded to me like all of NASCAR was overhead.

Salzar was shouting instructions in both English and Spanish, attempting to organize his men. He and Torres were at the side door that opened to the dirt helipad. Puke Face was in front of me, working at my cuffs. "You're going with them," he yelled over the noise and confusion. He released me from the shackles and jerked me to my feet. I dug in and refused to move. He gave me another jerk and I went limp, down to the ground. I wasn't going to make this easy. Hooker was on the roof, trying to get in. I just needed to last long enough. I could see the outline where the torch had carved into the metal. They were almost through. A second crew was working at the other end of the building.

Puke Face picked me up like I was a sack of flour and ran to the door with me. There was the sound of ripping sheet metal and a crash. Puke Face turned to look, and I saw that a big piece of roof had crashed to the floor. The torches were still whining overhead. The second piece was about to go. Ropes dropped through the hole in the roof and guys with guns were sliding down the ropes. I had a moment of disorientation when I thought the men were in SWAT dress. Where had Hooker gotten a SWAT team? And then I realized they were in leathers. Hooker had recruited a biker club. The second piece of roof went down, and Hooker came down with it.

Puke Face turned away from the chaos in the building and ran through gunfire to the big military helicopter. A handful of Salzar's men were defending the helipad area. The helicopter blades were in motion, picking up speed, kicking up dust in the predawn darkness. Salzar was already on board. Torres was at the helicopter bay door with an aide. They were waiting for me. I was their hostage. I was their last chance to get the canister.

Pukey had me at the door, trying to hand me off to Torres and the aide, but I had my feet braced on the lip of the open door. I heard Pukey do something like a grunt and a sigh in my ear, and then he released me and went over on his back with a crash. I curled my fingers into Torres's expensive suit jacket, gave a hard shove with my legs, and pulled Torres out of the helicopter. We both went flying and hit the ground hard, Torres on top of me. I was stunned and simultaneously utterly revolted. Having Torres sprawled over me was right up with spiders and leeches in my hair. I did a full body grimace, rolled Torres off and scrambled to my feet.

Salzar yelled for the chopper to *go* and the bird lifted.

There was a volley of gunfire from the ground, aimed at the departing helicopter. I shielded my eyes from the swirling dust, but even through the dust, I could see the flames shoot out from the chopper's undercarriage. The chopper hovered in place for a couple beats and then spiraled off, like a crazy airborne top. It went up and then it went down, crashing in the swamp. There were two explosions and fire jumped high in the sky and then settled into the water grasses.

Hooker came up behind me. He grabbed me and hugged me to him. "Are you okay?" Hooker yelled.

"Just got the wind knocked out."

"I was worried you were dead. It would have

been terrible. I would have cried in front of all these guys."

"There's no crying in NASCAR?"

"Hell no. We're manly men."

And then he kissed me with a lot of tongue, and his hand on my ass.

"Your hand's on my ass," I said when he broke from the kiss.

"Are you sure?"

"Well, *someone's* hand is on my ass."

"Guess it's mine then," he said.

I shoved Puke Face with my foot and rolled him over onto his stomach. He had ten darts in his back. The darts were big enough to take down a moose. Torres had three in the chest.

"I see you used the tranquilizer darts like we talked about," I said to Hooker. "Someone's a real marksman."

"Darlin', this is NASCAR. We're beer-drinkin', skirt-chasin', speed-crazy rednecks. *And we can shoot.*"

Someone threw a switch inside the garage and the outside was flooded with light, letting me see for the first time the full extent of the operation. I'd counted twenty-three men with Salzar. It looked to me like Hooker had sixty men. Maybe more. Hard to tell in the activity.

NASCAR uses big tractor trailers to transport their cars and equipment. One of Hooker's eighteen-wheel transporters was parked back by the garage doors. His service truck was next to the transporter. There was a herd of Harleys and half a dozen big-boy customized pickups parked in the same area. There are three sounds that give me goose bumps every time. NASCAR starting their engines, a well-tuned Porsche, and a Harley with Python pipes. The Harleys in the lot were totally pimped, Pythons included. No wonder it had sounded like thunder when they rolled in. A second transporter and service truck from another race team were backed up to the side of the building. Men were working, moving the welding equipment off the roof and onto the trucks.

The stench of burning aviation fuel hung in the air. The dust was settling over the helipad, and the frenzy of the attack was reduced to ordered confusion.

"It's over," Hooker said. "Salzar's gone, and we have Torres. We're turning Salzar's men loose in the swamp. Good luck there. Except for Puke Face. We have plans for Puke Face and Torres."

Hooker and I went back inside the building and watched Bill motor the forklift over to a rental van. Bill loaded the crated gold into the van and pulled away from the pallet. Hooker and I closed and locked the van doors. Then Bill drove around the building, and we loaded the still unconscious Pukey and Torres onto the forklift and dumped them into a crate in Hooker's transporter. Bill backed off with the forklift and jumped in to help Hooker nail the crate shut.

The deal Senator Gil made with his contact in Cuba was that they would trade Juan Raffles for the gold or for Salzar. Our choice. Senator Gil's Cuban contact had made it known that Cuba considered Salzar an enemy of the government, and the government would be happy to trade him for Juan. I suspected the Cuban contact would be even happier to open the crate and find Marcos Torres. Sort of like Christmas come early. One less political piranha for Castro to worry about. Castro would open the crate in the dark of night in Havana and maybe dispose of the contents. Not my problem.

We carefully tucked the canister, still wrapped in Judey's blanket, beside the crate containing Puke Face and Torres.

Judey was doing his nurturing thing for Maria. He had her in a chair, drinking coffee, eating a granola bar. I walked over and sat with them, taking a cup of coffee for myself.

"Are you okay?" I asked Maria.

"No permanent damage. Older and wiser."

"We've made arrangements for your dad."

"Judey told me," she said softly.

Maria's eyes filled, but she didn't cry. More than could be said for me. I was on emotion overload. I was willing to cry at the least provocation. I drank a cup of coffee in one gulp and ate a granola bar without even realizing it. I looked at the empty wrapper in my hand. "What's this?" I asked Judey.

"Granola bar," he said. "You ate it."

The garage doors were open, and I could see the motorcycle guys were leaving. The NASCAR guys were staying to help with cleanup, scouring the area, picking up darts that missed their mark, and collecting spent casings from real bullets. Police would be responding soon, chasing down the smoke that was still billowing from the downed helicopter. We wanted to be out before they arrived.

Hooker's public relations car had gotten rolled out of the transporter to make room for the crate containing Torres and Puke Face.

"I came in the transporter," he said, "but we can go back in the dummy car."

"Okay," I said, "but I get to drive."

"Are you crazy? I'm not letting you drive my car. You're a maniac."

"I'm *not* a maniac. Besides, it's just a dummy car. And *I* should get to drive because I've had a very traumatic experience."

"*I* should get to drive because I rescued you. I'm NASCAR Guy."

"If you want to get lucky you'll let me drive."

Hooker looked a little like Brian when presented with a spice cookie. "Really? All I have to do is let you drive?"

"Yep."

He wrapped his arms around me. "I'd get lucky anyway, even if I didn't let you drive, wouldn't I?"

I smiled at him. "Yep."

"Here's the deal," he said. "You can drive, but you have to be careful. No cowboying around. This is a race car. It drives different from a regular car."

"Really?"

"Have you ever seen the inside of one of these?"

I levered myself in through the window and flipped the switch. *Driver, start your engine.* "Just get in," I said. "I think I can manage."

Hooker's transporter pulled out first, followed by Hooker and me in the PR car. Bill and Maria were behind us, driving the van with the gold.

Judey and Hooker's crew chief were behind the van in a pickup. Everyone else was already on the road. The sun was visible on the horizon. The garage was deserted. Tendrils of smoke curled from far off in the swamp. So far, there was no indication that the swamp police were investigating. Hell, maybe helicopters crash there all the time and they only clean them up once a week.

We were all headed for Homestead Air Force Base, where we'd make the swap. The plane that brought Maria's father to American soil would carry Torres and Pukey back to Cuba. The military would take possession of the gas canister, and hopefully the SovarK2 would go to gas heaven. Juan Raffles would go home with Maria . . . and so would the gold.

We were almost at the juncture of Route 997 when a blue Crown Vic blew past us. Slick and Gimpy. Late for the party.

I whipped Hooker's PR car around, hung a U-turn, and dropped the hammer.

"Oh man," Hooker said. "Here we go again."

I caught Slick and Gimpy and pulled out to pass. I looked to the side and saw the horror on their faces as they stared into the PR car at Hooker and me.

"It's all in the timing and placement," I said.

Then I jerked the dummy car and clipped the Crown Vic, sending it careening off the road. It caught some air, hit the water with a *splash*, and settled into the swamp.

"Darlin'," Hooker said. "We need to talk. I get the feeling you've done this before."

EPILOGUE

Hooker was grilling barbecued ribs on board his boat. He was dressed in his usual rummage sale shorts and ripped motor oil T-shirt. His nose was pink and peeling. His eyes were hidden behind his Oakleys. He looked happy. I don't usually brag, but I thought I had something to do with the happy part.

Judey was in the fighting chair, watching Hooker grill. Brian was dancing in place, focused on the ribs. Bill, Maria, and Juan Raffles were in deck chairs. Actually, Bill and Maria were in the same chair. It was almost embarrassing, but hey, this was my brother Wild Bill. Todd was lounging on the rail with Rosa and Felicia.

We were having a party. We were celebrating

the fact that we weren't dead. We were celebrating Bill and Maria's new two-million-dollar boat, which was tied up in the neighboring slip. And we were celebrating Juan's freedom.

"Cigars for everyone," Rosa said. "I rolled them myself."

I took a cigar and lit up.

Hooker smiled at me. "Darlin', that's damn NASCAR."

"Special occasion," I told him.

"You are *such* a charm," Judey said to me. "Just look at you in your brand-new little pink skirt and adorable blond hair. Who would think you smoked cigars and overhauled carburetors? It's like you take metro-sexual to a whole new level. It's like you're Metro Girl."

Hooker rocked back on his heels, his cigar clamped between his teeth. "Yeah, and Metro Girl's gonna kick ass on my racing team."

Overhead, the sky was a brilliant blue. The hot Miami sun warmed hearts and minds and points south. A late-afternoon breeze rattled in the palms and caused the water of Biscayne Bay to gently lap against the boat hull. Life was good in Florida. And okay, so I was going back to working on cars. Truth is, I was pretty happy with it. I was looking forward to working on Hooker's equipment. I'd seen his undercarriage and it was damn sweet.

"You actually saw her?"

Lily nodded slowly. "She was crying. And she was afraid."

"Can you see her now?"

Her quick, deep breath sounded like a gasp. "No." She lurched from the chair and stumbled against the coffee table.

McBride's heart jumped to hyperspeed as he hurried to Lily's side. He caught her elbow. "Are you okay?"

Her head lolled forward, her forehead brushing against his shoulder.

He wrapped one arm around her waist to hold her up. Her slim body melted against his, robbing him of thought for a long, pulsing moment. She was as soft as she looked and furnace hot, except for the icy fingers clutching his arm. Her head fell back and she gazed at him, her eyes molten.

Desire coursed through him, sharp and unwelcome.

PAULA GRAVES

FORBIDDEN TERRITORY

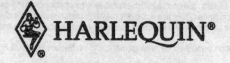

HARLEQUIN®

TORONTO • NEW YORK • LONDON
AMSTERDAM • PARIS • SYDNEY • HAMBURG
STOCKHOLM • ATHENS • TOKYO • MILAN • MADRID
PRAGUE • WARSAW • BUDAPEST • AUCKLAND

This book is dedicated to my mother, for not laughing
when I told her I wanted to be a writer; to Jenn, for
putting up with my doubts, my fears and my
dangling participles; and to Kris, for believing
in this story when I didn't.

ISBN 0-373-88700-0

FORBIDDEN TERRITORY

Copyright © 2006 by Paula Graves

ABOUT THE AUTHOR

Alabama native Paula Graves wrote her first book, a mystery starring herself and her neighborhood friends, at the age of six. A voracious reader, Paula loves books that pair tantalizing mystery with compelling romance. When she's not reading or writing, she works as a creative director for a Birmingham advertising agency and spends time with her family and friends. She is a member of Southern Magic Romance Writers, Heart of Dixie Romance Writers and Romance Writers of America.

Paula invites readers to visit her Web site, www.paulagraves.com.

Books by Paula Graves

HARLEQUIN INTRIGUE
926—FORBIDDEN TERRITORY

CAST OF CHARACTERS

Lily Browning—The reluctant psychic's visions of Abby put her in a killer's crosshairs.

J. McBride—The jaded cop with a tragic past—he doesn't buy Lily's vision but can't deny she's in danger.

Debra Walters—The ex-wife of Senate candidate Adam Walters is the victim of a deadly carjacking gone wrong.

Abby Walters—Debra's six-year-old daughter goes missing after her mother's murder.

Adam Walters—Abby's father is in a close race for the U.S. Senate—could his opponent be behind his daughter's kidnapping?

Joe Britt—Adam's campaign manager must keep his distracted candidate focused on the prize.

Gerald Blackledge—The incumbent senator is facing a tougher race than anticipated—how far will he go to win?

Paul Leonardi—Debra Walters's former lover wasn't happy about their breakup—could he be behind the murder-abduction?

Skeet and Gordy—Abby's kidnappers are deadly, but why don't they seem to know what to do with their little victim?

Cal Brody—The FBI agent thinks Lily knows too much not to be involved in Abby's kidnapping.

Rose and Iris Browning—Lily's sisters have special gifts of their own.

Casey—Why is this little girl showing up in Lily's visions of Abby?

Chapter One

The vision came without warning, a door bursting open in her mind.

Frightened blue eyes, red-rimmed from crying.
Freckled cheeks, smudged with tears and dirt.
Red hair, tangled and sweat-darkened.
A terrified cry. "Daddy, help me!"

Lily Browning pressed her fingers against her temples and squeezed her eyes closed. Explosions of light and pain raced through her head like arcs of tracer fire. Around her, a thick gray mist swirled. Moisture beaded on her brow, grew heavy and slid down her cheek.

She opened her eyes, afraid of what she would see.

It was just an empty schoolroom, the remains of the morning's classes scattered about the space—backpacks draped by their straps over the backs of chairs, books lying askew. The kids were still at recess.

"Lily?" A woman's voice broke the silence. Lily jumped.

Carmen Herrera, the assistant principal, stood at the entrance of the classroom, but it was the man behind her who commanded Lily's attention. His dark hair was crisp and close-cut, emphasizing his rough-hewn features and hard hazel eyes. His gaze swept over Lily in a quick but thorough appraisal.

The door in her mind crept open again. She stiffened, forcing it shut, her head pounding from the strain. Pain danced behind her eyes, the familiar opening salvo of a migraine.

"Headache again?" Carmen asked, concerned.

Lily pushed herself upright. "It's not too bad." But already the room began to spin. Swaying, she gripped the edge of the desk.

The man in the charcoal suit pushed past Carmen to cup Lily's elbow, holding her steady. "Are you all right?"

Lily's arm tingled where he touched her. Raw, barely leashed power rolled off him in waves, almost as tangible as the scent of his aftershave. It swamped her, stole her breath.

He said her name, his fingers tightening around her elbow. Something else besides power flooded through her. Something dark and bitter and raw.

She met his gaze—and immediately regretted it.

"Help me, Daddy!" The cry echoed in her head. Fog blurred the edges of her sight.

Swallowing hard, she fought the relentless undertow and pulled her elbow from the man's grasp, resisting the urge to rub away the lingering sensation of his touch. "I'm fine."

"Lily gets migraines," Carmen explained. "Not that often, but when they hit, they're doozies."

Lily heard a thread of anxiety woven in the woman's usually upbeat, calm voice. A chill flowed through her, raising goose bumps on her arms. "Has something happened?"

Something passed between Carmen and the man beside her. "Lily, this is Lieutenant McBride with the police. Lieutenant, this is Lily Browning. She teaches third grade." Carmen closed the classroom door behind her and lowered her voice. "One of our students is missing. Lieutenant McBride's talking to all the teachers to find out whether they've seen her."

Red-rimmed eyes.
Tearstained face.
Frightened cries.
Lily's head spun.

Lieutenant McBride pulled a photo from his coat pocket and held it out to her. She shut her eyes, afraid to look.

"Ms. Browning?" He sounded concerned,

even solicitous, but suspicion lurked behind the polite words.

Lily forced herself to look at the picture he held. A smiling face stared up at her from the photo framed by red curls scooped into a topknot and fastened with a green velvet ribbon.

Lily thought she was going to throw up.

"You haven't seen her today, have you?" McBride asked. "Her name is Abby Walters. She's a first-grader here."

"I don't have a lot of contact with first-graders." Lily shook her head, feeling helpless and guilty. The sandwich she'd eaten at lunch threatened to come back up, and she didn't want it to end up on the lieutenant's scuffed Rockports.

"You've *never* seen her?" A dark expression passed across McBride's face. Pain, maybe, or anger. It surged over Lily, rattling her spine and cracking open the door of her mind.

Unwanted sounds and images flooded inside. The lost girl, now smiling, cuddled in a man's arms, listening to his warm voice tell the story of *The Velveteen Rabbit.* Red curls tucked under a bright blue knit cap, cheeks pink with—

Cold. So cold.

Scared.

Screaming.

Crying.

Grimy tears streamed down a face twisted with

terror, hot and wet on her cold, cold cheeks. Panic built in Lily's chest. She pushed against the vision, forcing it away.

"We have reason to believe that Abby Walters may have been taken from her mother this morning," he said.

"Where's her mother?"

"She's dead."

The words sent ice racing through Lily's veins. She swallowed hard and lied. "I haven't seen this little girl."

McBride gave her an odd, considering look before he reached into his jacket pocket and pulled out a business card. "If you think of anything that might help us find her, call me."

She took the card from him, his palpable suspicion like a weight bending her spine.

Carmen had kept her distance while McBride talked to Lily, but once he turned back toward the door, she moved past him and took Lily's hand. "Go home and sleep off this headache. I'll send Linda from the office to cover for you." She glanced at the detective, who watched them from the doorway. "I can't believe something like this has happened to one of our kids. I'm working on a migraine myself." She returned to McBride's side to escort him from the room.

Lily thrust the business card into her skirt

pocket and slumped against the edge of her desk. Sparks of colored light danced behind her eyes, promising more pain to come. She debated trying to stick out the rest of the afternoon, but her stomach rebelled. She barely made it to the bathroom before her lunch came up.

As soon as Linda arrived to cover her class, Lily headed for the exit, weaving her way through the groups of laughing children returning to their classrooms, until she reached her Buick, parked beneath one of the ancient oak trees that sheltered the schoolyard. She slid behind the wheel and closed the door, gratefully shutting out the shrieks and shouts from the playground.

In the quiet, doubts besieged her. She should have told the detective about her visions. She couldn't make much sense of the things she'd seen, but Lieutenant McBride might. What if her silence cost that little girl her life?

Lily pulled the business card from her pocket and squinted at the small, narrow type made wavy by her throbbing head. The scent of his crisp aftershave lingered on the card. Lily closed her eyes, remembering his square jaw and lean, hard face. And those eyes—clear, intense, hard as flint.

She knew the type well. Give him the facts, give him evidence, but don't give him any psychic crap.

Lieutenant McBride would never believe what she'd seen.

BY MIDAFTERNOON, when Andrew Walters called from a southbound jet to demand answers about his missing daughter, McBride realized he faced a worst-case scenario. Less than one percent of children abducted were taken by people outside of their own families. Most child abductions were custody matters, mothers or fathers unhappy with court arrangements taking matters into their own hands.

But there was no custody battle in the Walters case. From all accounts, Andrew Walters had no complaints about the custody arrangement with his ex-wife. Over the phone, at least, he'd seemed genuinely shocked to hear his ex-wife had been murdered.

When he learned Abby was missing, shock turned to panic.

"Did you check her school?" he asked McBride, his voice tight with alarm.

"Yes." The memory of Lily Browning's pale face and wild, honey-colored eyes filled McBride's mind, piquing his curiosity—and suspicion—all over again.

"Is there any reason to think Abby might..." Andrew Walters couldn't finish the question.

"It's too early to think that way."

"Are you sure Abby was with Debra?"

"As sure as we can be." When they'd found Debra Walters dead on the side of Old Cumberland Road, a clear plastic backpack with Abby's classwork folder and a couple of primary readers had been lying next to her. Furthermore, neighbors remembered seeing Abby in the car with Debra that morning when she'd left the house.

Her car, a blue Lexus, was missing.

They'd held out hope that Debra had delivered her daughter to school before the carjacking, but McBride's trip to the school had turned up no sign of Abby.

McBride looked down at his desk blotter, where Abby's photo lay, challenging him. He reached for the bottle of antacid tablets by his pencil holder and popped a couple in his mouth, grimacing at the chalky, fake-orange taste. "We've set up a task force to find your daughter. An Amber Alert has been issued. Her photo will be on every newscast in Alabama this evening. We've set up a phone monitoring system at the hotel where you usually stay when you're in Borland, and a policeman will be within easy reach any time of the day or night. If you get a call from anyone about your daughter, we'll be ready."

"You don't have a suspect yet?" Walters sounded appalled.

"Not yet. There's an APB out on the car, and we've got technicians scouring the crime scene—"

"That could take days! Abby doesn't have days."

McBride passed his hand over his face, wishing he could assure Walters that his daughter would be found, safe and unharmed. But she'd been taken by carjackers who'd left her mother dead. McBride didn't want to think why they'd taken her with them instead of killing her when they'd killed her mother.

In the burning pit of McBride's gut, he knew he'd find Abby Walters dead. Today or tomorrow or months down the road, her little body would turn up in a Dumpster or an abandoned building or at the bottom of a ditch along the highway.

But he couldn't say that to Andrew Walters.

Walters's voice was tinny through the air phone. "Nobody's called in with sightings?"

"Not yet." A few calls had come in as soon as the Amber Alert went out. The usual loons. McBride had sent men to check on them, but, of course, nothing had panned out.

"Come on—when something like this happens, you get calls out your ass." Anger and anxiety battled in Walters's voice. "Don't you dare dismiss them all as crackpots."

"We're following every lead."

"I want my daughter found. Understood?"

"Understood." McBride ignored the imperious tone in Walters's voice. The man was a politician, used to making things happen just because he said so. And God knew, McBride couldn't blame him for wanting his daughter brought home at any cost.

But he knew how these things went. He'd seen it up close and personal. The parent of a lost child was desperate and vulnerable. A nut job with a snappy sales pitch could convince a grieving parent of just about anything.

"We're about to land," Walters said. "I have to hang up."

"One of my men, Theo Baker, will meet you at the airport and drive you to your hotel," McBride said. "I'll be by this evening unless something comes up in the case. Please, try not to worry until we know what it is we have to worry about."

Andrew Walters's bitter laugh was the last thing McBride heard before the man hung up.

McBride slumped in his chair, anger churning in his gut. The world was mostly a terrible place, full of monsters. Killers, rapists, pedophiles, users, abusers—McBride had seen them all, their evil masked by such ordinary faces.

A monster had taken Abby Walters, and the longer he kept her, the less hope they had of ever getting her back alive.

McBride picked up Abby's photo, his expression softening at the sight of her gap-toothed grin. "Where are you, baby?"

She wasn't really a pretty child, all knees,

elbows and freckles, but in the picture, the sheer joy of life danced in her bright blue eyes. People would notice a kid like Abby Walters. Even in the photo, she had a way about her.

Her picture had certainly affected Lily Browning, though not how McBride had expected. When he'd shown Abby's picture to others at the school, the grinning child immediately brought smiles to their faces. But Lily had looked ill from the start.

She was keeping secrets.

About Abby Walters? McBride couldn't say for sure, but sixteen years as a cop had honed his suspicious nature to a fine edge. He knew she couldn't have been in on the kidnapping; witness testimony had narrowed down Debra Walters's time of death to sometime between seven-twenty and eight-thirty in the morning. According to Carmen Herrera, Lily Browning had been in a meeting at six-thirty and hadn't left it until seven-forty, when students started trickling in. She'd been in class after that.

But he couldn't forget her odd reaction to Abby's photo.

On a hunch, McBride pulled up the DMV database on his computer and punched in Lily Browning's name. While he waited for the response, he mentally replayed his meeting with her.

He'd noticed her eyes first. Large, more gold

than brown, framed by long, dark lashes. Behind those eyes lay mysteries. Of that much, McBride was certain.

She was in her twenties—mid to late, he guessed. With clear, unblemished skin as pale as milk, maybe due to the headache. Or was she naturally that fair? In stark contrast, her hair was almost black, worn shoulder-length and loose, with a natural wave that danced when she moved.

She was beautiful in the way that wild things were beautiful. He got the impression of a woman apart, alone, always on the fringes. Never quite fitting in.

A loner with secrets. Never a good combination.

The file came up finally, and McBride took a look. Lily Browning, no middle initial given. Twenty-nine years old, brown hair, brown eyes— *gold eyes,* he amended mentally. An address on Okmulgee Road, not far from the school. McBride knew the area. Older bungalow-style homes, quiet neighborhood, modest property values. Which told him exactly nothing.

Lily Browning wasn't a suspect. She was just a strange woman with honey-colored eyes whose skin had felt like warm velvet beneath his fingers.

Irritated, he checked the clock. Almost four. Walters's plane would have touched down by now and Baker would be with him, calming his fears. Baker was good at that.

McBride wasn't.

He was a bit of a loner with secrets himself.

As he started to close the computer file, his phone rang again. He stared at it for a moment, dread creeping up on him.

Abby Walters's photo stared up at him from the desk.

He grabbed the receiver. "McBride," he growled.

Silence.

He sensed someone on the other end. "Hello?" he said.

"Detective McBride?" A hesitant voice came over the line, resonating with apprehension. Lily Browning's voice.

"Ms. Browning."

He heard a soft intake of breath, but she didn't speak.

"This *is* Lily Browning, right?" He knew he sounded impatient. He didn't care.

"Yes."

Subconsciously, he'd been waiting for her call. Tamping down growing apprehension, he schooled his voice, kept it low and soothing. "Do you know something about Abby?"

"Not exactly." She sounded reluctant and afraid.

He tightened his grip on the phone. "Then why'd you call?"

"You asked if I'd seen Abby this morning. I said no." A soft sigh whispered over the phone. "That wasn't exactly true."

McBride's muscles bunched as a burst of adrenaline flushed through his system. "You saw her this morning at school?"

"No, not at the school." Her voice faded.

"Then where? Away from school?" Had Ms. Herrera been wrong? Had Lily slipped away from the meeting, after all?

The silence on Lily Browning's end of the line dragged on for several seconds. McBride stifled the urge to throw the phone across the room. "Ms. Browning, where did you see Abby Walters?"

He heard a deep, quivery breath. "In my mind," she said.

McBride slumped in his chair, caught flat-footed by her answer. It wasn't at all what he'd expected.

A witness, sure. A suspect—even better. But a psychic?

Bloody hell.

Chapter Two

Heavy silence greeted Lily's answer.

"Are you there?" She clutched the phone, her stomach cramping.

"I'm here." His tight voice rumbled over the phone. "And you should know we don't pay psychics for information."

"Pay?"

"That's why you're calling, isn't it?" His words were clipped and diamond hard. "What's your usual fee, a hundred an hour? Two hundred?"

"I don't have a fee," she responded, horrified.

"So you're in it for the publicity."

"No!" She slammed down the phone, pain blooming like a poisonous flower behind her eyes.

The couch cushion shifted beside her and a furry head bumped against her elbow. Lily dropped one hand to stroke the cat's brown head. "Oh, Delilah, that was a mistake."

The Siamese cat made a soft *prrrupp* sound and

butted her head against Lily's chin. Jezebel joined them on the sofa, poking her nose into Lily's ribs. Groaning, she nudged the cats off her lap and staggered to her feet. Half-blinded by the migraine, she made her way down the hall to her bedroom.

The headaches had never been as bad back home in Willow Grove, with her sister Iris always around to brew up a cup of buckbean tea and work her healing magic. But Willow Grove was one hour and a million light-years away.

The phone rang. Lily started to let the answering machine get it when she saw Iris's face float across the blackness of her mind. She fumbled for the phone. "Iris?"

Her sister's warm voice trembled with laughter. "I'm minding my own business, drying some lavender, and suddenly I get an urge to call you. So, Spooky, what do you need?"

The warm affection in her voice brought tears to Lily's eyes. "Buckbean tea and a little TLC."

"Did you have a vision?" Iris's voice held no laughter now.

"A bad one." Lily told her sister about Abby Walters. "The detective on the case thinks I'm a lunatic." She didn't want to examine why that fact bothered her. She was used to being considered crazy. Why should McBride's opinion matter?

"What can I do to help?" Iris asked.

"Does your magic work over the phone?"

Iris laughed. "It's not magic, you know. It's just—"

"A gift. I know." That's what their mother had always called it. Iris's gift. Or Rose's or Lily's.

Lily called hers a curse. Seeing terrified little girls crying for their daddies. Broken bodies at the bottom of a ditch, rain swirling away the last vestiges of their lifeblood. Her own father's life snuffed out in a sawmill across town—

"Stop it, Lily." Her sister's voice was low and strangled. "It's too much all at once."

Lily tried to close off her memories, knowing that her sister's empathic gift came with its own pain. "I'm sorry."

Iris took a deep breath. "Do you want me to come there?"

"No, I'm feeling better." Not a complete lie, Lily thought. Her headache had eased a little. Just a little. "Sorry I called you away from your lavender."

Iris laughed. "Sometimes I listen to us talk and understand why people think the Browning sisters are crazy."

Lily laughed through the pain. "I'll visit soon, okay? Meanwhile, don't you or Rose get yourselves run out of town."

Iris's wry laughter buzzed across the line. "Or burned at the stake." She said goodbye and hung up.

Lily lay back against the pillow, her head pounding. Jezebel rubbed her face against Lily's, whiskers tickling her nose. "Oh, Jezzy, today went so wrong." She closed her eyes against the light trickling in through the narrow gap between her bedroom curtains, trying to empty her mind. Sleep would be the best cure for her headache. But sleep meant dreams.

And after a vision, Lily's dreams were always nightmares.

BY FIVE O'CLOCK, the sun sat low in the western sky, casting a rosy glow over the small gray-and-white house across the street from McBride's parked car. He peered through the car window, wishing he were anywhere but here.

When Lily Browning had hung up the phone, his first sensation had been relief. One more wacko off his back. Then he'd remembered Andrew Walters's demand and his own grudging agreement. Call it following every lead, he thought with a grim smile. He exited the vehicle and headed across the street.

Lily Browning's house was graveyard quiet as he walked up the stone pathway. A cool October night was falling, sending a chill up his spine as he peered through the narrow gap in the curtains hanging in the front window.

No movement. No sounds.

He pressed the doorbell and heard a muted buzz from inside.

What are you going to say to her—stay the hell away from Andrew Walters or I'll throw you in jail?

Wouldn't it be nice if he could?

He cocked his ear, listening for her approach. Nothing but silence. As he lifted his hand to the buzzer again, he heard the dead bolt turn. The door opened about six inches to reveal a shadowy interior and Lily Browning's tawny eyes.

"Detective McBride." She slurred the words a bit.

"May I come in? I have some questions."

Her face turned to stone. "I have nothing to tell you."

McBride nudged his way forward. "Humor me."

She moved aside to let him in, late afternoon sun pouring through the open doorway, painting her with soft light. Her eyes narrowed to slits, and she skittered back into the darkened living room, leaving him to close the door.

Inside, murky shadows draped the cozy living room with darkness. When McBride's eyes finally adjusted to the low light, he saw Lily standing a few feet in front of him, as if to block him from advancing any farther.

"I told you everything I know on the phone," she said.

He shook his head. "Not quite."

Her chest rose and fell in a deep sigh. Finally, she gestured toward the sofa against the wall. "Have a seat."

McBride sat where she indicated. As his eyes adjusted further to the darkened interior, he saw that Lily Browning looked even paler than she had at school earlier that day. She'd scrubbed off what little makeup she'd worn, and pulled her dark hair into a thick ponytail. Despite the cool October afternoon, she wore a sleeveless white T-shirt and soft cotton shorts. She took the chair across from him, knees tucked against her chest, her eyes wary.

Her bare skin shimmered in the fading light. He stifled the urge to see if she felt as soft as she looked.

What the hell was wrong with him? He was long past his twenties, when every nice pair of breasts and long legs had brought his hormones to attention. And Lily Browning, of all people, should be the last woman in the world to make his mouth go dry and his heart speed up.

He forced himself to speak. "How long have you been a teacher at Westview Elementary?"

She answered in a hushed voice. "Six years."

He wondered why she was speaking so softly. The skin on the back of his neck tingled. "Is someone else here?"

Suspicion darkened her eyes. "My accomplices, you mean?"

He answered with one arched eyebrow.

"Just Delilah and Jezebel," she said after a pause.

A quiver tickled the back of his neck again. "What are they, ghosts? Spirits trapped between here and the afterlife?"

A smile flirted with her pale lips. "No, they're my cats. Every witch needs a cat, right?"

"You're Wiccan?"

A frown swallowed her smile. "It was a joke, Lieutenant. I'm pretty ordinary, actually. No séances, no tea leaves, no dancing around the maypole. I don't even throw salt over my left shoulder when I spill it." She pressed her fingertips to her forehead. The lines in her face deepened, and he realized her expression wasn't a frown but a grimace of pain.

"Do you get headaches often?"

Her eyes swept down to her lap, then closed for a moment. "Why are you here? Am I a suspect?"

"You called me, Ms. Browning." He relaxed on the couch, arms outstretched, and rested one ankle on his other knee. "You said you saw Abby Walters—how did you put it? In your mind?"

She clenched her hands, her knuckles turning white.

"Why call me?" he continued. "Do I look like I'd buy into the whole psychic thing?"

"No." Her tortured eyes met his. "You don't. But I don't want to see her hurt anymore."

He didn't believe in visions. Not even a little. But Lily's words made his heart drop. "Hurt?"

"She's afraid. Crying." Lily slumped deeper into the chair. "I don't know if they're physically hurting her, but she's terrified. She wants her daddy."

McBride steeled himself against the sincerity in her voice. "How do you know this?"

Her voice thickened with unshed tears. "I don't know how to explain it. It's like I have a door in my mind that wants to open. I try to keep it closed because the things behind it always frighten me, but sometimes they're just too strong. That's what happened today. The door opened and there she was."

Acid bubbled in McBride's stomach, a painful reminder of too much coffee and too little lunch. "You actually saw her?"

Lily nodded slowly. "She was crying. Her face was dirty and she was afraid."

"Can you see her now?"

Her quick, deep breath sounded like a gasp. "No."

Tension buzzed down every nerve. "Why not?"

"It doesn't work like that. Please..." She lurched from the chair and stumbled against the coffee table. A pair of cut-glass candlesticks rattled together and toppled as she grabbed the table to steady herself. Out of nowhere, two cats scattered in opposite directions, pale streaks in the darkness.

McBride's heart jumped to hyperspeed as he hurried to Lily's side. He caught her elbow. "Are you okay?"

Her head rose slowly. "Go away."

"You can't even stand up by yourself. Are you drunk?"

"I don't drink." Her head lolled forward, her forehead brushing against his shoulder.

"Drugs?"

He could barely hear her faint reply. "No."

He wrapped one arm around her waist to hold her up. Her slim body melted against his, robbing him of thought for a long, pulsing moment. She was as soft as she looked, and furnace-hot, except for the icy fingers clutching his arm. Her head fell back and she gazed at him, her eyes molten.

Desire coursed through him, sharp and unwelcome.

Ruthlessly suppressing his body's demands, he helped her to the sofa, trying to ignore the warm velvet of her skin beneath his fingers. "What did you take for the headache?"

"I ran out of my prescription." She lay back and covered her eyes with her forearm, as if even the waning afternoon light filtering through the curtains added to her pain.

"I can call it in for you. Do you have any refills left?"

"Just leave me alone."

He should go, and to hell with her. It was probably another con. But she wasn't faking the pain lines etched across her delicate face. "I can call a doctor for you—"

"The prescription bottle's in the drawer by the fridge." Tears slid out from beneath her forearm.

Her weak capitulation gave McBride an uneasy feeling as he headed to the kitchen to find the prescription.

He was back in fifteen minutes, using the keys Lily had given him to let himself back into the house. It was a few minutes after six and night had fallen, cool and blue. He fumbled along the wall for a light switch, but couldn't find one.

Pausing to let his eyes adjust to the dark, he saw the pale sheen of a lampshade a few feet away, outlined in the glow coming through the windows from the streetlight outside. He felt his way to the lamp and turned it on. The muddy yellow circle of light from the low-watt bulb barely penetrated the darkness in the corner where it stood. But it was better than the unrelenting darkness.

Lily lay on the sofa, her arm still over her eyes.

"Ms. Browning?"

She didn't answer.

McBride crossed to the sofa and crouched beside her, watching the slow, steady rise and fall of her chest. She was asleep, without the benefit of the pills he'd just spent more than fifty dollars buying for her.

No matter. She'd probably need them when she woke up.

She shifted in her sleep but didn't awaken. Waiting for her to settle back down, McBride gave in to the male hunger gnawing at his belly and let his gaze wander over her body, taking in the tempting curves and planes. At some point in her sleep, the hem of her T-shirt had slid up, baring a thin patch of smooth, flat belly and the indentation of her navel.

Heat sluiced through him, unexpected and unwanted. Dragging his gaze from that narrow strip of flesh, he pushed himself to his feet and stepped away from her.

He distracted himself with a quick, cop's-eye survey of the living room. Clean. Spare. Simple furniture in neutral tones with just enough color to ward off boredom. He moved closer to the wall to study a framed watercolor, a delicate rendering of a tulip in colors that would be subtle even with full illumination. A neat signature appeared in black appeared in the bottom right corner: Iris Browning. Mother or sister?

Movement to one side caught his eye. A Siamese cat crouched, frozen, near a small iron plant stand, staring at him from between the leaves of a philodendron. McBride barely made out glowing turquoise eyes in a chocolate face.

A shudder ran through him.

Suddenly, a scream split the quiet, snapping the tension in his spine like a band. Off balance, he stumbled backward into the lamp, knocking it over. The bulb shattered, plunging the room into darkness.

With his heart slamming against his rib cage, he turned to the sofa, peering through the blackness. In the glimmer of light flowing through the window, Lily's face was a pale oval, twisted into a horror mask by her wide-stretched mouth, her scream rising and swelling like a tidal wave, chilling him to the bone.

LILY KNEW IT WAS NIGHT, black as pitch and deathly quiet except for whimpering sobs. She recognized Abby's soft cries.

"Abby?" she whispered.

The child didn't hear her, but stayed where she was, somewhere in the deep blackness, crying in soft little bleats.

Lily knew she was dreaming, that by waking

she could spare herself whatever lay beyond the door separating Abby Walters from her abductors. But she couldn't abandon the little girl.

She could almost hear Abby's thoughts, the panicked jumble of memories and fears—Mommy lying on the roadside, blood streaming down her pale hair, tinting the golden strands red.

Mommy, wake up! Am I going to die? Daddy, help me!

Lily heard the rattle of a doorknob and the scraping sound of a dead bolt sliding open. Bright light sliced through the dark room, blinding them both.

Abby screamed.

A whistle shrieked.

Second shift at the lumber mill. Daddy would be home soon.

As she did every afternoon, Lily shut her eyes and watched her father wipe his brow with his worn white handkerchief, then reach for the switch to shut off the large circular saw.

Bam!

A log slipped loose from the hooks and slammed into Daddy's back, pitching him into the spinning steel blade. A mist of red spun off the blade and spattered the sawdust on the table.

Daddy screamed.

Lily awoke in an explosive rush. Smothering

blackness surrounded her, her father's scream soaring, deafening her.

Then she realized the scream was her own.

Gentle hands emerged from the blackness, cradling her face. The couch shifted beneath her and a familiar scent surrounded her. Fingers threaded through her hair, drawing her against a solid wall of strength and warmth.

She felt a hammering pulse against her breasts, beating in rhythm with her own racing heart.

A low voice rumbled in her ear. "It's okay."

Her heart stuttered, then lurched back into a gallop as she realized the strong arms wrapped around her belonged to Detective McBride.

Chapter Three

Feeling Lily's warm body stiffen, McBride let her go. "I think you were having a nightmare." He stood and stepped back from the couch. "Do you remember it?"

She hesitated. "No."

"Think you can bear a little light?" McBride turned on the nearest of the two torchiere lamps flanking the couch. Golden light chased shadows to the other side of the room. "Okay?"

"Yes." She met his gaze, her eyes huge and haunted.

He frowned. "You sure?"

"I'm fine. No need to babysit anymore."

Though he had more questions to ask, he decided to let her stew awhile, wondering when he'd come back. "I put your pills on the kitchen counter. It cost fifty-six dollars, but since I broke your light, we'll call it even." He gestured at the lamp lying at a crooked angle, propped up by an armchair. "Sorry."

Her glimmering eyes met his. A pull as powerful as the ocean tide engulfed him, catching him off balance. He forced himself to turn away, move toward the front door.

Sofa springs creaked behind him. He felt her approach, the hair on the back of his neck tingling. When he turned again, he found her closer than expected. Close enough to touch. He clenched his fists. "Stay away from this case, Ms. Browning. There's nothing in it for you."

"Goodbye, Lieutenant." She opened the front door. Her skin glowed like porcelain in the blue moonlight.

Quelling the urge to touch her, he slipped out the door and hurried to his car. He slid behind the steering wheel and took several deep breaths. When he felt more in control, he dared a quick look at the dark facade of Lily Browning's house.

His lips tightened to a grim line. What the hell was wrong with him? Of all people, he knew better than to let a woman like Lily Browning get under his skin.

He'd learned that lesson the hard way.

SUNLIGHT KNIFED across Lily's bed, waking her. She squinted at the clock on her bedside table. Nine. All that sleep and she still felt as if she'd been run over by a truck.

She pulled her T-shirt over her head, breathing in a faint, tangy scent clinging to the cotton. It took her back to the darkness, to the feel of McBride's strong arms around her. She'd felt safe. Comforted by his solid body against hers, the soothing timbre of his voice in her ear, telling her everything was okay. God, she'd wanted to believe him.

Jezebel jumped from the dresser to the bed and rubbed her furry face against Lily's chin. Lily stroked the Siamese cat's lean body, from silvery mask to long gray tail. "Hungry, Jez?"

After feeding the mewling cats, she retrieved the Saturday morning paper from the front porch. Settling at the kitchen table with a bowl of cereal, she opened the newspaper.

Abby Walters's freckled face stared back at her. Former Wife of U.S. Senate Candidate Found Dead, Daughter Missing, the headline read in bold, black letters.

Abby Walters, age six, had gone missing after her mother was killed in a carjacking Friday morning. The article speculated the attack might be politically motivated. Abby's father and Debra's ex-husband, Andrew Walters, was a state senator running for the U.S. Senate.

The door in her mind opened a crack. Resolutely, she slammed it shut.

"IT WAS A ONE-TIME THING. She threatened to get a restraining order and I quit." The slim, nervous man sitting across the interview table from McBride pushed his wire-rimmed glasses up his long nose with a shaky finger. "My God, y'all don't think I had anything to do with it...."

McBride tapped his pencil on his notepad and let Paul Leonardi stew a moment. The man's dark eyes shifted back and forth as he waited for McBride to speak.

"I was out of town Friday. I left home at five in the morning. You can ask my neighbor—he saw me leave."

McBride pretended to jot a note, but he already knew all about Leonardi's trip to Lake Guntersville for a weekend of fishing and eagle watching. It had taken the task force most of Sunday to track him down after Andrew Walters had fingered Leonardi as the man most likely to leave his ex-wife dead by the side of the road.

"I loved Debra. I'd never hurt her or Abby."

"Lots of men kill the women they love. That's why it's called a crime of passion." McBride felt a glimmer of satisfaction when Leonardi's face went pale at his words. "I did check your alibi. The cabin manager said you didn't show up until noon. That's seven hours to make a two-hour drive to Guntersville. What did you do with the other five hours?"

"God, I don't know! I took the scenic route part of the time. I stopped for gas somewhere around Birmingham, I think. I stopped at an antique store in Blount County and picked up an old butter churn to add to Mom's collection for her birthday coming up. I went by the home store outlet in Boaz to pick up a pedestal sink for the guest bathroom I'm renovating at home." He raked his fingers through his thinning hair. "Damn, I knew I should have waited and done all that on the way back home, but I figured I'd be tired and just blow it off."

McBride wrote down the stops he mentioned, asking for more details. Leonardi couldn't remember the gas station in Birmingham, but he supplied the name of the antique store and the home center outlet. McBride would put a couple of the task force officers on the job of tracking down the man's movements on Friday morning.

"Back to Mrs. Walters for a moment—I understand you showed up at Westview Elementary one afternoon about a month ago, when she was picking up Abby." McBride watched Leonardi carefully as he spoke. The dark-haired man's eyes widened, dilating with alarm. Good. "That's what convinced her to threaten you with a restraining order, wasn't it?"

Leonardi looked down at his hands. "I just wanted to talk to her. I wanted her to tell me why she'd decided to end it."

"She said you were a transition, didn't she? Just a post-divorce ego stroke."

Leonardi blanched. "It was more than that to me."

"But not her. And you couldn't take no for an answer?"

"I didn't think she'd really given us a chance. She has these friends telling her she should go out, have fun, not tie herself down. 'Don't just settle for the first guy who comes along, Debbie. Have some fun, Debbie.'"

"How do you know what her friends said, Mr. Leonardi?" McBride leaned forward. "Did you tap her phones? Did you put a bug in her house? What?"

He pressed his lips tightly together. "I want a lawyer."

"You're not under arrest. Why would you need a lawyer?"

Leonardi's baleful gaze was his only answer.

"When you showed up at the school—how'd you know what time Debra would be picking up Abby? Had you followed her before?"

Leonardi didn't answer.

"Maybe you know somebody who works there," McBride suggested, tapping the folder on the interview table. He flipped it open, exposing an enlarged photocopy of Lily Browning's driver's license photo from the DMV database.

Leonardi's gaze shifted down to the table as McBride intended. His brow furrowed slightly as his gaze skimmed over the photo, but beyond that, he had no reaction.

Not what McBride had been expecting, but he wasn't ready to discount the idea that Lily Browning had a part in Abby Walters's disappearance. "Know what I think, Mr. Leonardi? I think you have a friend who works at the school. She told you when the first grade would be letting out in the afternoon so you'd know exactly when to show up. Did she know about your plans for Friday, too?"

Leonardi's eyes filled with tears. "I didn't kill Debbie. Don't you get it? I lost her, too, just like her friends and her family and her jerk of an ex-husband did. Why aren't you talking to him? Don't you always look at the husband first?"

McBride had already talked to Walters Friday evening, going over his alibi in detail. Over the weekend he'd been able to validate all the times and places Walters had supplied. Of course, it was possible Walters had hired someone to kill his ex-wife, but the autopsy report McBride had found sitting on his desk first thing that morning suggested that Debra Walters's skull fracture might have been accidental, the result of a struggle with the carjackers.

They couldn't even be sure it was anything but a random carjacking. Debra Walters's Lexus hadn't shown up anywhere yet.

Neither had Abby Walters.

McBride's captain had left it up to him to put together a task force for the case. After contacting the FBI and the local sheriff's department to supply their own officers for the team, McBride had picked six of the best cops on the Borland force to assist him.

Sergeant Theo Baker had the job of holding Andrew Walters's hand and keeping him from calling every few minutes for an update. McBride understood the man's anxiety all too well, but he didn't need that distraction.

Some of the task force members were canvassing the area where Debra Walters had died, hoping for witnesses who might have seen something on Friday morning. Some were fielding calls from tipsters, most of them crackpots and attention seekers.

Others were monitoring Friday morning footage from the handful of traffic cams scattered throughout the city of Borland, hoping they could track Debra's movements from the time she'd left her home to the time she'd stopped on the side of the road to meet her death. McBride didn't hold out much hope for that angle; where she'd died was a lightly traveled back road without any camera surveillance.

"How long do you plan to hold me?" Apparently having a cry put the steel back in Paul Leonardi's spine; he met McBride's questioning look with a steady gaze. "I know my rights. You can only hold me for so long before you either have to charge me or let me go. Unless you think I'm a terrorist or something."

McBride was tempted to toss him in the cages just to make a point, but he quelled the urge. "I'm going to be checking out your alibi, Mr. Leonardi. If everything pans out, no problem. But you shouldn't leave town anytime soon."

"I'm not going anywhere," Leonardi said. "At least, not until after Debbie's funeral. Do you know when it'll be?"

McBride's eyes narrowed as he stood and motioned for Leonardi to follow him out of the interview room. Either the guy was really innocent or he had cojones of titanium. "Check with her ex-husband. He's handling the arrangements."

Back at his desk a few minutes later, McBride grabbed the bottle of antacids on his desk and downed a couple to ease the fire in his gut.

His captain, Alex Vann, chose that moment to pop his head into the office. He eyed the bottle as he sat down across the desk. "You eat too many of those things."

Ignoring the remark, McBride gave him an update on his interview with Leonardi. "I don't know if he's good for it or not. He has all kinds of motive, but he just doesn't feel right for this thing."

"And the nutso schoolteacher angle?"

McBride arched his eyebrow at the description of Lily Browning. "He didn't really react at the sight of her photo." Nothing beyond the furrowed brow, which could simply mean he was wondering why McBride was flashing Lily Browning's picture.

"Why don't you take a break, McBride? Go get some lunch."

"I'll order something in."

"Not good enough." Vann's jowly face creased with concern.

McBride didn't pretend not to notice. He put down the papers and looked up at his captain. "I'm fine."

"Maybe you should work another case. Take your pick."

"I want this one."

Vann's gaze darkened, but he didn't comment as he walked out of the office.

McBride didn't expect the captain or anyone else to understand. Working the Walters case was like rubbing salt into an open wound, but McBride couldn't let it go. He had to follow it to the bitter end. Find the child. Capture the kidnappers.

See justice done this time.

THE DOOR IN LILY'S MIND flew open without warning, catching her in the middle of grading papers in her classroom while her students played outside at recess. Her pencil dropped from her shaking fingers, rolling to the floor and disappearing in the silvery fog that washed over her in the span of a heartbeat.

Instinct urged her to fight off the battering ram of images, but at the first glimpse of Abby Walters's tearstained face, her resistance fled. She gave in to the vision's relentless undertow and let it sweep her into the haze.

The mists parted to reveal Abby Walters on the other side, knees tucked to her chin, blue eyes wide and unblinking.

"Abby," Lily breathed.

The misty void deepened. Abby huddled in the looming darkness, covered with something musty-smelling. A blanket? She was trembling. Her teeth chattered.

Lily shivered, goose bumps rising on her arms. *Cold.*

She tried to touch the little girl. Her hand felt

as if it moved through cold molasses. "Abby, where are you?"

Lily smelled the musty blanket they huddled beneath. She felt vibrations under her, the carpet-covered hump of a drive shaft hard against her left hip. They were in a car.

"They're moving you, aren't they?" Lily felt the tremble beneath her fingers and realized she was finally touching the girl. "Abby, can you feel me here?"

The little girl went still. "Mama?"

Lily felt a surge of excitement. "No, Abby, I'm a friend."

"Help me!" she cried.

"Shut up!" A harsh male voice boomed in front of them.

Lily tried to get her bearings. She and Abby shared the floorboard behind the front passenger seat. The voice had come from there, so someone else was driving. There were at least two kidnappers. Did McBride know that?

Lily put her arms around Abby and concentrated on planting the sensation of touch in the child's mind—skin to skin, warm and soft. Suddenly, the little girl jerked out of her grasp, all contact between them disintegrating into gray mist.

As Lily tumbled into the void, she saw a hand smack Abby's face. The girl whimpered in terror.

Lily cried out as the door in her mind slammed shut, cutting her off.

She came back to herself with a jerk. It took a second to reorient herself. She was in her empty classroom. A glance at her watch confirmed that only a few minutes had passed.

A rap on the closed classroom door jangled her nerves. "Lily?" It was Janet, the teacher whose class was next door. The door cracked open and she poked her head in. "Everything okay? I thought I heard a shout."

"Broke a nail," Lily fibbed, forcing a sheepish expression, though her whole body seemed to be vibrating with tension. "Sorry—it was my longest one."

Janet laughed politely, although wariness darkened her eyes. "Just checking." She closed the door again.

Lily buried her face in her hands, unnerved by the close call. She wasn't used to her visions attacking without warning. What if one hit her while class was in session?

She waited for the tightening bands of a migraine, but they didn't come. She should be in agony after such a powerful vision. Why not this time? Because she hadn't had time to fight it off? Was the answer really that simple?

She replayed the vision in her mind, trying to

pick up more clues. She'd made contact. Beyond everything else she'd learned, that fact stood out. Never before had she made actual contact with someone in a vision.

But Abby had heard her. Maybe even felt Lily's arms around her. Though she'd been frightened this time, maybe it was possible to make Abby understand Lily wanted to help her. But that meant letting the visions come, whatever they might bring.

Panic bubbled in her gut, tempting her to retreat again, to lock the door in her mind and hide the key forever. Visions were bad things. She'd learned that lesson long ago. She wasn't like Rose, with her happy gift of predicting love matches, which she'd channeled into a successful job as a matchmaker and wedding planner. Nor like Iris, whose gift of empathy helped her ease people's pain and despair.

Lily's gift was darkness, terror, blood and death. She didn't want to explore her visions. She wanted to end them.

But the memory of Abby haunted her. Maybe she could make a difference in this case. If time didn't run out.

She just had to make someone believe her.

As McBride had suspected, Paul Leonardi had caused at least one incident at Westview Elementary, near the beginning of the school year. Unfortunately, if Lily Browning had any connection to Leonardi, neither the principal nor vice principal knew anything about it.

"I doubt it," Carmen Herrera told McBride in her office a little before noon. "Lily's something of a homebody—she doesn't socialize that much, even with other teachers. I doubt she'd have any reason to know Mr. Leonardi."

A loner with secrets, he thought, remembering his earlier assessment of her. Apparently he'd been spot on. "And there was only the one incident?" he asked.

"Yes, just the one. It wasn't really that big a deal—he didn't resist when security asked him to leave. I didn't get the feeling he was really dangerous. Just heartbroken." Carmen flashed a rueful smile. "We've all been there once or twice, haven't we?"

He thanked her for her time and headed for the exit, slowing as he reached the half-open door to Lily Browning's classroom. Today, it was full of children, who sat with rapt attention as they listened to Lily reading.

He wasn't familiar with the book she'd chosen, but as she told the rollicking tale of a girl and her pet cat braving a violent thunderstorm to reach the girl's injured father, he found himself seduced by her musical voice.

He paused outside the doorway to get a better

look at her. She was perched on the edge of her desk, legs dangling. Today she wore her hair up in a coil, with wavy tendrils curling around her cheeks and neck.

It was soft, he remembered. Sweet-smelling, like green apples. He could still recall how she felt in his arms, trembling from her nightmare.

"That's it for today, ladies and gentlemen," Lily announced as she reached a shocking cliffhanger at the end of the chapter. She closed the book, came around the desk and slid it into her top drawer. Scattered groans erupted.

"Aw, Ms. Browning!"

"Can't we read one more chapter?"

"If we finish the book today, what will we have to read tomorrow?" Laughter tinging her voice, she rose from her desk and started passing out sheets of paper. "Besides, Mrs. Marconi is waiting for you in the library. Let's go, single file."

McBride's lips curved. Years passed, things changed, but teachers still lined their students up single file. He backed away, hoping to make a quick exit without being caught eavesdropping, but he hadn't made it down the hall more than a couple of steps when Lily's voice called out to him.

"Lieutenant McBride?"

Busted.

Chapter Four

Anxiety rippled through Lily's belly. Why was Lieutenant McBride here? Had something happened? "Is there news?"

The single file line of students flowing out the door behind her began to devolve into chaos. Tamping down her fear, she quickly brought them back into order, glancing over her shoulder to make sure McBride hadn't left while she was distracted. "Please wait here—I'll be back in just a minute."

She headed up the hallway with her brood, quelling small mutinies with a firm word or a quick touch of her hand on a troublemaker's shoulder. Once they were out the door in the custody of the librarian, she hurried back to her classroom, afraid McBride would be gone. But she found him sitting on the edge of her desk, his expression unreadable.

"Is there news about Abby?" she asked.

"No. I was just following another lead."

She cocked her head to one side. "Here?"

"Ever met a man named Paul Leonardi?" His gaze focused like a laser on her face.

She frowned, searching her memory. "Not that I remember."

"He had to be escorted from the school grounds a couple of months ago, near the start of the school year."

"Oh, that guy." It had caused a big stink, generating a dozen new security policies. "Yeah, I heard about it, but I didn't see it happen."

He pulled a piece of paper from his pocket. "You never saw this guy?"

She glanced at the paper. It looked like a driver's license photo. The man in the picture was nice-looking in an ordinary sort of way. She shook her head. "Do you think he's one of the kidnappers?"

"One of them? You think there's more than one?" McBride's eyes changed color, from smoky brown to mossy green. "Why do you think there's more than one kidnapper?"

She licked her lips. "I had another vision. Abby in a car, huddled under some sort of blanket. One of the kidnappers hit her." McBride's hard gaze made Lily want to crawl into a hole, but she pushed ahead. "Whoever struck Abby was in the passenger seat, so someone else had to be driving."

He rose from the edge of her desk. "If you remember anything about Mr. Leonardi, let me know."

She caught his arm. "I can help you if you'd let me."

He looked down at her hand, contempt in his eyes. "I'm up to my eyeballs in help, Ms. Browning. Every crackpot in the state seems to know what happened to Abby Walters."

She dropped her hand quickly. "Including me?"

"Some of my people are handling the crackpot calls. I'll tell them to expect yours." He headed out to the hall.

Torn between irritation and humiliation, Lily watched him reach the exit and step outside. He couldn't have made it any clearer that he didn't want to hear what she had to say.

She'd have to deal with her visions of Abby her own way.

LILY HATED FUNERAL HOMES.

The newspaper had listed the time and place for the pre-funeral viewing. Her stomach churned at the thought of crashing the wake, but if she was going to find Abby, she needed to start with the people closest to her. Her father. Family and friends. Proximity to people who knew the subjects had always made her visions stronger in the past. It was one reason Lily had become something of a recluse in her personal life. Avoiding people was self-defense.

But this time, she needed the visions to come.

She spotted Carmen Herrera getting out of her car. Lily stepped out of her own car and met the assistant principal halfway to the door. "I was afraid I'd missed you."

Carmen smiled sadly, putting her hand on Lily's arm. "Thanks for volunteering to come with me. I hate wakes."

"Me, too." She followed Carmen up the steps to the funeral home entrance, distracted by a spattering of camera flashes.

"The press." Carmen grimaced. "Ghouls."

More flashes went off as they entered. The foyer's faux marble floors and gilt furnishings gave the room a cold, austere feeling. *Funereal,* Lily thought with a bubble of dark humor. She tamped down a nervous giggle.

The small viewing chapel was packed with a combination of mourners and a few people Lily suspected were reporters who'd hidden their agendas along with their notepads to get inside.

Not that Lily could quibble about hidden agendas.

She signed the guest book and went with Carmen to the front, forcing herself to look at the body in the coffin.

Had Debra Walters been as lovely in life as the powdered, waxed and beautifully coiffed body in the casket? Seeing her now, Lily realized she did look a bit familiar. Maybe Mrs. Walters had been at a parent-teacher event earlier in the year. Or maybe it was just the resemblance between mother and daughter that struck a chord.

"There's Mr. Walters." Carmen moved toward a well-dressed man surrounded by a handful of fellow mourners. His newspaper photo didn't do justice to his lean good looks, Lily thought.

She should join Carmen, take advantage of the opening to meet Abby's father and see if he'd be receptive to her unusual method of finding his daughter. But a combination of guilt and fear held her back. There was something unseemly about using these particular circumstances to approach him with her offer of help.

"They did a good job, didn't they?" a man's voice asked.

Lily jerked her attention toward the questioner, a familiar-looking man of medium height with dark hair and mournful brown eyes. He met her gaze briefly before looking back at the body.

"But they didn't capture who she really was." Sadness tinged his voice. "She was the most alive person I ever knew."

This was the man in the picture McBride had showed her, Lily realized. The one who'd come to the school looking for Debra. The hair on her arms prickled.

"Paul Leonardi. Debra and I dated a few months ago." He held out his hand. "You look familiar. Do I know you?"

"No." She made herself shake his hand. It was damp and hot, his handshake limp. She quelled the urge to wipe her palm on her skirt. "I'm Lily. I teach at Abby's school."

His expression darkened. "Horrible about the little girl."

Interesting, she thought. He'd said "the little girl" as if Abby were an afterthought.

Paul's eyes shifted away from her, his brow creasing. "Great. The cops are here."

Lily followed his gaze and met the narrowed eyes of Lieutenant McBride. She looked away quickly, her heart clenching. Of course he was here. She should have anticipated it. He'd be hoping for the killer to show up.

Paul gritted his teeth. "Can't I have one night to mourn her without the Gestapo breathing down my neck?"

"He has a job to do," Lily responded, surprised to be defending McBride. "Don't you want him to catch Debra's killer?"

"Of course." Paul directed his glare her way.

Unless you're the killer, she thought, her heart leaping into her throat. Obviously, he'd had feelings for Debra, and from the way he'd phrased things earlier Lily gathered the relationship had ended, probably before he was ready.

Not a bad motive for murder.

To her relief, Carmen Herrera approached, Andrew Walters a step behind her. She put her hand on Lily's shoulder. "Lily, this is Mr. Walters, Abby's father. Mr. Walters, Lily Browning."

To Lily's left, Paul Leonardi stepped away before she was forced to make an introduction. He blended back into the rest of the crowd.

"It was kind of you and Mrs. Herrera to come. Abby's teacher was here earlier to pay her respects, but it means a lot that you both came as well." Andrew Walters took Lily's hand, his expression eager. "Do you know my daughter well, Ms. Browning?"

Lily glanced at Carmen before she answered Walters's question. "I don't know her, really, but from all accounts she's a delightful child."

"She is." Andrew Walters's gaze softened.

Carmen put her hand on Lily's shoulder. "I'll be back in a sec. I see someone I should say hello to." She drifted away, leaving Lily alone with Andrew Walters.

"I hope you find Abby soon," she told him.

His expression hardened with determination. "I'll do whatever it takes to get her back."

She almost told him what she knew then and there. But the sight of McBride bearing down on them held her in check.

"Mr. Walters?" McBride's voice rose over the soft murmurs of conversation surrounding them. He stepped forward, taking Andrew Walters by the elbow and drawing him away. "I need to speak to you."

Carmen crossed to Lily's side. "Ready to go?"

"Yes."

"Is that Lieutenant McBride talking to Mr. Walters?" Carmen asked as they headed for the exit.

"Maybe," Lily replied, keeping to herself the fact that Lieutenant McBride's rough-hewn features and hard hazel eyes were indelibly imprinted in her memory.

"STILL NOTHING FROM the task force?" His voice laced with desperation, Andrew Walters shifted from one foot to the other.

McBride forced himself to look away from Lily Browning's retreating figure. "We're still following leads."

"Is Ms. Browning one of those leads?" Walters asked. When McBride remained silent, he added, "You seemed eager to get me away from her just now."

McBride took a deep breath through his nose. He should have known a politician would be perceptive. And since Lily Browning proved by coming to this wake that she wasn't going to back off, it was a good idea to inoculate Walters with the truth before she made her next attempt to contact him. "I wanted you away from her because Ms. Browning believes she's having visions of Abby."

Walters cocked his head to one side. "Visions?"

"Obviously she's a crank."

"But what if—"

The hopeful gleam in Walters's eyes made McBride cringe. "Don't do this, Mr. Walters. You want to believe she can help you. I get that. I do. You need somebody to tell you Abby's okay and she's coming back to you any day now. Ms. Browning will tell you she can lead you to her." Acid spewed into McBride's stomach. "But she can't. She doesn't know anything."

"And you do?" Walters's cold voice seemed to grate on McBride's spine. "*You* think Abby's dead, don't you?"

McBride couldn't deny it, so he said nothing.

"I don't believe that, Lieutenant." Walters lifted his chin. "And if Lily Browning thinks she can help me find my daughter, I want to hear what she has to say."

"There have to be better leads to follow. What about a political angle? Is that possible?"

Walters's look of resolve faltered. "Maybe. I have a very powerful opponent with powerful backers. I don't know what they're capable of."

"We're looking at Blackledge, I assure you." The savvy old senator was barely leading Walters in the latest polls. Probably because of his divorced status, Walters had made his relationship with his daughter the focal point of his campaign ads, stressing family values in an attempt to assure the conservative local voters he was a solid citizen they could trust in Washington.

Maybe Blackledge or one of his people had figured taking the daughter would ensure Walters dropped out of the race. After all, the doting father could hardly keep up the campaign while his kid was missing. A thin motive, but not out of the realm of possibility, especially where politics were involved.

Of course, the same could be said of Andrew Walters.

However, Walters had an alibi. And McBride couldn't see a motive for killing his ex-wife and getting rid of his daughter. Everyone McBride had talked to agreed that Walters and his ex had remained friends after the divorce. Walters never missed a child support payment, supplying more than the court-agreed amount.

He might have means, but he lacked motive and opportunity. And Walters couldn't possibly be faking the panic underlying every word he spoke.

"Mr. Walters, I know what you're feeling—"

The state senator narrowed his eyes. "I doubt it. Now, if you'll excuse me, I have other people to talk to."

Torn between sympathy and anger, McBride watched Walters leave. He hadn't been feeding him a line. He knew exactly what the man was going through.

Every excruciating moment of it.

McBride gravitated to the open casket and gazed down at Debra Walters. She was lovely in death, her pretty features composed and calm, as if she were merely asleep. Thick makeup designed to make the dead look better than the living covered the bruise on her temple.

McBride's stomach roiled. Laura's casket had been closed.

"How can you be working on a case like this?" Theo Baker joined McBride at the casket, his dark eyes full of concern.

McBride's stomach burned. "Abby's father has

to know what happened to her." Even if she was
dead. It was not knowing that killed you.

   An inch at a time.

DEBRA WALTERS'S FUNERAL was a brief, solemn
affair, held at graveside. A smattering of people sat
in metal folding chairs under a white tent that
shielded the casket from the bright October
sunlight. Several more filled out the circle of
mourners around the site, including dozens of
cameramen from local stations and national
networks. Another clump of people gathered
around a tall, silver-haired man Lily recognized as
Senator Gerald Blackledge.

   Strange, his being here. Or maybe not—the
senator's opponent had just lost his ex-wife to
foul play. Maybe Blackledge thought if he didn't
appear for the funeral, he'd look as if he had something to hide.

   And a public show of compassion couldn't hurt,
she supposed.

   Andrew Walters gave a brief, eloquent eulogy,
captured for posterity by the news cameras. Ever the
politician, he managed to come across both sad and
commanding, an achievement Lily couldn't help
but admire, though she found his self-control almost
as discomfiting as Gerald Blackledge's decision to
attend the funeral and turn it into a media circus.

But maybe politicians had no choice but to be "on" all the time, with so many cameras around, waiting for them to stumble.

A cadre of reporters hovered about, talking into microphones in hushed tones that might have been unobtrusive if there weren't a dozen other newspeople doing the same thing at the same time. Across from Lily, on the other side of the circle of mourners, stood Lieutenant McBride, his eyes hidden by mirrored sunglasses.

But she felt the full weight of his disapproval.

Too bad. She'd given him a chance to help Abby. Now she was handling things her own way.

She didn't have to approach Andrew Walters after the service; he sought her out almost as soon as the preacher finished his prayer and the casket was lowered into the ground.

"I spoke to Lieutenant McBride this morning." He kept his voice low, taking her elbow and guiding her away from the crowd. "He says you claim you had a vision of Abby. Is that true?"

Unprepared for his straightforward question, she stumbled, grabbing Andrew's arm to steady herself. A murmur went up among the reporters and they shifted toward them. Lily quickly let go of Andrew's arm. "Yes, it's true, but we can't talk about it here."

"Come by my hotel room tomorrow evening.

We'll discuss it then," Andrew murmured, before carefully stepping away.

Turning, Lily came up against a wall of black-clad men with earpieces. Bodyguards, she realized as the men parted like the Red Sea and Senator Gerald Blackledge strode through the gap, hand outstretched.

"Andrew, I'm so sorry to hear about your ex-wife and daughter. If I can do anything to help, you mustn't hesitate to use me. Understand? Politics has no place in this situation."

The irony of the senator's words, juxtaposed against the flash of camera bulbs and the sea of camcorders and microphones, forced a bubble of nervous laughter up Lily's throat. She swallowed it, looking for her chance to slip away. But before she moved a step, Blackledge caught her elbow.

"Please, don't go on my account, Miss…?"

Andrew's mouth tightened. "Lily Browning, this is Senator Gerald Blackledge. Senator, this is Lily Browning. She teaches at the school my daughter attends."

The senator enveloped her hand in a firm handshake. "A delight to meet you, Ms. Browning. My mother taught English for thirty years." He looked sincerely interested, but Lily imagined a man who'd been a senator for twenty years had probably honed his acting ability to perfection.

"Really?" Lily responded politely, catching a glimpse of McBride a few feet away. Unnerved by his scrutiny, she murmured an excuse and moved aside, trying to avoid the cameras ringing them. She'd almost made it to the parking area when someone grabbed her arm. Whirling, she came face-to-face with McBride.

He'd removed his sunglasses, exposing her to the full brunt of his fury. "Don't do this, Ms. Browning."

She jerked her arm from his grasp. "Did I break a law?"

He didn't answer.

"I didn't think so." She headed toward her car.

McBride fell into step, his long strides easily matching hers. "He's vulnerable and desperate. The last thing he needs is someone promising she can bring his baby back home to him when we both know damn well you can't."

She unlocked her car and opened the driver's door, putting its solid bulk between her and McBride. "I know you don't think she's still alive."

His only visible reaction was a tightening of his lips.

"But I know she is, and I'm not going to wait around for you to get over your knee-jerk skepticism before I do something about it."

She started to get into the vehicle, but he

grabbed the door before she could pull it shut behind her. Looking down at her over the top, he narrowed his eyes. "If you really know Abby's alive, answer me this—why have four days passed without anyone calling with a ransom demand?"

Lily's stomach knotted. She had no explanation for that.

"Think about it." He let go of the door and stepped away.

HE WATCHED FROM THE gravesite, his heart pounding. Who was this woman with the knowing eyes? What could she know about what had happened to Abby?

He'd planned so carefully. Worked out all the details, figured the odds. He'd visualized just what would happen, down to the lightly traveled shortcut Debra took every weekday morning on her way to Abby's school. He knew where to stage the surprise attack, and how quickly Debbie would be scared into compliance.

It was supposed to be fast. Grab the girl and go, leaving Debra to sound the alarm and put the rest of the plan in motion.

But she had fought back.

He hadn't thought she'd fight back. She'd always been such a marshmallow.

Everything had gone terribly wrong. And now

there was Lily Browning, with her strange gold eyes and her knowing look, claiming she'd seen a vision of Abby.

His heart twisted with growing panic.

What if she really had?

A PHOTO OF LILY, Andrew Walters and Gerald Blackledge made the front page of Wednesday's *Borland Courier*. The teacher's lounge was abuzz when she arrived at school that morning.

"At least it's a good picture. And they spelled your name correctly," Carmen Herrera pointed out when Lily groaned at the sight of her face above the fold.

"I didn't give anyone my name." There was no mention of her in the body text, at least. "I guess Mr. Walters told them."

"Or the senator," Carmen suggested.

That was also possible—a jab at Mr. Family Values, consorting with a new woman right there at his ex-wife's funeral. What would voters think?

Worse, what would Lieutenant McBride think when he got a look at her name and face plastered across the front page?

She half expected to find him waiting on her doorstep when she arrived home that afternoon, storm clouds gathering in his eyes, so she was almost disappointed to find no one waiting. But when she entered her house to find her phone ringing, she wasn't surprised. She was listed in the directory; any reporter with a taste for a trumped-up scandal could look her up.

Lily grabbed the phone and took a deep breath, steeling herself for unpleasantness. "Hello?"

"Lily Browning?"

She knew that voice. The kidnapper's harsh drawl was unmistakable. Lily's heart slammed into her ribs. "You have Abby Walters."

There was a long pause over the phone. When the man spoke, he sounded wary. "How'd you know that?"

"Is she okay?" Lily's mind raced, wondering what to do next. Nobody was expecting the kidnappers to call here; all the recording equipment was no doubt set up at Andrew Walters's hotel, waiting for a ransom demand. As she scrabbled for something to write with, her gaze fell on the answering machine attached to her phone.

The kind that allowed her to record incoming conversations.

She jabbed the record button with a shaking finger.

"She's fine, for now," the kidnapper said.

"You hit her, you son of a bitch!"

There was a brief silence on the other end

before the man spoke in a hushed tone. "What the hell are you?"

Lily ignored the question. "Let me talk to her."

"Don't be stupid."

Shivers raced up her spine, followed by the first hint of gray mist clouding the edges of her vision. Gripping the phone harder, she fought off the sensation. "Why are you calling me instead of Mr. Walters?"

"You think we don't know the cops have his phone tapped? We've been looking for a way to contact him away from his hotel." The caller laughed. "Then we seen your picture in the paper. Lucky break, ain't it?"

Lily sank down on the floor, tucking her knees close to her body. "You want me to pass along your demands to Mr. Walters?"

"Tell him it's time to pay up. We'll be in touch."

She heard a soft clicking noise. "Wait!"

But the man had already disconnected.

She slammed down the phone and covered her face with shaking hands. The door in her mind bulged, trying to force its way open, but she continued to fight the vision.

She had to call McBride.

With pain lancing behind her eyes, she checked the tape in the answering machine, terrified she'd pushed a wrong button and failed to record the kidnapper's message. But the harsh drawl was there. "Tell him it's time to pay up."

She shut off the recorder and dialed McBride's cell phone number. He answered on the second ring. "McBride."

She released a pent-up breath. "It's Lily Browning. The kidnappers just phoned me."

"What?" He sounded wary.

She told him about the call. "I managed to record most of it on my answering machine. Do you want me to play it for you?"

"No, I'm on my way." He hung up without saying goodbye.

By the time he arrived ten minutes later, her head was pounding with pain, the vision clawing at her brain. She didn't bother with a greeting, just flung the door open and groped her way back to the sofa, concentrating on surviving the onslaught of pain in her head. She wished she could escape to her room and let the vision come, but she had to stay focused.

McBride went straight to the answering machine. "What time did the call come in?"

She altered her expression, trying to hide the pain. "The phone was ringing when I got home— maybe three-forty?"

He listened to the tape twice before he pulled it from the machine. "I'll get this to the feds on the task force, see if they can clean it up a little, pick up some background noises. Maybe we can pinpoint where he was calling from. And I'll take a copy to Mr. Walters, see if he recognizes the voice."

"I recognized it," she said, keeping her voice low out of self-defense as the pounding in her skull grew excruciating. She tried to say *something* more, but the merciless grip of the impending vision tightened. Helpless against it, she sank into a whirlwind of dark, cold mist.

Chapter Five

The mist parted to reveal a small, blue-clad figure.
Lily's heart quickened at the sight of dirty red
curls. "Abby?"

The child didn't respond.

The mist dissipated, revealing a tiny room with
mottled faux oak paneling and faded yellow
curtains splotched with sunflowers. A tiny bed
occupied the entire wall under the metal-frame
window. A prefab house, or maybe a mobile home.

"Abby?" she whispered again.

The child sat on the cot, huddling in a ball
against the wall, tears sparkling on her grimy
cheeks. With horror, Lily realized one of the
smudges there was a bruise.

Abby stirred, her blue eyes darting around the
room.

"Abby, it's me. Lily. I talked to you the other
day. Remember? In the car?"

The little girl's eyes widened. Her pink rosebud

mouth opened, making words without sound. But Lily heard her thoughts, as clearly as if the child had spoken. "Are you a ghost?"

"No, I'm not. I'm not scary at all." Lily touched her. "Can you feel that?"

"Yes." Abby whispered back in her mind.

"Good. See, I'm not hurting you, am I?"

Abby shook her head.

"My name is Lily. I teach at your school. Maybe you remember me from there?"

"I can't see you," Abby replied.

Lily wondered if she could make herself visible to Abby. Was it even possible? She concentrated on seeing herself in the vision. She looked down at Abby's arm and visualized her own hand gently squeezing the soft flesh. But nothing happened.

Abby's eyes welled up. "I can't see you!" she whimpered.

Aloud.

"Shh, baby, don't say it out loud." Lily held her breath, fearing the arrival of Abby's captors. After a few seconds passed and no one came, she exhaled. "Remember, Abby, you have to *think* everything. We don't want the mean men to hear you."

"Why can't I see you?" Abby's thoughts were a frantic whisper. "Where are you?"

"I'm at my house, but I'm thinking real hard about you, and my mind is touching your mind." Lily didn't know how to make Abby understand. She didn't really understand it herself.

"Like a psychic?" Abby asked. "Like on TV?"

Close enough, Lily thought. "Yes."

"Can you tell my future?"

"I know you're going to be okay. I'm going to help you."

"I want to go home." Abby started to cry. Lily put her arms around her, surprised by the strength of the mental connection. She felt the child's body shaking against hers, heard the soft snuffling sound. Warm, wet tears trickled down Lily's neck where the little girl's face lay.

"Soon, baby—" Lily stopped short.

Something began to form at the edge of her vision.

Her eyes shifted to the emerging image, her grip on Abby loosening. She drew her attention back to Abby, but not before she saw a shape begin to take form in the mists.

Another little girl.

"Lily? Where are you?" Abby jerked away, her body going rigid. "They're coming!"

Suddenly she was gone, and Lily was alone in the fog.

But not completely alone.

In the distance, she still saw the hazy shape of the unknown little girl. But as she approached the child, the image shimmered and faded into gray.

The mists began to clear, and Lily found herself in her living room, slumped on the sofa. The afternoon sunlight had begun to wane, shadows swallowing most of the room. Maybe ten minutes had passed since the vision started.

Real time. I was really there.

But who was the other little girl?

"Ms. Browning?" The sound of Lieutenant McBride's voice made her jump.

He sat on her coffee table, his expression shuttered. He'd shed his jacket and rolled up the sleeves of his white dress shirt to his forearms. "Back among the living?" he asked dryly.

Her head pounded from the fight she'd put up to hold off the vision until she could tell McBride about the call. Staggering to her feet, she headed to the kitchen for her pills.

The detective followed. "Another headache?"

She swallowed a pill and washed it down with water from the tap. "If you're just going to mock me for the rest of the afternoon, go away. Don't you have a tape to analyze?"

"The feds are on the way to pick it up. They'll give Sergeant Baker in my office a copy to take over to Mr. Walters."

At least Mr. Walters would know why she didn't make their meeting tonight, she thought.

McBride sat down at her kitchen table and waved toward the chair next to him. "I'm all yours for the evening. So why don't you tell me what the hell just happened in there?"

"I need to lie down."

His eyes narrowed. "Fine. I'm not going anywhere."

She ignored the threat and staggered to her room, wincing as sunlight sliced through the parted curtains, shooting agony through her skull. Too ill to draw the blinds, she groped her way to her bed and lay down, covering her eyes with her forearm.

She heard quiet footsteps approaching on the hardwood floor. She could feel McBride's gaze on her. "You okay?"

"I just need to sleep."

"Do the headaches usually come when you have visions?"

"Only when I fight them," she murmured through gritted teeth.

"Why would you fight them?"

Couldn't he just leave her alone? "They scare me. I don't usually like what I see."

His footsteps sounded again, this time accompanied by the sound of drawing drapes. The thoughtfulness of the action surprised her.

His expression was hard to read in the darkness, but she thought she detected a hint of gentleness in his craggy features. "Thank you," she murmured.

His expression hardened. "Don't thank me yet."

He turned and left her alone in the dark.

"THE FEDS WILL BE bringing you a copy of the tape," McBride told Theo Baker over the phone. "Get it to Andrew Walters ASAP." Maybe Walters would recognize the voice.

And maybe pigs would fly.

McBride hung up and slumped on the sofa, tension banding across his shoulders. His gut churned like a whirlpool, but his antacids were at the office.

How convenient that a day after he'd mentioned the fact that the kidnappers hadn't yet called, Lily Browning should be the one contacted. Surely she saw how guilty it made her look. Yet she'd phoned him instead of Andrew Walters, who'd be far less skeptical about her motives.

What kind of game was she playing? And why had the caller sounded so spooked when she'd accused him of hitting Abby? "What the hell are you?" he'd asked. Either the guy was a heck of an actor or he didn't know Lily or what she claimed to be.

There could be an explanation for that, of

course. Maybe the kidnappers were hired thugs, and Lily's connection was to whoever had hired them to grab the girl. Paul Leonardi? McBride had watched Leonardi closely at the funeral home. When he'd approached Lily, it had seemed like a first-time meeting.

Gerald Blackledge? He'd made a point to talk to Lily at the funeral. And what kind of man would commandeer a solemn occasion to score political points? A man who thought abducting a little girl would drive her father out of the senatorial race?

McBride's belly burned like fire.

WHEN LILY WOKE, the clock on her dresser read 7:45 p.m. Around her, all was so quiet she wondered if McBride had given up and gone for the night. But when she padded barefoot to the kitchen, she found him sitting in one of the chairs facing the counter, where Jezebel perched like a stone statue, her blue eyes crossed in a baleful glare.

"I don't think she'd want you on the counter," McBride was telling the cat. "In fact, why don't you come over here and see me?"

Jezebel's eyes narrowed, but she didn't budge.

"Come on, kitty. Come see McBride. Come on," he crooned.

Lily bit back a chuckle of sympathy as Jezebel turned and started grooming herself.

McBride's voice dropped to a sexy rumble. "Got a big ol' lap here, puss. And I've been told I have talented hands. You don't know what you're missing."

A quiver rippled down Lily's spine.

"Oh, I see, you like playin' hard to get. You must be a female." McBride sat back and propped one ankle on the opposite knee. "That's okay. I'm a patient man. I can wear you down."

Lily decided to end the standoff before his sexy drawl melted her into a puddle in the kitchen doorway. "You're trying to seduce the wrong woman."

The detective's head whipped around in surprise.

"Jezzy hates everyone but me. It drives my sister Rose crazy." Lily picked up the cat and cuddled her a moment, smiling at his flummoxed expression when Jezebel melted in her arms, butting her face against Lily's chin.

She set her on the floor. "Delilah's the pushover."

As if Lily had spoken a command, Delilah entered the kitchen, tail twitching, and wound herself around McBride's ankle. He reached down and scratched the cat's ears. Delilah rewarded him with a rumbling purr of pleasure.

"Better?" Lily sat across from him, glancing

at the loose sheets of notepaper littering her kitchen table.

He gave her a considering look, gathering up the papers. His short hair was mussed and spiky, softening the hard lines of his face. His presence filled her kitchen, branding every inch of space he occupied as his own.

And a traitorous part of her liked the idea that he belonged here. With her.

The corded muscles of his forearms rippled as he stacked the sheets in a neat pile in front of him. When he spoke, his voice was gruff. "Headache better?"

"Yeah." Awareness shuddered through her, a magnet drawing her toward him. She'd already leaned his way when she caught herself. She rose from the table, wishing she hadn't closed the distance between them. "Have you eaten dinner?"

"No. Didn't realize what time it was."

She pulled sliced turkey, cheese and a jar of mayonnaise from the refrigerator. "I can make you a sandwich."

The legs of his chair scraped against the tile floor. She felt his body heat flow over her a second before he put his hand on her shoulder. "Sit down. I'll fix it."

She turned toward him, caught off guard when he didn't step back. Her gaze settled on the full

lower lip that kept his mouth from looking unap-
proachably stern. His square jaw was dark with a
day's growth of beard. If he bent his head now and
touched his cheek to hers, how would it feel?

Her legs shook as if she'd run for miles, and her
skin felt itchy and tight. She wished she could
blame her shivers on the events of the afternoon,
but she knew better.

Unlike Jezebel, she was beginning to find
McBride nearly irresistible. Much to her alarm.

His grip on her shoulder loosened, though he
didn't drop his hand away. His thumb brushed
across her clavicle, sending tremors pulsing along
her nerves. The moment stretched taut, the tension
between them exquisite. Her breath caught in her
throat, her lips trembling in anticipation of the
moment when he'd finally bend his head and end
the torture.

McBride's expression shifted and he stepped
back from her, looking away. "Where's the bread?"

She waved her hand toward the bread box and
retreated to the kitchen table. "Has Mr. Walters
had a chance to hear the tape?" she asked.

"He didn't recognize the voice."

"Why'd the kidnapper call me? I just met
Andrew Walters a couple of days ago. Abby isn't
even in my class at school." She allowed herself
a quick peek at McBride.

He put bread out on the counter and quickly started making a sandwich. "Good question. Any ideas?"

The hard tone of his voice made her wince inwardly. "No."

He set the sandwich on a napkin in front of her and took the chair opposite.

"Not eating?" she asked.

"Not hungry." He cocked his head, pinning her to her chair with the force of his gaze. She stared back at him, her breath trapped in her chest.

His features were too rough-hewn to be considered handsome. But he had amazing eyes, intense, clear and commanding. Their color shifted with his moods, almost brown when he was lost in thought, nearly green when he was working up a rage.

She wondered what color they turned in the heat of passion.

Trying to shake off the effect he'd begun to have on her, Lily leaned toward him across the table. "You obviously have questions for me. Let's have 'em."

"You had another vision?" His voice had a rumbling quality that made the skin on the back of her neck quiver. "Of Abby?"

She struggled to concentrate. "Yes. I think she was in a mobile home. The windows had metal frames and sills. And the room was tiny, with that boxy, prefab look some trailers have."

His gaze was dark and intense, impossible to read. "Anything that would help us identify it?"

"No. I only saw one room, and it was…ordinary." Though she tried to drop her gaze, she found herself unable to look away from him. He had a commanding quality about him, an air of strength and capability that elicited a primal response deep inside her.

It had been a long time since a man had made her feel this much like a woman. Why did it have to be McBride?

When he didn't respond right away, she felt herself begin to squirm, like a suspect under interrogation. She was pretty sure that was the point of his continuing silence.

"There was one thing—" She clamped her mouth shut before she revealed the odd appearance of the second girl. McBride obviously didn't believe she was having visions of Abby. Lily wasn't going to make things worse by mentioning a second child.

"One thing?" he prodded when she didn't continue.

"She talked to me this time."

He pulled back, his eyebrows twitching upward.

"I know it sounds crazy, but she heard me. She talked back. That's never happened before."

Maybe because Lily had spent most of her life running from the visions, she'd never really explored the limits of her ability. She still couldn't think of it as a gift, not like her sisters'.

"You get migraines when you have visions?"

"Except when I don't fight them."

He picked up a pencil and grabbed a fresh sheet of paper. He jotted something on the page in his tight, illegible scrawl. "That's right. You mentioned something like that before you zoned out."

"Before I had a vision."

"Uh, yeah." He twirled the pencil between his fingers. "You said you fight them because they scare you."

She swallowed hard. "Yes."

"How long have you been having visions?"

"Of Abby?"

He shook his head. "In general."

"Since I was little." The visions had been part of her life for as long as she could remember.

"And you've always had headaches?"

"Not always." Before her father died, she'd never had the headaches. But before then, she'd never had to fear her visions, either. "When I was younger, I didn't have headaches. But I didn't know to fight the visions."

For the first time he looked genuinely surprised. "They didn't scare you then? Why not?"

A flash of blood on jagged steel flashed through her mind. She closed her eyes, pushing it down into the dark place inside her. "I hadn't seen the bad things yet."

"Like what?" His voice lowered to a murmur. "Monsters?"

Was he making fun of her? He looked serious, so she answered. "I see people hurt. Killed. People in pain."

People like her father, bleeding to death on a bed of bloodstained sawdust...

"How do you know you don't have headaches when you don't fight the visions?"

"I had one the other day and didn't fight it. I didn't have any pain at all."

He cocked his head. "How can you know that's why?"

She sighed. "I suppose I can't. Does it matter? I'm going to keep trying to have them even if they hurt."

"Why would you put yourself through that?"

"Because Abby's still alive. I can still help her."

McBride looked at Lily for a tense moment. "Why are you having visions of Abby Walters? Why you in particular?"

"I don't know." The suspicion in his voice made her stomach cramp.

"When did they start?"

"Friday, at the school." The memory of those

first brief glimpses of Abby remained vivid. Frightened blue eyes. Tearstained cheeks. Tangled red hair. A terrified cry.

"Did you have the vision before or after you talked to me?" McBride touched the back of her hand, trailing his fingers over her skin, painting her with fire.

She swallowed with difficulty, resisting the urge to beg him to touch her again. "Before."

A muscle in his jaw twitched. "How soon before?"

"Just before, I guess."

He met her gaze for a long, electric moment, his eyes now a deep forest-green. "What did you see that first time?"

She related the brief snatches of that vision, then told him about later seeing Abby in the car. "I think they were moving her to wherever they are now."

He tapped his fingers on the table mere inches from her hand. She watched them move, wishing they would touch her again. Her fingers itched to close the distance between them, but she resisted, forcing herself to look up at him, away from that tempting hand. But the smoldering emerald of his eyes did little to cool the heat starting to build inside her.

She licked her lips and tried to focus. "Is it

against the rules for you to tell me how Abby's mother died?"

He didn't answer.

"I don't need details, I just…" She sighed, trying to explain the sensations she'd felt when talking to the kidnapper. "The man who called was desperate. I know he made a ransom demand, and maybe that's what they wanted all along. But I don't think they originally planned on a ransom call."

McBride cut his eyes toward her.

"He sounded scared. This wasn't how it was supposed to happen. Mrs. Walters wasn't supposed to die."

He caught her wrist. "Why do you say that?" His voice was tinged with suspicion, his eyes turning mossy brown.

"She fought, right?" Lily couldn't say how she knew that, but she did. "They didn't think she'd fight them. Maybe they don't have children of their own and don't know what a mother will do when her child's in danger."

He let go of her, but the heat of his touch lingered. She rubbed her wrist, trying to wipe away the tingling sensation his grip had imprinted in the tender flesh, as if every nerve ending had suddenly come alive. "That's how it happened, isn't it?" she asked.

He leaned toward her across the small table,

close enough for her to breathe in his warm, spicy scent. "Why are you really interested in this case?"

She lifted her chin. "I keep seeing that scared little girl in my mind. I have to try to help her."

"You can't," he said bluntly.

"Why not?" she asked.

"Because she's already dead."

Sharp-edged and stone-cold, his words slammed into Lily like a physical blow. She shook her head. "That's not true. The kidnappers just called—"

"What makes you think it wasn't a crank call?"

"I recognized the voice."

"So you say."

Lily shut her eyes, wishing she could shut out his words as easily. "I know it was him."

"I've been a cop for sixteen years. I've investigated five nonparental child abductions over that time." Weariness crept into his matter-of-fact tone. "Kidnappers don't take five days to make a ransom call. They know it gives the cops too much time to get involved."

Lily opened her eyes but saw nothing but blackness. A soft, pain-wracked voice filled the darkness. *She's gone!*

The darkness dissipated, the familiar decor of her kitchen coming back into focus, the echo of those two heartbroken words fading into the hum of the refrigerator behind her. Lily found McBride staring at her, his forehead creased with a frown.

He rose, his chair scraping against the tile floor. "I've put a patrol car outside to keep an eye on this place tonight. Tomorrow, with your permission, we'll tap your phone in case the man calls again." He didn't wait for her answer, making it halfway to the living room by the time Lily got her legs to work.

She followed him to the door, still shaking from the brief vision. Where had that woman's voice come from, pitched low with misery? Coming as it had in the wake of McBride's bitter words, was it connected to his own demons?

He had demons, without a doubt. Beneath his stony calm, Lily had sensed a misery so deep, so dark she could hardly bear to look at it.

She grabbed his arm as he opened the front door. "What if I don't want a tap on my phone?"

"Don't you want us to find out who's calling?" He stood close enough for her to see beard stubble shadowing his jaw. She could almost feel it, prickly against her skin, as if he'd rubbed his face against hers. His pupils were black pools rimmed by moss. Pure female response snaked through her belly, settling low and hot at her center.

"I'd also like to tap your cell phone," he added softly.

Right. Tapping the phone. "It's not listed

anywhere by my cellular company. But you can tap my home phone."

He didn't look happy, but he didn't press the issue. He stepped away from her and onto her front stoop, robbing her of his warmth. Her strength seeped away, leaving her enervated and bone-weary.

He turned back to her, danger glittering in his murky eyes. "You're playing a reckless game, Ms. Browning. Take care."

She watched him stride down the walk, his jacket flapping in the cool night breeze, every heavy thud of her heart echoing his solemn warning. The intent of his words may have been different than her own interpretation, but the truth remained: the people who had Abby knew who Lily was and where she lived.

She wasn't safe in her own home.

Chapter Six

Andrew Walters was on his cell phone when Lily arrived at his hotel suite Thursday afternoon for their rescheduled meeting. He took her raincoat and waved her in, slanting her a rueful look as he spoke into the receiver. "We'll have to blow that one off. The county party chairman will understand." He gestured at the sofa, moving into one of the rooms off the main living area to complete his call.

Lily bypassed the sofa and walked to the picture window spanning one wall of the living area. During the day, the McMillan Place penthouse suite would boast a panoramic view of the lush woodlands west of town, but rain and falling darkness turned the window into a mirror reflecting Lily's own bedraggled image back at her. She patted her rain-curled hair and straightened her skirt, wishing she looked more presentable.

It was important that Andrew Walters believe what she had to tell him.

He returned to the room, flashing an apologetic smile. "That was my campaign manager, Joe. We have to figure out how to manage the campaign while all of this is going on."

Lily tried to hide her surprise. She'd have thought the election would be the last thing on Andrew's mind.

"You think that's cold of me." He sounded resigned.

"No," she replied.

"People have invested a lot of time and money in my campaign. For their sakes, I have to go through the motions." He beckoned for her to join him in the sitting area. "It's good to have something constructive to focus on, to keep my mind away from the worst possibilities."

She sat where he indicated. "Understandable."

He sank into an armchair and slanted a considering look at her. "The FBI told me about the call from the kidnapper. Why do you think he called you?"

If Andrew Walters harbored the same suspicions as Lieutenant McBride, he hid it well. He looked desperate and anxious, but he didn't seem distrustful.

Lily wished she had a better answer for both of them. "I guess they saw my picture in the paper. From the funeral. My name was in the caption, and I don't imagine there are that many Lily

Brownings listed in the Borland phone book." It was the only explanation that made sense.

"I wonder how the press got your name in the first place."

She cocked her head. "I assumed you gave it to them."

"No." His eyes narrowed. "Probably Blackledge. He knew people would see us together and make assumptions. 'Andrew Walters didn't even let his first wife's body get cold before he found someone else.'"

She grimaced. "People won't think that."

He gave her a look that made her feel very naive.

She shook her head, appalled. "If my being there—"

"This is politics. Dirt gets flung. I'm becoming a little better at ducking these days." His face tightened with anxiety. "McBride says you've had visions of my daughter. What did you see?"

She told him what she'd seen in her visions, holding back only the appearance of the second little girl. Andrew Walters listened, his hands clenched in his lap, his sharp-eyed gaze moving over her face as if gauging her veracity. "What was she wearing?" he asked when she finished.

For a second, Lily's mind went blank. She remembered so much about Abby—the way she smelled, the tear tracks down her dirty, freckled face, the way one red curl hung just off center over her forehead. But what she was wearing?

Lily closed her eyes, recreating the most vivid scene, the one where Abby had been huddled in the back of the moving car. She heard the hum of the motor, smelled the musty odor of the blanket under which the child had crouched, cold and afraid. She saw the messy red curls, the chattering teeth.

The light blue overalls with a yellow rabbit on the front.

"Overalls." Her voice shook. "Pale blue with a yellow bunny on the bib. And she had a long-sleeved white turtleneck underneath."

When Lily looked up, Andrew's face had gone pale. His voice shook when he spoke. "My God, you *did* see her."

She released a shaky breath. She'd been afraid she was wrong, that her visions really were delusions, as McBride apparently thought. "That's what she was wearing?"

The man nodded, color slowly seeping back into his face. "A neighbor who saw her Friday morning remembered the outfit. She'd bought it for Abby on her last birthday."

"So you believe me?"

Andrew reached across the space between them and took her hand. His expression solemn, he nodded. "I believe you."

Relief swamped her. "Mr. Walters, I'll do whatever I can to help you."

He managed a smile. "Thank you. And please, call me Andrew."

She nodded. "Andrew—"

The shrill ring of the telephone interrupted her, the sound jarring her spine.

"The dedicated line." Andrew's voice sounded strangled.

"Answer it," she urged, breathless. Her nerves were so taut that she didn't recognize the signs until gray mist invaded the edge of her vision.

As the fog thickened, she glimpsed a man hunched over a phone in a dim room. She barely made out dark green walls and a computer nearby. The man's blond hair was thin and patchy, and his skin was milky pale. The glow of the computer screen made twin blue squares on the lenses of his wire-rimmed glasses.

It was the caller, she realized when he spoke.

"Mr. Walters, listen quick." Lily was certain she'd never heard the voice before. It definitely wasn't the harsh-voiced man who'd hit Abby, the one who'd called her home on Wednesday.

"Who is this?" Andrew demanded.

"We have your daughter."

"Is Abby there?" Andrew's voice was like a fly buzzing in her ear, oddly unreal, even though he was in the same room with her. "Let me speak to her!"

"You have until tomorrow afternoon to get five hundred grand together. When you do that, you'll talk to your kid. Got it? And if you call the cops, you'll never see your kid again." The caller shifted, his desk chair creaking.

Beyond him, Lily saw a bed with rumpled green sheets. A newspaper lay near the pillows. Abby Walters's freckled face stared up from its front page. But there was no sign of Abby. And the room didn't remotely resemble the one where she'd seen the little girl in her visions.

"I'll call back tomorrow to tell you where to drop the money." The caller's hand shook as he clutched the phone.

He's not one of the kidnappers, Lily thought. *They know not to call Andrew Walters directly.*

She struggled against the swallowing mists, trying to slam shut the door of her mind. She'd seen all she needed to see. She had to tell Mr. Walters what she knew.

She emerged with a jolt when he banged the telephone receiver into its cradle and bent over the table, sucking in several deep, steadying breaths.

Lily stumbled to the couch and sat, pressing her hand to her head. Fighting to end the vision before it was finished had a price; colorful lights crowded her vision, and the first twinge of pain shot up from the base of her skull. She fumbled in her purse for her pills and swallowed one dry, laying her head back against the sofa cushions.

Andrew turned to face her. "He wouldn't let me talk to her." Anxiety creased his handsome face.

"He doesn't have her." Lily lifted her eyes to meet his, hating to burst his tiny bubble of hope. She told him what she could remember about the vision. "It was a hoax. I'm sorry."

Andrew sank to the sofa next to her and buried his face in his hands. She touched his shoulder, unsure how to comfort him.

Someone rapped on the door. Andrew went to let two detectives into the room. "He wasn't on long enough for a trace, and his caller ID's blocked," one of them said.

Lily was no longer listening. She drifted on a river of pain, barely aware of the voices of the detectives talking or the trill of Andrew's cell phone when his campaign manager called back. Andrew's voice faded as he took the call in another room.

She wasn't sure how much time passed before a new voice roused her from her pain-washed daze. She struggled up from the depths of the soft couch and opened her eyes.

Detective McBride's stormy eyes stared back.

McBRIDE CROUCHED in front of Lily, trying to be angry. But she looked ready to collapse. Purple smudges bruised her eyes—headache, he guessed. "Walters says you think it's a hoax."

She hugged herself. The room was warm, but chill bumps dotted her bare arms. "I wish he'd kept that to himself."

"Why?" McBride lowered his voice to a gentle murmur.

Her eyes narrowed. "Aren't you angry I'm here?"

Tiny lines etched the skin around her eyes and mouth. Pain lines. He couldn't stop himself from touching a tiny crease in her forehead, gently smoothing it. "You have a headache?"

Her eyes drifted closed and she nodded, turning her head to give his fingers better access. Her body arched toward him, like a kitten responding to a gentle caress.

He dropped his hand with difficulty. "What did you do, fight your vision?"

Her eyes fluttered open. "I wanted to tell Andrew Walters about the hoax as quickly as possible." She stumbled over some of the words, as if she couldn't quite make them all fit together. "I fought to leave the vision before it was through."

And paid the price, he thought, then chided himself for letting himself get sucked into her delusion. Whatever had caused her headache, it damn well wasn't a psychic vision.

But she was right about the call being a hoax. Though smart enough to block his caller ID and keep his call too short for a trace, the man had blown it by not getting his business done in one shot.

Tomorrow he'd phone back and they'd get him.

"Can I go home now?" Lily leaned forward, bracing her hands on the sofa cushion. McBride stood to give her room to rise, but she moved faster than he did. Their bodies touched for a long, electric moment before he backed out of her way.

Maybe she *was* a witch, he thought, his body responding to her presence like fire to oxygen. He seemed entirely at her mercy, no matter how he tried to fight it. "Are you okay to drive?"

"I'm fine. The medicine's already working. And don't worry, officer. It's the non-drowsy formula." She gazed up at him, her eyes wide and glowing in the lamplight. Her body swayed toward him before she pulled herself up and slid past him, moving toward the door. McBride remained where he was, watching with clenched jaw as Andrew Walters closed his hand around Lily's arm and bent toward her, their faces intimately close as they spoke. Walters's grasp on Lily's arm became a gentle stroking, almost like a lover's caress.

McBride's chest tightened with anger.

"Lieutenant?"

McBride tore his attention away from Lily and Walters to look at the detective who'd contacted him after the call.

"Do you want to take the tape with you or do you want me to bag it and send it by courier?" the detective repeated.

"Courier," McBride answered.

As the two technicians headed out, McBride's eyes swung back to the door.

But Lily was gone.

He crossed to Walters. "You okay?"

Walters blinked as if startled. "Yeah. It's all just so crazy. Some creep playing with our minds." He shook his head. "How could someone do that?"

It's a big, bad world out there, McBride thought. Bigger and badder all the time. "We can't be sure it's a hoax."

"Lily's sure of it. That's good enough for me."

McBride's stomach sank as he dropped his hand from the other man's shoulder. "You know, Mr. Walters, we can't know for certain without a thorough investigation. I know Ms. Browning seems confident of everything she says, but—"

"She doesn't seem confident. I'd worry more if she did. But she's been right about everything so far."

"Like what?"

"She knew what Abby was wearing the day she disappeared."

McBride shook his head. "That was reported in the paper."

"Not the yellow rabbit."

"She knew about the rabbit?" Acid gushed into McBride's gut. The police had released a description of Abby's clothing—the blue overalls and white shirt—but held back the yellow rabbit decal to divide the crank calls from the genuine tips.

If Lily Browning had really described what Abby had been wearing, there was only one way she could have known.

She'd seen Abby Walters the morning she disappeared.

And he'd just let a person of interest walk out the door.

Chest tight with growing anger, McBride moved toward the exit. "I'm going to head out now and let our technicians handle things. Are you going to be okay?"

Walters looked exhausted. "I just want my daughter back."

"We'll find her." McBride heard the words, recognized his own voice, but couldn't believe what he'd said. He'd been raging at Lily Browning for giving Walters false hope, and here he was, adding his own lies to the mix.

He didn't believe the real kidnappers would call again, because Abby Walters was dead. Too much time had passed, with no sightings, and no clues but a harsh voice on Lily Browning's answering machine. Who knew whether that phone call was the real thing or just another of Lily's lies?

But he couldn't say that to Walters. Not yet. The man had to go through this part of the journey, the hopeful part. Next would come uncertainty, then despair, then the black anger that churned in the gut like a feeding frenzy of piranhas.

McBride didn't know what came after that.

AVOIDING THE CONGESTED perimeter highway, Lily took Black Creek Road home. It was a longer drive, but the winding road was lightly traveled, especially on a rainy night, and Lily was in no state of mind to deal with heavy traffic.

At least the migraine was almost gone.

But McBride's touch lingered like a fiery brand on her skin. She could still conjure up the tang of his aftershave, the intensity of his gaze sweeping over her as if he wanted to strip her bare of her defenses and find out what lay underneath.

Idiot. Trying to guess McBride's thoughts was a fool's game. If he thought of her at all, it was as a calculating con artist taking advantage of a wealthy but vulnerable man.

Whimsy wasn't Lily's style. She wasn't the fanciful sister; that was Rose, the hopeless romantic. She wasn't impulsive and daring like Iris, either. Lily was the eldest, the one with her head screwed on firmly. The one who'd taken care of her younger sisters when their mother died six years ago.

Lily didn't form ridiculous crushes on men who'd never return her feelings.

Mentally she dusted her hands of him. Done.

Her cell phone trilled, making her jump. She dug in her purse with her right hand and pulled out the phone. "Hello?"

"You never call, you never write." Her sister Rose's husky voice always reminded Lily of their mother. Iris, with her ebony hair and black-coffee eyes, looked the most like their mother, but Rose had her voice, low and just a little raspy, with a slow, sweet drawl that stretched her words like taffy.

"I talked to Iris just the other day."

"I always knew you liked her better," Rose said lightly. "I had a dream about you last night, Lil."

"Yeah?" Lily slowed her car as she approached Dead Man's Curve, where Black Creek Road formed a deep *S* as it followed the winding creek for a couple of miles.

"Yeah. Have you met a new man recently?"

McBride's rugged face flashed through mind. "Why?"

"Because you're going to fall in love with him."

A shiver ran down Lily's back. She ignored it, pressing her lips into a tight line. "Am not."

"Well, you also help him find his daughter. I'm not clear on whether you do that before you fall in love or after."

"Now I know you didn't dream that. Iris told you about my visions." Tucking her phone between chin and shoulder, Lily put both hands on the steering wheel as she navigated a sharp curve.

"Yes, she did, but I really did have the dream."

"Well, you're wrong on this occasion," Lily said firmly. "I've spent time with the little girl's father, and I assure you the last thing he's thinking about is falling in love."

Rose sighed. "It was a great dream. You were in the woods. There was a building with rickety wood steps. There he was—this incredible man, his arm around a little girl. He turned to look at you, and wow." Rose's voice dwindled to a contented sigh. "You were so in love with each other. It gave me chills."

Hair rose on the back of Lily's neck. If anybody but Rose were telling her these things, she'd laugh it off. But Rose's gift, predicting a successful love match, was as strong as Lily's, and much better developed. Still, Lily couldn't see herself with Andrew Walters. "What did this guy look like?"

"All I remember is dark hair."

"What about the girl?" Lily asked, thinking about Abby.

"I don't remember anything except she had big dark eyes that lit up when she saw you."

An image popped into Lily's head—of the dark-haired child at the edge of her vision of Abby. Lily shivered. Too creepy.

"So tell me about these visions you've been having."

Lily told her everything, including her new-found ability to make contact with Abby.

"She heard you? Cool! Any closer to finding her?"

Lily sighed. "I hope so. I'm worried, Rose. She's so scared. I feel helpless." She took a deep breath. "And during my last vision of Abby, I saw another little girl."

"The kidnappers have another little girl?" Rose asked.

"I don't think so. I think the little girl is somewhere else. Maybe nearby, though." Having spent so much of her life running from her visions, Lily had never figured out how they worked. Did the appearance of the new little girl have anything to do with Abby's kidnapping? Did the other child even exist, or was she a figment of Lily's imagination?

Maybe it was just a one-time thing. A fluke.

Crossed wires or whatever you called mixed-up psychic signals.

"I've gotta run, Lil—Iris is in the cellar boiling her eye of newt and I think I just heard something explode." The humor in Rose's voice assured Lily that her baby sister was exaggerating. "Don't be a stranger, okay?"

Lily laughed. The sound startled her. How long had it been since she'd heard herself laugh? "If there's still a house left by the time you and Iris get through with it, I'll definitely be home for Thanksgiving."

As she ended the call with her sister, she noticed headlights flickering in her rearview mirror.

HE GRIPPED THE STEERING wheel, his palms sweating inside his leather driving gloves. In the darkness ahead, all he could see of Lily Browning's car was a pair of taillights glowing like red eyes. He pressed the accelerator to the floor, eating up the road between them.

She knew too much. Saw too much.

She would ruin everything.

He was close enough to make out the shiny chrome bumper of her Buick and the rectangular sticker with Westview Elementary School printed in white block letters on a field of red.

A schoolteacher, he thought. Panicked laughter

rose in his throat. The most dangerous woman in his world was a bloody schoolteacher. How had this happened? How had everything gone so wrong so quickly?

No matter. It was going to end here.

Now.

WITH THE ON-RAMP to the perimeter highway backed up for more than a block, McBride went with a hunch and took Black Creek Road to avoid the snarl of traffic. If he was lucky, Lily Browning had taken the highway and he'd be sitting at her house waiting for her when she arrived. If not, he had a good chance of catching up with her on the winding back road.

Grabbing his cell phone, he called Theo Baker's direct line. "Call a meeting of the task force for first thing in the morning. I've had a copy of the phone call couriered over—"

"Right here in my hot little hands."

"Great. Get tech services to make a copy for everyone on the task force. Let's see if anybody recognizes the voice."

"Still think it's a hoaxer?"

"Ninety-nine percent sure." *But it's that one percent that could bite you in the ass,* McBride thought as he ended the call.

The weather was worsening; fog rising to meet

the pouring rain that was already cutting visibility to a few yards. McBride peered into the darkness, easing off the accelerator as he approached Dead Man's Curve. Rain sheeted across the blacktop and pounded his windshield, keeping pace with the wipers.

Ahead, two glowing red dots pierced the gloom. Taillights, he realized. Lily's car? Accelerating, he kept his eyes on the lights. As the road straightened for a long stretch, the taillights doubled. He squinted, trying to make sense of what he was seeing. Now two sets of lights traveled side by side on the two-lane road. One car passing a slower one?

Suddenly, both cars jerked violently to the right. His heart sped up. Was that a collision?

His cell phone trilled, sending his taut nerves jangling. He grabbed it and thumbed the talk button. "McBride."

"Lieutenant, this is Alli with Dispatch. You asked us to flag any call that came in from cell phone number 555-3252."

Lily's number.

"We've got a Lily Browning on with a 911 operator. She says another car is trying to run her off the road."

"What's her twenty?" On the road ahead, the pairs of taillights took another jarring lurch to the right.

"Black Creek Road, a mile before Five Mile Crossing."

McBride's heart jolted into high gear. He jammed his foot on the accelerator, ignoring the shimmy of the Chevy's tires on the slick blacktop.

Suddenly, the taillights ahead disappeared from view. McBride's breath caught. It took a second to realize the dispatcher was calling his name. "Yeah?"

"Sir, we just lost contact."

Chapter Seven

Lily threw her dead cell phone into the passenger seat, wishing she'd plugged the adapter into the cigarette lighter before she'd left McMillan Place. At least she'd managed to give her location to the operator before her phone went dead.

Gripping the steering wheel, she braced as the car beside her slammed into her again, sending her sliding toward the shoulder. She steered with the skid, managing to right the car before it went over the drop off into the thick woods.

With no streetlamps on the lonely stretch of road, she could make out little about the other car or its driver. It was a dark sedan, an older model judging by its shape, with tinted windows that hid the occupant from view. Not being able to see who was driving her off the road only amplified her terror.

What if her assailant rammed her down the steep embankment into the trees? Would another passing driver be able to see her vehicle from the road? And what would her attacker do if she was trapped and vulnerable at the bottom of the embankment?

She couldn't help but think of Debra Walters and Abby, alone on a stretch of desolate road, with nothing to protect them from the carjackers but Debra's willingness to defend her daughter to the death.

Was the person behind those tinted windows the harsh-voiced man from her vision? He knew where she lived; could he have followed her to McMillan Place, waiting to make his move?

Around another curve, her headlights outlined the concrete rails of a bridge spanning a narrow gorge. Lily didn't have to be psychic to know the other driver would double his efforts to send her off the road once they reached the bridge. And if she went over the side into the creek, she'd never survive the fall.

She sped up as she hit the bridge, praying her tires would grip the slick pavement long enough to get her safely to the other side. Her acceleration caught her tormenter by surprise, forcing him to gun his engine to keep from falling behind.

Lily's tactic gave her enough of an edge to cross the bridge unmolested, but as she reached solid ground again, the dark sedan bumped against the back panel of her Buick and veered hard to the right. She had no chance to recover as her assailant's maneuver sent her car spinning across the slippery road.

She held on, trying to keep from sliding over the opposite shoulder, but the momentum was uncontrollable. The world became a blur of dark and light as the Buick hit the shoulder and lurched backward down the fifteen-foot embankment, crashing into a tree with a bone-jarring crunch.

Lily's head whipped forward and slammed back into the headrest, setting off a brief fireworks display behind her eyes. When the lights and colors faded, she forced herself to shake off the shock and take stock of her condition.

The trunk of the Buick had taken most of the impact of the collision with the tree, leaving the front part of her car in pretty good shape. Her airbag hadn't deployed, though her seat belt had done its job, holding her in place while her car plunged off the road. She'd be feeling the bruises from the shoulder strap for days, and her headache was back with a vengeance. Beyond that, all her moving parts worked and she hadn't really lost consciousness.

Shaking wildly, she cut the engine. Her windshield wipers stopped at half-mast, their rhythmic swish-swish abruptly silenced. The void was filled by the heavy drumbeat of rain on the roof and the low moan of wind in the trees behind her, a lonesome sound that amplified her sense of vulnerability tenfold.

She peered through the water sheeting on her windshield, trying to see the road. The maneuver that sent her spinning had been a risky move for the other car. Had it met its own fate on the opposite side of the road?

She leaned over and opened the glove compartment, scrabbling through the contents until she found the cell phone adapter. She'd feel safer once she got the 911 operator back on the phone.

But when she finally located her cell phone on the floorboard on the passenger side, its plastic skin lay cracked and askew, wires spilling out through the opening.

Thank God she'd already called for help before the phone went dead. But it would take time for anyone to find her on the long stretch of winding road. And if her attacker hadn't spun out the way she had—

Light suddenly slanted across her windshield, splintered into glittering facets by the driving rain. She peered through the downpour, her heart in her throat.

Two powerful beams sliced through the gloom at the top of the embankment. They were steady and stationary.

Whoever it was had parked on the shoulder.

Panic zigzagged through her belly. What should she do? Stay put? Try to get out and hide in the woods?

She couldn't risk the former; she might as well be a rat in a cage, waiting to be fed to a snake. Her shoes weren't made for trekking through the forest, but she didn't have to survive out there for long. She just had to hope help arrived before her assailant found her.

Opening her door was harder than she'd expected; the car had sunk into the mud, leaving precious little room to maneuver.

She squeezed through the opening, grabbing her raincoat as she stumbled through the sucking mud. She lost a shoe right off and had to waste time retrieving it, crouching low in hopes that the occupant of the car above hadn't spotted her yet in the foggy darkness.

She took off the other shoe and squished across the soggy ground until she was well hidden in the trees. Flattening herself against the rough bark of a towering pine, she peeked back up at the roadway.

A dark figure stood at the edge, his large body backlit by the high beams. He seemed to be gazing down toward her car, his hands curled into fists. Then he began loping down the embankment, taking little care as he slipped and slid on the slick grass.

She could make out only his shadow now, large and looming, so close that she could hear the ragged hiss of his breathing. Terror coiled like a viper in the pit of her belly, spreading poison until her body froze with fear.

When he jerked the driver's door open, the glow of her dome light rimmed his profile, revealing the familiar set of a square jaw and tension lines carved on either side of his mouth.

Her knees buckling with relief, Lily dug her fingers into the pine bark to keep from sliding to the ground. A soft whimper escaped her throat as a splinter dug into her palm. "McBride."

He whirled around, peering into the woods. "Lily?"

She willed her legs to hold her upright for the few uneven steps it took to reach the clearing where McBride stood. She couldn't see his expression, now that the light was at his back again, but she heard his soft exhalation, saw his shoulders sag for a second before he closed the distance between them in two long strides and gathered her into his arms.

She wrapped hers around his neck as he lifted her out of the wet grass and into his tight embrace. His pulse hammered against her breast, keeping pace with her own racing heart.

"Are you hurt?" He started to release her, but she

tightened her grip around his neck, shaking her head. He lifted one hand to tangle in her hair, brushing the rain-drenched mass away from her face.

"Are you sure?"

She nodded. "I'm going to be a little sore, I think. But nothing permanent."

He glanced over his shoulder at her battered car, then back at her. Now that her eyes were adjusting to the darkness, she could see the angry set of his jaw and the glitter of leashed violence in his eyes. "Who did this? Did you get a look at him?"

She tried to gather her wits, though the combination of delayed reaction and McBride's hard body pressed against hers made coherent thought difficult. "It was a dark four-door sedan with tinted windows. I couldn't see the driver at all."

He uttered a terse profanity. "I saw it happening—I was about a quarter mile back when he started ramming you. But I couldn't catch up in time."

"That was you?" The lights in her rearview mirror. The ones that had given her hope for a brief moment. She pressed her forehead against his throat, her fingers digging into the muscles of his shoulders as she realized just how easily her fate could have gone the other way.

"Did you see what happened to the other car?"

"All I saw was his taillights ahead. He must

have spotted me coming, and gunned it. When I saw the skid marks on the grassy shoulder here, I stopped to see if you were hurt." He ran his thumb down her cheek, letting it settle at the edge of her lower lip. His voice softened. "You're trembling."

She was. And as much as she'd like to attribute it to shock, the main thing sending shivers down her spine was McBride's body pressed hard and hot against hers.

His gaze dipped to her parted lips, his breath quickening. She could see the struggle on his face, the need to resist. The sharp edges of her own doubts nicked her conscience even as she lifted her chin and met his mouth halfway.

Fire raced through her veins, surprising her with its wild intensity. McBride's arm tightened around her back, pulling her closer. His other hand tangled in her wet hair, curling into a fist until she was ensnared in his grasp.

He took his time with the kiss, giving and demanding in equal parts, stoking the flames in her belly. His tongue brushed over her lower lip, tasting her. Teasing her.

A low moan of pleasure rumbled up her throat. He tightened his arms around her in response, lifting her off her feet. One hand slid down her back, settling low, pressing her hips firmly against the hard ridge of his erection. Heat flooded her, settling at her center, warming her from the inside out.

He lifted his mouth away only long enough to blaze a trail across her jawline and down the side of her throat, nipping and kissing a path across her collarbone. She melted against him, a shimmering onslaught of need flooding her veins.

At the first faint sound of sirens in the distance, she tightened her hold on his shoulders, not ready to let him go. But he broke the contact, gently setting her back on her feet and taking a step away, breathing hard and fast. His gaze locked with hers, wary and oddly vulnerable, as the sound of sirens grew, piercing the drumbeat of rain.

After an endless moment, he held out his hand. "Think you can make it back to the road if I help you?"

Nodding, she grasped it, wondering if he could feel the tremors still fluttering through her from the kiss.

His big palm enclosed hers. "Need anything from the car?"

"My purse."

He let go long enough to retrieve the bag, and handed it to her. Then he took her hand again and helped her up the steep incline.

As they reached the road, a police car and an EMT unit were pulling up behind McBride's idling car. The two medics immediately took charge, separating her from McBride and helping her onto a stretcher in the back of the truck while they looked her over for any possible injuries. She leaned forward to peer around them, not ready to let McBride out of her sight.

He stood a few feet away, bathed in a wide shaft of golden light pouring from the EMT vehicle. He met her gaze with a reassuring smile before moving away to talk to the uniformed officers waiting by his car.

She sank back on the stretcher and closed her eyes, her mouth still tingling from McBride's kiss.

McBRIDE'S WATCH READ four-fifteen when he woke in the predawn gloom of Lily Browning's living room. Her sofa was built for a woman, sturdy enough but small. Cozy. Definitely not the ideal bed for a man of his size.

The EMTs had reassured him that the purple marks from the seat belt were superficial. Lily had been a little shocky, but a hot shower, dry clothes and extra blankets on her bed had fixed that.

She'd fallen asleep in his car on the way home and had roused only long enough to shower and crawl into bed. When he'd checked on her a little after nine, she'd been fast asleep.

Rubbing the ache in his neck, McBride let his

eyes adjust to the pale glow of light from a street-lamp seeping through the thin curtains on Lily's front windows. He stretched his legs out in front of him, trying to find a more comfortable position.

He shouldn't have stayed. A police car was parked outside, manned by two perfectly capable officers. Hanging around all night was overkill.

Not to mention dangerous.

He'd kissed her. Not a gentle, comforting peck on the cheek to reassure her that she was safe, either. No, he'd gone for long, wet and greedy.

Worse still, she'd tasted just as he'd expected— sweet with a tangy edge, like wild honey. The curves and planes of her body had fit perfectly against his, soft and hot despite the cold rain drenching them both.

How had he let this happen? Even now he felt the tug of her calling to him, just beyond the closed door at the end of the hall. If he went to her bed, would she turn him away?

He rubbed the heels of his palms against his bleary eyes. He was insane. She was a suspect, for God's sake! The attack on her tonight didn't change the fact that she had information only the kidnappers and cops should have. How did she know what Abby had been wearing the day she disappeared?

Maybe she really did see Abby in her mind, a treacherous voice inside him whispered.

No. He knew better than that. He'd learned that lesson the hard way. But could the trembling woman who'd returned his kiss with a sweet passion that made his head spin really be involved with murder and kidnapping?

He sat forward, burying his head in his hands. The idea seemed almost as insane as the alternative.

But those didn't have to be the only choices, did they?

Maybe the truth lay somewhere in between.

LILY CURLED UP IN BED with her cats, somewhere between sleep and wakefulness. Though sleep had done wonders for her, she felt sore all over from her nerve-wracking ordeal. And below the twinges and aches lay a relentless hum of awareness, a disturbing reminder of how her world had tilted upside down again with one shattering kiss.

Why in the world had she let herself lose control that way? She couldn't trust McBride; he still thought she was involved in Abby Walters's kidnapping. Lily had seen it in his eyes the day before in Andrew's hotel suite. And even if his doubts hadn't built an impenetrable wall between them, the man himself posed a grave danger to her heart.

The more she learned about the detective, the less she knew. He was a man steeped in secrets. Terrible ones, if the darkness she'd felt from him that night in her kitchen meant anything. What if being around him opened her mind to whatever horrors lurked within him? Could she bear it?

She shivered, cold despite the blankets piled atop her. Delilah nestled closer, a hot little knot against her side, but the shivers grew stronger. The darkness of the bedroom had already begun changing color and texture before Lily realized that she was having another vision.

She opened the door in her mind, both eager and afraid to see what lay beyond. As she pushed forward through the thick fog, she felt a warning pain behind her eyes and forced herself to let the vision flow around her, carrying her at its own pace.

Eventually the mists cleared to reveal Abby Walters lying on the lumpy bed where Lily had found her in her last vision. The child slept fitfully, her pale eyelids twitching with a dream. She looked cleaner than before. Lily took a deep breath through her nose and smelled soap.

Somebody had given Abby a bath, she thought with faint relief. Maybe that meant they were trying to take care of her.

Unless...

A darker thought forced her mind to a horrible place. Abby, naked and vulnerable in the hands of the man—men?—who had brutally killed her mother. Nausea rose in Lily's throat, making her eyes sting with acrid tears.

"What did they do to you, baby?" She stroked Abby's cheek, her fingers tracing damp tear tracks.

"It's okay," a child's voice whispered, very close.

Lily whirled around.

The dark-haired girl from her earlier vision stood behind her, clad in yellow-striped pajamas a size too small for her. She clutched a ragged stuffed toy against her chest, something round and tattered, its furry green body worn and thin.

She smiled tentatively at Lily. "I watched her for you."

Chapter Eight

Lily felt as if she'd gone mad. "You watched her?"

The little girl nodded. "I know you can't always be here, so I check on her sometimes to make sure she's okay."

Lily's mind reeled, threatening to suck her back to reality. She forced herself to stay calm, let the vision hold her in its gossamer web. "Who are you?"

"Mama calls me Gina, but I don't think that's my name. She's not really my mama, you know. My real mama's dead."

Lily noticed the little girl was almost transparent, unlike Abby. She wasn't actually in the same room, Lily realized. She was somewhere else.

But where?

"I can't stay much longer." The girl began to fade.

Lily reached out, wondering if she could touch her. "Wait, Gina! Are you sure Abby's okay?"

The girl's image rippled. "Yes."

Before Lily could move, the dark-haired girl was gone.

Lily slowly turned back to Abby. The child's eyelids had stopped fluttering and her soft, snuffling breath was even and deep. Relief trickled through Lily as she watched the child's peaceful slumber, until the fog began to swirl around her, drawing her back to the doorway.

She reached out to stroke Abby's cheek again before the door in her mind closed, hiding the child from her sight.

Emerging from the fog, Lily sat upright in the bed, hugging herself with trembling arms. The face of the dark-haired child remained etched in her mind, pale, heart-shaped, and so, so sad.

She shivered. Who was this solemn little girl?

BLUE MOONLIGHT BATHED the bedroom. The little girl blinked as she emerged from the haze to find herself huddled in bed.

She looked around quickly, just to reassure herself that she was back in her own room. She clutched Mr. Green more tightly to her, rubbing her cheek against his threadbare fur. Straining her ears, she listened for Mama. But the house was silent.

She pulled the covers more tightly around herself and stared at the cracked ceiling. She knew something was wrong with her mother. In her little-girl wisdom, she also knew Mama's trouble had something to do with her.

Mama called her Gina, but that wasn't her name. She was Casey. She had vague memories of someone calling her name. "Casey, baby, come here." The voice was deep. A man's voice. She liked the way it sounded, a little gruff but tender.

She knew the voice belonged to her daddy, but she barely remembered him. Only Mama, for just about as long as she recalled. The fuzzy memories that came at night, memories of being held in Daddy's strong arms, were little more than dreams.

Sweet dreams.

Nestled under the covers, Casey felt sleep creeping up on her. She closed her eyes, picturing Lily, the nice lady who was taking care of Abby. Casey smiled in the dark.

That smile carried her softly into sleep.

LILY OVERSLEPT, waking with bright morning sunlight slanting through her bedroom window. The digital alarm clock read seven twenty-five. She was going to be late for work.

She sat up quickly, gasping as pain rocketed through her entire body before settling in a hot ache in the back of her neck. Okay, work was out.

She reached for her phone and called Carmen Herrera's office number. "Carmen, it's Lily. I'm so sorry, I overslept and I haven't even had a chance—"

"Lily, thank God you're okay!" Carmen interrupted. "Lieutenant McBride called me this morning to let me know about the accident so I could arrange for a substitute for your classes. He said you were a little banged up."

Lily glanced at her reflection in the dresser mirror. Shadows circled her eyes, almost as dark as the vivid bruises slanting across her shoulder and chest where the shoulder belt had left its mark. "I'm a little bruised and sore, but I should be fine by Monday. Thanks for getting someone to fill in."

She hung up the phone and eased her sore legs over the edge of the bed. Jezebel glided in from the hall and wrapped herself around Lily's ankles, meowing.

"I bet you're hungry, aren't you, Jezzy?" She put on a bathrobe and hobbled down the hall to the kitchen, wondering if McBride had already left for the office.

But he was waiting in her kitchen, the morning paper spread out in front of him, a mug of steaming coffee sitting to one side. He looked up when she entered. "The nice cat has been fed. The psycho one refused to eat anything I gave her."

Lily glanced at the four open cans of cat food on the counter, her lips curving with amusement.

She picked up the tuna, Jezebel's favorite, and emptied it in one of the cat bowls. Jezebel went straight to it and started eating.

"Spoiled brat," McBride murmured.

"Thank you for calling in for me." Lily poured herself a cup of coffee and joined McBride at the table before taking a sip. Strong and hot, the coffee burned going down, making her eyes water.

"I figured you'd be too sore from the accident to deal with a bunch of eight-year-olds." His gaze dropped to her throat. "Do those bruises hurt much?"

"Not too much." She lifted a hand to her neck. He was being too nice to her. It made her feel self-conscious.

"I hope you don't mind, but I found your sisters' phone number in your address book and called to let them know you'd been in an accident. I talked to the one named Rose."

Lily bit back a smile at the look on his face. Two minutes on the phone with Rose had probably confused the hell out of him. Her ebullient sister was Lily's polar opposite.

Her smile faded. It hadn't always been that way.

"She said she would be here before noon."

Lily frowned. "I don't need a babysitter."

His expression became shuttered. "She insisted. Besides, I've got to get out of here soon—I have a meeting at nine. I've called for a patrol to come by your house every thirty minutes, just in case there's any trouble."

She set her coffee cup down, her stomach clenching. "Are you expecting trouble?"

He gave her a considering look. "You tell me."

Ah, there was the McBride she knew. Suspicious by nature. "I didn't imagine the phone call from the kidnapper. You heard him. You also saw that car run me off the road. Unless you think I arranged that, too?"

His only answer was a slight narrowing of his eyes.

"Because it makes so much sense to risk life and limb on the off chance that you left Andrew Walters's hotel room right after I did, and took the same detour I took."

"Well, you do claim to be a psychic," he pointed out.

"I don't claim to *be* anything." She picked up her coffee cup and took it to the sink, emptying the dark liquid down the drain. She'd had about all she could take of McBride and his coffee for one day. "All I've ever said is that I see things other people don't."

"Potato, potah-to," he murmured in her ear.

She turned and found him inches away. "What do you want from me?" Her own voice came out soft as a whisper.

His half smile faded. "I want you to stay away from Andrew Walters. His life is turned upside down, and he's clinging to anything that'll make his world stop shaking. Including you."

"What are you suggesting?"

"Walters thinks you can find his daughter. That makes you the most important person in his life right now."

Lily frowned, not liking what he was implying. "Look, I know you didn't like finding me at Mr. Walters's hotel, but I assure you—"

"What do you think will happen to Walters if you don't deliver Abby in the end?" McBride asked.

A flicker of uncertainty ran through her. What if she couldn't? Was she giving the man false hope?

"You're telling Andrew Walters that his little girl is all right, that there's still a chance he'll find her again. Do you really know that?" McBride edged closer. "What happens if tomorrow we find Abby's body in a ditch somewhere? How much harder is that going to be for the man?"

Her throat tightened, his soft words painting vivid pictures in her mind. "Stop it."

McBride suddenly looked tired. "I don't mean to hurt you, Lily. But there are too damn many odds against her." His voice was so flat and faraway, she hardly recognized it. "So please, don't give Walters any false encouragement. Okay?"

"Am I supposed to pretend I never heard of Abby Walters?" Tears blurred Lily's vision. "She's a scared little girl who saw her mommy die, and now she's all alone with two very bad men. I won't abandon her in that dark place."

McBride took a deep breath. "Then come to me instead of Walters. Tell *me* about your visions."

Wariness flitted through her. "Tell you?"

"I promise I'll look into everything you tell me." He looked queasy, but his gaze remained steady.

"Mr. Walters expects me to stay in touch."

"I'll tell him you're part of my investigation and you'll be reporting to me now." McBride took a step back. "Deal?"

She licked her lips, realizing that he'd just played her—and that it had worked. She would do what he asked. "You won't ignore what I tell you?"

"I'll follow every lead you give me."

She put her hand over her mouth, wondering if she was making a mistake. But when she dropped her hand, it was to say, "Okay, it's a deal."

The look of satisfaction in his eyes made her immediately regret giving in so easily. But she quelled her doubts; she could always break her end of the deal if he broke his.

She released a pent-up breath. "So what do I do, call you if I have a vision? And I guess you'll want me to write down everything I see, right?"

He seemed flummoxed by the question, as if he hadn't quite thought past manipulating her into staying away from Andrew Walters. Beneath the confusion, a darker emotion burned in his narrowed eyes.

"Is something wrong?" she asked.

He shook his head. "Yes, write everything down."

Lily pushed her hair back from her face. "Is this going to be a problem for you?"

He lifted his gaze to meet hers, his expression shuttered. "No. No problem."

She studied his face, trying to figure out what he was thinking. He could hide his emotions as well as almost anyone Lily knew, although he couldn't quite cover up the dark place inside him. It roiled, black and deep, just under the surface.

He took a step toward the doorway. "I should go. I need to head home and change."

She walked him to the door, leaning against the jamb as he took his jacket from the coat rack. He paused next to her, turning to meet her uplifted gaze.

"Call if you need me."

Heat bloomed deep in her belly. "I will."

He leaned in, and she rose on her toes to meet him halfway, as if drawn by a microscopic thread, the pull of his body intense and powerful. She curled her hand around his neck and brushed her lips against his. She'd expected combustion, but instead, the sweetness of the kiss washed over her in a river of warmth. She relaxed, giving in to the velvety caress of his mouth on hers.

When he gently broke away, coldness seeped into the marrow of her bones.

McBride stepped back onto the concrete stoop, gathering his coat around him to ward off the chill. Lily closed the door, needing the distance, the barrier between them.

But she remained there, her cheek against the door, long after she heard his car drive away.

ROSE ARRIVED AROUND TEN, laden with an overnight case, bran muffins and a thermos. "Iris sent buckbean tea." Rose hugged Lily. "You okay? McBride said you got a little banged up."

"I'm fine." Lily took the basket of muffins from her sister and led her inside. "My car's totaled, though."

Rose dropped her bag on the floor by the sofa and followed Lily to the kitchen. She glanced at the two coffee cups in the sink. "So, this Mc-Bride—is he cute?"

Lily put the muffins on the counter and gave her sister a warning look.

Rose bent and picked up Delilah, who had wound herself in a knot around her legs. "Hello, gorgeous." She rubbed the cat's ears until Delilah purred like a motorboat. "Iris would've come, but she's almost figured out some mix of bat's wings and eye of newt that'll relieve menstrual cramps in half the usual time, and far be it from me to stand in the way of such a miracle."

Lily pulled the plastic wrap off the basket and picked out a couple of muffins for herself and Rose. "Put my cat down and pour us some tea."

Rose poured two cups and joined Lily at the kitchen table, moving aside the newspaper McBride had left folded on the table. "So really—who is this McBride and why did he spend the night with you?"

Heat rushed up Lily's neck and spilled into her cheeks. She touched the edge of the newspaper at her elbow, trying to hide her reaction. But the paper only reminded her that McBride had sat here reading this paper only a few hours earlier, looking sleepy and disheveled and utterly irresistible.

"Ooh, Lil, you're blushing!" Rose leaned forward, her expression eager. "Spill it!"

Lily gave her sister a stern look. "McBride's the head of the task force investigating Abby Walters's abduction."

"Ooh, and you're working with him? Because of your visions?"

"Kind of." Lily caught her up with all that had happened since they'd spoken on the phone the night before.

Rose's eyes widened with horror. "Someone ran you off the road? McBride just said it was an accident."

"I don't know who it was or why he wanted to hurt me," Lily admitted. "It doesn't make any sense—the kidnapper who called me the other day seemed to want me to give Andrew a message. But maybe I spooked him when he realized I'd seen him hit Abby."

"Have you had more visions since then?"

"Yeah. A really strange one." Glad for a sympathetic ear, Lily told Rose about the second little girl who'd appeared in her visions of Abby. "It was so strange. It was like she'd been watching Abby and me."

Rose's eyes glittered. *"Creepy!"*

"It didn't feel creepy, though," Lily said. "At first, maybe, but after that it seemed sort of sweet. How she'd been watching over Abby."

"You think she knows Abby?"

"I think she's connected somehow. Maybe a cousin or something. Something about her looks familiar."

"Why would Abby's cousin come to you in a vision?"

Lily shrugged. "I'd love to ask Andrew Walters about the little girl, but I promised McBride I'd stay away from him."

Before Rose could respond, Jezebel jumped from the counter onto the kitchen table, knocking over Lily's tea.

"Jezzy!" Rose jumped up to avoid the liquid spreading toward her.

Lily shooed the cat away and crossed to the counter to retrieve a roll of paper towels to mop up the mess, while Rose grabbed the newspaper off the table to keep it from getting wet.

When Lily dumped the soaked towels and returned to the table, she found Rose gazing at the paper, a strange light in her eyes.

"What is it?" she asked.

Rose turned the paper around, showing Lily a front-page photo of McBride and a couple of detectives Lily didn't recognize, manning phones at police headquarters.

Rose pointed to McBride. "This is McBride, isn't it?

Lily nodded, chill bumps rising on her arms. The picture caption didn't identify him by name. "How'd you know?"

Rose's grin split her face from ear to ear. "Sugar, he's the man you're going to marry."

Chapter Nine

McBride watched the cable news interview through narrowed eyes, a little unnerved by how well Andrew Walters was holding together under the camera lights. The man was smooth, well-spoken and engaging. The camera loved him.

No wonder he was in politics.

"I'm grateful for everyone's support. I can't tell you how much it means to me." Walters looked straight at the camera, his chin up, his eyes soft with emotion. "Please remember to keep your eyes open. Be aware of who's around you. That little redhead you see in the grocery store could be my daughter."

"He's good," FBI Special Agent Cal Brody murmured.

McBride glanced at the agent. Brody was a lean, rangy man with the sharp eyes of a hunter. He said little and missed nothing. And he looked just as bemused as McBride felt.

"He has an alibi," McBride responded, aware

what the agent's dry words were implying. "And no discernible motive."

"What about his opponent?"

"If Blackledge was behind it, he screwed up. Walters's poll numbers are way up since his daughter disappeared." A niggle of unease crept under McBride's collar as he spoke.

"Motive." Brody echoed the path of McBride's thoughts.

McBride pressed his lips together, considering the idea of Walters as the mastermind behind his daughter's kidnapping. Was it possible? His alibi was airtight, so he'd have had to hire someone else to make the snatch...

No. Until this morning, when he'd arrived to find Walters up to his elbows in campaign discussions with his campaign manager, Joe Britt, McBride had never seen the man as anything other than a desperate, heartsick father.

But Walters had a job to do, just like McBride.

When Brody joined McBride and Walters that morning, he'd gone over the FBI's game plan. "We think we've figured out this guy's trace-blocking system, so we should be able to pinpoint him when he calls today. We get his location, we strike, we grab him." Brody had looked at Walters. "I understand you don't believe he's legitimate."

"Lily is sure he's a fraud," Walters had said.

"Lily?" Brody had asked.

"She's a psychic who's helping us find Abby," Walters had said before McBride could stop him. McBride had braced himself for the agent's reaction.

Brody's only response had been a quick glance at McBride.

Walters had managed to stay away from the topic of Lily for most of the day, distracted by a Birmingham television news crew who'd arrived to interview him about his missing daughter.

McBride wished he were as easily distracted. He couldn't seem to stop thinking about Lily Browning.

The crew wrapped up the interview, broke down their equipment and left. Walters went to change clothes, leaving McBride alone with Brody.

"How closely did you look at him?"

"Verified his alibi. Checked his bank account to see if there were any odd outputs of money, but he is in the middle of a senate run. There've been outlays. But they seem legit."

Brody shrugged. "From what I know about Blackledge, if Walters had any skeletons, they'd be out of the closet already."

Brody was right. Walters knew what it was like to live under scrutiny. It was only reasonable he'd hold up under pressure better than the average guy with a missing daughter.

Walters returned to the sitting room, minus his

jacket and tie. "I hope that earns us a few more eyeballs."

Odd phrasing, McBride thought. But the trill of a phone diverted his attention.

It was the dedicated line.

McBride glanced at Brody. The fed nodded. Andrew Walters sank onto the sofa and took a deep breath.

As they'd agreed, McBride answered the phone. "Hello?"

"Hello, Mr. Walters. Remember me?"

McBride recognized the voice from the surveillance tape. He squeezed the receiver tightly. "I remember." He smoothed his gravelly voice to sound more like Walters.

"We want five hundred grand in tens and twenties, dropped in the waste bin at the corner of 10th and Maple. Tomorrow night at eleven-thirty. We'll be watching, so don't be stupid."

"That's a lot of money to get together by then."

"Don't jerk me around, Walters. You're worth fifty times that. Eleven-thirty tomorrow night." The man's voice quavered despite his attempt to sound tough. "And no cops, got it? I smell so much as a whiff of bacon, the kid is dead."

McBride gritted his teeth. "You'll have Abby there?" He wondered if the FBI techs had been able to get a trace yet.

"Just be there." There was a click, then a dial tone.

A second later, an FBI surveillance tech burst through the door. "We've got him!"

LILY STARED AT HER SISTER. "I beg your pardon?"

"I said, you're going to marry McBride." Rose was matter-of-fact, as if she'd just said Lily was having waffles for breakfast. "I just now saw a true-love veil, your face over his. You know what that means."

Lily shook her head. No matter how attractive she found McBride, she couldn't believe he was her "one true love." They'd never find common ground enough to be together forever.

"He's the man in the dream I had, the man you're going to be madly in love with, remember? You find his daughter…." Rose stopped, frowning. "Does McBride have a daughter?"

"I don't think so." None she knew of, anyway. McBride wasn't the most forthcoming man she'd ever met. "I think you're off the mark this time." A queasy feeling settled in her stomach. "For all I know, he's happily married."

Which would shine a new, unwelcome light on their recent kisses, she realized with a sinking heart.

Rose frowned. "I'm never wrong about these things."

"Trust me, whoever the mystery man is, it's

not McBride." She changed the subject. "How's business?"

"Pretty good. Right now I'm working on a wedding in Willow Grove and one over in Talladega. I think—"

The jangling phone interrupted her. Lily shrugged apologetically and answered on the second ring. "Hello?"

"Lily? It's Andrew Walters. They traced the call!"

Lily's stomach flipped. "Really?"

"I'm heading to the station to wait for them to arrive with the suspect." Andrew paused, tension buzzing over the phone line. "Are you sure he doesn't have Abby?"

About to reassure him, Lily remembered McBride's warning. What if she was wrong? What if she built up Andrew's hopes, only to have all her visions turn out to be nothing but delusions?

It didn't matter, she realized. "McBride won't let anything happen to Abby." He'd die before he'd let her get hurt. It was the one thing Lily was sure about.

"Will you come to the police station? I need you there."

Lily hesitated, remembering her promise to McBride. But she needed to be there. Already she was pumped with adrenaline; sitting here in ignorance for hours, waiting for news, would be too excruciating to contemplate. "On my way."

"Where're you going?" Rose asked when she hung up.

Lily explained briefly. "I have to go."

"We'll take my car," Rose said.

"We'll have to," Lily said, her hands trembling as she thought about what awaited her.

AS UNIFORMED OFFICERS pulled him from the back of the squad car, Ray Biddle squinted at McBride. "You got the wrong man."

McBride smiled grimly. "We always do." He followed the tight little procession into the booking area. As the clerks began to process Biddle, Theo Baker came around the corner. He crooked his palm at McBride, motioning him to follow.

"What's up?" McBride asked as he reached him.

"Mr. Walters didn't stay put. He's here. So's your pretty little psychic friend and some other woman."

McBride uttered a succinct oath. "Where are they?"

"I took 'em to the office." Theo led the way, two stairs at a time, but McBride's longer legs propelled him ahead as they reached the detective division at the end of the hall.

Andrew Walters sat in one of the chairs in front of McBride's desk, talking to a woman McBride didn't recognize. Lily stood across the room, her head turned toward the windows. Late afternoon sunlight bathed her face with golden light, causing McBride to falter before he caught himself and continued into the room.

Walters met him halfway, his expression tense. "Well?"

"Phony, like you thought. There were newspaper clippings about Abby's kidnapping all over his house, but no sign that she'd ever been around. He's being booked."

"Can I see him?" Walters asked.

McBride passed his hand over his face, suddenly tired. "I guess so. Our guys will want to interrogate him first."

"Can I watch?"

McBride motioned to Baker. "Theo, take Mr. Walters with you to observe Biddle's interrogation." He crossed to his desk, pressing his hands to his weary eyes.

He expected Lily and the unknown woman to follow Theo and Walters out. But when he dropped his hands, the two women remained, Lily still standing by the window and the unidentified woman sitting primly in front of him, studying him with a pair of sparkling brown eyes.

"Who the hell are you?" he asked.

She laughed, and he saw the resemblance. He glanced at Lily. "She belongs to you?"

Lily's lips curved. "I don't usually claim her."

She gave a little wave. "My sister Rose. Rose, this is Lieutenant J. McBride."

Rose held out her hand. "Nice to meet you. What's the J. stand for?"

McBride ignored her question and her extended hand, his eyes still on Lily. "I thought you were going to stay away from Walters."

Lily didn't answer.

"You're right, he *is* a grouch." Rose stood and looked down her nose at him, a twinkle in her light brown eyes. "I'll leave you to your spat in a minute, but I have just one more question. Are you married?"

McBride stared up at her, flummoxed. "No. Why?"

Rose just gave her sister a knowing look. Lily lowered her head, color flooding her neck and cheeks.

When Rose was gone, McBride looked across at Lily. "You could have asked me that yourself."

She lifted her chin and met his gaze. "I should have asked before. Considering."

He clenched his left hand into a fist, haunted by a phantom memory of cool gold circling his left ring finger. "I was married. My wife died a little over five years ago."

Lily crossed to him, her wild-honey eyes soft with concern. "I didn't know. I'm sorry."

He'd never figured out how to respond to those two words. Did he say thank-you? Or, it's not your fault? As usual, he said nothing.

She touched his cheek. "I wish I'd been wrong about the hoax, too. I wanted you to find Abby safe and sound."

He took a shaky breath, wanting nothing more than to press his face to her stomach and hold her close. Her touch made him feel wide open and raw. He hadn't felt so much—good or bad—in a long time. He'd thought it was better that way, feeling nothing. But he was beginning to realize feeling nothing was its own kind of pain.

He closed his eyes, overwhelmed by her warmth, by the slow, rhythmic stroke of her fingers on his face. He couldn't find the energy to sound stern when he asked, "Why are you here?"

"Andrew phoned and said you'd traced the call." She slid her hand down his neck to settle on his shoulder.

He opened his eyes. Her wary gaze met his and he realized she had her own walls to breach. Somehow the knowledge only made him feel more vulnerable.

She stroked his shoulder, her fingers brushing against his neck. He leaned into her caress, unable to resist the comfort she offered.

She moved behind him, pressing her soft hands

against his skull, and began to rub his throbbing temples. When she drew his head back against her belly, he didn't resist. Her touch drove out the cold ache that had crept into his core when he'd arrived at Biddle's house and found no sign of Abby Walters. McBride hadn't realized until that moment just how much he'd been hoping he was wrong and that she would be there, alive and well, for him to rescue and return to her father.

"You must be exhausted." Her voice purred through him. "I know you couldn't have gotten much sleep on my sofa, and you've been on this case night and day."

"It'll be that way until all the leads are exhausted."

"Or until you find her."

He leaned his head back to look at her. "I wish I believed that."

"I know." She ran the back of her fingers down his cheek, her soft skin rasping on his day's growth of beard. "Rose is staying at my place tonight. Join us for dinner."

He smiled at the thought. "I suspect your sister is best experienced in small doses. I've had mine for today."

"Then tomorrow?" she pressed.

He tried to read her intentions behind those liquid gold eyes. "Dinner?"

"I'm not much of a cook, but I can come up with something."

He swiveled the desk chair, turning to face her. "Why?"

A flicker of fear passed across her face, and she took a half step back. But he read her answer in her wary eyes. He caught her hand, keeping her close.

"We could hurt each other in so many ways," he whispered.

Her lips trembled. "I know."

"We'd be crazy to even try it."

She nodded but took a step toward him, her legs sliding between his knees. She cupped his face between her palms. "Tomorrow night at seven?"

"Work is crazy. I can't promise to be on time."

"I'll keep dinner warm until you get there." She leaned in to kiss him.

The rattle of the doorknob gave them a second's notice before the door to the office began to open. Lily stepped away from him, robbing him of her warmth. She was on the other side of his desk by the time Theo, Walters and Rose walked in.

"He claims you got the wrong man." Walters's grim smile was chilling. "But he matches the description of the man in Lily's vision, so I know it's him."

McBride glanced at Lily. Her face was a porcelain mask, expressionless. "I'm sorry we didn't find her today," she said.

Walters looked at Lily. "We will."

McBride walked them down to the front lobby. While Rose led Walters ahead, Lily lingered behind. She lifted her face when they reached the front desk. "You could do with some rest, McBride."

He bent toward her, wishing they were in a less public place. "I'm glad you came here today."

For a split second bright light washed over her face, then was gone. It took another second for McBride to realize it had been the flash of a camera. He looked in the direction from which it had come.

A cluster of reporters were gathered around Walters and Lily's sister near the doorway. McBride strode over to the group, Lily on his heels. "Come on, guys, let Mr. Walters pass."

One of the reporters thrust his microphone toward Lily. "Ms. Browning, is it true that Mr. Walters has asked you to assist him in finding his daughter?"

Lily's face went pale, but she didn't answer. She tried to move away, but the crowd hemmed her in, separating her from McBride.

"Are you a psychic, Ms. Browning? Do you claim to have had visions about the kidnapping?" the reporter pressed.

Andrew Walters caught Lily's arm, drawing her

to his side. When he bent and said something in her ear, McBride felt his stomach coil into a hard knot. Old bitterness rose from deep inside, swamping him with doubt. Lily said she had only Abby's welfare at heart, but here she was, ready to work the cameras—

Only she wasn't. She was gazing at McBride, her eyes pleading, as if begging for rescue.

He pushed through the crowd and drew her out of the mass of reporters. "Ms. Browning has no comment." He bundled her through the front door, past the phalanx of newspeople.

Rose caught up with them at the bottom of the steps. "Wow, that was like a scene from a movie."

"Where's Walters?" McBride asked.

"He's giving the reporters a story. Said it might help him find Abby." Rose straightened her twisted blouse. "I think one of those reporters pinched my butt."

McBride glanced at Lily, a smile tugging at his lips. Her eyes met his, bright with amusement, and he let out a chuckle. A second later, Lily joined him.

Rose stared at them with mock outrage. "Yeah, well, it wasn't your butts."

McBride grinned broadly and held out his hand to her. "It's been nice meeting you, Rose Browning."

"Same here." She shook his hand firmly and headed toward the car, leaving him alone with Lily.

He turned and gazed into Lily's laughing eyes. "Anybody pinch your butt?"

She caught his hand, gave it a squeeze. "Sadly, no. Thanks for the rescue."

"Guess I was wrong. You're not a media hound, after all."

Her smile faded. She tried to let go of his hand, but he held on, keeping her close for a moment more.

"I'm sorry. I didn't mean to upset you." He caressed the back of her hand with his thumb. "I'll see you tomorrow night?"

Her smile returned. "Tomorrow night."

He let her go, and she began to walk away. When she reached the car, he spoke her name. "Lily?"

She turned to look at him. "Yeah?"

"Maybe we *will* find Abby safe and sound," he said.

She smiled slightly. "Maybe we will."

But it was a lie, he thought as he watched her get into her car and drive away. He had a sick feeling that if they ever found Abby Walters, safe and sound was the last thing she'd be.

Chapter Ten

The story made the Saturday morning newspaper: Psychic Joins Police In Search For Missing Child. Almost covering the top right corner of the paper, a candid photo captured Lily and McBride, heads close as they spoke. The caption implied she and McBride were conferring on the case.

Lily sank onto the sofa in dismay, paper in hand.

There were lots of quotes from Andrew Walters. Ever the politician, he knew how to turn the reporters' hostile questions into an asset. Though he never admitted that Lily was a psychic working to find his daughter, he made sure that the thrust of the article became a heartfelt plea for Abby's return.

Unfortunately, the journalist seemed to have done some background research on her, interviewing people from Willow Grove who'd known her when she was growing up. People whose names she barely recognized all had stories about those strange Browning girls and their odd ways. Worse, the article mentioned her job as a teacher at Westview Elementary. Now every reporter covering the case had her name and her occupation.

It wouldn't take long for them to hunt her down.

She was tempted to take Rose's advice and go home to Willow Grove for the rest of the weekend. But Lily needed to catch up on grading papers before Monday morning.

She saw her sister off after breakfast. "Call me to let me know you got home safely."

Rose gave her a hug. "Be safe yourself, Lil. Okay?"

After she left, Lily settled down with the stack of student papers Carmen Herrera had dropped off Friday. By noon, she'd worked her way through most of them and was considering taking a break for lunch when her spine started tingling.

Abby, she thought, relief mingling with the gray mist washing over her. She hadn't realized how much she'd needed to see the little girl again.

Seconds later, she was in Abby's tiny prison. The girl stood on her bed, peering out the small window. Lily strained to focus. "What're you looking at, Abby?"

The little girl whirled around. "Lily?"

"It's me, sweetie. Is there something out there?"

Abby turned back to the window. "I saw the mean man leave awhile ago, but he's back now."

"The mean man?"

Abby nodded. "He yells at me. The other one's nicer. His name's Gordy. The mean one's called Skeet. He hits me." She looked indignant. "Mama says you're not s'posed to hit people."

Lily wished she could put her arms around the little girl and never let her go. "Do they ever say where you are? Do they mention place names or street names?"

Abby's face crumpled. "I don't know. I'm sorry, Lily."

Her heart twisted. "It's okay, baby. You just try to listen and remember everything Gordy and Skeet say, okay? Then you tell me all about it. It'll be our little game."

"Can she play, too?" Abby asked.

The skin on the back of Lily's neck prickled. "She?"

"She means me," a child's voice said.

Lily whirled around. The mysterious dark-haired child of her previous vision stood in the shadows near the door. Gina, Lily thought, remembering what the girl had told her. *Mama calls me Gina, but I don't think that's my name.*

Gina smiled at Lily, her expression a heartbreaking mix of fear and hope. "Can I play, too, Lily?"

"Of course." Shudders rippled down Lily's spine.

The dark-haired girl sat on the edge of Abby's bed. "Abby can't see you like I can, Lily. Why not?"

"You can see her?" Abby's eyes were wide.

"Yeah. I can see you, too. But you can't see us."

"Why not?" Abby asked.

"I don't know," Lily admitted.

"I told Abby you have dark hair and gold eyes and you look like a fairy princess." The little girl sat next to Abby. The bed didn't shift physically, Lily noted with curiosity. Gina definitely wasn't there in the room with Abby.

"Gina, how often do you visit Abby?"

"My name's Casey," she replied with a frown.

"Why do you think that's your name?" Lily asked.

"Daddy talks to me in my dreams. He calls me Casey. He's going to teach me how to play best-ball." Casey's heart-shaped face screwed up in a serious frown. "What's bestball?"

"I think you mean baseball." Lily wondered how a child Casey's age could live in America and not know about baseball. "It's a game you play with a stick and a ball. Casey, do you ever hear the men who are holding Abby?"

"No. You want me to try? Is that how to play the game?"

Lily stared at her, overwhelmed by the strangeness of her presence in the vision. Where did

Casey come from? Was she a real child or something else? A ghost? Abby's guardian angel? Lily grasped for an explanation that didn't include committing herself to an asylum.

Not a guardian angel, she decided. Gina—Casey—had her own troubles, including a mother who called her the wrong name.

But her daddy called her Casey.

The mists tugged at Lily, pulling her toward the real world. Her struggle was brief, the slightest resistance causing pain to shoot through her skull. "I'll be back," she promised the children as the gray fog swallowed her. Abby faded right away, but Casey lingered, a forlorn watcher in the mist.

Lily came back to herself slowly, her sluggish mind trying to make sense of the pale, geometric patterns on the ceiling above her. Sunlight reflected through the blinds on her living room windows, she realized after a moment. She was on the sofa. She'd been grading papers when the vision hit....

"Back among the living now?"

Lily jumped at the rumbling sound of McBride's voice.

He sat a few feet away in a boxy armchair too small for his frame, legs stretched out in front of him. His arms draped over the sides of the chair, fingers almost brushing the floor. His chin rested against his chest as if he was napping, but his eyes were open.

Watching her.

Her heart hammered in her chest.

He sat up, arms sliding forward to rest on his thighs. His gaze never left her. "I knocked. You didn't answer."

She cleared her throat. "What time is it?"

"Noon." McBride rubbed his jaw, his palm making a whispery scraping sound against his cheek. "Guess you saw the paper."

She rubbed her own face. "Yeah."

"You just had a vision," he said flatly.

She swallowed hard. "Yes."

He said nothing else, his gaze narrowed.

Then Lily remembered something Abby had told her. "Their names! Abby told me the names they use. Skeet and Gordy."

He sat back, his eyes wary. "Abby told you."

Her heart sank at his reaction. "At least check it out."

"I will." He rose from the chair, moving toward the door.

Lily intercepted him, closing her fingers around his arm. "Please don't do this."

He didn't pretend not to know what she was talking about. "I told you this would be a problem for us."

"You also told me to come to you with what I see."

"I'm not talking about the case. I'm talking about this." He laced his fingers through hers, pulling her closer.

"You don't believe. I knew that going in."

"How long before you resent me for it?" He lifted his hand to her cheek, his fingers sliding along the curve of her jaw. He bent close, his breath whispering across her lips. "How long before this isn't enough?"

McBride's mouth slanted across hers, hard and hungry. She slipped her hands up his back, tracing the contours of his spine, the flare of his shoulder blades. She smoothed her hands down his rib cage, over the small of his back, down to the curve of his buttocks. Squeezing gently, she urged his hips into the welcoming softness of her belly.

His breath exploded into her mouth, his body's response unmistakable. His arms tightened around her, lifting her up and propelling her backward.

Her knees hit the edge of the sofa and she fell back, pulling McBride with her. He caught himself with his arms to keep from landing with his full weight atop her. She stared at him, her breath bursting from her lungs in short gasps.

Time stood still.

Then he bent his head again, closing his lips over hers.

This kiss was different from any they'd shared before. It was slower, more thorough. Lingering, nipping, suckling. He brushed her chin, her cheeks with his lips, planted soft, sweet kisses on her eyelids and the tip of her nose. Her heart swelled, snared in the flood of passion sweeping over them.

McBride closed his hand over her breast, his palm circling gently, stroking her through her T-shirt. She moaned as her nipple tightened in response.

He rose over her, gazing down at her as if to memorize every freckle, every eyelash, every tiny line of her face. In his desire-darkened eyes, she saw her own reflection, the tangled hair and passion-drunk eyes of a woman falling in love.

He lowered his mouth to hers, slowly, tenderly. Her lips softened. Heat spread through her in great, velvety waves.

Suddenly, something hit McBride from behind with surprising force, and he drew away from her, uttering a loud oath. Lily blinked with surprise and found herself looking up at two sets of eyes—McBride's and Jezebel's.

He rolled away from her, the cat clinging to his shoulder. Lily scrambled to her knees and reached for the feline. "Jezzy, no!"

Jezebel clung for another moment, then released her death grip and bounded away. McBride reached over his shoulder, his fingers probing the small tears the cat's claws had left in his cotton dress shirt.

Lily gazed at the torn cloth with horror. "I'm so sorry, I don't know what came over her. She never acts that way."

He rubbed his shoulder, looking more frustrated than angry. "Probably thought I was trying to hurt you."

She put her hands on his shoulders, turning him so that she could check his wounds. "Cats aren't like Lassie. They figure we can take care of ourselves." Her lips curved. "But they are territorial. She's usually the one on top of me."

McBride looked toward the windowsill, where Jezebel sat like an Egyptian statue, turquoise eyes glaring at him. "Sorry."

Lily laughed softly and rose from the sofa. "I have some antibiotic ointment in the bathroom."

By the time she got back, he had his shirt off. She'd known he was muscular, but the shirt had hidden just how well built he really was. He was leaner than she'd expected, his muscles well defined but not bulky.

She crossed to him, ointment in hand, wondering how she could possibly touch him again without throwing him back down on the sofa. Somehow she managed to apply the ointment to his scratches without letting her hands wander. "There."

He looked at her, his eyes dark with lingering passion. She touched his cheek, her heart squeezing as he rubbed his face against her palm and pressed his lips against the fleshy part of her thumb.

She cradled his head and bent to kiss him.

But he gently pulled away, rising from the sofa. "I realize it's a little late to remember this, but I'm still on duty." He lifted her hands to his lips, kissed her knuckles lightly and took a step away from her. "How are you going to get to work Monday?"

"I guess I need to rent a car." She should have done it while Rose was here to drive her around.

He shook his head. "I'll drive you to work Monday and we can see about renting a car that afternoon when I pick you up. What time do you need to be there?"

"I try to get there by six-thirty."

He grimaced but nodded. "I'll be here at six."

"Okay." Lily walked him to the front door, her body buzzing with unfulfilled need.

McBride nodded toward Jezebel, who still glared at them from the window ledge. His lips curved slightly. "I think she's still looking for an apology," he murmured, dropping a quick kiss on Lily's cheek before he left.

Closing the door behind him, Lily turned and glared at the animal. "Forget getting an apology from me, brat cat."

She should probably be grateful that Jezebel had stopped them before things went too far. With all the obstacles to their tenuous relationship, jumping into sex this quickly was probably a very bad idea.

But damn, it had felt like a good one at the time.

LILY HAD THOUGHT she'd be glad to be back at school. But as much as she'd missed her kids, she found it impossible to concentrate on work.

All she could think about was McBride.

They had come so close to making love Saturday. The memory of his mouth on hers was so vivid it made her body grow warm and liquid with need.

But that had happened two days ago, and since that time she'd had a chance to think long and hard about what was going on between them.

The truth was, she and McBride were wrong for each other. There wasn't a chance in hell they'd ever form a lasting relationship together.

Because she was a psychic.

There. She'd admitted it.

She was a psychic. She'd spent most of her life hating the word, hating the idea, but the truth was she couldn't change what she was, no matter how much she wanted to.

And for the first time, she didn't think she wanted to.

She had a gift, just like her sisters. Like most gifts, it came with strings attached. What she saw in her visions often brought her pain. There would be many visions she'd rather escape. But if her recent visions of Abby had done nothing else, they'd taught her that sometimes her gift could be a blessing as well as a curse.

She'd helped Abby. She'd comforted the child, helped her not be so afraid. God willing, her visions would lead her to Abby soon. Lily could never turn her back on her gift now.

Not even for McBride.

She sensed that something dark and horrible had happened to the detective. Something that made belief impossible for him.

So she had a decision to make. She could either take what she could get, knowing that it wouldn't end well, or stop playing with fire now before she got burned.

Which was it going to be?

By the time the school bell rang at three, she was no closer to an answer. And McBride would be there soon, forcing her hand. She tried to distract herself by getting a head start on grading the day's papers while she waited.

But by ten to four, McBride still hadn't shown.

Carmen stuck her head through the doorway just after four, her expression full of curiosity.

"Got a call from Lieutenant McBride. He's stuck in traffic, but he's on his way. You want to call him, tell him I'll give you a ride?"

Lily knew she should probably take Carmen up on the offer, but realized that by avoiding McBride, she'd be only delaying her decision. "I'll be fine. I'm sure he'll be here soon."

"Okay. Everybody else has left, but Roy's in the gym sweeping up, and Mabel is over at the portable classrooms if you need anything." Carmen left with a little wave.

Lily passed the time preparing her own classroom for the next day's lessons. The air was thick with silence, the deep hush that could be found only in places like schools, as if the remembered sounds of children laughing and talking somehow made the rare quiet tangible.

When the classrooms emptied, the thermostat had been turned down. Lily shivered and pulled her warm cardigan more tightly around her, looking out the window toward the school entrance. She wished McBride would hurry.

She was about to turn away from the window when she saw a car pull into the parking lot. She thought it was him for a moment, until she realized the vehicle was the wrong make. It disappeared beyond the building.

The hair on the back of her neck rose.

She dipped her hand into her purse and pulled out her keys. A small vial of pepper spray was attached to the key chain; she unsnapped the safety tab from the vial and slipped into the dark, deserted hallway.

Her footfalls sounded like thunder in the void, rivaled only by the roar of her pulse in her ears. She forced herself to take deep, steady breaths as she walked quickly to the second-grade classroom that faced the faculty parking lot. She slipped through the door and hurried to the window.

The car was a light-colored sedan, maybe a Ford. The driver's door opened and a man stepped out, a baseball cap low over his face. Lily back-pedaled slowly, watching the man move furtively toward the side door, disappearing from sight.

Her heart racing, she wondered if the door was locked, and decided she didn't have time to make sure it was. She whirled and ran from the room, heading for the front entrance. There were homes across the street; if she could get there safely, she could knock on doors until she found someone to help her.

She hit the front door running, but it didn't open. She pushed again, rattled the metal panel, but it was locked. So was its mate.

She banged her hand against the second door with frustration. The sound echoed through the empty hall and died away, supplanted by her ragged breathing.

And a furtive noise down the hall.

Lily held her breath.

There it was again. A soft scraping noise, metal on metal. A soft, hollow rattle.

He was opening a window.

Okay, don't panic. There has to be another way out.

The gymnasium. Of course.

Carmen had said Roy was there, cleaning. The gym was on the far side of the building, and the sounds she was hearing indicated the intruder was somewhere between.

But there was more than one way to the gym. And she had the advantage of familiarity.

Lily sped silently toward the lunchroom doors halfway down the hall. She could no longer hear the window rattling, but surely he hadn't had time to crawl through yet.

She covered the last few yards and was reaching for the door handle when she saw him. All in black, from dusty boots to the knit ski mask he must have donned on his way in, he filled a doorway ten yards to her left.

He froze, surprise evident in his stiff posture. She went still as well, just for a second.

Then she bolted through the cafeteria door.

The door swung shut behind her, hitting him with a soft thud as he followed her. She kept her back to the cafeteria wall as she scooted across the room, knowing his eyes wouldn't adjust to the dark for a few seconds. He'd probably waste time feeling for a light switch that wasn't there, not knowing it was on the side of the room where the faculty sat, so that mischievous students couldn't play games with the lights.

She was almost to the end of the cafeteria before she heard him closing in behind her. She sped up, knees knocking into chairs as she skimmed past tables in her frantic dash for the door.

Her fingers brushed the cool metal handle but missed. She groped again, but it was too late. Arms like tree trunks crushed her, squeezing the air from her lungs.

"Where you goin', Lily?" His breath burned her ear. She smelled stale cigarettes and peppermint. The combination almost made her gag. She didn't recognize the voice, so it wasn't the one Abby called Skeet. The mean one.

Lily clutched the little vial of pepper spray in her hand, wondering if she could get far enough away from him to use the spray without also incapacitating herself.

"What do you want?" She could barely gasp out the words.

His grip tightened, constricting her air further. He lifted her half off her feet, jerking her toward the door. "I was gonna leave a little note for you in your classroom, but since you're here, I'll deliver it in person."

He whirled her around and pinned her to the wall. Her elbows banged against the porcelain tile, pain shooting down to her fingertips and threatening her grip on the pepper spray. But she gritted her teeth and held on.

"Stay away from this thing." He spoke slowly. Clearly. "I know the feds are watching your house. They've tapped your phone by now, haven't they? Do you really want the headache of being involved in this case?"

She wrinkled her nose at the sour smell of his breath. Fear still pulsed through her veins, but anger was catching up.

I know something, too, she thought, lifting her chin. "You don't know as much as you think you do. Like, at this very minute, there's a policeman on his way here to take me home."

"Don't try to bluff me, Lily."

"Didn't you notice my car wasn't in the lot?"

He jerked her to her toes and slammed her back against the wall. "Your car was totaled the other night."

Her heart caught. "You drove me off the road."

"And you still didn't get the message, did you?" He tightened his grip on her. "So I'll deliver it face-to-face. Stay away from this case. Tell Walters you're through. Tell that cop you want out. Got it?"

She bit back the pain radiating from her bruised spine. "What are you afraid of? That I know who you are?"

He let her go suddenly, as if her skin had sent out an electrical pulse. Taking advantage of her momentary freedom, Lily lifted her hand in a smooth arc and pressed the top of the pepper spray dispenser. A noxious cloud of stinging spray filled the air, some of it floating back toward her even as she ducked and ran.

Her eyes stung and began to tear up, but she didn't slow down, weaving through the maze of tables and chairs toward the lunchroom door. She heard coughing and cursing behind her, closer than she liked. The ski mask the man was wearing must have blocked some of the spray.

She hit the lunchroom door with a thud and burst through, darting to the left.

With a crunch of shattering glass, her attacker slammed through the door behind her, too close.

Lily turned the corner and ducked into the male faculty bathroom, locking it. She retreated to the back stall and crouched in the corner, her breath coming in harsh rasps.

She'd just run herself into a trap.

Chapter Eleven

McBride pulled into the paved circle in front of the school, cursing himself for taking the expressway. He was almost an hour late, after making such a big deal over driving Lily to school for her own safety. If she'd rented a car on Saturday as she had suggested, she'd be safe at home instead of sitting alone in an almost empty school, waiting for him to arrive. She was probably ticked off at him, with good reason.

He headed up the walkway to the front door and pulled the handle. The door rattled but didn't open.

Locked.

He frowned. Had she found a ride home?

He walked around the building toward a cluster of portable classrooms, where a tall, handsome black woman was locking up. She gave a start as she turned to see him.

"Sorry. I'm looking for Ms. Browning to give her a ride home, but the front door is locked."

The black woman smiled. "Oh, Ms. Herrera always locks that door when she leaves. Roy and me—Roy's my husband—we clean up after hours and go out the back doors when we leave. Ms. Herrera told me Lily was waiting on somebody. Says you're a policeman." She peered at him. "Mind if I see your badge?"

He smiled and showed her his shield.

She pulled a set of keys from a ring on her belt, led him around to the front and unlocked the door. "Lily's room is that way." She pointed. "Fourth one on the left. Y'all come get me when you leave, and I'll lock it up." She headed back around the building.

McBride hurried down the hall to Lily's class-room. He stepped through the door, already opening his mouth to apologize. But the room was empty.

"Lily?" He took a quick look around to make sure he wasn't missing a hidden closet or cloak-room. He saw her purse lying open on top of her desk. But no Lily.

He stepped back into the hall and looked down the darkened corridor. He was about to call her name when he heard a muted scraping sound. He went still, instinct taking over. Easing the 9mm Smith & Wesson from his holster, he held his breath, listening carefully.

He heard another soft rattle, then a brittle

banging noise, like something hitting a window. His stomach clenched with tension and the beginnings of fear as he crept toward the noise.

The sounds were coming from a room two doors down.

By the time he reached the doorway, he hadn't heard any sounds for several seconds. He readied himself just outside the door, straining to hear any noise, however tiny. He looked down to ground himself, sucking in a deep preparatory breath.

And saw the splatters of blood.

Blackness poured into his brain. He fought through the fear and braced himself, running through police procedure like a mantra. *Go in low, cover your back, stay alert.*

He had to do it. He had to do it now.

He burst into the room, pistol held firmly in the correct two-hand grip. He swept the room with the gun and his sharp eyes, quickly ascertaining that it was empty.

At least, it was empty now.

He crossed to the open window, careful to remain low. He saw movement outside, a blur of cream. A car, he realized, speeding out of the parking lot too fast for him to get more than a cursory look at the make and model, much less anything like a license plate. It careened down the street, ran a stop sign without even slowing and disappeared from sight.

McBride holstered his gun and turned away from the window. He had already taken a couple of steps toward the door when he noticed the smell.

Pepper spray, sharp and burning in his nostrils.

For the first time, he saw the dark lump on the floor. He fished a pen from his pocket and lifted the object. The acrid pepper odor intensified.

It was a black knit ski mask.

Acid spewed into McBride's stomach. He dropped the mask and ran to the door. "Lily!"

The sound echoed down the empty corridor.

"Lily!" He peered through the gloom at the spatters of blood, trying to follow their trail. They weaved down the hall in widely spaced droplets. Whoever had been bleeding had ducked into each room, as if searching for something.

Or someone.

McBride followed the trail around a corner to the men's bathroom. Several drops of blood marred the tile floor in front of the door, as if the injured person had stood there for several seconds. The next drop of blood was about five feet down the hall.

The trail of blood ended at the door of the cafeteria. The glass window set in the door was broken. McBride found a torn fragment of black fabric on one of the jagged shards of glass still in the window.

He bent closer, trying not to disturb the shattered glass on the floor. The fragment looked like leather—from a glove?

Panic buzzed down his spine. He pushed the fear away and forced himself to focus. There'd been an intruder. There was blood—probably from the perp, he reassured himself, looking at the broken glass.

But where was Lily?

There was no way the intruder could've gotten through that window with Lily. If she were conscious, she'd have been kicking and screaming. And if she were unconscious, she'd be too unwieldy to pull through such a small space.

She had to be here somewhere.

He retraced his steps, following the blood spatter. At the door to the men's bathroom, he again noted the extra blood outside the door. He gave the door a push.

It didn't budge.

"Lily?"

A jingling noise startled him. He whipped his gun up.

A tall, thin black man dropped his key ring to the floor with a clatter and lifted his hands, his eyes wide with shock.

McBride lowered his weapon and flashed his shield. "Police. Got a key to this bathroom?"

LILY HAD BARELY registered the sound of McBride's voice outside the bathroom when the door in her mind exploded open, sucking her through the portal into raw fear edged with the coldest, blackest darkness she'd ever known. Emotions battered her—terror, despair, guilt, grief, hate. Darkness filled her lungs and seeped into her skin, covering her, drowning her.

A woman's voice inhabited her mind so completely that the words she muttered seemed to be her own. "She's gone, McBride. Clare's gone. I can't find her. Clare!"

Lily sobbed with anguish. "Oh, Clare, my baby!"

She felt hands on her shoulders, hot against her freezing flesh, dragging her from the whirlpool of grief. Eyes opening, she saw McBride's face close to hers. She clung to him as he drew her out of her dark vision, gasping for air as the blackness released her from its grasp.

But the anguish remained, pouring out in a tormented cry. "She's gone, McBride. Clare's gone!"

McBRIDE RELEASED Lily's arms and staggered backward into the bathroom wall. The room swam as he stared into her vacant eyes, his ears ringing with her anguished words.

She's gone, McBride. Clare's gone!

The voice had been Lily's, but the tone, the inflection, the anguish had been Laura's. Grief had etched his late wife's words into his soul. There could be no mistake.

He barely heard the janitor's voice. "Good Lord, Lily!"

A few feet away, Lily bent over the urinal, retching and crying. The janitor hovered over her, waving his hands ineffectually, apparently unsure what to do.

Battering down grief to the dark place inside him, McBride walked to the sink, wet several paper towels and took them to Lily, who hung over the urinal, fighting dry heaves.

He crouched next to her and bathed her flushed face.

"It was the man who ran me off the road," she said.

McBride sat back on his heels. "Are you sure?"

"He said I didn't get the message that time, so he decided to deliver it face-to-face. Did you see him?"

"Just a glimpse of his car." He brushed her sweat-dampened hair away from her cheeks, looking for injuries. "Did he hurt you? There was blood—"

"I think he put his hand through the lunchroom door."

DNA, McBride thought, trying to focus on his job. He'd get the crime scene unit to gather samples. "He left his mask behind. Did you hit him with pepper spray?"

She nodded.

He gently wiped her mouth. "Did he say why he was here?"

"He wants me to stay away from the case." She shivered.

McBride slipped his arm around her to warm her, although he felt so cold inside he wasn't sure it would do much good. He helped her stand and led her out of the bathroom into the dark hallway.

She wrapped her arms more tightly around her trembling body. "I'm sorry I'm not much help," she murmured.

Torn between wanting to hold her and wanting to run as far away from her as he could get, McBride compromised by doing neither—and doing his job. "Did you get a look at him?"

"Before he entered the building. He's tall, about your size." Her teeth chattered. "He already had the mask on, so I didn't see his face or his coloring, except he was Caucasian. I wasn't close enough to see the color of his eyes except when he caught me in the cafeteria, and then it was too dark."

"He caught you?" The thought of the masked man touching her sent rage flooding through him.

She rubbed her upper arms. "I was running

from him. He grabbed me and pinned me against the wall."

McBride reached for her. She wrapped her arms around his waist and pressed her face to his throat.

The janitor cleared his throat. "I'm gonna check and see if Mabel's all right. We'll call the police."

"Ask for Captain Vann in the detective bureau," McBride said. "Say McBride told you to call and that it's connected to the Walters kidnapping."

The janitor's eyes widened. "I'll do that."

McBride cradled Lily's face between his hands, searching her pale face. "Are you sure you're all right?"

She nodded. "I'm just a little shaky."

He had a feeling Lily wasn't shaken nearly as much by the intruder as by whatever the hell had happened in that bathroom, when she'd cried to him in Laura's grief-stricken words.

Had she really seen that horrible scene from his past?

No. It could have been a calculated guess. That was the game the phonies played, wasn't it? Take a few facts, make some savvy guesses and play it up big time.

He'd seen it before.

But how could Lily have known about Clare? From newspaper archives? Could she have pieced things together, made some smart guesses and created a scenario to match past reality?

No. Lily wasn't that cruel. She wasn't playing games.

But if she wasn't, then she was telling the truth about her visions. Something McBride wasn't ready to believe.

THE BLUE GLOW OF streetlamps poured through the windows of McBride's office, holding back the darkness but not the late autumn chill. Shivering, Lily leaned back from McBride's desk and rubbed her burning eyes. He was in the captain's office across the hall, conferring with his task force. He'd apologized for not being able to take her straight home. "We have to go over everything that's happened today."

She'd waved off his apology. "Go."

Now she was beginning to miss him. She was safe enough—who would come after her in a station full of armed cops?—but the silence was starting to get to her.

So it was with relief that she heard the door across the hallway open and footsteps move toward McBride's office. McBride entered the room, closing the door behind him. "You holding up?"

She nodded, wishing he would touch her. She

needed to feel his hand on her skin, reassuring her that everything was all right.

He crouched beside her, placing his hands on her knees. She shivered, her body leaping in response to his light touch. "Let's get you home."

"Agent Brody wanted to talk to me, didn't he?" She wished McBride would kiss her. The heat of his mouth over hers would chase away the chill that had settled into her bones.

"I told Brody it could wait." He touched his lips to her forehead, then pulled her out of the chair and into his arms. Bending his head, he kissed her lightly. "We'll stop by my place so I can get some clothes, and then I'll take you home."

She looked up, trying to read his expression. Though his kiss had been sweet, she'd detected a hint of distance in his posture. No big surprise; he'd been shaken by what had happened today. By her ordeal, certainly, but also by what had occurred when he'd found her in the bathroom.

She would never forget the look on his face when she'd surfaced from her hellish vision with another woman's words on her lips. For a moment, he'd seemed like a dead man, eyes empty, soul vacant. He had recognized the words, the pain.

Tomorrow, she decided, she'd make him tell her about Clare.

MCBRIDE SLEPT WITH LILY that night. Just slept, neither of them thinking about passion after the day's ordeal. McBride woke every few hours, unable to sleep for very long before being awakened by dark, twisted nightmares he didn't dare remember in the light. Each time, he found Lily sleeping peacefully beside him, her cats curled behind her like living bed warmers.

When he woke for good around 6:00 a.m., Lily was awake, sitting next to him with the cats in her lap. She greeted him with a sleepy smile. He sat up, rubbing his eyes. "What're you doing up so early?"

"I still work for a living."

He shook his head. "You're not going back there today."

"I have to go back sometime."

"Not today. You're exhausted."

"I'm fine." She cocked her head. "You look wiped, though."

He grinned. "I always look this bad."

"Not *always*," she murmured with a slight arch of her eyebrows and a devilish grin. "Sometimes you're almost okay-looking. I live for those moments."

He grinned at her. "Sweet-talker." He started to lean toward her when his cell phone shrilled.

Groaning, he grabbed it from the night table. "McBride."

It was Captain Vann. "Just got a call from Walker County. They've got a juvenile Jane Doe, red hair, blue eyes, about five or six years old."

McBride's stomach sank. "How fresh?"

"Under twelve hours, they think."

Abby Walters, he thought immediately.

"They're e-mailing us the morgue photos in about half an hour," Vann said. "I'd like the whole task force here, just in case."

"I'll be there in fifteen minutes." McBride hung up the phone and looked at Lily. She gazed at him, her brow wrinkled with concern. He tried to keep his expression neutral, but she saw through him.

Her face went white. "Abby?"

McBride sat beside her and took her hand. Her fingers were icy. "Walker County cops have found a juvenile Jane Doe. They're e-mailing photos in a little while. The captain wants the task force present."

She shook her head mutely.

"It might not be her," he said, wishing he believed it.

She nodded but didn't look convinced. "Go on. I'll get one of the FBI agents outside to drive me to work."

McBride stroked her hand. "You can't go back

to school today. You'll just bring the press flocking there, disrupting the students."

She sighed in frustration, but he could see her accepting the inevitable. "Okay. I'll call Carmen."

Lily walked McBride to the door. "Phone me when you know something."

He kissed her brow. "I will. Try not to borrow trouble."

As he was getting into his car, his cell phone rang. It was Special Agent Cal Brody. His voice was grim. "I just got the message. Think it's her?"

"I hope to God not." McBride cranked the engine, steeling himself for what was about to come.

THE PHOTOS LOADED SLOWLY on the computer screen, revealing pixel by pixel the harsh face of death. Though he sat in the middle of a climate-controlled police station, McBride could feel the cold air of the morgue in the images, felt it seep under his jacket, spreading chill bumps across his flesh. He studied the pictures, forced himself to be thorough, before he turned away from the screen. "It's not her."

He got up and paced across the room, breathing deeply to drive out the imagined odor of death. He leaned against the door frame, longing for a double bourbon straight up, though he hadn't had a drink in years.

Special Agent Brody joined him. "Got a cigarette?"

"Don't smoke."

Brody's grin was horrible. "Neither do I."

McBride rubbed his face, unable to escape the image of that tiny white body lying on the metal slab. "You have any clue who that little girl could be?"

Brody shook his head. "Maybe she hasn't been reported missing yet. The M.E. says it looks like she was raped and strangled."

McBride closed his eyes. Sharp, dark pain ate at his gut.

"Did Walters know about this call?"

"No."

"Good." McBride crossed the room to Theo's desk. His colleague looked up at him, silent compassion warming his dark brown eyes. "Theo, give Walker County a call and let them know that's not our girl."

He gave a nod and picked up the phone.

"I've got some new stuff on Paul Leonardi." Brody followed McBride back to his office. "Looks like his alibi is solid. We've tracked down people at every place he gave us, and between their register receipts and their personal memories, everything checks out."

"Damn." McBride dropped into his chair.

"What about the woman?" Brody added.

McBride slanted a look at the FBI agent. Brody's expression was hard to read, but he already knew the man shared his skepticism about all things paranormal. "I don't think she knows anything we can use."

"I meant, what about her as a suspect?"

McBride picked up the bottle of antacids on his desk, shaking a couple straight into his mouth. "She didn't call herself. She didn't drive herself off the road, and she didn't attack herself at the school yesterday."

"She could have an accomplice."

McBride couldn't argue. Lily's part in this whole mess was the one thing he couldn't make sense of. How was she involved? If she wasn't in on the kidnapping, why were people trying to hurt her? Because they believed she really was a psychic and were afraid she'd figure out who they were?

He rubbed his aching temples. "Nothing about her adds up."

"I'm just saying, it's awfully damn convenient that she seems to be right where the action is, every time." Brody gave him a hard look before going to talk to Captain Vann.

As the rest of the task force dispersed to their planned duties for the day, McBride picked up the phone and called Lily. She answered on the first ring. "It's not her," he said.

He heard her soft exhalation of relief. But a moment later, she said, "But it was somebody."

"Listen, I'm going to have to be here awhile longer. I'll call you later." He hung up, running a hand over his eyes.

Just hearing her voice tempted him to race back to her house and her waiting arms, but Brody was right. Lily was the big unanswered question sitting right in the middle of his investigation, and until he made sense of her part in the case, he had a feeling they'd never find out what had really happened to Abby Walters.

McBride grabbed Brody as he was about to head out. "You going to see Walters?"

"Yeah."

"I'll drive." Resolutely putting Lily out of his mind, McBride followed the FBI agent out of the office.

Chapter Twelve

"I'm sorry—I've been listening to the tape over and over, but I just don't recognize the voice," Walters said. "What does Lily say?"

McBride glanced at Brody. The agent's eyebrows twitched upward as McBride struggled for an answer that wouldn't sound crazy. "She thinks the caller was on the up and up."

"Did she recognize the voice?" Walters pressed.

McBride sighed, out of wiggle room. "Yeah, the voice on the phone. Not the one at the school, though."

Walters looked from McBride to Brody and back. "At the school? Someone contacted her at the school?"

Ignoring Brody's frown, McBride told Andrew Walters about the intruder at the school. "She's fine, just a little shaken."

"Thank God." Walters looked shaken himself. "I don't think I could live with myself if something happened to her because of what I've asked her to do."

Reassuring Walters that Lily was fine, McBride steered the interview back to the tape. "Maybe the kidnapper's connected to you somehow. Maybe a supporter you met at a rally."

"More likely a supporter of my opponent," Walters said blackly. "I knew he liked to play dirty, but—"

"Are you suggesting Senator Blackledge is connected to your daughter's kidnapping?" Brody's voice was quiet and grim.

Walters sighed. "I didn't say that."

Some of the task force had been dogging Gerald Blackledge for days as the savvy old senator beat the bushes in search of more votes. But given the way Walters was surging in the polls thanks to the sympathy vote, McBride couldn't see how kidnapping Abby would serve Blackledge's purposes. If he'd hoped that Walters would quit the race, he'd miscalculated badly.

Walters's cell phone rang. He glanced at the display panel. "I've got to get that."

"We'll see ourselves out," McBride said.

In the elevator down to the lobby, Brody gave McBride a measuring look. "I get Walters buying into the psychic business—but you don't, do you?"

"Of course not," McBride answered. But guilt

nagged at him, giving his gut a nasty little tweak, as if he was being disloyal to Lily for scoffing at her visions.

He and Brody were back at the station by eleven-thirty. On his way to his office, he checked in with Alex Vann to tell him about the interview with Walters regarding the tape from Lily's answering machine. "Walters says he doesn't recognize the voice and he has no idea what the man means about finding a way to contact him."

As McBride headed out the door, Vann pushed up out of his chair. "McBride, wait, there's something you need to know—"

McBride stopped short at the open door, his eyes widening when he saw the woman standing in the doorway across the hall. Her shiny blond hair glistened like silver in the glow of the overhead fluorescent lights.

His gut twisted. "Delaine."

THE FBI AGENT Lily convinced to drive her to the rental car place was happy for the change of scenery; surveillance was a pain in the ass, he'd confessed on the drive to the rental place. And he took a great deal of pleasure shaking the handful of reporters who'd mobbed them as they made their escape.

She'd picked out her clothing with care,

settling on a pair of slim-fitting olive-green wool pants and a figure-hugging sage cashmere sweater. By the time she'd chosen just the right suede sling-back pumps to complete the look, she'd started thinking of the outfit as her coat of armor. Because once she picked up a rental car, she was on her way to McBride's office to slay a dragon.

Today, she was going to ask him about Clare. And she wasn't going to leave his office until he told her.

She picked another Buick, similar to her totaled car, needing that sense of familiarity. She gave in to Agent Logan's demand that he follow her to the police station, but shooed him away when he tried to stay until she'd finished her business inside.

"Lieutenant McBride will see me home," she promised. Logan looked reluctant, but did as she asked.

She was halfway up the stairs to McBride's office when her cell phone rang. Torn between impatience to get the coming confrontation over with and relief to have the inevitable fireworks postponed, Lily hesitated only a moment before answering.

It was Andrew Walters. "Lily, thank God you're all right! Lieutenant McBride told me what happened to you."

"I'm fine," she assured him.

"I think you should do what the man said. I don't want to be responsible for something bad happening to you."

Lily frowned. "You don't want me to help you anymore?"

"You could have been killed." Andrew's voice was a curious mixture of anxiety and persuasiveness.

No wonder he's a politician, she thought.

"The police haven't had any luck finding anyone with the names you gave them, and the scenes you've described from your visions are too vague to help them pinpoint her location."

She tried not to take his words as a rebuke of her abilities. She knew what she was seeing was real. In time, she'd come up with the clue to help them find Abby.

If they had time.

Andrew's voice grew gentle. "I don't want you hurt."

There was nothing threatening in the tone of Andrew's voice. But the hair on the back of her neck rose, anyway.

"I'll think about it," she agreed.

"Good." He rang off quickly, as if he'd accomplished what he'd set out to do. She hung up the phone more slowly, considering Andrew's request.

Could she turn her back on Abby just because things were getting a little dangerous for Lily herself?

McBRIDE STARED AT Delaine Howard, fighting the urge to run. He'd never expected to see her again. God knew he didn't want to, especially on a day like today. But Delaine had always seemed to know when he was at his weakest.

He looked around the office to see if any other cops were there to run interference. But the rest of the day shift appeared to be out on calls. He closed the distance between them, noting with dark satisfaction the anxiety in her eyes. "What do you want?"

"I'm here about the kidnapping."

McBride thought the acid in his stomach was finally going to burn a hole all the way through. He moved past her and entered his office, grabbing the bottle of antacids from his desk. He crunched a couple between his teeth. "I suppose you've had a vision?"

"No." She paused in the doorway to his office. "I know you could never trust my visions again. Not after—"

"Cut the crap, Delaine. What do you want?"

She licked her lips and crossed to stand in front of his desk. "The woman on the news—Lily

Browning—you have to listen to her. She can help you find that little girl. She has a powerful gift."

His gut rebelled. "I don't work with psychics."

Delaine frowned. "But the news said—"

"It's Andrew Walters's idea. He's a father whose little girl is missing." McBride impaled her with his hard glare. "People believe all kinds of crazy things when they're desperate."

A tear slid down her cheek. "I thought Clare would be where I told you."

"But she wasn't, was she?" McBride rose to his feet, bitter rage surging. "She wasn't anywhere you told us we could find her. Do you have any idea what you did to us? Laura's dead because of you! I might as well be. And *you* did that, Delaine. You kept our hopes alive until they destroyed us." His voice rang through the office, dying away into silence.

Then he realized he and Delaine were no longer alone.

Lily stood in the doorway, gazing at him with stricken eyes. "Clare was your daughter."

The sympathy in her voice was too much for him to bear. He backed away from her and held up his hands. "Don't."

Delaine caught Lily's arm. "Give him a minute."

Lily jerked her arm away. "Don't tell me what to do." She turned to McBride. "I'm not her. I didn't do this to you."

McBride looked at Delaine. "You need to go now."

Tears filled Delaine's eyes. "I am sorry, McBride. You have to know that I never meant for things to go so wrong—" Her voice broke on a sob and she hurried out of the office.

McBride dropped heavily into his chair, trying to control his emotions before he did something rash. He looked at Lily. "You should go, too."

"No."

The look of understanding in her eyes nearly made him come undone. He balled his fists at his sides, afraid of losing himself completely to the blackness inside him if she stayed much longer. "You can't lead me to Abby Walters. I don't believe you. I never will. And no matter what you say, I don't think you can live with that in the long run."

She closed her eyes, pain drawing lines in her forehead.

"Look at me," he demanded.

She squeezed her eyes more tightly shut, shaking her head.

He lurched from his desk and grabbed her arms. "Look at me, damn it!"

Her eyes flew open, wide and afraid.

"This is what happens if you're wrong. This is what Andrew Walters will become when he finally learns the truth about Abby." McBride gave her a hard shake and let her go.

She backed away, eyes shiny with tears. "Andrew wants me off the case."

A sliver of surprise worked its way into the darkness inside him. He'd thought that Walters would cling to false hope to the bitter end. "Good. Then it's settled."

"I can't back away from this."

"That's your problem." Anger receded, sucking him back into an icy black abyss. He sank onto the edge of his desk. "As far as I'm concerned, it's over. I'm through."

She stared at him, dumbfounded.

"Go home, Lily."

"McBride, you can't just—"

He cut her off. "I'm done."

Her unflinching gaze held his for a long, painful moment. Then, suddenly, she looked away. Her lips began to tremble. She turned and hurried out the door.

He groped for his chair and sat, burying his head in his hands, giving in to the shakes he'd held off ever since Lily had walked through the door and into the middle of his nightmare.

He needed a drink. One shot of Jack Daniels after another, burning a path down his gullet until he forgot about the big, black hole in his heart.

He dragged himself to his feet and grabbed his coat. It was time to reacquaint himself with an old, reliable friend.

HER HEAD POUNDING with the force of another vision, Lily struggled to reach her vehicle. The last thing she wanted to do when McBride was in this state was go into a trance in the middle of his office.

Racing down the front steps of the police station, she managed to slide behind the wheel of her rental car before the vision sucked her through the door in her mind, into the mists. She didn't fight it, letting the flow of the vision soothe away the burgeoning ache in her head.

She emerged into an old-fashioned parlor sheltered from the midday sun by juniper bushes growing outside. A woman sat in a rocking chair near the hearth, holding out her hands as if warming them in front of a fire. But no fire was lit.

"You came." Hearing the small voice, Lily turned around to find Casey in the doorway, a smile carving dimples in her cheeks. "I called," the dark-haired girl said. "Did you hear me?"

"Is this where you live?"

The child nodded, her smile fading. "That's Mama." She gestured toward the woman. "She's in one of her moods."

Lily moved closer to the figure in the rocking

chair. She was a thin, pale woman about ten years older than Lily. She looked as though she'd been pretty once, but illness had slackened her jaw and glazed her blue eyes.

"I had another mama, but she died. My daddy couldn't take care of me, so I came to live with her." Casey knelt in front of the woman, pressing her cheek against her knee. "She didn't used to be so sad." Casey stroked her outstretched arm, but the woman didn't react.

Chills raced down Lily's spine. Was Casey even there? Or was she a ghost, the remnant of a child long dead? Had the woman gone crazy from grief? Was she paying no attention to Casey because Casey wasn't really there?

"I'm not a ghost," Casey said. "You have to be dead to be a ghost, and I'm not dead." She turned her head and looked at Lily, the directness of her gaze unnerving. "Are you dead?"

"No."

Casey smiled. "It would be okay if you were. I like you anyway. You're not scary."

Lily touched the girl's cheek, wondering if Casey would be able to feel it. The child rubbed her cheek against Lily's palm, her little-girl flesh soft and warm. Lily caressed the solemn, heart-shaped face.

"Will you come play with me?" Casey took her

hand. Lily squeezed the small fingers, marveling at how real they felt.

Casey led her down a narrow hall to a tiny room decorated in fading pink and white. "This is my room," she said proudly.

Lily looked around the tiny, cluttered space, her heart aching. It was grimy, despite obvious attempts by someone to keep it tidy. How long had this child lived with her mother's madness, trying to carve out some semblance of a normal life?

Lily sat on the bed by Casey, who picked up a book from a rickety bedside table. "My favorite book," she said.

Lily recognized the bright cover; she'd been reading the same book to her class for the past couple of weeks. *"Boots and Belinda,"* she murmured. "It's one of my favorite books, too."

She settled on the side of the bed and listened, her heart aching, as Casey carefully read the first chapter aloud. She read well, under the circumstances, though she mispronounced some of the more unfamiliar words. Lily wondered how she'd ever learned to read at all. Did she even attend school?

How could the world be full of so many lost little girls like Casey and Abby? Like McBride's Clare?

The vision seemed to last forever, through two more chapters of the book, through the lengthening of shadows in Casey's tiny bedroom. Just as

Lily realized how long she'd been there, the door in her mind opened, beckoning her back to reality.

"You have to go." Casey put down her book and picked up her tattered stuffed frog. "It's okay. My daddy gave me Mr. Green to watch after me."

"I'll try to come back," Lily promised.

The sun-warmed vinyl seat of the rental car replaced the dank mists swirling around her. She opened her eyes to bright sunlight, her heart pounding against her rib cage. The dashboard clock read four-fifteen. Two hours had passed, just as they had in her vision.

Lily pressed her face into her hands, trying to reorient herself in a world that seemed surreal after the sweet cocoon of time she'd just spent with the sad-eyed little girl who called herself Casey. Who was this child? Why did she have such a strong connection with Lily, strong enough to draw her to a misty netherworld and keep her there for almost two hours when most of Lily's visions lasted no more than five or ten minutes?

She had to find out who Casey was, try to make sense of her part in what was happening to Abby Walters.

But first she had to deal with McBride.

McBride LEANED OVER his kitchen table, his hand barely touching the smooth side of the unopened bottle of Jack Daniels. He couldn't remember buying it, couldn't even remember how or when he'd arrived at his house.

All he could remember was how hot and strong the whiskey had always felt as it washed down his throat and filled his stomach, numbing the pain, if only for a while.

He flipped another page of the photo album lying in front of him. He didn't remember bringing it out, either. He hadn't looked at it in a long time. He didn't know why he was doing so now. Every photograph was a fresh stab in the heart.

Clare at birth, tiny, red and wrinkled. Laura holding Clare, joy lighting her face from the inside. Clare's first birthday, when she'd put out the candle with her hand...

McBride shoved the album away and clutched the bottle of whiskey between his palms, rubbing the smooth glass surface to warm the golden liquid inside. Four years of sobriety were about to head out the window. He needed numbness so badly he thought he might die if he didn't take one drink.

He wanted it almost as much as he wanted Lily.

He'd thought that once he ended it, he could just walk away. But she was like a splinter, driving deeper the more he tried to extract her. He bled inside from wanting her.

Like the alcohol, she promised heat and release.

Relief from pain, at least for a while. He could almost taste her on his tongue, feel her slick heat welcome him deep inside her.

He could pour the Jack Daniels down the sink and the craving would eventually leave him alone, at least for a while. But even though he'd chased Lily away, he couldn't escape her. And that scared the hell out of him.

The front doorbell rang. He ignored it and tore the paper seal around the neck of the bottle.

The bell rang again, long and persistent.

"Go away!" he yelled.

The person at the door started banging. Hard. Relentlessly.

Anger poured through McBride, the first thing he'd felt besides grief in hours. He liked the feeling. He lunged to his feet, slamming the bottle of whiskey down on the kitchen counter on his way to the living room. He threw the dead bolt latch and jerked open the door, ready for a fight.

The sight of Lily hit him like cold water in the face. He staggered back from the door.

She took a step toward him, her expression wary. "You don't get to end this by yourself."

He took another step back. "Go away."

"No." She crossed to him and took his hands. Hers were soft and warm, her touch sending sensations coursing through him like a powerful drug.

He stiffened, resisting. "No."

She lifted one hand to his face. Something inside him cracked and spilled out, spreading warmth through his chest. In the face of her tender persistence, his resolve began to crumble. When she slipped her arms around him, he leaned heavily against her and let her lead him to the sofa.

She stroked and soothed him, cradling his face between her palms. She drew his head down and kissed him, her lips warm and incredibly soft. The coldness inside him began to recede, coiling back into its hidden lair. She deepened their kiss, touching her tongue to his. He opened his mouth to her gentle invasion, gave in to the electric sensations sparking in his belly and loins.

Lily curled her fingers into the fabric of his shirt and murmured his name. He covered her mouth with his, swallowing the word. Desire scorched through him as he drew her to her feet, pulling her with him toward his bedroom.

They didn't make it out of the living room.

Chapter Thirteen

McBride pressed Lily against the living room wall and ran his hands down her thighs, drawing them apart to cradle the hardening ridge of his erection. Heat pooled in her center as he rolled his hips, baring his teeth in primitive satisfaction when she gasped at the electric sensation.

He rocked against her, the friction shooting sparks along her spine. Unbearable anticipation built inside her.

Tightening his grip on her with one hand, he tugged open the zipper of her pants, then pushed both jeans and panties over her hips to bare her flesh to him.

She needed more. Now.

He tangled his hand in the curls between her thighs, his fingers teasing the sensitive flesh until she shook with need. Kicking away the clothes tangled around her feet, she opened herself to his touch. He knew how and where to stroke her, when to tease and when to torture. When he slid two fingers inside her, she clutched his shoulders and growled his name.

He silenced her with another hard kiss, unzipping his own pants. Savage need coiled inside her as he grasped her hips and held her steady. His gaze locked with hers, his eyes black with passion. Her breath caught in her throat. Then he rose between her thighs and drove into her in one long, hard thrust. She dug her fingernails into his back, gasping at the sudden fullness.

He went still, searching her face. "Lily…"

She kissed away the uncertainty her soft cry had elicited. "Please," she whispered, sliding her hands over his shoulders and down his back. She pressed her palms against his buttocks and pulled him deeper into her. A low groan of pleasure rumbled up her throat.

He stroked her breasts lightly through her blouse, his thumb teasing her nipples to aching peaks. She arched against him, felt him stir deep inside her. Her belly quivered and softened as he began to move within her.

He unbuttoned her blouse, unsnapped her bra and pushed both garments aside, covering her bare breasts with his palms. As he stroked her, gentled her with his caresses, she relaxed, accepting more of him with each thrust.

A delicious tension began to build in her core. She found his rhythm and rocked with him, stoking the fire spreading through her belly.

He pulled her thighs up, lifting her feet off the floor. She held on to him tightly, wrapping her legs around his waist as he pinned her against the wall. He soon lost control, his thrusts hard and frantic, and she realized he was going to finish well ahead of her.

He gave one final upward lunge and his body went rigid as he found release. Her name trembled on his lips, soft and desperate as a prayer, and she didn't care that her own body still buzzed with tension, unfulfilled. For this moment, at least, she'd given him exactly what he needed.

It was what she'd come here to do.

McBRIDE DIDN'T KNOW HOW much time passed before he was able to move again. Lily's fingers convulsed against his back, her hips still moving slightly against him. He stroked her hair and brushed his mouth against hers, tasting her tears. "It's okay," he whispered, wondering if it was. It had been a long time since he'd been with a woman, but not so long that he had forgotten what it felt like when she reached her climax.

Lily hadn't.

He lowered her feet to the floor and pulled away

from her. She made a soft, rattling noise deep in her throat, and clung to him, not letting him release her.

He stroked her cheek, growing alarmed. "Lily?"

She lifted her hand to his face. "Shh."

Her gentle touch felt like an accusation. He could hardly bear to look at her. "I'm sorry. I just—I needed—"

She pressed her lips to his. "I know."

He should have gone slow, taken time to find out what pleased her. To make love to her with his hands and mouth, readying her for him, giving her pleasure before taking his own.

She took his hand and moved toward the hallway. When he resisted, she met his gaze, her eyes dark with need and a hint of laughter. "Don't dawdle. You have unfinished business."

His heart stopped, then restarted at a jackhammer pace. Grasping her hand, he led her to his bedroom.

FULL DARKNESS HAD FALLEN when Casey woke. She hadn't meant to fall asleep, but she'd kept reading after Lily left, and suddenly her eyes just wouldn't stay open. She sat up and yawned, looking at the thin crack of light under her closed door. Was Mama awake?

She crept to Mama's bedroom. The door was open, and she slipped inside. Mama was on the bed, still clothed, her shoes on her feet. She lay atop the covers, but Casey could tell by the slow rise and fall of her chest that she was asleep.

Maybe that was good, Casey thought. Maybe when morning came, Mama would be like she used to be, before her spells.

Casey tiptoed back to her bedroom, changed into her pajamas and curled up on the bed, cuddling Mr. Green close. Still groggy, she closed her eyes and tried to go to sleep. But she had a hollow feeling in her chest, as if she was all alone in the world. The feeling made her sad and a little scared. She wished she could go find Lily. Lily would make her feel better.

Or maybe Abby, she thought with a sudden smile. Abby probably had that empty, all-alone feeling, too. She was a lot littler than Casey, and she was always real scared because of the mean men who took her away from her daddy and mommy. Abby would probably like Casey to come see her.

Casey didn't have words or thoughts to explain how she could visit Abby and Lily in her mind. She just could. She had thought they might be like her other friends, the ones she played with in her mind. There was Fern, who had a white poodle named Juliet. And Sam, who had a cat named Moonshine and a daddy who was a sea captain.

She'd read about all her friends, knew what they looked like from the pictures in the books or from her own imagination.

But she'd never read about Abby or Lily. Lily had appeared to her first, a brief flash in her mind as she lay in bed, somewhere between sleeping and waking. Curious, Casey had followed her through the gray mists to the room where Abby stayed. Casey had left when Lily did, but the next time she'd stayed and talked to Abby. Abby told her about her daddy and mommy and about how the bad men had grabbed her and hit her mommy and how her mommy had fallen down and gone to sleep.

Casey hadn't said the word *dead* to Abby, but that's what she thought. Abby's mommy was dead, like Casey's real mama.

But what about Daddy?

Casey could still hear his voice in her head sometimes. *Sweet baby marshmallow, close your bright eyes....*

Casey grabbed Mr. Green and squeezed his lumpy body to hers. She curled into a little knot, her forehead creasing with concentration. She tried to imagine the mists surrounding her, like on a foggy day, when she couldn't see her hand in front of her face. She drifted through the fog, looking for Abby.

She found Abby's room, smelled the musty, dirty scent. But Abby wasn't in there.

Fear coiled in Casey's chest. Was she with the bad men?

Then she saw the open window. The sunflower curtain rippled in the cool breeze flowing through it. Casey let herself float to the window to look out at the meadow of tall grass stretching to the edge of thick, dark woods. She spotted Abby, a speck of light in the darkness. She'd crawled out of the window! She'd gotten away from the bad men! Casey clapped her hands and laughed. Yea, Abby!

Suddenly, the door behind Casey banged open. She whirled around and saw a man filling the doorway. He had sandy hair, a mean, scowly look on his face and a big gun in his hand. Beyond him, two men lay on the floor. Something red pooled around them, as if they'd spilled cherry Kool-Aid and taken a nap in the middle of the mess.

Only Casey knew it wasn't really cherry Kool-Aid. It was darker and thicker and it smelled funny, like the bright pennies she collected in a little pink piggy bank on her dresser. She didn't like the way it smelled. It made her tummy feel all squirmy and hot.

The big man in the doorway rushed toward her, sending panic shooting through her veins. She crouched in terror, trying to make herself as small as she could.

He walked right through her, and she remembered with a gush of relief that she wasn't really there in the little room with the messy bed and the open window.

He peered out the window. Could he see Abby?

Casey joined him at the window, keeping her distance even though she knew now that he couldn't see her. Outside, Abby had disappeared from view. Relief washed through Casey, making the room glitter like fairy dust and almost disappear.

She focused her mind on staying in the room, braced by her growing worry about Abby alone in the woods. Now Lily wouldn't know where to find her. And anything could happen to a little girl all alone. Didn't Mama always tell her that, back when Mama used to talk to her more?

She had to follow Abby so she wouldn't be alone. That was all there was to it. And later, maybe she could find Lily and tell her where Abby was now. Lily would know what to do. She'd know how to stop the bad man with the scowly face and the gun.

Lily would take care of them.

LILY NESTLED NEXT TO McBride under the warm quilt and listened to his heartbeat beneath her cheek. She could never turn back now. Making love to him had only sealed their fate. She just had to figure out how to make things work for them outside the bedroom.

"This isn't how I thought today would end," McBride murmured against her neck.

"You're not sorry, are you?"

He sat up, drawing her into his arms. "No. You?"

"No." She pressed her mouth against the faint cleft of his chin. "But since you brought up the subject of today…"

He drew away slightly. "Do we have to talk about it?"

She wasn't going to give in. McBride needed this. She scooted to the headboard and draped her arm around his broad shoulders. "Start with Laura. Where did you meet her?"

He turned to look at Lily, his features tinged with reluctance. But after a moment, he relaxed a little, leaned into her embrace.

"College," he answered. "She was great at math. I was good at history. We sort of bartered with each other. She helped me in math and I got her through Western Civ."

"What did she look like?"

He smiled, his eyes distant. "Cute. Not movie star pretty, but cute. She had the prettiest skin, very fair. I remember she always wore about a ton of sunscreen whenever she walked out the door. Clare had the same kind of skin."

Once McBride got started, the story poured out of him. He told Lily about the friendship that had turned into romance. The marriage right after graduation. Laura had taught junior high math and he'd gone straight to the police academy. After three years of marriage, they'd started trying to have a baby, but Laura couldn't carry to term.

"A fertility expert finally found a deformity in her uterus that other doctors missed. It was a fairly simple surgical procedure. Next thing we knew, we had Clare."

His mouth tightened when he said his daughter's name. Lily squeezed his shoulders, wishing she had her sister Iris's gift. Iris could have absorbed his pain and eased his suffering. Lily would've given anything to take away McBride's pain.

But all she could do was see things that other people couldn't, a gift McBride loathed. And after seeing him with Delaine this afternoon, hearing how the woman's broken promises had ripped his life apart, Lily understood why.

"How old was Clare when she disappeared?" she asked.

"Barely three."

Just a baby, Lily thought.

"She was there, playing in the yard one minute, and the next..." His voice grew faint, as if he couldn't believe it any more now than he could six years ago. "Gone. Just like that."

"Nobody saw anything?"

He shook his head. "It was a weekday. Most of the families on the street had older kids, all in school. Laura had been teaching Clare to ride her tricycle when the phone rang. Laura ran inside to get it. She wasn't gone more than a minute or two. We had a fenced-in yard." His voice broke. "She didn't think anything could happen."

Lily closed her eyes, heartsick. Maybe she'd been wrong to make him tell her these things.

He drew his legs up to his chin, curling in on himself. "It was Laura's idea to work with a psychic, but I didn't argue. I'd have done anything to find Clare."

"So you found Delaine."

"She found us. She came to the station and said she'd had a vision about Clare. She knew what Clare had been wearing and about a scrape on her chin where she'd fallen off her trike. She knew about her favorite toy. God, we wanted to believe her," he said bitterly.

"Of course. You wanted to find your daughter."

"We wanted somebody to tell us that she was all right, even after weeks passed without any leads." He rubbed his jaw with a shaky hand. "I'm a policeman, Lily. I knew the truth. It was staring me in the face, but I couldn't deal with it. Delaine convinced us that she'd seen Clare, that she was living with another family and all we had to do was find out who those people were. She kept having visions, getting closer and closer, and I believed every single word she said.

"I followed every clue, stayed up all night for days on end, going over every detail, considering all the possibilities. If she saw a rose in her vision, I'd make a list of all the florists and nurseries in the state. I'd even look for the name Rose in the phone book, just in case. I did legwork and more legwork, knocked on doors, made phone calls, hounded my fellow cops until they were ready to have me put away, and finally—finally!" His laugh was the most horrible sound Lily had ever heard. "Delaine had a breakthrough. She saw Clare in a green-and-white house over in Rockwell, just over the county line. She even gave us a name. The Graingers."

"So you found the Graingers?" Goose bumps scattered across Lily's bare shoulders.

"We converged on the place. Two cars from here, plus the county sheriff over in Rockwell. Lights flashing, sirens going. Scared the hell out the poor Graingers, who were having a birthday party for their little girl."

"Who wasn't Clare."

"Who wasn't Clare." His voice sounded dead. "Because Clare was dead. I think I realized it the instant I saw the little Grainger girl with her pigtails and pretty green party dress. Holly Grainger was alive. My baby was dead."

"I'm so sorry." Tears spilled down Lily's cheeks.

"After that, I told Delaine to stay away from us. I forbade her to go anywhere near Laura. I made sure she wasn't allowed at the station house." He sighed. "What she did to us was the cruelest thing she could've done. She should have just killed us instead."

Lily felt sick, understanding so much that had puzzled her since she'd first met him. She wondered how he could bear to be around her after his experience with Delaine. No wonder he wanted her to stay away from Andrew.

Yet she knew Abby Walters was alive. She *knew* it.

But had Delaine been equally sure about Clare?

"After the incident at the Graingers', Laura started seeing Clare everywhere. At the grocery store, the park, at church. She'd drive by schools and swear she saw her playing on the swings or climbing the monkey bars." His chest heaved, as if the mere effort to breathe was too much for him. "One day, she thought she saw Clare across Beaumont Parkway. She didn't even look before she ran into the street. There was a car—"

Lily couldn't bear to hear any more. She pressed her hand over McBride's mouth. "Please!"

He pulled her hand away as if compelled to

finish. "I got to the emergency room just before she died. The last thing she told me was that she'd seen Clare. She wanted me to go get her." His face crumpled. "I couldn't do the last thing she wanted me to do. I couldn't go get our baby."

A hard, gasping sob exploded from him, wrenched from the dark place Lily had sensed in him almost from the first. She held him, aching for the child he had loved and she'd never gotten the chance to know, while he emptied himself of six years of darkness.

His shudders subsided gradually, and he drew away from her. She let go, giving him time to compose himself. He sat on the edge of the bed with his back to her, his hands moving over his eyes to wipe away the evidence of his grief. "I'm sorry."

"Don't be."

He looked at her over his shoulder. "I know you believe you're really seeing Abby Walters when you go into your trance or whatever it is. I know that."

"But you don't believe it."

"I don't have it in me anymore." He ran his hand over his jaw. "I'm sorry."

"It's okay."

He turned away from her. "You'll start to resent me."

Was he right? At this moment, in his bed, with

his body warm and solid beside her, she couldn't imagine it. But what would happen the next time she had a vision of Abby?

Lily had run from her gift her whole life, had hated it, feared it. Now she'd finally begun to trust herself, to believe she had been given this special ability for a purpose. She could use it to help people, find scared little girls like Abby.

She couldn't turn back now. Even when she had run from it, the gift had been a fundamental element of who she was.

It defined her.

McBride turned and touched her face. "Let's not think about any of this tonight, okay? We'll think about it later." He lay down and pulled her into his arms, his breath warm against her cheek. She heard his breathing deepen as he drifted off to sleep, his body relaxed and content behind hers.

But she lay awake, wondering if their newfound intimacy could outlast her next vision.

Chapter Fourteen

Casey couldn't feel the cold as she followed Abby into the woods, but she knew the smaller girl had to be freezing. She wore no coat and only a pair of thin, dirty socks on her feet. Older and wiser, Casey felt the weight of responsibility for her friend. She had to help Abby find a warm, safe place to stay until Casey could find a way to reach Lily.

"Abby!" she cried. Abby kept running.

She must be scared of the scowly man with the gun, Casey thought, straining to catch up. She glanced over her shoulder to see if the man was following. She couldn't spot him, but she heard crashing noises in the woods behind her. Fear rose in her chest, hot and sharp. It tasted like pennies, reminding her of the men she'd left behind in the trailer.

Ahead, Abby dashed through the woods, tripping on tree roots and getting tangled in the low bushes blanketing the forest floor. She somehow stayed just out of reach, and Casey couldn't figure out why. After all, Casey was floating along like a butterfly, easily staying clear of the stumps and vines that made Abby fall down over and over.

"Abby, you've gotta hide! I can help!" Casey screamed into the darkness. *Oh, God, please help her hear me,* she prayed fervently. *Make her hear me.*

Abby tripped over another root and sprawled forward, hitting the ground with a thud. She made soft, gasping noises that scared Casey into a final spurt of effort.

"Abby, are you okay? Abby, can you hear me?" Casey finally touched her friend.

The little girl managed to draw a few short, struggling breaths. The wheezy sounds subsided and her eyes widened. "Casey?"

Casey felt like cheering. "Shh! Yeah, it's me! You got away from them but somebody's coming after you!"

Abby started crying. "I heard a bang-bang noise, Casey. I think it was a gun!"

Casey thought of the weapon she'd seen in the scowly man's hand. It had looked gigantic, like a cannon.

"They're gonna find me," Abby mewled. "They're

gonna come after me and shoot me!" She choked on her sobs. "Tell me what to do, Casey! I'm scared."

"You've gotta be quiet, like Lily tells you, 'member?"

Abby's sniffles sounded like thunder in Casey's ears. "I want Lily!" the little girl wailed. Even though the words came from Abby's mind, not her mouth, Casey held her breath, afraid the scowly man had heard.

"It's okay," she promised, her own thoughts a whisper. "Lily will be here, you wait and see."

BY MIDNIGHT LILY WAS still awake, too tense to close her eyes. Her stomach growled, reminding her she'd skipped dinner.

Without waking McBride, she extracted herself from his grasp and slid out of bed. Cool air washed over her body, raising chill bumps, so she slipped on his discarded shirt and picked up the extra blanket that had fallen on the floor during their lovemaking, wrapping it around herself before heading to the kitchen to find something to eat.

The pantry wasn't well stocked. After moving a few boxes and cans, she found a pack of crackers that didn't look too old. She grabbed a glass from the draining rack by the sink, filled it with water and carried her snack to the table.

Halfway there, she felt the shivers hit. She made it to the table, falling into one of the chairs just before the door in her mind crashed open and she was sucked into the mists.

Casey appeared in the fog in front of her. "Oh, Lily!" She flung herself into her arms.

"What is it?" Lily squeezed her close.

"There was a gunshot, and a bad scowly man had a gun, and I think he killed the bad men who took Abby, and she got away but she's all alone in the woods and it's cold and she's scared, and he's looking for her, and I don't know what to do!" Casey squirmed out of Lily's embrace and tugged her hand urgently. "You've got to help us!"

Lily didn't wait for Casey's words to sink in, tightening her grip on the child's hand, she followed her through the mist.

MCBRIDE LAY BETWEEN dozing and waking, waiting for Lily to return to bed. Though her scent lingered in the sheets and on his skin, he missed the feel of her next to him.

He pressed his face against her pillow and breathed deeply, remembering the way her soft, spicy-sweet scent had washed over him during their lovemaking. She had been both generous and demanding, trusting him enough to let him know when he was pleasing her and when she needed more. She'd given back to him in return, eager and willing to please him, as well.

And afterward, she'd given him what he'd needed most, letting him share the darkness he'd kept inside for so long.

He had been terrified of letting go of his grief, as if in doing so he would lose what small connection he had left with Laura and Clare. But he hadn't lost them, after all. For the first time since Clare's disappearance, he found he could think of his daughter and smile, too.

Clare had been a happy child, full of joy and laughter. She could flash her dimples at him and make his heart melt. He had almost forgotten that over the past six years.

How could he have let his rage and grief steal Clare's smiles from him?

Thanks to Lily, he had those memories back again.

Tired of waiting for her to return to bed, he slipped on a pair of pants and followed the light to the kitchen, where he found Lily sitting at the table, her back to him. He padded across the cold linoleum and lifted her hair, pressing his mouth against the side of her throat. "Hungry?" he asked, noting the crackers sitting in front of her.

She didn't answer.

Then he saw the glass lying on its side, water

dribbling off the table and puddling on the floor at her feet. The skin on the back of his neck tingled. "Lily?"

He crouched next to her. Her forehead was creased, her eyes open but unseeing. A whisper passed between her soft pink lips, but he could make out no words.

She was having another vision.

Ignoring the spilled water, he sat across from her, his heart in his throat. He hadn't expected to have to deal with this part of her so soon. After all they'd just been through, he still couldn't—wouldn't—believe she had some sort of supernatural ability to "see" people and places beyond her own reality. Yet neither could he believe she was a liar, a charlatan putting on an act for his benefit.

So the only other option was what? Madness?

Her sightless eyes stared toward the kitchen window, but he knew she wasn't seeing her reflection in the darkened panes.

With growing unease, he waited.

"THERE SHE IS!" Casey pointed and tugged Lily's hand.

The mists in Lily's mind parted to reveal Abby, crying quietly in the middle of a dense, dark wood. The trees loomed over her like spindly monsters, dwarfing her tiny body. Lily intensified her concentration and touched the frightened child's tearstained face. She felt the dampness beneath her fingertips.

"Lily, you came!" Abby's face lit up with a smile. A now-familiar ripple of wonder shot through Lily. She knew that in reality she was sitting in a chair in McBride's kitchen, but she could feel Abby's soft skin as surely as if she were truly there in the dark, cold woods.

She soothed Abby as she concentrated on seeing more of the child's surroundings. The forest stretched into blackness, but she heard sounds in the distance, something—someone—crashing through the underbrush. Lily clenched her jaw and focused her mind on seeing beyond the void, but she could only hear the noises. "Abby, you need to hide."

"There's a big bush over there." Casey pointed.

Lily led Abby to the bush and crouched beside her. "Abby, I need you to be quiet as a mouse. Can you do that?"

The little girl nodded.

Casey hunkered down beside them, her wide hazel eyes fixed on Lily's face, as if waiting for the next instruction. The full weight of responsibility crashed down on Lily's shoulders.

The noise behind them grew louder, and Lily finally caught sight of the source. Though the darkness rendered him little more than a hulking shadow, she could tell by his build and his powerful movements that he was a man.

She peered through the gloom, wishing her gift of clairvoyance came with a built-in spotlight. She couldn't get a good look at him in the dark.

Until he came close enough to touch.

A thin beam of moonlight pierced the canopy of trees overhead, revealing his sandy hair and stocky build. Around forty, he wore dark clothes and carried a large gun.

Lily tightened her grip on Abby. The child went still.

The man crept closer. Lily held her breath, terrified he'd find Abby's hiding place.

After an excruciating length of time, he passed the bush where Abby was hidden. The little girl started to get up, but Lily held her in place, allowing herself to breathe again. She waited, caressing Abby's small arm, until the man was well away. Then she whispered, "Do you think you're ready to keep walking, Abby?"

"Sure she is." Casey took one of Abby's hands. "We can make it together, can't we?"

Abby blinked away her tears and nodded.

Lily helped Abby up. "Honey, you need to think hard, okay? Think hard about Casey and me holding your hands. Do you feel it?"

Abby nodded.

"Okay. Do you remember which direction you came from, sweetie?" The last thing Lily wanted was to lead the little girl back to her abductors.

Abby looked around. She lifted one plump arm and pointed. "Over there."

"She's right, that's the way we came," Casey agreed.

Lily tightened her fingers around Abby's hand. "Let's go."

By focusing sharply, she could see about fifty yards ahead of her at any one time, but thought it would be enough. She just had to keep Abby putting one foot in front of the other until they came to some sign of civilization.

After a long walk, Abby said, "I see a light."

Lily peered into the gloom, seeing nothing. "Which way?"

The little girl gestured to her left. She tugged Lily's hand, urging her to quicken her pace.

On the other side of Abby, Casey's image was wavery, not quite there. All of Lily's concentration was on Abby, which meant that Casey was sustaining her presence almost completely on her own. Lily wondered if the little girl was clairvoyant.

How was she ever going to explain this to McBride?

Suddenly, ahead, she saw it. A yellow light. It

flickered as they approached, sometimes shielded by tree limbs but growing ever closer. Soon, Lily could make out the edge of a clearing, then the dark outline of some sort of building.

"It's a house!" Abby started running toward the light.

It was, indeed, a house. Made of natural pine clapboard, it nestled in a clearing in the woods, with a wide porch that spanned the entire front.

Abby almost tripped but caught herself, her little legs churning as she hurried forward.

Excitement surged through Lily as she realized that Abby was really going to be safe. She would knock on the door of that house and nice people would come to the door and help her.

Wouldn't they?

Or was Abby about to walk into the lair of an even more heinous monster?

Lily pushed her doubts to the back of her mind. Abby couldn't last out in the cold much longer. She had to take a chance on the people in this cabin. "Abby, knock on the door. Tell whoever answers that your name is Abby Walters and that you were kidnapped. Tell them to call the police, and tell them about yourself, okay? Can you remember all that?"

Abby nodded, her eyes bright with tears of nervous excitement. "Are you coming with me?"

"I can't, honey. But I'll come find you soon, I promise." She let go of Abby's hand.

As soon as the contact was broken, she felt the mists swirling around her, blurring the edges of her vision. Frantically she clung to the vision, watching Abby climb the three steps to the porch. Lily looked for some kind of distinguishing mark on the house so she could tell the police where to search for her.

As the mists encroached on the clearing around her, she caught sight of a painted wooden plaque hanging on the wall next to the front door of the house—geese flying in tandem, a wide blue banner stretched between their beaks. In neat script on the banner was written The Marlins.

Then the mist swallowed her. She emerged from the grayness a few seconds later.

But she wasn't in McBride's kitchen.

She was in Casey's bedroom.

"You're going to leave me now, aren't you?" Casey stood before her, arms tight around her tattered green frog.

"I promise I'll try to come back. Maybe you can help me do that."

Casey smiled. "I don't feel alone when you're here."

Lily tried to hug the little girl, but the tug of reality at her back was too strong. Arms still outstretched to Casey, she was sucked back through the door in her mind.

Casey gazed out at her from the doorway, tears trickling down her cheeks. Then the door slammed shut and Lily was back in the kitchen. Looking at McBride.

She gave a little start.

His touch on her arm was tentative. "Are you okay?"

She clutched his wrist. "McBride, Abby got away from her kidnappers!"

His forehead creased with a frown. "Lily—"

"Please, you have to listen to me just this one time! Abby escaped through the window of the trailer home where they were keeping her. There was a man—I think maybe he killed Abby's kidnappers, and now he's looking for her in the woods. He has a gun. I helped Abby hide until he went past us, then we walked in the other direction and found a house in the woods. The last I saw of Abby, she was knocking on the door."

Brow furrowed, McBride stood up and took a step away from her.

She followed, closing the gap he'd opened. "You've got to call the FBI or somebody! What if the people at that house aren't nice?"

"You sound…crazy."

"Damn it, McBride, if you don't call someone,

I'm going to do it. She's at a house in the woods. I couldn't get a good bearing as to where it might be, but I think it's here in this county. The terrain looks kind of familiar. The house is one-story, pine clapboard, with a big veranda-style porch. And there's a plaque on the wall by the front door, two flying geese carrying a banner with The Marlins printed on it."

He grabbed her hand. "Lily, listen to me—"

Before he could say another word, the phone rang.

A bubble of hope rose in Lily's throat. Had the people in the house already called the police?

McBride didn't move for a moment. She could tell by his expression that the timing of the call spooked him a little. He looked from her to the ringing phone.

"Get it." Her stomach tightened with anticipation.

He crossed to the phone. "McBride."

Seconds later, myriad emotions darted over his face—disbelief, anger, confusion, consternation, realization, bewilderment and, finally, a mixture of fear and hope. "Okay, I'm on my way." He hung up the phone.

"It's Abby, isn't it?"

He walked slowly toward her, looking stunned. "A man named Jerry Marlin called the county sheriff. A little girl knocked on his door in the middle of the night, said she was Abby Walters and they were supposed to call the police."

It took a second for McBride's words to sink in. Then shivers rolled over Lily. She groped behind her for the chair and sat. "She's okay?"

"Best they can tell." As McBride closed the distance between them, he opened his mouth, then closed it again, as if he didn't know what to say.

Neither did she.

He stopped a foot in front of her. "Agent Brody is headed out there already. I've got to go."

She pushed away from the table. "I'm going with you."

MCBRIDE CONCENTRATED on the dark, winding road. Jerry Marlin's address was a rural route box, but the sheriff had given him good directions. They were less than a mile away now.

Lily had been silent during the drive. Just as well. McBride didn't know what to say to her. The world was upside down, nothing making much sense. He was a man who dealt in facts. The facts of the Abby Walters case were that the little girl apparently was alive, after all. She'd apparently escaped her captors, made her way through the woods and knocked on the door of Jerry Marlin's cabin.

And Lily Browning had told him every single fact well before the phone rang.

He was afraid to believe that he was about to see Abby Walters alive and well. He'd been sure they'd find her in a ditch or a Dumpster somewhere around the county. He'd been rehearsing the words he would say to Andrew Walters.

He was afraid to believe until he saw Abby for himself.

He pulled off the highway onto a gravel road that led deep into the woods. The gravel soon gave way to dirt. "Almost there," he murmured, the first words he'd said in ten minutes.

Next to him, Lily was tense and pale. She turned to look at him, her eyes glittering in the dashboard lights.

"How you doing?" he asked. "Warm enough?"

She nodded. "Did anybody call Andrew Walters?"

He shook his head. "We want to wait, make sure this isn't a hoax or a false alarm." The Chevy's headlights suddenly picked up the reflector paint on a county sheriff's car, then the pine cabin looming just beyond. McBride parked behind the sheriff's cruiser and turned to Lily. "Ready?"

She unbuckled her seat belt and nodded.

They converged in front of the car, Lily sliding her hand into his. He tightened his fingers around hers and walked with her up the shallow porch steps. Immediately he saw the wooden plaque beside the front door. Even in the waning moonlight, he could make out the pair of geese and the printed banner. "The Marlins," he murmured.

Lily's hand trembled in his. He looked down at her and saw her staring at the plaque. "It's really here," she breathed.

He squeezed her hand and knocked on the door. It opened and a lanky black sheriff's deputy greeted him. "You McBride?"

"Yes." He indicated the shield on his belt, then released Lily's hand. "This is Lily Browning. She's been helping us on the case. Where's the child?"

The deputy waved toward a doorway to the left. McBride went through the wide archway, Lily right behind him.

Three people sat at the kitchen table. A burly man with steel-gray hair was in one chair, a short, plump woman with pink curlers in her bleached hair across from him.

And in the middle, her grubby little hands wrapped around a stoneware mug, sat Abby Walters.

McBride's stomach tightened into a hard, hot ball. He took a couple of tentative steps toward the child, then closed the rest of the distance in a dash, reaching out to touch the little girl's face. "Abby?"

She blinked rapidly, startled by his sudden approach.

Her skin was warm and unbelievably soft. He drew a swift breath. "Tell me your name, honey."

She wiped her cheek with one grimy hand. "I'm Abby Walters, I live at 524 Winslow Road and I want to go home."

"Your daddy will be here soon. But I need you to tell me everything you remember about tonight."

Abby's face crumpled. "I heard a bang. It sounded like a big firecracker going off. I pushed and pushed at the window and it opened, so I climbed out and ran."

McBride glanced over his shoulder at Lily. She stood in the kitchen doorway, her arms wrapped tightly around her stomach, tears in her eyes as she stared at Abby.

She had been right about everything. Skeet, Gordy, Abby. This house and the geese on the plaque on the porch...

He looked back at Abby, who was saying, "It was real high and I was scared I'd fall and break my neck like Mama always says, but I was more scared Skeet'd come get me and hit me like he hit my mama, and so I opened the window and I jumped."

Her gaze shifted, looking beyond him.

He heard Lily's voice, soft and trembling. "Abby. It's Lily."

Abby's face lit up. She leaped from the table, pushing past McBride.

He turned in time to see the little girl fling herself into Lily's arms. Lily crushed the child to her, tears streaming down her cheeks.

"You came, Lily, you came!" Abby cried.

Chapter Fifteen

Lily tightened her arms around Abby. She was really here, really okay. Not just a tiny freckled face in the mists of her mind, but solid little arms and legs wrapped around her.

Abby patted Lily's cheeks with her hands. "You're so pretty! I never could see you."

Lily stroked Abby's red curls. "I'm so proud of you. You were such a brave girl to get away."

"Mama will be real proud of me, won't she?"

Lily's heart broke. She glanced past Abby to McBride, who leaned heavily against the table, watching them. He looked as if a truck had hit him.

All his firmly held, highly logical beliefs had just been blown apart. Abby was alive and well, and Lily had been dead on target. His whole sense of reality was probably off-kilter right now.

Agents Brody and Logan entered the kitchen behind her. Brody glared at Lily. "What's she doing here?"

"We've got a lot of ground to cover." McBride pushed himself away from the table edge. "Has anyone called Walters?"

Brody ignored Lily and smiled at Abby, his stony face softening. "You must be Abby."

The little girl tightened her grip on Lily.

"It's okay." Lily stroked the child's tousled curls. "Mr. Brody just needs to ask you some questions."

"About Gordy and Skeet?" Abby asked solemnly.

Lily threaded her fingers through Abby's hair. "Yes, honey. Let's go sit at the table and talk to Mr. Brody and Mr. Logan." She carried Abby to the table and set her in the chair.

"Ms. Browning?" Logan took Lily's arm as she started to sit by Abby. "I have some questions, if you don't mind."

"She was with me all night," McBride interjected.

Brody and Logan both turned to look at him, then back at Lily. A blush rolled up her neck and into her cheeks.

"Humor me," Brody said finally.

McBride started to protest, but Lily put her hand on his arm. "It's okay."

She followed Agent Logan to the parlor. He waved at the overstuffed settee by the window and took the paisley armchair across from her. His broad shoulders knocked awry the lace doily draped over the chair back. "Ms. Browning, tell me what happened after you left your house this evening."

"At least part of what I did is none of your business."

She was pleased to see that some men were still capable of blushing. "So tell me the part that is my business," he said.

Stifling a smile, Lily complied.

"YOU ACTUALLY HEARD LILY in your room, Abby?" Brody's voice was gentle, but McBride detected the steely edge.

"She wasn't really *in* the room." Abby's mouth tightened with impatience. "She was in my *mind,* helping me hear her."

"Did Lily tell you she was just in your mind?"

"Yeah, 'cause at first I thought she was a ghost voice and I was scared. But then she said she was in my mind, and I wasn't so scared. She hugged me and made me feel better."

"Hugged you? You felt her touch you?"

Abby frowned. "Well, sorta. It was like butter-flies, you know? Like a hundred hundred butter-flies flapping their wings against me. But it made me feel like I wasn't alone."

"And she helped you find this house?" Brody asked.

"She and Casey did. Lily said go knock on the

door and tell them I was Abby Walters and to call the police." Abby nodded solemnly. "And I did."

McBride drew a shaky breath. Had Lily been with Abby in her mind, helping her find safety? What other explanation was there? Lily hadn't been out of his sight for fifteen minutes. Short of thumbing a ride on a passing helicopter, she couldn't have gotten to these woods and back in that short a time.

"Who's Casey?" Brody asked.

"She's this kid who came to visit me. I couldn't see her, either." Abby spoke as if she were saying nothing unusual.

Goose bumps rose on McBride's arms.

Brody glanced up at him, one brow cocked so high it almost reached his hairline. He looked back at the little girl. "Abby, are you sure Lily was never really in your room?"

"Yes, I'm sure. Neither was Casey. I told you." Abby's bottom lip puffed out and tears welled in her red-rimmed eyes. "I don't want to talk anymore. I wanna go home." Tears trickled from her eyes. "I want to see my mommy."

"Come on, Brody, she's had enough for tonight." McBride put his hand on the fed's arm. Brody motioned for McBride to follow him while Mrs. Marlin entered the room and comforted Abby.

"Who do you think this Casey is?" McBride asked as they stepped into the dark hallway.

Brody ignored the question. "Is Mr. Walters on his way?"

McBride nodded. "I sent a uniform to drive him here. He sounded too shaky to get here under his own steam."

"Good." Brody nodded and walked toward the open parlor door, a rectangle of light in the narrow, gloomy hall. McBride followed him. Inside, Lily and Agent Logan sat across from each other, both silent and tense.

"Mike, I'd like to see you out here for a minute," Brody said.

As Agent Logan came out of the parlor, McBride went inside and crouched next to Lily. "Everything okay?"

She nodded. "How's Abby holding up?"

"She's doing great. She thinks you're the best, you know." He didn't ask about Casey. Not in front of the agents. He'd save that for later.

Lily smiled. "I'm just glad she's okay."

"McBride, can I see you a moment?" Brody asked. He and Logan stepped away from the doorway, forcing McBride to follow them. Brody's grim expression made McBride's gut coil into an aching knot. The FBI agent lowered his voice. "We just got a call from your men. They found the trailer where Abby was being kept. We also found Debra Walters's missing Lexus."

McBride could tell there was more. "And the kidnappers?"

"Dead from gunshot wounds."

McBride remembered Lily's earlier words. A man with a gun.

Lily had seen a killer.

HE'D NEVER KILLED BEFORE.

It wasn't like he'd thought it would be, the kick of the gun in his hand or the sound ringing in his deafened ears. And the blood. God, the blood.

He'd had to do it. Make a mess to clean up the mess.

Blood spatter dotted his clothing, a fine red spray on the dark wool. But he'd been prepared for that possibility. He stripped off his latex gloves and wadded them up with his sweater, pants and shoes, shivering as the cool October breeze whipped across his bare skin. Tucking the blood-stained clothes into a small garbage bag, he tossed them into the Dumpster in the alley.

Donning the spare clothes he'd brought with him, he closed the top of the trash bin and returned to his car, his heart pounding with growing apprehension.

Had Abby seen him? He didn't think so. Even

if she had, she was just a little girl, easily confused. And his alibi, should he need one, was rock solid.

Maybe it was finally over.

WALTERS ARRIVED at the Marlins' house around the time that Brody and Logan were briefing McBride on the two murders, so McBride missed the reunion between father and daughter. Walters was bundling the sleepy little girl into his arms when McBride and Lily reentered the kitchen.

Walters looked at Lily, his eyes bright with tears. "I don't know how…"

She shook her head and squeezed his hand. "Not necessary."

"Mr. Walters, I'd like to put you both in protective custody until things get settled."

Walters's blue eyes narrowed. "Settled how?"

McBride glanced at Abby, who'd already fallen asleep on her father's shoulder. Quietly, he told him about the murders.

Walters looked shocked. "My God. Why?"

That was the big question. Who would want to kill the kidnappers and why? "We're looking into that right now."

"And you think Abby's in danger?"

"She didn't see whoever shot the men, and as far as we know, he didn't see her. But we shouldn't take any chances." It was possible the sandy-haired man didn't consider Abby enough of a threat to go after her, but McBride wasn't ready to risk her life on that assumption. "We can provide twenty-four hour guard at your hotel room."

Walters shook his head. "I don't want her to stay in another strange place. Debra's sister agreed to take Abby until I can settle everything here. I'll send half my security detail with them. It'll free you up to find out who did this and why."

McBride would have preferred to keep Abby where he could make sure she was safe, but he understood Walters's need to get the girl into a familiar place with someone she knew and loved. "We may need to talk to her again."

Walters didn't look happy, but he nodded. "Understood."

McBride motioned Theo Baker over and briefed him on the plan, making it clear that he was to treat the trip back to the hotel as a protective detail.

McBride and Lily walked Walters and Abby out to Theo's car. The sergeant headed back around to the driver's seat. "You coming in to the office now?" he asked.

"I'm going to see Ms. Browning home." McBride didn't like the idea of leaving her alone, now that she was a murder witness.

Theo grinned. McBride's stern look only made his grin widen. "Just leave your cell phone on, Romeo."

When they'd left, McBride slid his arm around Lily's waist, leaning his head against hers. He was overjoyed to see Walters and his daughter reunited, but couldn't suppress a tinge of jealousy and resentment. Why hadn't he had a happy ending, too? He took a deep breath, careful to hide his feelings. "Hell of a night."

Lily slipped her arm around him. "A lot's happened that you need time to assimilate."

He looked at her. *Assimilate? Nice tidy word to describe having your entire mind turned inside out.* "You think?"

"Are you mad at me?" she asked.

He rubbed his face, ashamed of his snappishness. He was the one who'd been wrong, after all. He'd been wrong from the beginning, accusing her of being a liar and a fraud, then later thinking she was delusional.

Well, no avoiding it now. Lily was the genuine article, a visionary, a psychic, a clairvoyant—all those words he'd struck from his vocabulary years ago.

He just wished he felt better about it. Life had been simpler when he could bury himself in skepticism.

"I'm not mad." He touched her cheek. "I just need time."

"To assimilate." Her voice held a hint of amusement.

"Yeah."

Once they were back on the road, he asked the question that had nagged him since he'd listened to Abby Walters's story. "Lily, who's Casey?"

Her eyes glittered in the blue glow of the dashboard lights. "Abby mentioned her?"

The hair on his neck crawled. "She said Casey's a kid who visited her sometimes, but she never actually saw her."

"Casey is a little girl, about nine or ten. She lives with her mother, who's…odd." A thread of sadness ran through Lily's low voice. "I think maybe she's adopted, because her mother calls her by a different name."

A finger of unease ran down McBride's spine. "What name?"

"Gina."

An old, familiar ache of disappointment settled in his chest. "Where does she live?"

"I'm not sure. It could be anywhere."

"How'd she get to Abby's room?" He dreaded the answer.

"I think she's clairvoyant, too."

Great. "How many times have you seen her?"

Lily's eyes dropped. "A few."

"And you didn't tell me about her?"

She slanted her gaze at him in silent accusation. Of course she hadn't. He'd have seen her story as proof she was a liar or a lunatic. "Why was Casey visiting Abby?"

Lily's voice darkened. "Maybe she's just a lonely little girl with a special gift, and she found Abby like you might find a particular radio station by flipping channels."

He fell silent and cranked the car, too wrung out to process one more strange, impossible fact tonight. Instead, he fell back on what he knew best. "You saw the man who killed Abby's kidnapper."

"I know. But he doesn't know that."

"If he reads the papers, he knows you're a psychic who was looking for Abby. That might be enough to put you in danger."

Her brow furrowed. "Then so is Casey. She saw him."

"But he couldn't see her, right? You said she wasn't really there."

His words elicited a faint smile. "I don't suppose anybody on your task force is eager to talk about her, either."

"No," he conceded. "But maybe you should talk to a sketch artist. Do you think you could describe the man you saw?"

She nodded. "But it won't be admissible in court. I can't exactly testify that I saw him in my mind."

Once again discomfort shuddered through him. He tamped it down. "I'd still like to see what you saw."

"So you believe me?"

The wary eagerness in her voice made his chest hurt. "Let's just say I'll consider the possibility," he answered. "I'll give Jim a call tomorrow morning and set something up."

"Not tonight?"

"It's almost 2:00 a.m. I think it can wait till morning."

"What *about* tonight?" Lily asked.

"You're coming home with me."

"Under protective custody? Or do you have something else in mind?" A smile curved her lips.

He shot her a heated gaze. "Oh, I have lots in mind."

BY THE TIME LILY ROLLED away from McBride, the glow of dawn was washing his bedroom, painting the walls and ceiling pink. Lily stared at the light patterns on the ceiling, trying to catch her breath.

McBride pushed her hair away from her face with a trembling hand. "See what you do to me?"

She smiled. "I love what I do to you. And I really, really love what you do to me."

He laughed. "Wanton hussy."

"I feel like a wanton hussy." She lifted herself onto one elbow. "I don't even know your first name."

He made a face. "I never use it. McBride's fine, really."

"Oh, come on. What is it?" She ran her finger down the dark line of hair that bisected his stomach.

He caught her hand and shook his head. "That dog won't hunt, sugar. Nobody calls me by my first name. Ever."

"I'll bet I can guess." She leaned on his chest and rubbed her chin against his sternum. "Is it James?"

"Nope."

"Jeremy, Joseph, Jud, Jed, Jeremiah, Jacob, Jesse?"

"Not even close." His smile broadened.

She frowned, frustrated. "Why don't you just tell me? For heaven's sake, you'd think it was Jubal or something!"

His grin collapsed like a pricked balloon.

Her eyes widened. "It's Jubal?"

He made a face. "Jubal is an honored McBride family name."

"Jubal." Grinning, she tried it out.

"Lily, nobody calls me Jubal."

"I'm starting to like it. Jubal." She pressed her mouth against his collarbone. "It could be my secret name for you."

His forehead creased. "Define 'secret name.'"

She nibbled the thick muscles of his neck. "Jubal," she whispered, flicking her tongue against his flesh. She dropped nipping little kisses along his neck and jaw, punctuating her soft murmurs. "Jubal, Jubal, Jubal—"

"Okay, I surrender." Laughing, he gently nudged her away from him. "You can call me Jubal. But only when we're alone." He held up a stern finger. "And only you. Nobody else knows."

"Not even my sister Rose?"

He looked horrified. "Especially not her!"

"Okay, it's our little secret." She bent to kiss him again, groaning when the phone on McBride's bedside table rang. "Damn it, who calls so early in the morning?"

"Goes with cop territory." He answered. "McBride."

Lily propped herself on her elbow again, watching the furrows in his brow deepen as he listened to whoever was on the line. "Okay, thanks. Stay in touch."

"What's up?" she asked when he hung up the phone.

McBride sat up and swung his legs over the side of the bed. "Let's find something to eat. Then I'll tell you all about it."

MAMA WAS ACTING FUNNY again, so Casey retreated to her bedroom, curling up with Mr. Green and escaping into *Boots and Belinda,* one of her favorite books. She'd read it so often now it was nearly falling apart, but if she turned the pages very carefully, she could still read it. She liked to pretend she was Belinda, who had a smart and brave cat named Boots.

One time Mama had brought home a kitten for Casey. They'd named him Patches because he had black and white spots all over. Mama had taught Casey how to hold him—not too tight, not too loose, but just right. That was back when Mama was a lot better.

But not long after that Mama started having more spells. Sometimes she'd forget to feed Patches or let him inside when it was cold. Patches finally left for good and Mama had never gotten Casey another cat.

But I'd never forget to feed a cat, Casey thought, draping the open book across her chest. *I'd feed her and change her water and brush her hair like Belinda brushes Boots.*

She smiled at the ceiling. She'd name her Lily, she thought. And maybe the real Lily would come visit. Then Casey could show her the kitty and say, "See, I named her after you! So you'll have to come visit all the time and play with her."

Casey rolled onto her side, suddenly sad. She had that all alone feeling again, now that Abby was back with her daddy and Casey couldn't find her anymore.

"Gina?" Mama's voice sliced through Casey's melancholy. She stood in the doorway, her blue eyes wide and strange. "I don't want you talking so loud anymore, young lady!"

Casey frowned. Talking loud? "I wasn't talking, Mama."

"Don't yell at me, young lady!" Mama lurched toward her. "If you can't behave, you'll just have to stay in here."

Casey clutched Mr. Green more tightly to her. "But Mama—"

Mama grabbed the doorknob and stepped back into the hall, pulling the heavy door shut behind her.

"I can't take any more of your screaming!" The door muffled Mama's voice. Casey heard a scraping noise, metal on metal. "I can't take it anymore!" Mama's voice rose with hysteria. Casey heard great, wracking sobs through the door.

She ran to the door and pressed her ear against it. She heard Mama's shuffling, unsteady footsteps retreat down the hall, accompanied by loud hiccups.

Quietly, carefully, Casey tried to turn the doorknob. It rattled uselessly in her hand. Locked.

She tapped cautiously on the door. "Mama, can you hear me?"

Nothing but silence.

She rapped more loudly. "Mama, I'm scared. Please let me out." She pressed her ear to the door and waited for her reply. Still there was nothing.

She hugged Mr. Green closer and looked around the room, wondering what to do. There was no other door, no way out. She couldn't get out the window because it was painted tightly shut.

A shiver wracked her body. Daddy would know how to get her out. He'd say, "Sit tight, Casey, and I'll have you out in a jiffy." Yes sir, that's what he'd say if he was here.

But he wasn't here. Nobody was here but her and Mama.

"Mama, please come open the door. I'm hungry and I'm scared and I've got to pee."

Still nothing. No answer, no noise.

Little Abby found a way out, Casey reminded herself. She'd just climbed out her window and run for help, big as you please.

But she had had Casey's help. And Lily's.

Lily would know what to do, if only Casey could figure out a way to reach her. Clutching the stuffed frog against her chest, she squeezed her eyes shut and concentrated hard.

Lily!

"THEY IDENTIFIED THE bodies in the trailer as Rick 'Skeet' Scotero and Gordon 'Gordy' Stevens. Two-bit career criminals with records going back twenty years." McBride hunted through the cabinets for something to eat.

"Any idea why they took her?" Lily asked.

"Brody thinks someone hired the men to threaten Debra Walters and her daughter. They're rounding up Senator Blackledge and his campaign staff as we speak." He turned to look at her. "I called the sketch artist. He'll meet us at your house at ten this morning. But don't tell anyone else you saw the man in the woods. We don't know who he's connected to. No point putting yourself in more danger. Agreed?"

"That makes sense." Lily started to push aside the blue binder on the table when she realized it was a photo album. Curiosity battled dread. But she was incapable of leaving it closed. She shot a glance at McBride. He was crouched by the cabinets next to the sink, sorting through some cans.

Hands trembling, she opened the album to the first photo.

It was an eight-by-ten family portrait. McBride, Laura and a small baby. *Clare,* Lily thought, her tears blurring the chubby little face. She wiped them away.

All three were smiling, McBride's face carefree

and unlined. She hardly recognized him like that, so happy and lighthearted, as if he were king of the whole, wide world.

Pain clutching her heart, she turned the page. More family pictures. Laura and Clare. McBride and Clare. All three of them at the beach, in the kitchen, in front of a Christmas tree. Clare alone, grinning at the camera, her face smeared with what looked like strained carrots. Lily laughed and cried at the sweet, funny little face.

With each successive photo, Lily watched Clare grow. First a crawling baby, then a wobbly toddler, then a sassy two-year-old. The very last picture in the album was another eight-by-ten portrait. It was Clare at age three. Probably the last photograph McBride had of his daughter, Lily realized.

She studied the picture, looked at every inch of the little girl's face, trying to commit her to memory. Clare had her mother's fair skin and quaint heart-shaped face. Her daddy's dark hazel eyes.

Lily's heart flip-flopped. Her fingers tightened on the album and she drew a sharp breath.

That face.

She'd seen it, leaner and sadder, without the little-girl chubbiness. She'd seen those hazel eyes, no longer sparkling with childlike wonder, but serious and worried. Lily plucked at the peel-away covering holding the photo in place and pulled it free from the sticky backing, managing not to damage the picture. Her hands shook as she flipped the photo over to see if anything was written on the back.

"Katherine Clare McBride, age three."

Katherine Clare.

Not Casey, Lily realized.

K.C.

She released a shuddering breath, afraid to move. She remembered the little girl's words. "Daddy calls me Casey."

Daddy calls me K.C.

Casey was Clare McBride.

Chapter Sixteen

McBride turned to look at her. His gaze dropped to the album in her hands. A dozen different expressions flitted over his face before he finally settled on a sort of sad acceptance. "That's Clare."

Lily's chest tightened, afraid that what she was about to tell him would be more than he could take. "She's beautiful."

"Is it horrible that when I saw Andrew Walters run to his little girl, all I could think was, I wish that was me?" McBride sat down at the table beside her, taking the photo from her hands. He ran his fingers over it and looked up at her. "I wish you could have found Clare for me."

When Lily reached out to touch his face, her hand was shaking. "What if I told you I could?"

"Find Clare?"

"Yes."

He looked puzzled. "Why are you asking this?"

Her stomach clenched. "Would you believe me?"

"Is this some kind of test?"

Lily shook her head. "I just need to know."

Silence stretched between them for a long moment. Lily's tension rose to the snapping point before he finally spoke. "If you looked me in the face and told me you knew where Clare was, yes, I'd believe you." In his murky eyes she saw a depth of desperation she'd never seen before. "I'd give my soul to believe Clare was still alive."

She lowered her trembling hand and asked the question she dreaded most. But it had to be asked, because there was always a chance she was wrong about who Casey really was. "What if I told you I could find Clare, but it turned out I couldn't?"

McBride's face shut down as if somebody had turned off the lights. Lily had her answer before he said the words. "I think I'd hate you the rest of my life."

The coldness of McBride's reply gave her chills. Her trembling increased, vibrations rolling along her spine.

Gray mist began to swirl.

The door in her mind banged open and she heard her name as clearly as if someone had called to her across the room.

"Help me, Lily!" Casey's pale face appeared in the mist. She held out her arms.

Without a second thought, Lily went to her. The mist dissipated, revealing Casey's bedroom. Lily gently lifted the little girl's face. "Are you hurt?"

"Mama locked me in here and she won't let me out and I can't hear anything. I'm hungry and I'm scared and I need to pee. Please, Lily, help me, please!" Tears streamed down Casey's face. "Please, Lily, I'm scared!"

"Shh, sweetie, it's okay. I'm here and I'll help you, okay? But I need you to calm down and help me, too."

Casey made a visible effort to calm herself, rubbing her tear-reddened eyes. "Okay."

"Your mother locked the door and you can't get it open?"

"No, I can't."

"Show me."

Casey went over and tried to turn the doorknob. Lily heard the rattle as it refused to move. For some reason Lily didn't want to think about too closely, the door locked from the outside. "Casey, how was your mother acting?"

"She kept yelling at me to stop screaming, but I wasn't, Lily. Honest, I wasn't screaming at all."

The woman must have been having a psychotic episode, Lily thought with trepidation. Casey might be safer locked in her room for now. But how long until the woman came back?

Lily scanned her surroundings for anything that could help the child escape. "What about the window?"

"I can't open it."

"Try it for me again." Maybe it was just stuck.

Casey moved toward the window. The sill was only a couple of feet off the floor, so Casey had no trouble gripping the handles and giving the window a jerk. But it wouldn't budge.

Out the window, Lily saw a short stretch of unkempt grass before the surrounding woods took over. The window was low enough to the ground that Casey could climb out, if they could ever get it open. "Casey, I need to come to where you are. Do you know the name of your town?"

She shook her head. "Mama never lets me leave here. I can only go to the edge of the woods."

Lily frowned. "You don't go to school?"

Casey shook her head. "But I know how to read. Mama taught me, before she got so sick."

Lily sensed the child wasn't far away; the woods and general terrain looked familiar. "Are you in Alabama?"

"Yes!" Excitement shone in Casey's eyes. "Mama taught me a song. 'My home's in Alabama, no matter where—'"

A sharp crack interrupted Casey's slightly off-key rendition. Her eyes widened. "What was that?"

Lily stared back, her heart racing. She feared she knew exactly what that sound had been.

A gunshot.

McBRIDE SAID LILY'S NAME. She didn't respond.

A chill ran down his spine as he sat back from her, unsure what to do. A few moments ago, she'd just...left. Her eyes had gone glassy, her face flushed, and then she was gone to wherever it was she went when one of her visions hit.

Was it what he'd told her? He hadn't meant to be so harsh, but she'd said she wanted the truth. He didn't know if he could ever forgive her if she convinced him once more that Clare might still be alive, only to fail to deliver on her promise.

But it was a moot point, wasn't it? He'd accepted a long time ago that his little girl was dead.

McBride touched Lily's face, wondering if it was bad for her to have her visions interrupted. Would it give her one of those horrible migraines? He didn't know how it worked.

"No!" An anguished wail poured forth from deep inside Lily, setting McBride's teeth on edge.

Suddenly, her eyes blinked rapidly and focused, then widened in alarm. She gripped his arms. "McBride, we've got to find her!"

She was still having visions of Abby? "We've already found her, Lily. Abby's safe with her daddy."

"Not Abby!" Lily clutched his shoulders and pulled herself to her feet. "Clare's in trouble. We have to help her!"

Blood roared in McBride's ears. "Clare?"

Lily's gaze pierced his heart. Her lips moved soundlessly for a moment, as if she were searching desperately for words. Then her voice broke through, raspy and quivering. "She's alive, McBride. Clare's alive."

He felt the blood drain from his head. "No."

"She's alive and she needs our help." Lily touched his face, her fingers hot and dry. "I know you're afraid to believe, but we don't have time."

He pushed her hand away. "Lily, don't do this."

"You said you'd believe me if I told you I knew where she was. I know the risk I'm taking." She grabbed his chin and forced him to look into her eyes. "I know it can destroy us."

He swallowed hard. "You saw her just now?"

"She's the little girl I told you about." Lily pointed to Clare's photo. "This is her. Only she's older—nine or ten."

His body went numb. "But she said her name was Casey."

"K.C., McBride. Katherine Clare. You called her K.C., didn't you?"

He gazed at Lily, his heart in his throat. "We

called her Clare, after her aunt Clare. But sometimes I called her K.C."

"It's your daughter, McBride. She's not dead."

Tears filled his eyes. He slowly lifted his hands to his face. "Not dead."

"She's in trouble. We have to find her."

He looked up, a fresh agony of despair rolling over him. "How? You don't know where she is."

Lily told him everything she'd seen of Casey in her visions—the old-fashioned parlor, the small bedroom, the distant and disturbed woman Casey called Mama. "Does it ring any bells with you at all?"

"Maybe she just looks like Clare." He wobbled on the edge of belief, afraid to take the final plunge.

Lily released a sigh of pure frustration. "There has to be something…" Her eyes suddenly lit up. "You gave her a stuffed frog. Mr. Green. You said he'd watch out for her."

McBride's heart skipped a beat, then hurtled into hyperspeed. He could see the green frog as clearly as if he'd bought it just the day before.

Doubt left him, washed away in a bittersweet flood of hope.

Casey was his daughter, Clare. And Lily was going to help him find her.

PARFAIT-PINK WALLS, cracked in places and peeling...

It took Lily a few moments to realize she was seeing the morning sun reflected off the dingy walls of Casey's tiny bedroom instead of McBride's kitchen. Panic clawed her insides. Where was the girl? Had the madwoman done something to her?

"I'm here." Casey crouched in the corner, clutching her toy frog.

"Why are you on the floor?" Lily asked.

Casey waved at the bed. Lily saw that the sheets were wadded into a ball in the middle of the lumpy mattress. She smelled something sour.

"I couldn't hold it." Casey sniffled. "I tried to find something to use, but I couldn't hold it anymore."

Lily crossed to her quickly, stroking Casey's face. "It's okay. Your daddy and I are going to get you out of here."

"Daddy?"

Lily smiled at the sudden rush of hope she saw in Casey's face. "Your daddy's with me right now, honey. He never wanted to let you go. Nobody gave him a choice. But I told him about you. We're going to help you, but you have to help us do it."

Casey nodded eagerly. "How?"

"I want you to put on warm clothes. Do you have warm clothes in this room?"

"Yes." Casey rose quickly and started rummaging through the battered chest of drawers near the window. She donned fresh underclothes, a pair of jeans and a too-snug sweater.

"Put on another sweater, and at least two pairs of socks," Lily directed, at the same time trying to listen for any noises from outside the room.

Casey did as she said.

"Now, wrap that other pair of blue jeans around your arm and hit the window as hard as you can."

Casey's eyes widened. "What if Mama hears?"

Lily didn't know what to say. She wasn't sure if the woman was even alive anymore. Or if she was, maybe she was too far gone to hear anything, lost in the depths of another catatonic episode. Lily almost hoped so. If the woman were to come into this room and do something to Casey while Lily was there watching...

She shuddered, feeling the door in her mind trying to open and pull her back to reality. She clenched her teeth and fought it like a mother tiger. Concentrating on Casey, she was able to stay in the vision, but already her head was beginning to ache.

"Hit it, Casey."

Casey planted her feet in front of the window and took a deep breath. Lily could see her nibbling her bottom lip in preparation. At that moment, she looked just like McBride.

Then she struck the window with her padded hand. The glass rattled but didn't give.

They both waited a few seconds, breaths bated, listening for any noise from outside the room.

Nothing.

"Hit it again," Lily said.

Casey slammed her hand into the window. This time, one pane broke, sending shards flying.

"Again, Casey!"

The girl banged the windowpane next to the broken one. It shattered as well. She hit each pane with increasing force, smashing them until the bottom six panes were broken.

"Now, Casey, here's the hard part. Strike the wooden part as hard as you can. Strike it until it breaks."

The little girl made a soft growling noise deep in her throat, then started hammering away at the wood. Pieces splintered outward bit by bit until she'd made a space large enough to crawl through. Lily felt the biting cold October air pouring through the opening.

She told Casey to drape more clothing over the ragged places to protect herself. Then the girl crawled through the opening and tumbled to the ground.

Lily envisioned herself following through the window, and she was suddenly outside, where

Casey was picking herself up and dusting off her jeans. Sunlight pierced the wall of trees in the east, washing everything in gold. The child started running toward the sunlight and Lily tried to follow, but her throbbing head slowed her. "Wait, Casey! Where are you going?"

Lily felt the door in her mind opening, drawing her back. Desperately, she looked around, trying to memorize every detail. The one-story house, white paint with green shutters. Sagging gutters. Unkempt yard. Trees all around.

Then she saw the spire. It rose against the eastern sky, little more than a dark silhouette just above the treetops, but she thought it might be a church steeple.

She kept her eyes on the spire until the mists surrounded her, dragging her back to her own time and place.

Lily jerked in her chair, nearly toppling over. "McBride!"

He was right beside her. "What is it?"

She grabbed his arm. "I saw her! She's out of the house, and I think I know how we can find her!"

He caught her shoulders. "What did you see?"

He made her go over everything she'd experienced, sifting the facts carefully, looking for hidden clues. She gritted her teeth against the pain in her head and told him everything she could remember. He latched on to the spire, of course. It was probably the best clue they had.

"It was like a church steeple," she said. "I couldn't see it all that well, but what else could it be?"

"Okay, let's look at what we've got." He pulled a notebook from the kitchen counter and wrote as he spoke. "The house is in a small clearing. It's one-story, white with green shutters. The gutters are sagging and it looks to be isolated. The back of the house faces what direction?"

She closed her eyes, fighting pain as she tried to picture the scene that had played out before her eyes. "South."

"Okay, the front faces north, then. And the church spire is in the east…" His voice trailed off suddenly. She looked at him, and found his eyes wide.

"What is it?"

"I think I know where that church is!" His voice shook with excitement. "It's in the middle of the woods, like you said. If I find the church, I can backtrack to the house." He kissed her quickly and started toward the bedroom.

"Wait, I'm coming with you." She tried to stand, but her head swam. She stumbled into the table.

He was at her side in a second, arms circling her. He caught her chin in his hand and lifted her face to his. "Did you fight the vision?" he asked, looking surprised.

"It was trying to bring me back before I was ready. I wouldn't let it."

"Are your pills in your purse?"

"I'll get them. You go."

"I'll be back soon." Brushing her hair aside, he kissed her forehead. "How will I ever be able to thank you for this?"

She caught his hands. "Just bring Clare home."

THE GRAVEL ROAD LED to the Barclay United Methodist Church, a small white clapboard building in the middle of Barclay Woods. McBride parked the car and got out, staring at the tall steeple. His heart banged against the back of his throat as he looked toward the spot where the spire seemed to prick the veil of heaven.

She's here somewhere, isn't she?

He closed his eyes and opened his heart, calling to his little girl with every ounce of love he had inside him. *Daddy loves you, K.C., he loves you so much.*

He called her name aloud. "K.C.!"

The sound echoed in the early morning quiet of the woods. Only the soft chirping of birds and the chatter of squirrels answered him.

God, please don't let this happen again.

"K.C.?"

The silence compelled him forward, into the forest. He jogged through the tangled under-brush, sometimes stumbling, sometimes sliding, always moving west toward the house he knew had to be just beyond the next stand of trees. He called his daughter's name as he ran, his voice ragged and shaking.

When he saw the edge of a clearing through the wall of trees, he staggered to a halt. The sound of his breathing was harsh in the stillness. He took a step forward, then another. His strides sped up and he finally broke into the clearing, where he halted again and stared.

There it was, just as Lily had said. A small, one-story white house with green shutters. Overgrown grass, sagging roof.

This was it! She was right.

Hope surged through him like new blood, pro-pelling him forward. He ran around the side of the house, heedless of any possible danger, his heart, mind and soul set on one goal: finding his daughter. He turned the corner and ran a few steps more before his feet caught up with his eyes.

The silence swallowed him whole.

Bile coursed upward through his esophagus, gagging him. Squeezing his eyes shut, he turned his head and retched, falling to his hands and knees. Ice seemed to replace his blood as his stomach emptied, leaving him stiff and cold.

Finally, he stopped retching and found the strength to turn his head again, clinging to one last sliver of hope. Maybe adrenaline had played tricks on him. Maybe he'd been so afraid of having his hopes dashed again that he'd created his own worst nightmare.

He slowly opened his eyes. His heart sank.

The entire front of the place was a blackened ruin, gutted by a fire long since extinguished. This house hadn't been occupied in years.

McBride hung his head, wishing he were dead.

LILY SLEPT FITFULLY, dark dreams disturbing her slumber. She was in a black space, blacker than night, blacker than death, and she could hear McBride calling his daughter's name.

"K.C.!"

The sound echoed in her head, a hard, brittle noise. It sounded like blood tasted, she realized. Sharp and metallic.

"Liar!"

She twitched in her sleep as McBride's voice stabbed her in the heart.

"You said she was alive! You said I could find her, but you were wrong!"

She ran from the malignant thickness of that

voice, crying as she ran. Her tears were acid, burning her cheeks. She couldn't escape the fiery heat of McBride's hatred.

"I hate you for what you've done!" McBride's voice pursued her in her nightmare.

Lily jerked awake with a cry, clawing at the bedcovers that held her prisoner. Her heart caught as she realized McBride was sitting in a chair next to the bed, looking at her with eyes as dead as winter.

"Oh, God." Lily choked on the words.

He looked away from her.

"You didn't find her." Her heart plummeted.

McBride didn't glance at her again. "You're right. She wasn't there."

"Did you find the church?"

"Yeah. I even found the house. But Clare wasn't there."

"You mean you didn't find her at the house." Lily felt a glimmer of hope. "McBride, I told you that she ran away. She was probably out in the woods, hiding. If we just go back, I'm sure—"

"No." McBride's voice sounded hollow. "I found the house. Dirty white with green shutters, sagging roof—everything was just right. But it was gutted by fire a long time ago. Nobody's lived in that house in years."

Lily shook her head. How could that be? "But Abby saw her, too."

"You were in Abby's head, Lily. She probably saw whatever you saw."

"Why would I see your daughter if she wasn't there? Before yesterday I didn't even know you had a daughter. And I didn't see a three-year-old. This was a grown-up nine-year-old." Lily shook her head. "Maybe we were wrong about where the house was in relation to the church. Or maybe we had the wrong house."

"Stop!" He doubled over as if in pain. "Please, just stop, Lily. I can't do this anymore."

But I wasn't wrong about Abby, she thought, desperately clinging to that fact. Abby had been right there where she'd seen her. She couldn't understand why McBride hadn't found K.C. "I don't know what happened. After we found Abby, I was so sure…" Hot tears sprang to her eyes.

"I'm not saying you don't have some kind of ability," McBride said. "Finding Abby was proof of that. But you were obviously wrong about Clare."

The one failure he'd never be able to forgive. He'd said as much. Tears trickled down Lily's cheeks. "I'm so sorry, McBride."

He nodded, but he still didn't look at her. "I know you believed you had found Clare. It's really not your fault." He rubbed his jaw. "It's my fault. I knew better than to let myself believe again. I knew all the risks, what it was going to cost me, but I did it anyway. I should've known better."

The pain in her head had faded, but her heart was ripping apart. "You want me to leave."

He didn't answer for a few seconds, and she almost dared to hope. But then he nodded slowly. "I know I'm not being fair to you. But I know now that I can't do this. I've called Theo to follow you home. He's waiting outside."

She could tell by the sound of his voice that she'd never be able to convince him otherwise.

Tamping down despair, she stood, legs wobbling as she crossed in front of him, barely able to keep her hands from reaching out to touch him. She went to the closet, where she'd put some of the clothes from her overnight bag.

"I'll do that," he said. "Your head's still hurting."

She leaned against the frame of the closet door, her chest aching with pent-up grief. She had known the risks as well. She'd known that trying to find Casey could cost her the chance of being with McBride.

But she'd been so sure.

How could she have been so wrong about Casey when she'd been so right about Abby? Lily just didn't know how the visions worked. She didn't know what caused them, how to control them or what they meant. It had been arrogant to think she did.

She pushed herself upright and turned to McBride. He stood near the dresser, folding her clothes and putting them into the overnight bag. He avoided looking at her, as if the sight of her was more than he could bear.

She sought the strength to ask him one hard, dreaded question. "Did you ever love me, McBride? Even a little?"

A muscle in his jaw jumped. He turned and looked at her, his gaze cold, his expression nearly blank. "I just knew I was going to find her today. I thought I could feel her with me. It was like I could reach out my hand and touch her. And I thought, Lily did this for me. She brought my baby back to me."

Lily gritted her teeth, holding back a sob.

McBride shut his eyes. "Then I found that burned-out house." His shoulders rose and fell with a deep sigh. "You want to know how I feel about you? I don't feel anything, Lily. I just don't…feel." He turned away, pulling out the dresser drawer where she'd put some of her belongings.

Unable to find anything else to say, Lily joined him by the dresser and started putting her clothes into the overnight bag. They moved in slow, silent concert, methodically erasing all evidence that she'd ever been part of his life.

She closed the case, and McBride took it from her, heading toward the hallway. He walked her out to her rental car, pausing as she slid behind the wheel. "You'll probably want to get out of town for a while," he said. "I'll take care of it with Brody. There'll be reporters hunting you down if you hang around."

She looked at him, studied him one last time. She wished she had a photo, some memento she could pull out when the nights were long and lonely. Something to remember him by. But they hadn't been together long enough for love notes, dried roses or any of the forget-me-nots that accompanied lost love.

All she would have was the memory of this moment to haunt her for a lifetime.

McBride waved at Theo Baker who sat behind the wheel of a dark sedan idling at the curb. Then he finally looked at her one last time, his dark gaze unfathomable. After a moment, he turned and started walking back to the house.

She slumped in the driver's seat and shut her eyes, aching with misery. Casey had been so real to her. She could still see her little face, still hear her voice in her head.

What if she was really out there somewhere? Maybe not McBride's daughter, Clare, but somebody, some scared little girl, lost and all by herself?

Lily didn't know. She didn't know if finding Abby had been a fluke, a once-in-a-lifetime lucky break. She didn't know if her gift was reliable. She didn't even know if there ever was a little girl named Casey who was hiding in the woods, waiting for her daddy and Lily to come rescue her. She didn't know anything anymore.

Chapter Seventeen

When Lily arrived home a little after ten, Agent Logan stood on her front stoop talking to a dark-haired man with a bushy mustache. The sketch artist McBride had called, she realized, spotting the sketch pad under the stranger's arm. She'd forgotten all about the meeting.

Agent Logan smiled in greeting. "I'll be down the street if you need me, Ms. Browning." He headed down the driveway, stopping briefly to speak to Theo Baker.

The mustached man introduced himself as Jim Phillips. Waving off her offer of something to drink, he went right to work, listening to her description of the man she'd seen in the woods. His charcoal pencil flew across the paper as she viewed the results and helped him tweak the sketch.

Within a half hour, he'd managed to draw a very good likeness of the man she'd seen following Abby.

"That's him," she finally declared.

Jim closed the sketch pad and shook her hand. "Thanks for the input—you have a good eye. I'll be sure McBride gets this ASAP."

His mention of McBride felt like a stab in the heart, but she kept her chin up until she'd ushered him out the door.

She glanced down the street, looking for the FBI van. It was no longer where it had been parked earlier. A niggle of unease tickled her spine, but she pushed it away. They were probably hidden from plain view. The FBI was good at that, she'd heard.

Still, she thought as she closed the door, she'd feel safer if she could see them.

Slumping on her sofa, she tried to coax her cats to her lap, but they kept their distance, glaring at her from the doorway. "It was overnight, not a week," she protested. "I left you plenty of food and water."

They didn't budge from the doorway, gazing at her with pure feline disdain. Lily gave up and sat back, closing her eyes.

A knock on her front door jerked her upright, nerves jangling. Her cats scattered.

McBride, she thought, her heart leaping with hope.

But it was Andrew Walters who stood on her doorstep.

CAL BRODY WAS WAITING for McBride when he arrived at the station. The agent took his own sweet time vacating McBride's desk chair, which only darkened McBride's already pitch-black mood. But he welcomed the rush of anger. After the past couple of hours, it was good to feel anything, even rage.

"I've gone over the evidence retrieval in this case, and I've got to hand it to you, Lieutenant, it's damn good," Brody commented. "You've got good people here."

"Did you think this was Hooterville or something? Of course we did a good job." McBride glared at him.

"Didn't mean any offense." Brody quirked his thick, dark brows. "Your captain has refused further FBI assistance in investigating the deaths of the two kidnappers, and we've already found forensic evidence that Rick 'Skeet' Scotero killed Debra Walters. So we're done here. We're heading back to Birmingham."

McBride's brow furrowed. "What about your surveillance unit at Lily Browning's house?"

"We packed them up an hour ago. She's not a witness, and we're pretty sure that the men who called her are dead." Brody's eyes narrowed. "Unless you want us to continue investigating her as a possible accomplice?"

McBride's patience snapped. "Oh, for God's

sake, Brody. She's not a suspect. You know it. I know it. Now get out of my office so I can get some work done."

"By the way, Walters called to say thanks again." Brody actually smiled, although the expression looked strange on him. "Nice that at least part of this mess ended well."

After Brody left, McBride passed his hand over his face, feeling sick. He didn't want to think about Andrew Walters with his beautiful, healthy little girl, while McBride was sitting here, wondering why he had to keep going through hell over and over again, losing everyone and everything that gave meaning to his life.

He grabbed his bottle of antacid tablets and twisted open the top. He crunched two tablets, unsure if they'd be strong enough to calm the acid bath churning in his gut. Reaching for his phone, he arranged for a patrol unit to watch Lily Browning until he could figure out what to do with her next.

No matter how much he was hurting right now, letting her go home alone had been damn near a dereliction of duty.

"How'd you manage to evade the reporters?" Lily asked as she settled in the armchair across from Andrew Walters.

"I'm used to it by now. I've learned the tricks."

Andrew stretched one arm across the back of her sofa. "Abby sends her love. She's with my ex-wife's sister in Tellerville."

"I'm sorry I didn't get to say goodbye." Lily tamped down her disappointment. "But I'm so happy she's safe."

"Thanks to you." Andrew leaned forward. "I'm hoping you can answer something for me. Abby keeps talking about someone named Casey. Do you know who she's talking about?"

Tears stung the back of Lily's eyes. "She's a little girl who showed up in some of my visions of Abby."

"Showed up?"

"She wasn't physically there in the trailer with Abby. She just…appeared."

"Appeared? How?"

"I think maybe she's clairvoyant, too."

Andrew shook his head, his lips curving in a half smile. "This is all so…"

"Weird?" Lily supplied.

He nodded. "Abby says Casey's the one who told her about the man with the gun."

Remembering McBride's warning, Lily played dumb. "What man with a gun?"

"I believe it must be the man who killed the two men who took Abby. Abby said he was following her in the woods."

Lily feigned surprise. "I heard the men were dead, but…"

"The FBI think it may have something to do with the senate race." Andrew's expression oozed dismay, but he couldn't hide a tiny glimmer of satisfaction in his blue eyes. Anything that cast doubt on his opponent would aid his bid to become the next senator from Alabama, Lily realized. That was politics.

"Horrible," she murmured, not really sure what else to say.

"So you never saw the kidnappers or anyone else in your visions? Just Abby?"

"Just Abby," she lied. "And Casey, of course."

"What does Casey look like?"

Lily's stomach tightened. "She's just a little girl," she said, being deliberately vague. "A little older than your daughter. I didn't see that much of her. I was more focused on Abby."

"I see." He sounded disappointed. "I'd have liked to thank her, too. Abby said Casey was a great source of comfort."

"I don't think I'll be seeing any more of her." Lily's throat tightened with misery. Andrew's questions only reminded her of all she'd lost.

A shudder ran down her back, sprinkling gooseflesh across her arms and legs. Another shiver washed over her, giving her less than a second's notice before the vision slammed open the door in her mind and pulled her inside.

The gray mist dissipated with shocking suddenness, and Lily almost tripped over Casey. The little girl was huddled in a dark place, hands tucked into the sleeves of her sweater. She was shivering, but her color looked good, Lily noted with a rush of relief. She said Casey's name.

The little girl's dark hazel eyes lifted. She scrambled to her feet. "Lily, I thought you'd gone away forever!"

Lily wrapped her arms around the child and hugged her tightly, tears streaming down her face. "It's okay, Casey. I found you."

MCBRIDE HEARD FROM the patrolmen he'd sent to check on Lily just before eleven. "Andrew Walters arrived a few minutes ago, and Ms. Browning let him in," the officer related. "Want us to stand by?"

"Stay a little up the street," McBride ordered. He didn't want Lily to feel like a suspect.

He hung up the phone and tried to finish some paperwork. But minutes later, he pushed aside his keyboard and admitted what he'd been avoiding since Lily walked out his door.

He loved her.

He didn't want to love her. His life would be less painful and less scary if he didn't feel anything for her. He had pushed her away, let himself blame her for his pain, but she refused to leave his heart.

Now he knew she never would.

Loving her made him question his own skepticism, the hard, cold anger he'd carried inside him after Clare disappeared, even his treatment of Delaine Howard, a woman who'd only been trying to help him. Maybe she'd given them false hope about Clare when caution would've been kinder, but she'd tried to help, just as Lily had. That counted for something.

In Lily's case, it counted for everything.

She had been right about Abby Walters. No way to deny that; the little girl was living proof. Yet Lily had been so wrong about Clare.

McBride rubbed his burning eyes. Okay. She had made a mistake in identifying the little girl. But he didn't think she'd invented the story of Casey.

So if she wasn't Clare, who was she?

The door to his office opened and Theo Baker entered, his eyebrows nearly meeting his hairline. In his wake strode Senator Gerald Blackledge and his security detail. "The senator would like a word with us," Baker said.

Blackledge didn't wait for an invitation to sit. He laid a manila folder on McBride's desk and dropped into the chair across from him. "I realize your case just got a whole lot harder for you, so I'm here to simplify things a little bit."

McBride opened the folder and found page after page of polling data. "This simplifies things?"

"Look at the dates and the polls. Those are my campaign's internals, notarized by the independent polling firm we hired to gather the information. They will be willing to testify to the time and date stamps and the veracity of the information."

McBride scanned the pages, checking the notary marks as well as the dates, before he went back to look at what the polls revealed. He had to go over them twice to be sure he understood what he was seeing. "You were pulling way ahead."

"Exactly," Blackledge said with a nod. "We knew that three weeks ago. Why on God's green earth would I try to put Andrew Walters's name back on the front page of the newspaper, especially in such a sympathetic light?"

He wouldn't, McBride realized. The notarized polling data erased what nebulous motive he might have. "I'll be following up with your polling company."

"I'd expect no less." Blackledge stood and motioned for his entourage to follow him out.

"Wait a second, Senator." McBride crossed to the doorway. "Do you think the Walters's campaign had the same polling information?"

Blackledge's brown eyes glittered. "I would think so."

McBride watched the senator leave, his own eyes narrowed.

"If Walters knew about those polls…" Baker began.

Before he could finish, Jim Phillips stuck his head through the open doorway. "Got a minute for me, McBride?"

McBride cocked his head. He'd forgotten about sending the sketch artist. "Did you see Ms. Browning this morning?"

"I did." Jim handed McBride his sketch pad. "She's got a good eye for detail."

McBride gazed down at the sketch, taking in the sandy hair, fleshy features and prominent forehead of the man in the sketch. Recognition dawned, followed quickly by a flood of cold dread.

Son of a bitch.

IGNORING THE GRAY MIST curling closer, beckoning her back to reality, Lily started looking around her, seeking some clue to Casey's whereabouts. The room was dark and dusty, pierced in places by slivers of light peeking through cracks in the walls and clean patches in the filthy windows. She couldn't make out many details, but the setup was unmistakable. Casey was in an old, abandoned schoolhouse.

"Casey, tell me everything you can remember about how you got here. Did you notice any landmarks, anything unusual?"

Casey shook her head. "It was just woods, lots of pines and dead trees. I saw squirrels and birds—wait!" Her eyes brightened. "I had to cross a stream! I was so proud 'cause I got across on the rocks without getting my feet wet."

That might be a help if Lily could narrow down the possibilities. But there had to be dozens of old, abandoned schoolhouses in Alabama. She glanced about, seeking something that could tell her for certain where the child was. "Casey, help me look around. See if you can find anything that has a name written on it. Look in the desks."

Casey crossed to the nearest desk and opened the top. She jumped and squealed when a spider darted across her hand, but quickly shook it off and started searching through the yellowed papers. Lily peered through the gloom but could make out none of the faded words. "Try the next one."

In the fifth desk they hit pay dirt. There was an old primer with a faded blue stamp in front. "Willow Wood School," Casey read aloud.

Not ten miles away, Lily realized with wonder. She grabbed the girl and hugged her tightly. The fog thickened around her. "I know where you are, baby," she told Casey as the mist began to separate them. "I'll be there soon, I promise."

She came back to herself in a rush.

"My God, Lily, are you okay?"

She blinked, surprised to find herself in her living room, sitting across from Andrew Walters.

"What just happened? Did you have a vision?"

She pushed herself to her feet, her knees wobbly. "Andrew, I'm sorry—I have to go. I'll be in touch, I promise."

He followed her to her car. "Are you sure you're okay to drive? I can take you wherever—"

"I'm fine." She slid behind the wheel and started the engine with shaking hands, backing down the drive and out onto the street with reckless speed, racing time and her pounding heart to get to McBride's daughter.

HE KEPT HIS EYES ON Lily Browning's rental car, forcing down the panic rising like a gusher in his throat. She'd seen him. And so had some kid named Casey.

Who the hell was she? How had she seen him?

He kept pace with Lily as she raced down the street, but didn't get too close. He couldn't risk spooking her before she led him to wherever the little girl was hiding. *Please, let her take me there!*

Then he could finally tie up the last loose end.

"I'm not going down for this. This was your idea."

He ignored the pale-faced man next to him. They'd come up with the plan together and they would finish it together.

"What if she's not going after the kid?"

"She is," he growled.

She had to be.

She'd seen him in the woods, while she was helping Abby get to safety. She and the kid named Casey. They were the only ones who could bring the whole mess crashing down on his head.

They had to be stopped.

MCBRIDE GRITTED HIS TEETH with frustration at the sea of red taillights forming about two miles down the interstate. Flashing blue and cherry lights in the distance marked the site of the accident that appeared to be snarling traffic.

He didn't want to wait. He had to get to Lily now.

Between McBride and the sea of taillights ahead was an exit onto Boudreau Road. It was probably fifteen minutes out of his way, but the interstate traffic would take at least that long to clear. Yanking the wheel to the right, he headed for the exit.

Boudreau Road stretched for six miles through beautiful, wild terrain thick with towering green pines and hardwoods already changing colors and losing their leaves.

His stomach ached. It looked like the road he'd traveled on his way to the church in Barclay Woods.

Just beyond the bridge over Tuttle Creek, the road began winding downhill, giving McBride a panoramic view of the valley beyond.

His breath caught.

Just a mile or two ahead, glistening in the midday sunlight, a white spire rose above the pines.

He heard Lily's voice in his mind. *It was like a church steeple. I couldn't see it well, but what else could it be?*

A schoolhouse, he thought, gazing at the bell tower. It could be a schoolhouse.

The car shimmied as he pulled off the road. His heart pounded wildly in his chest. It couldn't be. Could it?

He took a second to get his bearings. It was after noon now, so the sun was inching toward the western sky. Best he could tell, he was due west of the tower. If Lily had been right, there was probably a road to his left.

Of course, that was a big if. But he had to know.

He drove another half mile before he caught sight of a side road winding into the woods. He braked quickly, almost skidding, and turned down the dirt road. He had gone about twenty yards when his mind registered the mailbox that had been directly across from the turnoff.

McBride backed to the edge of the pavement, jerked the car into Park and got out. He walked back to the roadside and looked across the blacktop at the rusted mailbox. Corroded brass numbers climbed the wooden post, hanging askew. Stick-on letters on the box spelled out one name: Grainger.

McBride drew a swift breath, chill bumps breaking out on his arms and back.

This was the mailbox Delaine Howard had seen in her vision all those years ago. *This* Grainger.

This is it, he realized, his pulse thudding in his ears.

He raced back to the car.

The road became almost unnavigable the deeper he went into the woods. He clenched his teeth and wrestled with the steering wheel, holding the Chevy on the bumpy dirt drive. When he was almost ready to park the car and walk the rest of the way, the road smoothed out and he saw the edge of a clearing just ahead.

Stifling the urge to gun the engine, he drove on. Now he could see a white building peeking through the trees.

A white clapboard house with faded green shutters.

Clearing the edge of the woods, he pulled into the high grass behind the house. His whole body clenched as he cut the engine and got out. He hesitated, struck by how similar this house looked to the one he'd come across just this morning. The shape was different, the green paint on the shutters darker. But it matched the general description Lily had given.

He looked to his right. Above the trees, lit by the bright sun, loomed the top of the schoolhouse bell tower.

This is what Lily saw, he thought. He took a deep, bracing breath and walked slowly through the high grass, rounding the corner of the house. He was half prepared to find another burned-out shell. But the house was intact.

He pulled open the shabby, ripped screen door and knocked. There was no answer, so he knocked again. Still no answer. He tried the doorknob and was surprised when it turned easily in his hand. "Hello?"

Then the smell hit him. Sharp. Metallic.

Blood.

His heart hammered as he pulled his Smith & Wesson from his shoulder holster and rushed inside. He was being reckless as hell, but fear eclipsed reason as he remembered the gunshot Lily said she'd heard in her vision.

Had the woman done something to his baby girl?

He burst through the kitchen doorway into the

hall and almost slipped as his feet hit a sticky wet patch. He grabbed the doorjamb and stared at the dark pool of blood at his feet.

Just in front of him lay the body of a woman.

The cop in him took over for a second, surveying the scene with clinical detachment. Head shot, probably instantly fatal. From the looks of the scene, self-inflicted.

Then his heart overcame the initial numbness and he darted past the body, heedless of how he was compromising the crime scene. He tried each door down the hall. At the very end on the left, he found a locked one.

He hit the door with several sharp shoulder blows, ignoring the pain. The wood finally splintered and he burst inside.

It was a child's bedroom. It fit Lily's description, right down to the broken window.

Clare's alive, he realized, his heart in his throat.

He raced back down the hall, past the body and out the door. He ran past the car and plunged into the woods, keeping his eyes on the schoolhouse bell tower.

LILY PULLED OFF THE ROAD onto a dirt track leading into the woods. The uneven terrain put the rental's shocks to the test, jostling her around despite the seat belt holding her in place. She went as far as the road would take her and finally pulled over, heading the rest of the way on foot. The woods were thick with underbrush, making the path to the old schoolhouse hard to travel, but Lily crashed ahead, heedless of the twigs and vines that slapped against her legs as she ran.

She made enough noise that she almost didn't hear the rustling underbrush behind her.

Almost.

A finger of fear sketched a cold path up her spine. She darted to her right, taking cover behind a thick-trunked pine. Heart pounding, she took a quick peek at the woods behind her.

A sandy-haired man pushed through the heavy underbrush, a large pistol in one hand. And next to him, brow furrowed with determination, walked Andrew Walters.

School.

Chapter Eighteen

McBride raced through the woods, calling his daughter's name until he was hoarse. It was taking longer than he'd expected to reach the schoolhouse, but he didn't want to risk missing Clare hidden behind a bush or tangle in the thick underbrush. Within minutes, he was close enough to see the shabby white clapboard building peeking through the tree trunks as the woods thinned out. He started jogging toward the building, something unseen but powerful tugging at his heart.

He burst into the clearing and stared at the schoolhouse. It was dingy white, set about four feet off the ground on a natural stone foundation. Sagging pine steps led to a narrow porch in front of the double doors. McBride saw the door was open a crack. "Clare?"

He stood very still, listening. His heart lurched at a faint rustling sound coming from inside. He tried to temper the surge of adrenaline, reminding himself the noise could be a squirrel or a bird trapped in the building.

But deep inside, he knew.

"K.C.!" he called. "K.C., it's Daddy!"

He heard the soft rustle again. His heart banged against his ribs as he stared into the gloom beyond the partially opened door. He wanted to dash up the stairs but feared they wouldn't bear his weight. He stopped at the bottom and peered into the darkness. "K.C.?"

A small oval face seemed to materialize from the darkness inside. McBride took a swift, shuddering breath.

A dark-haired wraith emerged from the schoolhouse, her hazel eyes huge in her pale, heart-shaped face. McBride sank to his knees, his mind whirling.

"Daddy?" Her voice was faint.

He held out his arms. "Yes, baby, it's me."

She shook her head, suspicion written all over her. "You're not the one who's supposed to come get me."

McBride pushed himself to his feet. Clare took a swift step backward. "No, honey. It's okay. I'm not going to hurt you. I'd never hurt you."

"Mama said you didn't want to take care of me anymore," Clare said, accusation in her voice.

The memory of the dead woman lying in her

own blood flashed through his mind. "She didn't know what she was saying, Clare."

"My name's Casey," she said firmly.

"I know. I used to call you that. Casey." He said her nickname the way she said it. "I didn't give you away, Casey. I love you. I'd never give you away. You were taken from me."

"Mama said my real mommy was dead."

"She is, sweetie." He thought of Laura, and ached with the knowledge that she'd gone to her grave without seeing her little girl again. "But I'm alive and I never gave you up."

As he said the words, he felt guilt hit him like a freight train. He *had* given her up, hadn't he? Five years ago, he'd let her die in his heart and mind. If it hadn't been for Lily, she'd still be dead to him.

If for no other reason, he would love Lily forever for giving his daughter back to him.

She was so beautiful, he thought, looking at his child. She wasn't the cute little three-year-old he'd lost, but a tall, thin girl fast approaching the edge of adolescence. He'd lost six years of her life.

He noticed the ragged stuffed toy she clutched against her chest. Mr. Green had changed, too, he thought with sadness. "I see you still have old Mr.

Green. Has he been taking good care of you, marshmallow?"

Her eyes widened and she took a step forward. "Sing the song," she demanded.

He blinked with surprise. The song?

Then he remembered. Laura had made up a lullaby and they had sung it to Clare every night. He closed his eyes and willed the long-buried words to come to mind. Suddenly, he could hear Laura's sweet, clear voice in his ear, giving him the words.

"Sweet Baby Marshmallow, close your bright eyes,
Old Mr. Sunshine has left the night skies,
He's gone to a picnic on the far side of Mars—"

Clare's soft, little-girl voice finished it for him. "But he left Mrs. Moon to watch over the stars."

She scampered down the steps and flung herself at him. He caught her, certain he would die from the feeling of her solid warmth snuggled against his chest.

In his pocket, his cell phone trilled. He felt Casey's body twitch against him. For a second, he considered shutting it off, but the caller could be Lily. He grabbed it. "McBride."

It was the patrolman he'd positioned outside

Lily's house. "Sir, we've been following Ms. Browning since she left her house about twenty minutes ago. She just drove into the woods and parked on a dirt road."

Clare's voice in his ear was soft and slurred. "I told her where to find me, Daddy."

McBride's heart caught.

"Sir, Mr. Walters and another man headed into the woods behind her about three minutes ago. Should we follow?"

As McBride's blood ran cold, Clare suddenly went stiff in his arms. He held her away from him, searching her pale face. She was staring somewhere beyond him, her eyes fixed. Sightless. It reminded him of Lily during one of her visions. A shudder ran through him.

The patrolman's voice buzzed in his ear. "Sir?"

"Follow," he said tersely, disconnecting.

Casey went limp in his arms for a second, then reached out her little hands to clutch at his shirt. "Lily's in trouble!" she cried, a ragged edge of panic to her voice.

"Lily's in trouble?" he repeated, trying to understand.

Then he heard a gunshot.

He caught Clare's chin in his hand, made her look at him. He kept his voice soft, trying not to scare her. "Baby, I need you to do something for me."

LILY HEARD A CRACK behind her, and a whistling sound fly by her ear. Adrenaline exploded inside her, spurring her to greater speed. She had to draw them away from the schoolhouse.

Then she heard something else. "Lily!" It was Casey's voice, as loud as if the child was right beside her. Lily stumbled, almost falling.

"Daddy's here," Casey whispered in her ear. "He says run to the schoolhouse. He'll take care of us."

Lily shook her head. "They want to hurt you."

"He's here! He said to tell you his name is Jubal and he'll take care of us. Hurry!"

His name is Jubal. Lily's heart skipped a beat as hope flooded her, nearly knocking her off her feet.

"Hurry!" Casey's voice began to fade.

Another gunshot shattered the calm of the woods. The tree next to Lily exploded in a shower of wood splinters, peppering her face and arms.

Her heart pounding in her throat, Lily changed course, racing toward the schoolhouse spire barely visible through the pines.

McBride's there with Casey, she chanted with each pounding step. *He'll take care of us.*

MCBRIDE HELD HIS DAUGHTER close, peering out the schoolhouse window. He called in more backup, including Theo Baker. McBride had his gun and a second clip in his pocket—*never leave home without 'em,* he thought with a grim smile—but he couldn't keep Lily safe if she didn't show up.

Two long minutes later, he saw a flurry of movement in the woods. Lily burst through a gap in the trees into the clearing, flying at a full run toward the schoolhouse.

"Stay here," he admonished Clare. He ran out on the porch. Aiming his gun toward the rustling sounds coming from the woods, he fired two quick shots while Lily took the rickety schoolhouse steps two at a time.

He caught her outstretched hand and pulled her inside, tucking her between him and his daughter. "Are you hurt?"

She shook her head, her golden eyes moving from his face to Clare's and back again. She went pale as a ghost for a second, and he put out a hand to keep her from toppling over.

"You found us!" Clare threw herself at Lily.

Lily's arms tightened around McBride's daughter. She buried her face in the little girl's dark hair. "You're here." She looked up at McBride. "How?"

He spared a second to glance at her. "I believed it was possible."

Her smile spread over him like sunshine, giving him a surge of confidence. He peered out the window, watching for movement. His cover fire had apparently given Lily's pursuers pause.

"I saw the sketch," he told her. "The man you saw in the woods is Joe Britt, Andrew Walters's campaign manager."

"Andrew Walters is with him." Lily's voice darkened. "Abby's own father was in on it."

McBride stared at her in shock and revulsion. He reached for Clare, running his hand over her slim back. She leaned against him, shattering his heart into a million little pieces.

Suddenly, he heard a soft, scraping sound at the back of the schoolhouse. He whirled, peering through the gloom of the darkened room toward the slivers of light at the far end, where the weathered pine had buckled and split over the years, letting in daylight. A dark shadow passed across one of the boards and stopped.

"One of them is back there," McBride murmured. "Cover your ears."

He aimed his weapon at the dark shadow still evident across one of the openings. Taking a deep breath to steady his aim, he fired. A howl of pain answered.

The front steps of the schoolhouse creaked. McBride flattened himself against the wall, his heart racing. He hoped his first shot had taken out the man at the back, because until help arrived, he was outmanned and possibly outgunned.

"Sirens," Clare murmured against his arm.

"Shh, baby," he whispered. Then he heard them. Sirens. At least two cars, probably three, moving in their direction.

The cavalry had finally arrived.

The creaking on the front porch stopped. A second later, McBride heard something crashing through the underbrush. He edged to the doorway in time to catch sight of Andrew Walters running away.

Part of him wanted to pursue, to run Walters down and beat the hell out of him. It was bad enough he'd put his own child in danger for God knew what reason. He'd come here to kill Lily and Clare. McBride had no doubt about it.

But first he had to neutralize Joe Britt as a danger.

"Pull those desks in a circle and hide under them," McBride told Lily. She went right to work, while he slipped outside and crept around the back of the schoolhouse.

He found Joe Britt on the ground, curled up in a ball of agony. His kneecap was a bloody mass of tissue, bone and singed Italian silk. He didn't even try to go for his gun as McBride bent to retrieve it.

He was checking Britt for other weapons when he heard footsteps rapidly approaching. He whirled around, gun trained.

Theo Baker held up his hands. "Whoa, Tex."

McBride lowered his gun. "Finish searching this piece of sh—" He bit back the rest of the curse, aware of his daughter just inside the schoolhouse.

As Theo took over, McBride went around to the front of the schoolhouse. Eight uniformed policemen swarmed the area, two of them holding Andrew Walters by his upper arms. His hands were cuffed behind his back. He met McBride's gaze for a brief second before lowering his head.

Rage boiling in his gut, McBride forced himself to keep his voice calm. "Lily? You and Clare can come out now. It's over."

Lily emerged from the schoolhouse, her arm around Clare's thin shoulders. She met his eyes with a look so full of emotion it made his breath catch. She joined him at the foot of the steps, her gaze moving past him to settle on Andrew Walters.

Before McBride realized what she was going to do, she'd thrust Clare into his grasp and launched herself toward the politician, her small fist connecting with his jaw. The blow was hard enough to snap his head back.

As a couple of officers grabbed her to keep her from landing a second blow, Lily growled, "You heartless son of a bitch! Your own daughter!"

"Nobody was supposed to get hurt," Andrew blurted.

"Have you read him his rights?" McBride asked as the officers holding Lily handed her over to him.

"Yes, sir!" one answered with a grin.

McBride couldn't return the smile. He just gathered Lily and Clare close, thanking God he'd gotten to them both in time.

THE EMERGENCY ROOM DOCTOR assured them Casey was in good health, though he wanted to keep her overnight for observation. But McBride wasn't convinced, hovering by the bed long after the little girl had drifted off to sleep.

Lily had already been debriefed by Theo Baker and now sat in an armchair on the other side of the bed, her fingers still entwined with Casey's. The events of the day had begun to sink in, crushing her beneath the mingled joy and horror.

What was going to happen to Abby? Poor baby, to have lost her mother so horribly, to go through the fear and the abuse she'd suffered at the hands of her kidnappers, only to have her father taken away when she needed him most.

Her body thrumming with exhaustion, Lily almost missed the tingle radiating from her spine. But when the door in her mind swept open, she hurried into the mist, hoping she'd find a pair of blue eyes waiting on the other side. She found herself in a dark room, sitting on the edge of a soft mattress.

Abby sat in the middle of a mound of pillows, her knees tucked up to her chest. Lily touched her. Abby gave a start. "Lily? Did you hear me calling?"

Lily caught her up in her arms. "I'm here."

"I was afraid you'd gone forever," Abby whispered.

"I told you she'd come. She'll always find us."

Lily looked up and met the eyes of McBride's daughter.

Lily stroked Abby's hair, wondering how much her aunt had told her about her father. "Are you okay, Abby?"

"Aunt Jenn says I'll be staying here with her and Uncle David 'cause Mommy's in heaven and Daddy's got to go away for a while." Abby sniffled, her tears warm against Lily's neck. "But Casey promised you'll come see me."

Lily exchanged a glance with Casey, whose solemn little face looked old for its years. "You bet I will." She felt the tug of the mists at her back. Clinging to Abby as her head began to pound, she tried to hold on.

"We have to go, Abby." Casey crossed to Lily and took her hand. "We'll see you again, I promise."

Lily let Casey lead her back through the enveloping mists. When she opened her eyes, she was in the hospital room, her hand still curled around Casey's. The girl's sleepy eyes gazed up at her.

McBride's voice rumbled in her ear. "Where'd you go?"

Lily squeezed Casey's hand. "Abby needed to see us."

McBride's happy expression faltered. "Poor baby. How will her life ever be normal again?"

Lily wasn't sure if he was talking about Abby or his daughter. Maybe it didn't matter. "She's with people who love her enough to get her through it, whatever it takes."

Theo Baker stuck his head in the hospital room doorway and beckoned for them to join him. Lily gave Casey's hand another squeeze and followed McBride to the door.

Theo lowered his voice. "Britt's telling everything he knows. He wants to make sure Walters doesn't put it all on him. Seems Walters was down double digits in his campaign's internal polls, like Blackledge said. He and Britt got desperate."

And they'd gone for the sympathy vote, using his own daughter. Lily's heart clenched as she thought of Abby.

"Britt hired Gordon and Scotera to carjack Debra Walters. It was supposed to make the papers, garner public sympathy."

"But Debra fought back," McBride guessed.

"Once that happened, Gordy and Skeet went

rogue. Walters and Britt didn't know where to find them till they called Lily."

"That's why Andrew Walters wanted me on the case," Lily realized. "They used me to find their missing accomplices."

Theo nodded. "When the kidnappers called you but didn't leave instructions for the ransom drop, Britt figured they were giving Walters a message on how to contact them. They'd had a preplanned meeting place to hand over Abby, so Walters went and left a note for the kidnappers there. When Scotero showed up to check for a message, Britt was there, hiding. He followed Skeet to the trailer."

"And killed them there." McBride's expression turned grim.

"They wanted more money. He decided they were a risk."

"What about when Britt was chasing Abby in the woods?" Lily asked.

"Britt swears he wasn't going to hurt her. He just wanted to find her before she could talk to anyone else, in case Skeet and Gordy had said something to her about what was going on."

"Politics." McBride grimaced. "I hope they nail Britt and Walters to the wall." He looked over his shoulder at his daughter, his expression softening. She'd fallen back to sleep.

Theo put his hand on McBride's shoulder. "I'm glad about Clare. It's a real miracle."

McBride slanted a warm look at Lily. "Yes, it is."

Theo flashed a smile at Lily and left them alone.

McBride walked back to his sleeping daughter's bedside. He touched a wisp of hair curling on her cheek. "You found her, Lily. Just like you said." His voice was thick with emotion.

"No, Casey found me." They'd decided to call her Casey to make her feel more comfortable. Lily had a feeling it would be Clare's name from now on.

A new name for a new and happier life.

Pulling her close, McBride kissed Lily, his touch setting off a thousand little fires up and down her spine. Releasing her mouth, he whispered, "Forgive me for everything I said this morning."

"I understood." She tried to reassure him, but he pressed his fingers to her lips, shushing her.

"No, I need to say this. I realized it didn't matter whether you were right or wrong. You tried to help me. I could never hate you for trying to help me." His lips curved. "I love you too much."

"I love you, too." She touched his cheek. "I can't believe you stumbled onto Casey by accident."

"It wasn't an accident."

She cocked her eyebrow, surprised.

"I think I was supposed to take that exit instead

of staying on the interstate. I was supposed to find her."

She shook her head, smiling at the irony. "That's mighty unskeptical of you, Jubal McBride."

He grinned. "I know. I don't think Delaine Howard was a fake, either." He told her about the mailbox he'd found. "The woman who had Clare was named Grainger. Just like the people I told you about, the family with the little girl that Delaine thought was Clare. When I saw the mailbox, I remembered something about those Graingers. The little girl's father had been divorced a few years earlier, after his three-year-old daughter, Gina, died of leukemia. It was one reason we thought he might have Clare, having lost a little girl like that."

"The woman who had Clare was Mr. Grainger's ex-wife."

McBride nodded. "I think so."

"So...what? Mrs. Grainger happened to be walking by and saw Casey playing alone in the yard?"

"I doubt we'll ever know, but I'm going to look into it."

"So you believed Casey was alive all on your own, huh?"

He grinned. "Yeah, I did." He tightened his arms around her. "I saw a miracle today, Lily," he murmured in her ear. "I saw my dead daughter walk out of that schoolhouse alive. I watched that little girl send you a message clear across the woods, and now I'm looking at you both here with me, safe and sound. I'll never scoff at your visions again."

She tilted her head back. "McBride..."

"Marry me, Lily. I can't imagine the rest of my life without you."

She arched an eyebrow. "Is that a question or a command?"

He laughed. "Whichever gets you down the aisle with me."

She chuckled. "Oh, I've had it on good authority for a while that you're the man I'm going to marry. Rose told me so days ago. And I never argue with my sister about such matters."

"Rose told you?" His brow furrowed.

"Did I forget to tell you both of my sisters have special gifts of their own?"

He looked down at her in mock horror.

She laughed. "It appears to run in both our families."

He looked back at Casey. "She does have a gift, doesn't she? Laura always swore her side of the family had 'the sight.'"

Despite his earlier assurances, Lily's stomach tightened as she searched his expression. "Are you okay with that?"

"She saved you with her gift. And you saved her with yours." He claimed her mouth with a deep kiss that drove away the last of Lily's doubts. Her gift—her amazing gift that she'd too long seen as a curse—had brought her more joy and hope than she'd ever imagined possible.

He released her and lifted her face, gazing into her eyes. A smile carved lines into his rugged cheeks. "Thanks for showing me how to believe again."

She wrapped her arms around him and rested her head on his shoulder, looking past him to where his daughter—soon to be hers, too—lay sleeping.

My pleasure, she thought.

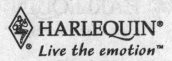

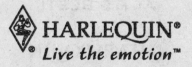

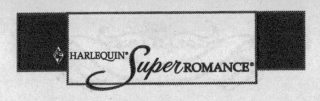
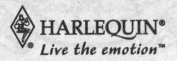

Harlequin Historicals®
Historical Romantic Adventure!

From rugged lawmen and valiant knights to defiant heiresses and spirited frontierswomen, Harlequin Historicals will capture your imagination with their dramatic scope, passion and adventure.

Harlequin Historicals . . . they're too good to miss!

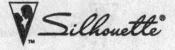

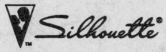